I0818082

REVENGE OF THE EMERALD MOON

Also by Nathan W. Toronto

Saga of the Emerald Moon

Rise of Ahrik
Revenge of the Emerald Moon
Redemption of the White Planet (available July 2023)

Bullet Points

Military science fiction anthologies edited by Nathan W. Toronto, with stories from new and established authors.

Volume 1

Stories from David Drake, Tony Ballantyne, Walter Jon Williams, James C. Glasss, Nathan W. Toronto, and more.

Volume 2
(available December 2022)

Stories from Joe Haldeman, David Drake, Ian R. MacLeod, Shannon Fay, Eric Fomley, T. Fox Dunham, and more.

Revenge of the Emerald Moon

Nathan W. Toronto

Toronto International Media

This novel is entirely a work of fiction. The names, characters and incidents portrayed in it are the product of the author's imagination. Any resemblance to actual persons, living or dead, or events or localities is entirely coincidental.

Hardcover edition, first impression, July 31, 2022
ISBN 978-0-9976550-7-0 (hardcover)

Created in the United States of America.

The Arabic block *noon* colophon is a trademark of Toronto International Media.

Cover design by Nancy Wride. Cover © 2022 Nathan W. Toronto as a collective work. Cover image courtesy of NASA (public domain).

Other editions: ISBN 978-0-9976550-6-3 (paperback)—
ISBN 978-0-9976550-5-6 (ebook)

For the meek,
And those that mourn

Typeset using LaTeX.

Wengi Me'en
Fly Together

I went to the mountains
In darkest day,
Where man would no longer
Steal nor slay.

I went to the stream
Of water sweet,
Where Woman gave people
Dreams of peace.

I walked to the ocean,
Gray as slate,
Where Humans found the will
To bury hate.

I flew through the sky
With a boson drive,
And saw what it meant
To be alive.

We soared to Moon,
Green and wide,
And together we learned
From war to hide.

Contents

1	War Among the People	1
2	Lines of Communication	20
3	Subsistence	31
4	Moral Force	51
5	Danger in War	63
6	Strategic Reserve	86
7	Friction in War	108
8	Methods of Resistance	124
9	Night Fighting	150
10	Boldness	172
11	Criticism	196
12	Tension and Rest	216
13	Surprise	239
14	Battle	253
15	Superiority of Numbers	267
16	Effects of Victory	292
17	Cordon	321

18 Stratagem 336

19 Invasion 353

20 What Is War? 372

Extras **390**

Redemption of the White Planet
Book 3: Saga of the Emerald Moon
Chapter 3, "Sierra Vista" 390

Acknowledgments 405

About the Author 406

1 War Among the People

THE PITTER-PATTER OF FEET STOPPED ANDA, his hand poised to cycle the airlock. With a smile, he set down his helmet and knelt down to gather his daughter in an embrace. "Up already, Sera?"

She coughed, then hugged her stuffed *dubbi* tight. "I can't sleep, Abbi."

She hadn't slept well since falling ill, and Anda was not surprised to see her up before he headed out to the tanks.

"Can you go to Imma's bed?" He stroked Sera's long auburn hair and smiled, but inwardly he steeled himself for another fit of coughing.

He and Esh'a had tried everything they could to help Sera fight this mysterious illness, but weeks of healers and treatments had done nothing. Sera still suffered from coughing fits. Anda gritted his teeth. Every day she grew weaker, it seemed. *Why can't I help her?*

Sera shook her head and gave him a stern look. "Not back to bed. Story."

Anda sighed. "A short story. I have to check the algae before Homerise."

He sat on the heated stone floor and pulled Sera onto his lap. "Do you know the story of the *pter'a* flower?"

Sera shook her head, then yawned and cuddled into the crook of his arm.

Anda squeezed Sera close, and the little girl clutched her *dubbi* to her chest.

"Many thousands of years ago, before The War, the *pter'a* flower grew all over," he said.

"On Moon, Abbi?"

"No, Serit, this was on Home. Back then, there were no people here."

Sera yawned. "Moon is now, and Dom is Home." She looked up at Anda with sleepy eyes. "I'll go Home someday."

Anda pursed his lips. "Home is not a good place now. Many people die there." He shifted Sera on his lap, with a pause to indicate that he would continue the story. "They said the *pter'a* flower had magical properties, that it could heal any wound."

"Could it cure me, Abbi?"

Anda stroked his chin, as if considering the possibility. "I bet it could, Serit," he said, trying to build both myth and hope at once, "but it's been two thousand years since anyone has seen the flower on Home." He stroked her hair and squeezed her shoulder. "But I believe it's out there, somewhere."

"I'll find it." She coughed. "Then I'll get better."

All Anda could do was smile. He hadn't the heart for much else.

Footsteps shuffled toward them, and Esh'a leaned against the dome wall next to the airlock. Her bloodshot eyes told Anda that she, like Sera, had not slept well. Esh'a shivered and pulled her nightgown close, then glowered and shook her head in a slow arc of displeasure. The small wooden vial of vanilla hanging from her neck swayed with the motion. Her raven hair cascaded over her shoulders, as if it too disagreed with what Anda was doing.

Her eyes narrowed with skepticism. "Telling her about the *pter'a* flower again?"

Anda pled with his eyes, but Esh'a met his gaze with cold despair. *Have hope,* he wanted to say, but he worried that they would lose Sera, and then afterwards Esh'a would succumb to the mercilessness of loss and fate. If Sera died, it would destroy them.

Anda gazed at his wife. He could not remember the last time they kissed each other good morning.

"I have to go check the tanks," he said, nudging Sera toward Esh'a and unfolding himself from the floor. *We have to pay for these treatments somehow.*

He stepped to the airlock once again, but Sera tugged on the thigh pocket of his exosuit. "Abbi, will I die and never be found, like that flower?"

A lump formed in Anda's throat. He bent down to look Sera in her pale eyes, red-rimmed and weary from pain and illness. Anda stroked her hair once again. "Not if I can help it, Serit."

He didn't dare look at Esh'a before cycling out through the airlock. He knew he would see only scorn and bitterness on her face. He did not begrudge his wife her pain, her longing for what should have been, but Sera needed hope now more than ever.

The healer at the nearest outpost had told them yesterday that there was nothing more he could do. "They're starting a new trial this week down in Kalevo," he'd said. "Treatments every month. I'll see if I can get her in." The healer had given them a grim look. "But even if she gets in, I don't know if it'll work."

Anda bounded out to the algae tanks in Home's lowgrav. With every leap, he screamed into his helmet, frustration and anguish boiling over. *How can I pay to go to Kalevo every month? How can I give my wife hope? How can I save my daughter?*

The light of Homerise over the horizon fed his anger. On Home, Sera would be cured by now, he was sure of it. But he and Esh'a couldn't go Home. They were marked. They'd be hunted and executed if they went back. It would do Sera no good to have her health, but no parents.

The tanks came into view, seven squat cylinders of dull steel, each twenty meters across. The algae they cultivated served two purposes. The gasses the algae emitted made Moon's thin atmosphere more breathable, but, more important, the algae helped feed Moon's population, over two million now. They said the atmosphere would be breathable in less than twenty years, but Anda only cared about today. About getting his daughter better.

Homerise cast its blue-gray pall over the broken landscape. Moss grew thick on Moon's rocks and boulders. The wispy haze of clouds tinted Homerise a dozen shades of green.

Anda used to love this time of morning. No matter his problems, he could lope out here and find peace, peace of recognizing how small he was to the cosmos, and of sensing the presence of some greater plan.

But that was gone, faded into an unreachable past. Without his family, he was nothing. He wanted to believe that the universe had a plan for him and for Esh'a and for Sera, but now he felt like he stared into blackest night.

At least he had his algae crop. That was something.

He made one final leap and wrapped gloved fingers over the rim of the first tank, three meters from the base. His feet jammed into the footholds on the side of the tank with practiced skill. He pulled himself up and peered over the side.

He froze.

Instead of a deep green, the surface was a pale, almost thin blue. Black rimmed the inside of the tank. He checked the water temperature reading on his helmet display. Normal. He synched his exosuit's compiler to the tank's system and checked bosonic heaters, acidity, gas proportions, radiation retention. All readings normal. Except biological activity, which sat at sixteen percent, too low to sustain life.

How? Algae production was the oldest form of agriculture on the Emerald Moon. Tanks didn't just fail like this.

He scrambled down from the rim of the tank. Nervousness climbed up his chest. If one tank failed, so could the others. *Everything I own is here, in these tanks.*

Anda bounded to the next tank, leaped up, and pulled himself to the rim. His heart sank. The surface of the algae in the second tank was even paler than the first. Anda checked the readings. Bioactivity at nine percent.

Frantic, he leaped to the ground and bounded to the next tank, and the next, and the next. Every one, dead. At the last tank he crumpled to the ground, a vacant husk of despair.

What was I supposed to do differently?

Despair turned to agony, and agony to fury. He balled his fist and slammed it into the ground, over and over and over again, until his suit sounded the oxygen alarm. *Rupture in right glove,* the display read. *Oxygen levels at 28 percent.*

Anda took in a deep breath. It wouldn't take that long. To die. To let the cold heart of space take him.

27 percent.

He took in another breath and searched for a reason to smile. Then Home cleared the horizon. Emerald light crawled over the ground.

25 percent.

He pushed himself off the moondirt and took a single bound toward home, then another, and another. He could almost feel the oxygen leaving his exosuit.

15 percent.

Oxygen levels in his exosuit stood at zero when he cycled through the airlock and tore his helmet off. The artigrav kicked in.

When Sera ran up to throw her arms around him, he smiled. He couldn't help it.

Ahrik tapped a finger on his desk and licked his swollen lip. He wondered how long the violence would last. Zharla woke up from her coma fourteen years ago, but gone now was the joy of being together. Of seeing each other's greatest hopes fulfilled. Their erstwhile joy did not bear up under the weight of childlessness and the burden of governing a planet. The violence she inflicted on him became more frequent when Nayr started asserting his influence. Ahrik worried for the future.

He still loved his wife—that would never change—and he thought she loved him, deep down. After all they had lived together, she must still love him. She must.

He stared down at the square of paper on his desk and pondered the implications of signing it. His eyes wandered over the statuettes commemorating a career's worth of deployments, victories, and even one or two defeats, regimented on his desk as if at parade. His eyes flicked to the far corner of his desk, where his *qasfin*, his greatest fear, lay concealed. He knew the blade would still be sharp, even after all these years, but how Ahrik had enjoyed its repose. He considered the paper Zharla wanted him to sign. He could not bear to unleash the demons of war once again.

Signing the paper would change everything with Nayr, his stepson. Ahrik worked for years to build this relationship. Conceived in pain, Nayr was the only child Zharla ever had, and Ahrik raised Nayr like his own. She must know what signing this order meant. Nayr was still their greatest hope for the future, but signing this order now was, for all intents and purposes, an invitation for Nayr to start a civil war.

Ahrik saw it. Every day, Nayr consolidated his power, positioned his forces, and cultivated the favor of those on the Council of Elders. One of those Elders was particularly close to Nayr: Sheresh Shehur-li, Nayr's greatest champion.

Sheresh. The only person in the world Ahrik truly hated. Sheresh had started the War for the Emerald Moon seventeen years earlier, and in order to make peace Ahrik and Zharla had shuffled the truth of his role under the rug. Sheresh had the blood of hundreds of thousands on his hands, but Zharla wanted peace, and Ahrik could do nothing about it.

Ahrik snapped the paper taut to take one more look at it. It beggared belief. Ahrik wanted nothing more than to make Sheresh pay for his crimes, but to do so now, like this, would come at catastrophic cost.

Injustice was the cost of peace. Get along with the criminal who started the last war. Now, Sheresh was using his position on the Council to groom Nayr for power. If Sheresh and the Council put Nayr on the throne, Sheresh would control the world. Ahrik and Zharla needed more time. More time to teach Nayr wisdom. More time to prepare for the inevitable transition.

Sheresh was already an old man when the War for the Emerald Moon started. Ahrik and Zharla needed more time for Sheresh to die. But Sheresh needed to die naturally, not like this, under an executioner's blade.

Ahrik set the paper on the desk. He saw their dilemma, as plain as the full moon on a clear night. He didn't know why Zharla refused to see it.

He pushed himself to a standing position and stepped over to the window, his hover chair sliding out from under him. The stone buildings of Meran gleamed in the morning sun, reflecting off the bay. The glimmering light prompted memories of the battles he and his sons had fought to protect this fair city.

The Emerald Moon stood high in the morning sky. How long Ahrik had fought to keep the moonie rebels at bay. He looked back at the paper on his desk. And now this.

His wife, Queen Zharla, had been awake for fourteen years of peace, but in a coma for the three years of the War for the Emerald Moon before that, three years that saw the Ketel of Ahrik, his sons, spread over Dom and the moon, in an effort to preserve what remained of women's rule, fighting the forces of sedition, hate, and prejudice, those forces that Sheresh raised in secret so long ago.

She's coming, said a voice in his head. The voice cast into his mind over the tendril link, his connection to his sons, his clones. He grew up with them, fought with them, and bled with them. Of the ten thousand he started the last war with, only two thousand remained. 2,158, to be exact. What a price his 10,000 sons, his clone warriors, had paid to preserve women's rule. To defend Zharla's reign. And now she dared to trespass on his domain, to see if he did her bidding, to pursue that folly of statecraft, to thrust an entire planet into war once again.

Thank you, Hawk. Hawk was the only member of Ahrik's command group that remained from the halcyon days of first combat, in the War for the Emerald Moon. The rest of the old command group were either broken and retired or rotting in the ground, their remains scattered throughout the worst places in the world, on the moon, and in space. He and his sons realized soon after the War for the Emerald Moon began that combat held no glory, only pain and an unknown grave. Zharla had given up little to achieve her power, by comparison to Ahrik and his sons. Her comfort and delusion blinded her to the horrors of war.

He studied the glimmering bay, to think on something other than war. To delay the inevitable war planning for just a bit longer.

Footfalls sounded behind him. He did not acknowledge her, but he heard the paper rustle from his desk. He felt her hand on the small of his back. Almost, he wanted to believe they could have what they once did. Her touch surprised him, that she would dare after what she had done just the day before, and because her touch still sent a tingle down his spine.

She leaned into him, ever so slightly. "Dear, don't we want to sign this order?"

Her voice still electrified him, even though he knew what she really was, a half crazed monarch who endangered her people with pointless obsessions. "You say 'we', but we agreed on a division of labor: you rule, I govern."

She smiled and rubbed his back. "Ah'ke, I . . . Oh."

She stared at his lower lip and took out her handkerchief, but Ahrik jerked his head back. He moved away from her, his face incredulous. He nodded toward the paper in her hand. "Tell me what this is really about."

She played dumb, an unbecoming charade, then dabbed her handkerchief at her forehead. "How do you mean?"

"I mean, why do we need to put Nayr's mentor on trial for crimes against the race?"

"He unleashed a bioweapon on the Emerald Moon three months ago, near some remote outpost called Kalevo." Zharla's face feigned disbelief and affront. "He violated the treaty with the moonies. He endangered the peace. How can we ignore that?"

Ahrik knew she cared neither for moonies nor the peace. He stepped around the desk, ostensibly to view the holos on the wall, but also to put the desk between them. She tended to lash out whenever they discussed her obsession, Shahl, his long dead brother, and Ahrik sensed that he was about to come up. "This order endangers the peace," he said. "Ignoring the behavior of Sheresh keeps us safe, Zhe'le. You do know that he started the last war, right?" Ahrik paused to consider what he was about to say. His eyes half-closed with pain. "Some of us remember what the War for the Emerald Moon was like."

Zharla glared at him. "You call this peace, Ah'ke? We rule all of Dom, an entire planet, but ghouls haunt our dreams."

Ahrik frowned. "He's dead, Zhe'le."

She looked out the window and into the morning sky, then twisted her handkerchief in her hands. "We'll find him, Ah'ke. He's out there on the moon. Somewhere."

Ahrik padded over and worked the piece of paper out of Zharla's hand. "You're asking me to sign a declaration of war," said Ahrik. He steeled himself for the half-truth he was about to utter. "Nayr and his clones are coming of age, and he loves power too much. This trial is an attack on his mentor's honor. This is all the excuse Nayr will need to . . ."

Zharla shifted her weight and eyed a challenge in his direction. "To what, Ah'ke?"

"Nayr is unstable." He paused for emphasis. "Nayr loves his mentor very much."

Zharla snorted. "Love, Ah'ke? He loves his mother." Her lower lip quivered. "He loves me more than anything."

Ahrik wondered if that was true, but he dared not try to disabuse her of the notion now, when she might strike again. "He's not . . ." Ahrik pursed his lips and shook his head. "He's not ready to rule."

"You have to give up power sooner or later, Ah'ke."

"He's using you, Zhe'le. Sheresh is using you."

She scoffed. "That's ridiculous. Sheresh is weak. He needed me to keep him on the Council of Elders."

"You did that against my advice."

"I have this under control. Sheresh overreached, and now we'll put him in his box, where he belongs."

"You're asking for war. Begging for it."

She gave him a condescending smile and stroked his shoulder. "Power has gotten to your head, dear. Maybe we should start thinking about a transition."

Ahrik ripped his shoulder away, but his eyes flashed with the sting of her remark. "You know me better than that."

She knew he wanted only to serve his people, but now she was accusing him of selfishness, when he was anything but. She couldn't see that, either.

He glared at her with finality. "War is nothing to be trifled with, Your Majesty."

A glazed look passed over her face, as if she had heard none of what he'd said. She turned to look up into the sky. "If Shahl is up there on the moon, Sheresh may have killed him with his bioattack."

Ahrik threw up his hands. Blood pumped into his neck. "And there we have it. Your obsession with my dead brother drives us into a war we can ill afford."

She stepped to him and caressed his face, but her eyes glinted like obsidian. Ahrik stiffened, but forced his body to welcome her advance. He needed her, if he was to succeed. The people loved her, almost worshiped her. She leaned in and kissed him, and he was equal parts revulsion, submission, and exultation. "I'm very sorry about your mouth, dear. It won't happen again."

She always said that, the day after.

She rubbed his arm, and a strange look whispered into her eyes. "If you don't want to sign the order—"

He narrowed his gaze. "You already signed it, didn't you?" He looked away, into the unforgiving middle distance. "I'm so sorry, for us all."

She froze at the accusation in his voice, then gave a slow nod and looked up at the moon again. She stepped to the door, but paused before palming it open. Her hand hovered over the reader. "I . . . I told him. About you."

Ahrik's eyes grew wide, and a chasm of fear opened in his gut. "You told Nayr?" Ahrik stumbled to his desk and slumped into his hoverchair, expression vacant, head light. "Zharla, what have you done? Your son doesn't need any more reason to hate me."

From his hoverchair he reached for the secret compartment set into the far corner of his desk, an intricate tremor in his hand. He pressed his fingertip onto the miniature reader next to it. The compartment cover dissolved to reveal his *qasfin*, resting on soft velvet the color of blood. Face grim, heart longing not to do so, he lifted his cherished and reviled *qasfin* by its hilt and took in the gleam of its tight crescent blade, as sharp as the day it was forged. Biriq.

He tested its weight in his hand. Fourteen years since he hid Biriq in this place, and now he lifted it out once again, much earlier than he hoped he would. Its name meant Lightning, that it might fly with speed and power.

"Zhe'le," he said, still focused on his blade. "Do you know what this means? Zhe'le?" He looked up. She was gone.

Hawk, he cast over the tendril link, *mobilize the* ketel. *Quietly.* Maybe there was still a chance to avoid a war with Nayr and his 100,000 supersoldiers.

Nayr palmed open the cabinet to the sparring weapons and thought, for a moment, if he'd be justified in using a sharpened *qasfin* instead. He was seventeen years old today, just a few weeks from his *qer'ish* day, and for every single day of those seventeen years the person he called father had lied to him. And if Nayr was anything, he was honest, with himself and with others. He expected nothing less from those he loved.

Used to love.

He frowned and padded across the room. His soft-soled sparring boots gripped the glimmering wooden floor. Afternoon sunlight streamed through the window facing Meran Mountain and bounced off the floor, a king's ransom worth of wood here on Dom, this dry, rocky world.

He rested his palm on the reader next to the combat weapons cabinet, the one with the sharpened weapons, and asked himself if the world would notice if he incapacitated Ahrik, the man he once called father.

No liar deserved to rule the world.

Nayr dissolved the cabinet cover and examined the gleaming combat *qasfina*. The morning light caught their curved steel blades, atomic-sharpened to wicked edges. He lifted one off its rack and hefted its familiar weight. The leather-bound hilt creaked in his grip. So many years of training, and now he was close to his *qer'ish* day, midsummer's night after his seventeenth birthday. He was about to come of age, to make his own decisions, and he would finally be able to use a *qasfin* for real.

But now he contemplated using one against an enemy he never knew he had. Someone must protect Mother, and the world, from Ahrik's lies.

The door dissolved with a whoosh behind him, and he grabbed a cloth from the rack inside the cabinet.

"Hello, son."

Ahrik's voice raked over his ears like teeth grinding ice. The word "son" stood in the air like a monument to Ahrik's disloyalty. Nayr shuddered at how Ahrik could command his *ketel* all these years while lying like that.

Ahrik pulled off his combat boots. "Sorry I'm late."

Another lie. "No problem. I was just polishing the *qasfina*."

Ahrik grunted as he slipped on his own sparring boots. "You know, the palace has servants to polish those."

Nayr wondered what drove Ahrik to lie. The power to rule a planet was surely an intoxicating drug, but it was not worth selling one's soul. Ahrik had to be stopped.

Nayr replaced the combat *qasfin*, but a twinge of doubt interrupted the action. Maybe now was the right time, after all. He could surprise Ahrik while he focused on his sparring boots. No, Nayr decided. He wasn't sure what Mother would think. No point in killing or maiming Ahrik until he was sure the Queen wouldn't disagree.

Nayr walked back across the room, nodding in acknowledgment of Ahrik's comment about the servants. "A man dependent on others isn't free," said Nayr. "Isn't that what you always say?"

Ahrik raised an eyebrow and stood to choose his weapon from the sparring cabinet. "What's wrong, son? Is it the talk you had with your mother?" His face shifted, like a weasel. "We can talk about it."

Nayr paused before reaching for his favorite sparring weapon, a *qasfin* with a heavy oak hilt and soft iron blade. The extra weight made him stronger, for when he'd need to wield a blade for real.

His thoughts wandered once again to the combat *qasfina*. He could switch one out for a sparring blade later. He and Ahrik sparred every week. Ahrik wouldn't notice the switch until it was too late.

Nayr hoped he wouldn't regret his indecisiveness today. He frowned. Ahrik would assume it was in response to his question.

"Son—"

"Don't call me 'son'," said Nayr, pulling on his sparring gloves.

Ahrik pulled on his own gloves, then looked away. He pretended like he was in the throes of some inner turmoil. "So, she really told you."

The old man was holding something back. Nayr shook out his arms and legs, but narrowed his eyes in distrust. "What else are you keeping from me?"

Ahrik stood and pursed his lips, then bored his gaze into Nayr. Yet another lie hid behind his eyes. "Let's spar."

The old man could only hide so long from the truth. Nayr's wrist compiler chimed. He frowned. He forgot to remove it. He looked down, though, and his head swam.

A message scrolled up the tiny display, from Sheresh, his closest mentor and friend: *Just arrested. Accused of crimes against the race. Order came from the palace.*

Ahrik. No one but Sheresh's oldest rival would have signed the order.

Nayr's blood boiled. He sensed this day would come. Long ago, Sheresh was Ahrik's first supervisor. In private, Ahrik accused Sheresh of starting the War for the Emerald Moon seventeen years earlier, before Nayr was born, but Nayr spoke with Sheresh often about it. This was another one of Ahrik's lies. And now Ahrik had trumped up charges against Sheresh, the wisest man Nayr knew. His closest friend.

Nayr threw his wrist compiler into his bag, strapped on his arm guards, and picked up his sparring *qasfin*. "Yes," he said. "Let's spar."

No sooner had they crouched into their stances than Nayr flew at Ahrik with fury and motion. Ahrik dodged and parried. Sparks glanced off his arm guard when Nayr's blade struck. Ahrik grunted with the effort, and Nayr caught a satisfying sheen of worry on the old man's face.

They usually started slow, but Nayr was in no mood to go easy. Let the old man have a heart attack, for all he cared. It would save Nayr the trouble.

Ahrik regrouped and swung his blade, but Nayr dodged and leaned back to cut Ahrik's legs out from under him with a kick to the back of the knees. Ahrik spun out of the way, but Nayr relished the look of surprise on Ahrik's face.

Nayr couldn't understand why Ahrik had done it. Why lie about being his father for all these years? Why invent charges against Sheresh? Why lie to Mother in order to consolidate his rule?

Ahrik launched another counterattack, but Nayr was smaller and quicker. He used Ahrik's momentum against him. Nayr tucked into Ahrik's attack and slammed an arm guard into his ribs. Then, as Ahrik's blade rushed toward Nayr's head, he slid out of the way, spun, and brought his own blade onto the small of Ahrik's back.

Ahrik cried out in pain and crumpled into a roll away from Nayr. He gave a withered grunt. Bosonic springs under the floor cushioned most, but not all, of the fall. Their subatomic hum groaned under Ahrik's weight. Ahrik crouched on all fours, like a tiger ready to spring, but Nayr leaped first. Ahrik tried to dodge, but Nayr's knee connected with Ahrik's gut, along with a squelch and a satisfying rush of air leaving Ahrik's body.

Ahrik slumped onto his back, the fight gone out of him. He lay still. His breath heaved, his eyes looked stern, and he examined the ceiling. "I . . . deserved . . . that."

Nayr scoffed and threw his practice *qasfin* to the ground. He was furious enough still to ignore the basics of blade safety. He just didn't care. One day his life was just like he wanted it, and the next he faced a different future, fraught with uncertainty and self-doubt. "Who decides what we deserve or don't deserve?" Nayr asked. "At least you had a choice."

Ahrik sat up. "Now wait a minute, Son . . . Nayr."

Nayr ripped off his arm guards and gloves. "Why?"

Ahrik's shoulders sank toward the floor. "You sure you don't want to go another round? Settle your mind a bit?"

Nayr tore off his sparring boots. "Why didn't you tell me?"

"I wanted to . . ." Ahrik looked off. He avoided Nayr's piercing glare, then focused on the floor. "It doesn't change anything. People may say your military blood isn't pure, but you and I both know that doesn't mean a thing."

"You're not my father. By law, I shouldn't have 100,000 clones to command." Nayr slammed a fist into his bag. "My life is built on a lie. How can I lead my sons? I am a liar."

"No, Nayr. Your *keteli* clones are yours forever, because of your tendril link with them. No one can change that," said Ahrik. He slipped his own blade onto its rack and stretched his back. He sighed a look at Nayr. "You're the Queen's son. She has no daughters, nor will she. You're next in line for the throne. What worries you?"

Nayr guffawed, then shook his head. "You don't get it." He took his wrist compiler out of his bag and slapped it on his wrist. The wrist compiler reminded him why he was so furious. "Just because you're obsessed with power doesn't mean I am, too. I care about my sons and about serving Mother, not about ruling this dessicated rock."

Ahrik started to peel off his gloves. "Service and rule are one and the same, Nayr. We hoped you'd have learned that by now."

Nayr sealed his bag shut with a ferocious swipe. His thumb and forefinger pressed together like a vice as he ran them across the two sides of the biomesh seam. "Don't bring Mother into this." He drilled his glare into Ahrik and took a step forward. He thought about finishing what he'd started. "Your lust for power blinds you. You can't see the evil you sow."

Ahrik narrowed his eyes, but kept his demeanor calm. Nayr trusted him like a viper guarding a bird's nest.

Ahrik nodded in his direction. "I can help you, Nayr."

Nayr shouldered his bag. "Help me what? Betray Mother? Execute my mentor?"

"Ah," said Ahrik. He looked away with a hint of guilt. "So this is really about Sheresh."

Nayr stepped to within an arm's length of Ahrik, but Ahrik didn't move a muscle. So arrogant. Nayr poked a finger into the old man's chest. "I will expose your lies, Ahrik Jeber-li. Stay away from my friends and family."

Nayr shouldered his bag and stormed out. As he did, he accessed the internal compiler implanted in the base of his skull. This tech was the privilege of every *ketel* commander in the Army. The internal compiler gave him the tendril link to communicate with, command, and control his clones. His sons.

The internal compiler also let him store vast amounts of information, accessible only to him and encrypted to his unique genetic code. He created a new file, named it "Revenge," and put a single word in it: "Ahrik."

Anda and his family trundled along in the hold of the farming co-op's cargo freighter, deep green blocks of freeze-dried algae stacked all around them. There were fewer blocks in this harvest than before the Black attacked Moon's algae tanks, so Anda drew special comfort from the rich pungency of the cargo wafting around them. They jostled back and forth as the freighter navigated the uneven terrain on its antiquated hover system.

Anda and Esh'a were still in debt for their tanks and seed algae, and with the failure of their crop they couldn't afford to take the subtransporter to Kalevo, much less a shuttle. Anda wondered if he and Esh'a had made the right choice, all those years ago, to run from Home and live in self-imposed exile on Moon.

He looked down at Sera, sleeping peacefully despite the bumpy ride, nestled between him and Esh'a. He smiled. Without their choice to marry and live here on Moon, they would not have their beautiful daughter. Now, ten years after they chose exile, seven-year-old Sera was in a healing trial, so their trip to Kalevo would serve two purposes: start Sera's new treatment, and find a way to keep their farm afloat. They would make this work, just like they had every time before. Even after he had discovered the dead tanks yesterday, Anda had still felt a sliver of hope.

Esh'a shifted her weight. She caught Anda looking at Sera. Her eyes softened and she smiled at him. He reached an arm around and squeezed her shoulders, but she didn't lean into him like he desperately wanted her to. Still, his heart sang at the smile he'd gotten out of her.

"I'm glad she finally got to sleep," he whispered.

Esh'a's eyes grew serious and studied the steel-grate floor of the freighter. "She'll need all her strength to fight this."

She always saw challenge where he saw opportunity. Even after all these years, it surprised Anda how different they could be. They loved each other. This was just a rough patch.

Anda shrugged to concede her point. "We'll go to the healing clinic first thing, then over to Yosi's place. He'll be able to help us with another loan."

Anda could tell by the way Esh'a looked back at him that she thought Yosi would be as much help as a meteorite shower. She fiddled with the vanilla charm at her neck and smiled again, but this time it wasn't deep and heartfelt, like before, but a brave face for an unwelcome future, like she didn't have a choice. "Sera," she said with a note of concession, "is the priority."

The freighter jerked up and then jolted forward, knocking Anda and Esh'a against the algae blocks. The blocks rattled violently inside their steel bindings, and Esh'a looked at Anda in alarm as she used her arms and body to stabilize Sera. The girl stirred, but remained asleep. The bindings held, and Anda and Esh'a both breathed a sigh of relief.

"Sorry!" the pilot yelled from the front.

Anda cast a confident eye at his wife. "We can do this."

Esh'a's face tightened with worry, and her eyes welled a deep red. She breathed in, then let it out slowly, looking anywhere except at Anda. She patted his knee. "Sometimes, Anda, hope is not enough. Sometimes, we have to make hard choices."

Panic flushed through Anda as he realized what she was suggesting. "We already made the hardest choice. We're here, on Moon, as a family. Don't undo that."

She closed her eyes in frustration. "We can starve together, or I can do what we both know has to be done."

Anda just shook his head, not daring to speak or look at his wife. For a long while, they rode in silence, until the pilot called back, "Five minutes!"

Anda gave his wife a tender sigh. "Let's try with Yosi, but . . . if it comes to splitting up . . . let me go instead of you."

Sera began to stir, and Esh'a laughed off his request. "You know as well as I do that my chances of survival down there are much better than yours. Too many people know who you really are."

Sera yawned and rubbed her eyes. "Abbi and Imma, I'm hungry. Are we there yet?"

Anda squeezed Sera and smiled. "Almost there, Serit."

Esh'a locked eyes with him again, and, as if in compromise, said to Sera, "We'll go to the healer first, so he can help you get better."

When they cycled through the airlock at the Kalevo clinic, the receptionist's face was grim and frazzled. The waiting room was packed. A deep sense of unease tunneled its way into Anda's chest. Kalevo was small, an outpost on the outskirts of a settlement, not even a town. Nothing like the city at Moon Station Prime. It was midmorning here, much too early for this many people to be at a healer's office.

"I didn't know Kalevo had this many people that could get sick," he whispered to Esh'a. They didn't even have an appointment. Their lives, this far out from Prime, didn't require that much planning.

The receptionist sighed when they told him they were there for the trial. "That's pretty important," he said, searching for something with bloodshot eyes as his fingers whisked over the compiler display. "Let me check with the healer about getting you in."

He came back a minute later and motioned for them to follow him. "Shouldn't an orderly take us back?" whispered Esh'a to Anda.

Anda shrugged, but his worry deepened. He gripped Sera's hand and followed the receptionist to an examination room.

After too long a wait, the healer entered and motioned for them to sit. He remained standing, a mask of exhaustion on his face, and leaned against a counter. He showed his palms in exasperation. "I'm sorry, but

I'm not the healer running the trials. Can you come back tomorrow? Get here just after Homerise?"

"What's going on?" asked Esh'a, her brow furrowed, her voice wary.

Beside them, Sera fidgeted.

The healer pursed his lips. "The healer who was leading the trial and two of the orderlies left this morning, without warning. You know how it is when people leave."

Anda, wondering why this should matter, leaned forward and rested his elbows on his knees. "They left Kalevo?"

The healer avoided eye contact, then paused. "They left Moon."

Anda's breath caught in his throat. No one ever left Moon. Those that left were sellouts. "They went to Home?"

The healer nodded.

Esh'a shifted uncomfortably in her chair, her demeanor incredulous. "What the sunfire for?"

"Safety," said the healer, his tone measured and uncertain, as if he wasn't sure they could handle this information.

Anda looked at him, confused. "Why would anyone want safety there? People come here to escape Home, not the other way around."

The healer looked at them like they'd been hiding under a rock for the last ten years, which was, in a way, true. He sighed like he would have to explain something to a child. "Most of the people out there in the front waiting room have symptoms like your daughter's, but your daughter was one of the first reported cases. That's why she qualified for the trial."

Sera cleared her throat and smiled at the healer. "Thank you," she said, hugging her *dubbi* tight.

The healer cocked his head. A smile broke on his face as he looked down at her. "For what . . . uh . . . Sera?"

"For helping me get better."

He pushed himself away from the counter and crouched down so his eyes were on a level with Sera's. His eyes conveyed a barely disguised wonder. "Promise me something, Sera. Always be this positive, okay? No matter what."

She nodded like she'd never consider anything else. "Sure."

The healer looked up at Anda and Esh'a, and his brow furrowed with concern. "I have to be honest. In the last two weeks, this illness has begun draining Moon of its population. There are reports of crop failures in the outlying districts, and just today even rumors of failures closer to Prime, and some people say they're connected to this Moonlung or Creeping Cough or whatever it is they call it."

"The Black." Anda's shoulders slumped.

The healer rolled his head with uncertainty. "No one really understands it, but one thing's for sure: Prime is a sweltering hive of despair right now, since there are a lot more people who want to leave than can."

Esh'a stood and squeezed her hands with impatience. "So, you'll be here tomorrow when we come to start the trial?"

The healer gave them a sheepish smile. "Maybe. Maybe not. I put in an application, too."

The air seemed to rush from the room, and an empty, woozy feeling opened up in Anda's mind, as if the artigrav had shut off all of a sudden. They'd come to Moon ten years ago to get off the grid, for peace and safety, for a better life, but they couldn't really live on Moon if everyone else simply left.

Esh'a muttered a curse and sliced out of the door. She was in the airlock before Anda even thanked the healer and prepped Sera's helmet.

They bounded toward Yosi's place, the three of them hand-in-hand. Esh'a commed Anda on their private channel, the one they used when they didn't want Sera to hear. "It's started again, hasn't it? We won our independence, and we're winning the peace, so they're trying to cut us back down to size with another war."

Anda frowned at the prospect. "Let's not jump to conclusions."

She hissed in annoyance. "Don't be naive."

Anda couldn't meet her eye. "A war would be so pointless."

"I'd rather fight a pointless war and die than give in and die anyway, Anda. If they can do this to Moon, then they'll stop at nothing."

An uncomfortable moment passed. Anda could tell Esh'a had something else to say, but didn't know how to say it. He almost agreed with her about fighting. When it came to the goodwill of the people on Home, Anda's reserve of hope ran precious thin.

Yosi's place came into view, three small domes peaking over the horizon. Home was about to set, and Anda was glad they would spend the night with Yosi and his family. It would do them good to be with friends again. Yosi was the closest thing Anda and Esh'a had to family.

Sera, between them, squeezed their hands and commed over the general channel, "I'm hungry."

"Almost there," Anda and Esh'a said in unison.

When Yosi's place was only a few bounds off, Esh'a commed Anda over their private channel again. "Do you think your brother had anything to do with this?"

Her question stopped his blood cold. He didn't want to believe it could be possible, but he knew if Home had anything to do with the illnesses and the crop failures and the mayhem at Prime, then there was a good chance that Ahrik knew about it, at least, even if he may not have ordered it done.

Anda knew his brother and his rash, impulsive heart. He could have ordered this. Anda frowned back at Esh'a. "Let's see if Yosi has any answers."

Yosi received them like old friends always do, with food and a warm embrace, his eyes sharp and discerning, but his face otherwise armed only with a gregarious smile, like one would expect from someone who makes his living convincing people to give him money. His gaggle of kids swarmed around them, and Sera, hunger forgotten, blended right into the mix, frolicking and running from one dome to the next, which were connected by a bewildering circuit of tunnels. Yosi's wife, fecund, plump, with her head shaved like almost all women from Moon, those like Esh'a excepted, admonished the children as they bolted past, time after time.

After they ate a simple meal, the children's ruckus reignited, but Yosi and his wife laughed it off as the four adults sat around the table. "So, Esh'a and Anda," asked Yosi, scratching his bald pate, "how's the farming?"

Esh'a looked at Anda and pursed her lips. Sera coughed as she ran by, and Esh'a called, "Serit, why don't you take a break?"

Anda shifted in his seat and drew in a breath to buy time, unsure how to broach what was coming. "That's one reason we're here, Yosi."

"Oh?" asked Yosi, his eyes narrowing and head leaning to one side in a gesture of mild curiosity.

Anda's shoulders and eyes fell. There was no mincing words. "The crop failed."

Yosi shared a sharp glance with his wife, then laughed, nervous. Yosi had lent them the money for their farm, and the loan was still years away from being paid off. A crop failure would sting Yosi, too. "Ah, you mean that one of your seven tanks failed, right?"

Esh'a got up and ran after Sera as she flew by.

Anda sighed and shook his head slowly in Yosi's direction. "The whole crop."

"All seven tanks?"

"All seven tanks."

Yosi slumped back in his chair and examined the ceiling. "Anda, I—"

Anda waved a hand to cut off what Yosi was about to say, words Anda suspected he didn't want to hear. "We have a plan, Yosi. Just float us for one more cycle, then we'll be in a position to—"

Yosi stood, cutting him off in turn, and cast a desperate look at his wife, then back at Anda. Anda's breath caught in his throat. Esh'a returned and stood in the doorway to the dining dome, Sera clutched by the hand, huffing from the exertion of play, on the verge of another coughing fit. They always started when Sera ran too much.

"We can't give you any more money," said Yosi, with forbidding finality. "You both did great things for independence. You fought bravely in the war, and we know that Home wants nothing more than for you to walk out the wrong end of an airlock. I know how important the farm is to your lives." He stared at the floor. "But the markets are wild now. The exodus from Moon is making demand for algae erratic. We've lost"—he looked at his wife again—"a lot."

"I . . . I know," said Anda. "You've done what you could."

"The truth is," said Yosi's wife, huffing and working herself out of her seat, "we applied for refugee status. Yosi here didn't have the heart to tell you." She frowned and looked from Anda to Esh'a and back. "He knows what Moon's independence means to you."

Anda exchanged a knowing glance with Esh'a, still standing in the doorway. She fingered the canister of vanilla at her breast, then looked away, worry lining her face.

Sera walked over to Anda, glided it seemed to him, and took his hand in her frail fingers. She coughed, and her body convulsed with the effort. Anda winced and rubbed her back, helplessness coursing through him.

The coughing continued, and Sera climbed into his lap. After the coughing had subsided and her body had gone flaccid from the effort, she took a few breaths and gave him a weak smile. "Abbi," she said, "are we going to Home now?"

Anda didn't dare look at Esh'a, for fear that emotion would overcome him. In his mind's eye, she was covering her nose and mouth with her hands and turning away from the door so that Sera wouldn't see her tears or hear her sobs. The image alone nearly sent Anda over the edge.

"No, Serit," said Anda, clinching the lump in his throat with force of will. "Just Imma. You and I will stay here."

2 Lines of Communication

ZHARLA PADDED DOWN the corridor toward her son's room. She walked on eggshells with him lately, and she still hadn't talked to him about Sheresh or the attack on the moon, even though it had been a week since the blowup in the sparring chamber.

She knew she should talk to Nayr. Ahrik would never let her hear the end of it if she didn't. Ahrik always went on about confronting one's problems and not letting them fester.

Maybe he was good for her, but she wasn't so sure, with how they fought lately.

She didn't used to hit him. She couldn't recall when that had started.

Zharla nodded good morning to a few passing servants, then stopped in front of the door to Nayr's chambers. She drew in a long, deep breath and pressed her palm to the chime.

No answer came at first, but she did hear rustling inside. Then, a weak voice called, "Yes?"

Zharla didn't know whether to interpret that for the silly question it was—would someone chime, unless they wanted to come in?—or as an invitation to enter. She chose the latter. She was the Queen, after all. No door should remain closed to her.

A wall of darkness and the stuffy smell of stale human met her as she crossed the threshold. Through the lugubrious air, she saw a rumpled clump on the bed move to a sitting position. Probably the source of the rustling.

He coughed and moaned, as if ill.

Zharla rushed to his side. "I didn't realize you were still sleeping." She pressed her open mouth to his forehead, to check his temperature, then pulled back and rubbed his shoulder. "Are you unwell?"

He almost shrugged, then brought his hand to his mouth and covered another cough. She wondered if he was faking. She suppressed the thought. Zharla knew her own son would never deceive her.

Nayr gave a wan smile. "Just a little tired. That's all."

"It's been a busy week, hasn't it?" She cradled his chin with her hand. She didn't want to bring up Sheresh and the moon, but Ahrik wanted her to. "Nayr dearest, there's something we need to discuss. I spoke with your fath . . . sorry . . . Ahrik about last week's sparring session."

Nayr's eyes perked up. "What did he do now?"

"What do you mean?"

"He got us into this mess, right? He signed the order to try Sheresh?" asked Nayr, eyes boring into Zharla. "Ahrik insisted on being treated like my father for all these years, right?" Nayr threw off the covers and yanked his chin out of her grasp, an angry motion that belied a fragile physical state.

Zharla reached out a longing hand. "Nayr, wait. That's—"

"He lies about everything, Mother. Why do you still trust him?"

Guilt niggled at Zharla's gut. She couldn't let him believe such untruths. She pushed back against the confusion bubbling up inside her, then realized that these were convenient untruths, at least for her. She'd done what Ahrik asked. She'd spoken with Nayr, and she knew she couldn't press the issue with Nayr without endangering her relationship with her son.

Still, she couldn't undermine Ahrik. She fidgeted with her handkerchief. "I trust others so that I can rule, son."

Nayr sighed and grasped Zharla's hand. "You don't need him to secure the throne, Mother. I have come of age. My sons and I can—"

Zharla gasped and gave Nayr a look of shocked understanding. A sensation of cold fear rippled down her spine, and silence clamped down on the space between them. She twisted and worked her handkerchief, as if releasing her unease by degrees. Midsummer's night was still a few weeks away, but Nayr wanted to be treated as if he'd come of age already. Slowly, carefully, she stood, her back ramrod straight and her eyes fixed on a point just to the right of where Nayr sat.

"What are you suggesting, Nayr?"

"You don't need him. We both know it."

"He's a good man." Zharla furrowed her brow. "Why is it always a competition with you two?"

"Every day of my life he's lied to me, telling me he's my father when he's not."

"We thought—"

"No!" He sprang from the bed, his body a fountainhead of intensity. "He drove you to it, Mother. He's made you . . . do things . . . that you wouldn't otherwise have done."

Fire glowed behind his eyes, but the lie behind his words stabbed at her heart. She couldn't remain silent. "Tha . . . that's not true, Nayr. I was forced to choose him, in the beginning, but it's different now." She looked away. "I . . . I lov—"

Nayr grunted and shook his head with frightening vigor. "He should have been there for you, Mother. He should have been more loyal."

Zharla sighed and took in her son for a beat. "How I rule is my concern, Nayr." She tried to embrace him, but his body felt rigid and stiff with pent-up emotion. She peered into his eyes. "He wants what's best for you."

Nayr pulled away and stormed to the door. He palmed it open and turned with an expectant look on his face, of impatience mixed with pity, a clear signal that her time to leave had arrived.

He narrowed his eyes at her. "He wants to control you."

Zharla shrugged and looked away again, unable to meet his gaze. Maybe Nayr was right. Maybe she'd been Ahrik's pawn for all these years. She trusted Ahrik with everything, and it would be easy, so easy, for him just to take over.

She stopped and caressed Nayr's cheek as she went by. "I . . . I'm sorry. I didn't mean to upset you."

She stepped into the corridor. The door resolved behind her. As she walked off, she thought she heard voices wafting from Nayr's chambers, laughter and a tone of triumph.

But she couldn't be sure. Now was not the time to confront Nayr. She would tell him later that she had decided to make Ahrik demobilize his ketel. Nayr would be pleased about that.

Renla tugged at her short-cropped curls and gazed through the transluced hull. The planet Dom shrank away beneath the shuttle. Sunshine slanted across the horizon, framing the receding continent of the Eshel below with light.

After seventeen years of submitting her will to the army, the army was finally giving her her due, after a fashion. That week, Renla had finished a grueling, six-month advanced space infantry training course at Queen Zharla Station, the first of twenty-four elevator stations nearing completion around Dom. Her reward? Orders to catch this shuttle, bound for the Emerald Moon, home to all the lying, stealing, murdering human refuse that Dom had long ago rejected. Sure, she was getting a command, but who wanted a command surrounded by a bunch of moonies?

She squashed into a jump seat along with twenty or so other soldiers, her ruck stuffed between her knees, and wondered how long her anonymity would last. This was the army, and combat engineers, or diggers, were a smart bunch. They could sniff out presumed authority with the best of them.

Renla drew in a breath and smiled, content to let her anonymity live as long as possible. She looked down at the square of stiff paper nestled in her palm. Her command was the 2,000-strong Fighting 11th, a combat engineering hand that traced its lineage back over thirty years, to the War of Unification, when the Army of the Eshel unified the planet and secured women's rule. That was when Ahrik's father died, when Renla was still a snot-nosed thug in the depths of in-mountain Meran.

Renla looked into the faces of the others in the shuttle, to see if there were any clones. The Fighting 11th Hand was the first hand of *hayla*, or non-clone volunteers, to integrate clones into its ranks after the rise of Ahrik, during the War for the Emerald Moon, when Ahrik fought the secret clone army that Sheresh used to endanger the Esheli republic. Few knew what really happened back then, but Renla knew: that war was all Sheresh Shehur-li.

Renla had fought the moonies in that war, and in most of the years since. Mostly gunrunners and criminals since the war, but she'd sent a fair number of moonies to a better place, at least according to her. Now, the moonies she was about to meet up there would put a target on her back when they realized she had their relatives' blood on her hands.

She looked around the shuttle for the telltale clone markers: largish ears, mouth, or nose, or some other feature that didn't quite seem to fit. In the days before the last war, the army had given them traits for use in battle, like sharper senses, better endurance, or specific tactical abilities like the ability to climb walls or jump high. But after Ahrik revealed the secret clone units, human cloning was banned for real. A lot of the soldiers in the shuttle wore unit markings from the Fighting 11th on their shoulders, but none were clones, as far as she could tell.

Lady knows I don't need to deal with mindless freaks for two years in command. Clones are almost as bad as moonies.

Down on Dom, wispy clouds floated over the rugged, shrinking mass of the Eshel, the continent she once called home.

The person next to her leaned in. "If you think it looks good now, wait till you're on the way back."

Renla turned and saw a woman beaming at her, disciplined eyes framed by a classic digger haircut and determined jawline. The sort of person you wanted next to you in a fight. Renla shrugged, unsure if she wanted to strike up a conversation. "No, I was just . . ." She admired the view once more and let her gaze drift away. "Yeah, it's pretty amazing."

The other woman stuck out her hand. "I'm Lyn. Where do you dig?"

Renla, in the traditional greeting between women, touched her fingertips to Lyn's. "Renla. I just gradua . . . What?"

Lyn's eyes grew as wide as saucers. "Oh, you must be the new boss." Lyn's face brightened even more, which Renla hadn't thought possible. "I'm your two, ma'am."

Lyn gave a salute, made awkward by the straps holding her down, which also attracted the gaze of most of the shuttle. Renla groaned within, but immediately assumed the mask of command. What little peace she'd been looking forward to on the transfer to the moon receded like the planet below them.

Renla glanced back at the Eshel. They were moving fast now.

Lyn rustled in her seat. She pointed a thumb at Renla but addressed the rest of the shuttle. "The new boss."

Calls of "Ho, boss!" and "Dig on!" echoed around the cabin.

Renla raised a fist in greeting and leaned over to whisper in Lyn's ear. "Are you always this devious?"

Lyn smiled, but ignored the question. "Ma'am, a lot of the diggers . . . uh, soldiers . . . in the command group are here. We went gravside for an immigration crisis simulation . . . excuse me, ma'am."

Someone on the opposite side of Lyn leaned over to interrupt. They exchanged a few furtive words. Lyn turned back to Renla, adjusted her ruck to give her commander just a bit more space, and narrowed her eyes in a way that showed deepest admiration. "Ma'am, one of the standard commanders thinks you might be *that* Renla."

Renla's cheeks turned an embarrassing shade of crimson. Her face grew hot. She'd hoped it would take a bit longer for her new unit to figure it out. Renla cleared her throat and shrugged in mock guilt. "The same."

As proof, she held up the small square of cardstock with her orders.

Lyn sucked in her breath and squealed with giddy delight. She snatched the card out of Renla's hand and passed it down the line. "He even signed it himself!"

Renla wondered if she had a discipline problem on her hands, furrowing her brow at what this augured for her command assignment. Two years would pass slowly if she had to deal with hero worship every day.

Lyn, her face harboring a mix of awe and aspiration, turned back and broke into Renla's thoughts, something Renla imagined would happen a lot in the coming months. "What's he like, ma'am?"

He was Ahrik, king consort to the Queen, and the object of many a young woman's fantasies. Even Renla, who knew Ahrik as a friend, had been drawn by such flights in the past. Ahrik had been petulant and unforgiving before Queen Zharla took him as her husband, but now he commanded her armies, humble, bearing the cares of so many on his broad shoulders. If he weren't married to Renla's oldest friend . . .

Renla bit her lip, then reasserted her professional composure. She also knew how Ahrik and Zharla had struggled with their marriage over the years. She would never endanger her longest friendship for some momentary trifle of romance.

She looked down at the wispy tattoo over her right thumb, one word: *cheret*. Freedom. Most people in the Army knew Renla as a rising star under Ahrik's command, back in the early days after the War for the Emerald Moon, but almost no one knew the closely guarded secret that she had been Zharla's personal bondswoman for ten years prior to joining up. She got the tattoo after Zharla freed her, just before Zharla became Queen and freed all the bondswomen and men by decree.

Renla sighed, her face plaintive with the mask of command. Those friendships were a fading memory now. She hadn't seen either Zharla or Ahrik in . . . six years, at least. Zharla's impish son Nayr despised Renla, probably because she competed with him for the attention of Mother Dearest.

Her orders card made its way around the shuttle. When Lyn plopped the orders card back in her hand, Renla rubbed a thumb over Ahrik's signature. *When did the three of us start to drift apart?*

She cocked an eyebrow at Lyn to hide the regret she felt over her old friends' estrangement. "Well, Ahrik's out of our league, that's for sure!"

Chuckles rippled around them and Lyn gave the episode a merciful death with a polite smile. Lyn leaned into Renla once again and, with a conspiratorial air, said, "Did they tell you what to expect at our digs on Moon?"

"Just the standard infopack. Keep an eye on the portal to the White Planet. Keep life support systems running. And we're supposed to manage an influx in residence, or refugee, applications." The bilious thought of being surrounded by moonies surged back. Renla scowled. "I heard that a few dozen moonies per day apply to transfer gravside. Any idea why?"

Lyn shrugged. "Some applicants say they're sick, but I don't put much stock in it. The crisis sim we just attended gravside won't be any help managing the influx, either."

Renla smiled. "That's the army way."

Renla looked out the rear hull. Dom was small enough that they should almost be at the moon. As if on cue, the pilot's voice came over the comm. "Dock in two. With the mystery illness, I am *not* staying long, so prepare for rapid debark."

"See," said Lyn, leaning in at a whisper, "even the pilot thinks there's something going around."

The soldiers seated in the shuttle secured the sheath clasps on their qasfina, checked their distillers, and gathered up their rucks. Renla slipped her orders card into a breast pocket and checked her own gear and weapons. She unstrapped her restraints and stood, then hitched her ruck to the latch under her distiller pack, shifting her body back and forth to make the weight settle evenly.

"Lyn, lead us off," said Renla, motioning toward the rear hatch. The army, and every soldier in it, prided themselves on making any landing as smooth as a combat insertion. Go light. Go fast.

They couldn't be too careful, either. The human terrain might be hostile on the moon. Renla lined up behind Lyn, who motioned post-landing sector assignments to the soldiers behind them. Of the soldiers on the shuttle, a third would go right, a third left, and a third to the middle.

"Thirty seconds," said the pilot over the comm.

"Ma'am," said Lyn, turning back to Renla, "our command post is just off the platform at Station Prime. This'll be quick. The platform's not busy this time of day."

Renla nodded and smiled. She went through the landing checklist in her mind: *Exit. Observe. Move. Secure.*

The shuttle settled to a stop and the light over the rear hatch switched from red to green. The hatch dissolved open. A stale, wretched stench rushed into the shuttle. Instead of an open path to the command post, Renla saw hundreds of moonies packed onto the platform. A line of soldiers, their mouths and noses covered with hygiene masks, cast worried looks behind them as they tried to keep the surging mass of people at bay, distillers at the ready. Many in the crowd had red-rimmed eyes. Some, farther back from the shuttle, were doubled over in fits of coughing.

Renla recoiled at the smell and raised her distiller in reflex. *Where do these moonies think they're going?*

Lyn hesitated before debarking, just for a moment, but it was enough time for Renla to grab her two from behind with one hand and shout, "Diggers, hold!" Renla tried to exude confidence and suppress outward expressions of hatred for the gawking moonies. She unhitched her ruck, rummaged around for her health pack, and called out, "Masks."

"Ma'am," said Lyn. Her face bore a look of apology and uncertainty. "I should have known tha—"

Renla cut her off with a look. "Looks like we have an immigration crisis on our hands, Lyn."

Nayr shifted his gaze from one clone to the other. One was a clone of Ahrik, and the other was one of Nayr's. Number 26735, according to the number tape on his chest. The two clones sat behind the stone desk of the prison reception area, in a staring contest over whether Nayr should go in.

Nayr fixed the older, Ahrik clone with a steely gaze. "Do you know who I am?"

The old clone broke his stare with 26735 and swiped at his compiler display. He avoided Nayr's gaze. "Sorry, sir. New orders. Prisoner four-five-zero-six is in strict isolation."

The old clone evidently thought himself in charge by virtue of age, or the lack of a keteli accent in his speech. He cleared his throat and returned his attention to his desk compiler, as if that settled it. Nayr scanned the area and assessed his options. He had come here every day for a week, ever since his mentor Sheresh was detained on a false accusation of crimes against the race.

Ahrik couldn't win that easily.

The prison reception area was hewn of rough stone. The entrance faced the setting sun, on the opposite side of Meran Mountain from the bay, shielded from the sea breeze by the mountain's lee. The afternoon waned, and light from the sunset streamed into the reception area. It cast an orange hue over stony-hard waiting benches, polished countertops, and the single door behind the desk, the only access point to the prison.

The stink of cheap disinfectant worked in vain to cover the hypocrisy of Ahrik's so-called justice, with its white-washed lies and stale legitimacy.

Nayr reached out on the tendril link to find 26735. His next generation internal compiler allowed him to reach much more of his ketel than Ahrik and his generation could. Since Nayr's was the last ketel grown, he had a decided advantage in command and control over any other ketel commander. He used it whenever he could.

Keteli 26735 was certainly much newer to prison guard duty than the Ahrik clone. After Ahrik's lies came to light last week, Ahrik agreed to integrate his ketel with Nayr's ketel in the bureaucracy. Nayr presumed this was an effort to placate him over Ahrik's outrageous lies. Ahrik was a fool for making such a concession, with nothing in return. His guilt probably drove him to it.

Nayr smiled at the old clone. "I want to speak to your supervisor."

The old clone sighed and closed his eyes as if communicating over his own tendril link to the Ketel of Ahrik, then opened his eyes and glared in annoyance. "She asked not to be bothered, sir."

The old clone was obstructing, and someone had ordered him to obstruct. Ahrik. He would stoop low to cut Nayr off from his allies and friends. Just to cling to power.

Nayr leaned over the counter. "What's your number, keteli?"

The old clone gave Nayr a glance, then pretended to organize some papers. He avoided eye contact once again. "Sir, I don't want trouble, but she's off the grid. No more comms today."

"Go get her," said Nayr. He stabbed the counter with his finger.

The old clone looked at 26735. "You go get her."

Nayr cast to 26735 over the tendril link: *Pretend like you don't know how to find your supervisor.*

Check, responded 26735.

Keteli 26735 shrugged. "I don't . . . remember how to get there."

The old clone huffed and pushed himself up from the edge of the desk. "Fine, I'll get her myself. But don't let him through."

The keteli just nodded.

After the old clone left, Nayr pulled a general access form from his breast pocket, signed by the Queen. He had slipped it into a sheaf of papers and kept it in his pocket for the last week, just in case.

Nayr pointed at the lower half of the form. "Stamp here."

The clone complied without hesitation. Nayr grinned. Soon enough, his sons would control the bureaucracy. They would introduce Ahrik's clones to a graceful retirement, or to something more permanent. Nayr originally agreed to this side-by-side scheme between his sons and Ahrik's clones so that his sons could learn how to perform the essential functions of the bureaucracy. Now, Nayr saw a golden opportunity for himself and his loyal sons. He thought of it as an investment in the future.

Nayr took the form from 26735 and strode through the door. At each new access point, he showed the form and guards waved him through. The advantage of bureaucracy was also its greatest weakness. Decision processes broke down into manageable steps in the name of efficiency. This meant that to bypass one step was a green light to all the others. Two could play at Ahrik's game.

Nayr descended into the depths of the underground prison. This carved, murky deep was the face of power that Ahrik didn't want anyone to know about. The ugly morass swirling beneath his pristine rule over the world.

Ahrik's rule lived on borrowed time. Even if the rest of the world thought the Queen was in charge, Nayr made sure his 100,000 knew the truth: Ahrik controlled it all. As soon as he slipped up, Nayr would be ready to slip in.

Nayr showed his pass at the fifth and final checkpoint and entered the isolation section. Prisoners only came out of the isolation section on a stretcher, or in a bag. And Nayr was determined to see his mentor, Sheresh, walk out under his own power.

The unwitting guard dissolved the door to Sheresh's cell. He stopped short. "What th—"

Nayr pushed past the guard and gave a cry of dismay. He slid to the ground next to his aged mentor.

Nayr cradled Sheresh's frail head and neck in his lap and stroked his short-cropped gray hair. The older man's eyes were bruised and bloated. Two gaps stared through his teeth. Those gaps weren't there yesterday. Crusted, dried blood clung to one ear.

Nayr fought back tears of anger. "Dear sweet Sheresh, what have they done to you?" Nayr stroked his cheek, but turned a fierce glare on the guard. "What is the meaning of this?"

"S . . . sir," the guard stammered, "he was fine last I check—"

"Silence!" Nayr's eyes flared. He turned back to Sheresh. "I'll make sure they pay for this. I'll move you to home confinement, where people who love you can look after you."

Sheresh gasped a breath and shook his head in a heavy arc. He patted Nayr's arm with a frail hand. "No, my dear Nayr . . . time is near." He winced a painful breath and clutched his ribs. "Ahrik's . . . lackey . . . transferred?"

A tear of rage slid down Nayr's cheek. "Renla? Yes, Ahrik was easy to convince."

Sheresh merely smiled, bloody and toothless. His eyes fluttered closed. "Out . . . of . . . way."

Footsteps sounded outside the cell. A lot of them. Nayr glanced up. Another of the old clones gasped in surprise at the doorway. A squad of his clone comrades flanked him. Their faces looked hard. They wanted to enforce Sheresh' isolation, but they figured out Nayr's ruse too late.

Their determination turned to surprise when they surveyed the scene. The old clone called for a healer team. He gave Nayr a guilty look. "Sir, we will conduct a full investigation."

"Monsters," said Nayr. "You'll do no such thing. You did this." He scowled. "You. Tortured. Him." Nayr leaned down to kiss his mentor's forehead. When he pulled away, Sheresh's forehead glistened with Nayr's tears. "They will pay, Sheresh," Nayr said. He set his jaw for the revenge he would exact. "I will make them pay."

Sheresh gave a wan grunt. He closed his eyes with a labored breath. Nayr checked his pulse. Weak. The healer team rushed in. Nayr rested Sheresh's head on the ground with tender care and eyed the healers. "I pray you're not too late." He eyed the others. "For all your sakes."

Nayr accessed the file called Revenge in his internal compiler and updated it: "Make Ahrik pay."

3 | Subsistence

IN THE WEE MORNING, Anda sat down at his compiler station and scanned his thumb to open up the command line. He blinked through the commands to access messages, jittering in his rickety hoverchair, hoping, as he had for the week since Esh'a left, that she had sent word.

But just as the messages came up, the display went blank.

Alarm crawled over Anda's mind, and his heart thumped. He swiped his fingers across the display, to make sure it hadn't slept prematurely, then he shoved his hoverchair out to crouch down beneath the compiler station.

The chair creaked and squealed as the antiquated hover mechanism faltered. Anda winced. The racket might wake Sera.

Sure enough, after he checked to be sure it wasn't a local power supply issue, Sera padded up behind him, a yawn in her voice. "What's wrong, Abbi?"

He turned and gathered her up in a hug. "I'm sorry to wake you, Serit. Can you go back to sleep?"

She scrunched up her mouth and peered this way and that. "I can't find my *dubbi*."

Anda forced down the urgency to check for a message from Esh'a and sighed at his daughter with soft eyes. He held out his hand to her. "Well then, let's find it."

The little stuffed animal was right where he expected it to be, on her bed, so he tucked her in and laid down next to her.

"Abbi, will you sing me a song?"

Her tender innocence was all that kept him from falling into the abyss of concern for his wife. If not for Sera, he would not have lasted one day alone out here, on the edge of humanity, but Sera always needed something, and he was happy to give her whatever he could give her. It kept him from second-guessing their decision to send Esh'a to Home.

"I only know one song, Serit. Is '*Wengi Me'en*' okay?"

"Mm-hmm." She yawned again, then rubbed her eyes.

Anda sang, conscious that his rendition followed the slow, complex melody only loosely, but content to know that Sera didn't care.

Hasfer jebela-li
Bi-aqmet yom,
Ef regel en mesk
U-en qetl bi-Dom.

Hasfer nara-li
Yesh ma khali,
Ef Amma te'a doma
Khulma salam-li.

Hamshe behar-li
Qemet ka-khajer,
Ef doma esh'hu raqbi
Maslia-li li-khofer.

Hangi bi-sema-li
Meh makne quwani,
U-hesh'het mahna-li
Li-qu hayani.

Hanungi li-Simhale-li
Khidar u-was'e,
U-me'en hanalem
Men mahrik li-khaf'e

Anda waited until Sera's breathing fell into a deep rhythm, then eased himself off the bed and over to the nook where his exosuit hung. There, next to his exosuit, previously hidden by his helmet, hung Esh'a's vanilla charm. He hadn't been outside since Esh'a left, so he hadn't noticed it before. He wondered why she hadn't taken it.

He sighed, sleep now a complete stranger, the fatigue of being without his wife already a psychological drain. He lifted the charm off its hook and slipped it around his own neck. As he did so, the specter of never seeing his wife again coursed through him like a ghost brushing his soul.

He shivered, even though their little dome's climate was well-controlled, the one thing that managed to work out here.

He thought of how little money they had left, what little they'd saved to get them to the next harvest. If that ran out before Esh'a sent more, Anda would have to go to Station Prime and risk working on the formal economy. Ahrik and his men might still be hunting him down, even after all these years. The war was supposed to be over, but then the Black came, and Sera got sick, and Esh'a left. He wouldn't count anything out.

He looked at the blank compiler display in its niche. He had to know what was going on. Esh'a could be in trouble, Sera needed to be cared for, and Anda wanted, more than anything, to keep his family together.

He pulled on his exosuit. If the blank display wasn't a local power issue, then the grid might be down. He sealed the suit up his front with a slurp, then eased his helmet off its peg and over his head.

When he cycled the airlock, the world went silent. His breathing filled the suit, and he could hear every creak and crackle in the suit's aging crevices. The external airlock door slid open. It was one of the older door models, designed before the dissolving boson tech came online. Anda felt the lift when he stepped out of the artigrav field. He took a deep breath and bounded out toward the gridnode, on a vector fifteen degrees north of the algae tanks. Or, what used to be the algae tanks.

He saw the dead, cylindrical husks, all seven of them, off to the south. They gave off no light, showed no sign of life. Frustration moldered in his chest. He'd done everything he could.

He bounded toward the gridnode, a squat metal pillar that connected a number of the homes in that sector to the network. He furrowed his brow. The node shouldn't be hard to find, especially before Homerise, since the tip of the pillar usually shined a brilliant blue.

He checked his suit's wrist compiler, to make sure he had the coordinates right. The gridnode should be right h—

His heart stopped cold.

The gridnode pillar stood not two meters away, dead. He should have seen it a thousand meters off, but he'd nearly stumbled right onto it.

He turned on his exosuit lamp, then sucked in his breath. The gridnode pillar wasn't just dead, but black as night, with squishy black tentacles spiraling out from the pillar and into the light green bracken. He cast his light all around, and to his horror he saw that the deadly Black had spread all over the ground, under his feet, toward his dome.

Moon was dying. Anda had never seen a death this grim or agonizing.

He sprang off toward their dome, leaping farther and farther with each bound, driven by the horror behind him and the imperative of facing the uncertainty that their future held.

He skidded to a stop at the airlock, heart pounding, and cycled through. He ripped off his helmet and began to think of everything they'd need, at least what they could carry.

Sera still slept. He hated to wake her, but he knelt by her bed and stroked her shoulder. "Serit? Get your exosuit on. Pack your *dubbi*."

"What's wrong, Abbi?"

"We have to leave for Prime. Now."

Ahrik flipped through the training reports. His alarm grew. Ahrik's suspicions had spiked after the incident at the prison the other day. He smelled a setup, and these training reports confirmed it. He finally had what he needed to make Zharla see what was really happening. To make her see what Sheresh had done to Nayr.

He shook out his wrist, the metal band wrapped around it reminding him of his fallen sons. His wrist still ached from his sparring match with Nayr last week, when his suspicions about Sheresh and Nayr first started. If such rage lurked within Nayr at the simple news of his true parentage, then he would stop at nothing to achieve his aims.

Ahrik stared at the yellow flowers of mourning placed around his office. The untimely passing of Sheresh at the prison put so much in flux. Ahrik peered down at his handheld compiler display and fought to still his disbelief over the training reports from the Ketel of Nayr. He refused to believe what he read.

Nayr had conducted three off-cycle mobilization exercises the week before, of ten thousand men each. His assault troops, not his support units. That meant that most, if not all, of his best-trained forces were concentrated and ready to move at a moment's notice.

Zharla would never believe that her son's intent was hostile, but Ahrik knew it couldn't be anything but. This was too much to pass off as coincidence.

He closed his eyes and reached out to Hawk over the tendril link: *Hawk, describe current deployment of Ketel of Nayr.*

A pause. The tendril equivalent of stroking one's chin in thought. *Latest reports have Ketel of Nayr dispersed over twenty base locations.*

Ahrik rattled his handheld compiler in frustration. *What about these training reports?*

Sir, they reported a return to their bases after the hasty mobilization exercises last week.

They reported?

Another pause, this time accompanied by a rising sense of discomfort on the other end. Ahrik could almost hear Hawk gulp, if a gulp could be sent with thoughts. *We'll investigate right away.*

I want eyes on every unit of his. Ahrik was about to sign off when he caught an intimation of something left unsaid. He narrowed his eyes. *What is it, Hawk?*

An orderly just handed me another training exercise request.

Let me guess. From the Ketel of Nayr.

Yes, sir. Planned in two days.

Ahrik flipped wildly through his handheld display. The pressure in his chest intensified with every report and form he flipped through. *Why don't I see the request on my end?*

It's a paper form, sir.

"What?" Ahrik stood up at his desk and slapped his palm on the polished stone. The pain rippled up his arm like an electric current.

He gritted his teeth and closed his eyes in concentration. Why would Nayr file a pap—

Of course. Ahrik made sure Biriq was secure at his hip and stashed his handheld in his thigh pocket, then burst out of his office. Once in the corridor, he sprinted to the *birza*, where Zharla was to be holding court with the most prominent matrons of the Eshel. He had to get to her before Nayr did.

He huffed from the unexpected exertion, and his blood boiled with anger. He skidded to a stop outside the gleaming metal door to the *birza*.

The steward rose from her chair and looked at him in surprise. "Your Highness?"

"Is she in there with the matrons?"

Her eyes darted toward the *birza* and back. "She granted a private audience to her son."

Ahrik looked around the empty waiting area. "Where did the matrons go?"

"He ordered them sent away."

His eyes saucered wide. The air went out of his lungs. He slapped his palm to the reader next to the door and moved to pass through.

The door didn't dissolve open. At the last moment, he jammed his other hand up to keep from smashing his face into the shimmering metal surface. "What th—"

He turned furious eyes on the steward. The arrogance once ingrained on her face slurried into helpless fear. "I . . . I had no choice." She staggered back. "The prince locked it from the inside."

Ahrik unsheathed Biriq and moved to the side of the door closest to the palm reader. "Stand clear. The Queen is in danger." He took a deep breath and planted his feet. *Hawk,* he cast, *order the ready patrol to the* birza.

He jabbed at the palm reader with Biriq. The metal of the reader mechanism groaned and flayed against the battle-hardened steel, and in a few seconds the glittering connectors to the dissolution mechanism lay exposed. He flipped Biriq's killing point around and worked the steel in between the connectors, cutting all he could find, to see if it would dissolve the door.

Nothing happened. Precious seconds ticked away.

Finally the door shivered and dissolved. Ahrik flipped Biriq back to its slashing position and pushed into the *birza,* ready for combat.

Nayr's ripcord figure slunk back from the reader mechanism on the inside of the door. His own blade slithered from its sheath. Zharla sat sniffling on her throne at the far end of the hall. Her shoulders shook. She looked up when Ahrik entered, but gave no hint of recognition or awareness of danger.

On instinct, Ahrik circled to get the wall at Nayr's back. "Stow your blade, Nayr."

Nayr slid in turn, a snake searching for an opening. "You have no right to rule, Ahrik."

Ahrik slashed at the air in frustration. All these years working with Nayr, and he still hadn't learned that Ahrik meant to give power away, not keep it for himself. He shook his head. "You're wrong, Nayr." He nodded in Zharla's direction. "She rules. I only govern."

Nayr scoffed and glided to position himself between Ahrik and Zharla. "A distinction without a difference."

"Stop it, you two."

They paused and turned their attention to the Queen, each keeping an eye on each other.

"Put your little knives away."

Nayr moved his blade from defense to rest.

Ahrik sheathed Biriq, a wary eye on Nayr. He took a tentative step toward Zharla. "Are you okay? Did he harm you?"

Nayr gave a victorious chuckle and stowed his qasfin, clicking the clasp into place.

"Hurt me? What?" Zharla asked, confusion swirling on her face. "No." She pointed a finger at Ahrik. "If anything, you have."

"Me?" asked Ahrik. "I'm here to—"

"Silence!" She glared at him.

Nayr crossed his arms and set his lips in a triumphant curl.

Ahrik raised an eyebrow at Zharla, but waited. When the woman made up her mind about something, trying to dislodge the idea was a dangerous proposition.

"You," she said, jabbing her finger toward Ahrik, "you drove my son away from me."

A foreboding premonition descended on Ahrik, a future vision of the destruction that Nayr would effect in the service of some perceived good, or at least what Nayr could convince Zharla was good. The world that Ahrik had spent two decades building and defending was now under threat. Anger tightened Ahrik's chest. He would die before he let an upstart youth of seventeen maul the future with pretensions of greatness.

Winning the Queen was the key. "You don't have to choose between him and me, Zharla." Ahrik pled with his eyes. "Give me more time."

"Do you know what he told me, Ahrik? He told me that you said you never wanted to be his father."

"It wasn't like that. I—"

A hand clapped his shoulder

"Give up, old man," said Nayr, his eyes insolent. "Admit defeat." Nayr tossed his head, chuckled, and walked through the vaulted doorway of the *birza*, his step light and confident.

Ahrik knew it was an act. The fight was coming, and this was the calm before the storm. Nayr was preparing the psychological battlefield so that when he struck, the Queen would think he was the victim, and Ahrik the perpetrator.

Two could play at that game. Ahrik whipped his handheld out of his thigh pocket and rushed forward to show it to Zharla. "He's up to something. See, he's begun to mobili—"

"Short exercises, to test the readiness of his men." She gave a sage, approving nod. "He told me about that."

"Okay, but he just submitted a request for a ketel-wide exercise."

Zharla shrugged. "So?"

"He submitted it on paper so he could get his flight paths cleared, butalso keep me from seeing it until it was too late."

Zharla sighed and examined her fingernails. The ensuing silence filled a beat of impending doom in Ahrik's heart. So many years of work and effort were about to be frittered away because the Queen couldn't stand up to her son, and because that son was obsessed with winning. Nayr was drunk on power.

"Zharla," he said. "Say something."

"He declared himself independent of me." She turned red-rimmed, accusing eyes on him. "It's his right. He's close to his *qer'ish*. He'll come of age on midsummer's night. But it hurts."

"Zharla, Nayr is about to overthrow the government and make you a puppet."

She shrugged again.

Ahrik shook his head. "I won't let him. We'll fight. Freedom has a price, and we're about to pay it."

Anger flared in Zharla's eyes, and she stood with a vigor he hadn't seen for a decade. "You did this, Ahrik. You drove him from us with your overbearing ways and your disdain for his dreams."

Ahrik couldn't fathom how Nayr filled her mind with such lies.

Ahrik slumped down onto the king consort's chair next to the throne. His handheld clattered onto the polished stone floor as strength left him. He let out a dull groan, and with it the hope of a peace they deserved but would no longer enjoy. He couldn't look at her. "I tried to be the father he needed me to be. I really did."

"He was always destined to rule."

She could not possibly see what that would mean. "He's not ready."

"Stand aside, Ahrik. Let him take his place, there"—she nodded at the chair where Ahrik sat—"beside me."

He searched her face for any sign that she knew what was coming. Even an iota of judgment. Finding none, he eased himself out of the chair and gave it one last, long look. Then he fixed Zharla with a stare of pity, mixed with scorn. "How many lives can you carry on your conscience, Your Majesty?"

She returned his look, but added to it disdain. "How dare you suggest I lack the fortitude to—"

Ahrik shrugged. "Getting people to die for you is easy."

She sneered. "You seem to have no trouble with it."

He poked his own chest. "My women and men die for something." He cocked his chin at her. "When millions lie rotting across this planet, to quench your beloved son's endless thirst for power, then you'll remember my words."

"How could you kno—"

"Then you'll wish you hadn't told me to stand aside."

She stomped her foot and glared down at him from her dais. "No. You have no way of knowing what he'll do."

"If we fight him now, many will die, but we can win. If we wait, then we'll have to bathe this planet in blood to dislodge his hate and his arrogance."

"Shut up, Ahrik." She crossed her arms in defiance. "You don't know what you're talking about."

Ahrik sighed and stepped toward the doorway, then thought better of it and turned to face her once more. "Do you know how I know that you've just sentenced millions to die?"

She gave a flourish with her hand and rolled her eyes away. "Enlighten me with your wisdom."

"He's me. Eighteen years ago. He couldn't be more like me if I were his real father. If I'd been given power without having to learn what it costs, like you're giving him, I would have destroyed anything or anyone in my way."

"Leave me, Ahrik."

Ahrik stood his ground. "It'll never be enough for him. He'll get a little power, then he'll want more, and more, and more, until his rage and hatred fill Dom and the moon with the pitiful detritus of lives once lived."

Zharla drew up to her full height and leveled a challenging stare at him. "I said, leave." She sniffed. "And demobilize your ketel."

Ahrik trembled with anger. His mind drained blank as slate. She was about to unleash a monster upon the world.

He stumbled away from her throne. The ready patrol rushed to the door of the *birza* as he exited. He motioned for them to stand down and return to the barracks. His dread grew with every step he took back to his office.

On the way, Ahrik fought to calm his breathing. When he finally succeeded, to some degree, he cast: *Hawk, demobilize the ketel.*

Sir?

Demobilize, and send observers to every one of Nayr's units. I want to know every move he makes.

Yes, sir. A pregnant pause.

What is it, Hawk?

Sir, I just got a comms report. The moon just went dark.

Renla?

Not sure if it's on our end or hers.

Ahrik sucked in a breath. Nayr might be behind this, too. *Hawk, make sure our old base outside Meran is stocked with weapons and supplies.*

That base hasn't been used in almost two decades, sir.

It will be. It will be.

Ahrik pressed into his office and collapsed into his hoverchair for a moment, then rose to clean his distiller and sharpen his qasfin.

Nayr sucked in the sweet smell of ammonia and tried not to think about the loss of Sheresh. He tried to think, instead, of the victory he'd won that morning, when he put Ahrik in his place in front of the Queen. He smiled at that thought and squeezed the trigger inside his distiller.

"Whoo-wee, 2," he said. "I will never get tired of mashing targets with the command company."

"Check, Father," said 2 as he sent the last of his own charges downrange. *Thu-thu-thunk. Thu-thu-thunk.* "Nothing like it."

Clouds of elemental gas hovered over the target area, five hundred meters away. Every week, the one hundred or so members of the command company met to practice tactical skills, be it to destroy targets at the range or engage in hand-to-hand or compete in athletics. This week: moving targets at medium range. The *thu-thu-thunk* of distillers echoed up and down the line and puffs of dust blossomed in the target area. Often enough, a target exploded with a splendid red *poof.*

Nayr emptied his chamber and smiled as his last charge created a red *poof* of its own. His distiller charged down with a mellow buzz. He peered up at 3, his ops chief. It was his turn to organize the week's competition. "Hey, 3. How many charges did I get out of my pack this week? Felt like a lot."

3 raised the gauge to his eye and examined the reading. He nodded. "Check, Father. Five hundred and twelve charges."

Nayr shook his arm out of his weapon and jumped up. "That's an eight percent improvement in efficiency over the last two months." He clapped 2 on the shoulder. "Put in a commendation for the research company. We need advantages like this."

The rest of the command company finished emptying their chambers and began to unfold themselves from their prone positions and compare results with their peers. The last *thu-thu-thunk* sounded down the line, and a stiff breeze off the ocean north of Meran blew another whiff of ammonia mixed with fetid algae back toward the command group. Nayr stroked his chin and sauntered over to 3. "Who won this week?"

3 smiled. "Father, a better question would be, who came in second, check?"

A twinge of loneliness stabbed at Nayr. A loneliness he couldn't show, not to his men, his sons. Every week he won. He worked as hard or harder than any man in his ketel at tactical skills, but he always came away with the nagging impression that his sons let him win. "C'mon, 3, don't tell me my command group is going soft on me."

His attempt at humor felt flat and hollow. His sons still laughed. Nayr wondered what it would be like to truly have someone enjoy what he said.

2, Nayr's aide, took the gauge from 3 and gazed through it. "Check, Father. You hit eighty-eight out of the 750 targets. The command company as a whole only took out 648 targets.

Nayr narrowed his eyes. The equipment wasn't working right. He couldn't question the numbers now, though. "648? Is that a new ketel record?"

His intel chief, 4, walked over, rubbing down his weapon with a scrap of cloth. "Father, it's a new command company record, alright." He chuckled. "But two companies in the 45th Hand are tied at 691 in mid-range moving targets. Six forty-eight ranks us fifty-first out of 500 companies in the entire ketel."

Nayr cocked his head and stared. "Thanks for being such a killjoy, 4. You know our company is less than half the size of most other companies, right?"

"Just giving the numbers, Father." He cast down his eyes, but Nayr knew it was an act. 4 never shied away from speaking his mind. Honest to a fault.

Nayr gave him a playful punch on the shoulder, but even that felt awkward. "That's why you're my intel chief." He turned to walk back to the shuttles and motioned 2 over. "I'm going into the city tonight. Announce leave for the command company, for breaking our record, but make sure personnel are rotated on short shifts to maintain minimal staffing at headquarters."

2 nodded. "Check, Father. We'll hold down the base until you get back."

Nayr waved to his command company and hopped into the bay of his personal shuttle. He grabbed a handhold in the rear cabin. "Pilot," he called. "Meran. Shtera Umqi."

"Check, Father."

Nayr's legs wobbled as the shuttle lifted off. He called up a jump-seat to sit on. As he sat down, he noticed his hand shake, the hand that had just been inside the distiller.

The pilot stole a nervous glance back at Nayr. *You okay, Father?* he cast over the tendril link.

Nayr put up his closed fist to show that he was okay. When he brought his fist back down, he removed his glove and flexed his fingers back-and-forth. He stopped flexing, but his hand still shook. He slammed his fist into his palm in frustration, certain that he had hit only one target, not eighty-eight.

The shakes in his hand were becoming more frequent.

He removed his yellow armband, sign of mourning for Sheresh, and his frustration grew. As he changed out of his uniform, he wondered why Ahrik had Sheresh tortured with such cruelty. Sheresh was on death's door anyway.

He couldn't melt into the press of humanity fast enough when he arrived at Shtera Umqi. He hated the masses of people here in the heart of in-mountain Meran, but he was finally alone here. In the midst of his 100,000 clones he was a celebrity that everyone adored but no one really wanted to understand, a somebody but a nobody. But when he descended to in-mountain Meran he was just himself, a nobody, but a somebody. No one else looked like him, dressed like him, or thought like him. People jostled him and didn't apologize, and shouted at each other without even looking in his direction, much less offering a look of submission or apology. Thousands upon thousands of sweaty bodies eddied to and fro in the station. They swirled in and out of Meran's warren of tunnels and vice. These people didn't care who was from the palace and who wasn't.

He could get lost in the danger down here. He never felt so alive as when he came down here. He hated it down here.

He drank in the sights, sounds, and smells of in-mountain Meran. This was the beating heart of the city, not stuffy and entitled out-mountain Meran, where Mother and Ahrik lived. Here, the Mothers of the Eshel fled from the horrors of The War thousands of years ago. Now their city thrived in-mountain and out-mountain both, in spite of Mother's rule.

He would change that. He would save Mother's legacy. She would never regret telling Ahrik to stand aside. Nayr would never regret causing her to.

The crowds began to thin as he passed through the spice market. The air smelled ripe with the tang of saffron and cinnamon. Some vendors called out their wares, but most were already closed for the day. On his left, he passed the social hall where Mother and Ahrik were almost killed in a rebel attack at the start of the War for the Emerald Moon. The rebel weapons sourced from the White Planet destroyed the doorway, now a lighter shade than the surrounding rock, the rest of the tunnel wall darkened by two thousand years of grime and hot breath.

He pressed on, from the spice market to the pottery market, and then to the tech market, where the crowds wore especially thin and the lights grew dim. He fingered his qasfin, cloaked at his thigh, just in case he had to defend himself.

He turned down an alleyway, dim and dank. The eyes of shadowy figures followed him as he slipped through the alley and stopped at a poorly-lit storefront for off-the-shelf handheld compilers, aerialbots, and surveillance equipment. The thick man behind the counter glared at him. The man's forehead gleamed with sweat, and he worked a wad of something foul in his cheek. "Whadda yuh wunt?"

Nayr stuffed his shaking hand into his pocket and cocked his chin at the man. "I haven't seen you here before." Nayr narrowed his eyes. "Do you know who I am?"

The man stood to his full height and moved around the counter with a menacing air. He looked down on Nayr, then spat into a corner behind him. The man flexed his neck. Veins popped. "Yuh'z one'f th'little prunce's pusky clones. State yur buz'ness quick, or I'll pound yuh down t'size."

Nayr pounced. His fists flew in a lightning, seven punch combination, then he danced out of the way of the man's lumbering counterattack, slow but deadly. Nayr crouched, then sprang up and caught the man with an uppercut. The man's head whipped back and he tottered toward the counter. As his head recoiled, Nayr grabbed the man's hair and slammed his head onto the stone surface. Something cracked, and blood spurted from the man's nose.

Nayr shook the pain out of his knuckles and brought his mouth close to the man's ear. "Looks can be deceiving. Call the Healer for me. Now."

The man rose up on his forearms. He cast stunned and ponderous eyes about, as if trying to figure out what just happened. He shook his head, a hint of fear and confusion in the movement. He held his nose. "No one culls th'Healur. He comes whun he wunts."

Nayr juked a fist in his direction, and the man flinched. The man held up one hand in surrender and the other on his nose, then backed to the wall. He reached toward a shelf and placed his hand on a reader hidden there. Not twenty seconds later, a door behind the man dissolved. He nodded Nayr inside while blood dribbled from his nose.

Red light illuminated the room inside. Old, stained carpets hung on the wall, and the room felt cold and wet, but it smelled of alcohol and cleaning agents. A couch sat against the far wall, an ankle-high stone table reposing before it, and on the couch sat the Healer, a red-robed man with considerable shoulders and a baritone hum to his voice, eyes piercing and amber.

"Come, Nayr. I'm sorry for my man out there. I just brought him on, and he hasn't quite learned the ropes yet." The Healer's voice gurgled like a pleasing, in-mountain brook. He patted the couch cushion next to him and smiled in his deceptive, unassuming way, then sighed. "Some people can't tell a cheap imitation from the real thing."

Nayr plodded over to the couch. Emotion welled in his gut. He felt cut off from so much, from so many. And Sheresh. Dear Sheresh. He sank onto the couch and nestled close to the man, who reached around and caressed Nayr's shoulder.

Nayr took a deep breath and stared at his trembling hand. His anguish swirled and fought for release. "They killed him."

The Healer squeezed Nayr close. "Even Sheresh could not cheat death."

Nayr pulled away and shook his head, eyes sad. "No. Too soon."

The Healer pierced Nayr with his look, as if searching for some well of inner resolve in the young man's heart. The Healer pursed his lips and produced a small felt bag. "Perhaps it's time we discussed revenge."

Nayr choked back a sob and snatched at the bag, but the Healer moved it out of the way with the deftness of a panther. "First, Nayr, promise me you won't overdo it."

Nayr's eyes shot through with red and his breath came quick and shallow. He whispered, "Anything."

The Healer gave the bag to Nayr, who tore open the leather tie and pushed his fingers through the opening. With his unmatched dexterity, hand steady and even, Nayr pinched a tiny pill, withdrew it, and gazed at it with keen adulation. He opened his mouth to receive this gift.

Saliva trickled from the corner of his mouth.

The tiny pill dissolved with a fulfilling tingle as soon as it touched his tongue. Nayr caught an aroma sweeter than any left by a distiller. He sank back into the couch, body flaccid for a moment, and drew in a deep draught of air.

After a moment, Nayr reached out and entwined his fingers through the Healer's. Nayr sighed with contentment. "You know me so well."

The Healer squeezed Nayr's hand in return. "You are a gem, Nayr. Now let us discuss how we will overthrow Ahrik Jeber-li, the Usurper, and end his unholy reign of terror."

Nayr smiled, really smiled, for the first time since Sheresh died. "My thought exactly."

From her place registering moonie vagabonds on the Station Prime platform, Renla furrowed her brow. The way her two strode up, wading with single-minded determination through the detritus and hum of exasperated moonies, Renla could tell Lyn was a special kind of frustrated. No, frustrated and worried. Lyn planted her feet next to the table where Renla sat.

Lyn put her hands on her hips. "Ma'am?"

Lyn glanced up and down the platform, foot tapping a nervous beat, avoiding Renla's gaze. She was only barely keeping it in. Renla motioned with her head toward her office, and Lyn responded with a quick, almost imperceptible nod of the head, making her hygiene mask jiggle. Her two wanted a private word.

A moonie family standing nearby, waiting to be registered, turned their heads to the newcomer. Moonies were scruffy and ragged, and they smelled of rotten algae, but they gave Renla and her diggers a wide berth. No one had tried to kill her—yet—but Renla had tasked her diggers with improving the moon's system of bunkers and launch tubes soon after she'd arrived, just in case things got testy.

She didn't trust these moonies, not one bit.

Lyn called them refugees, the moonies squatting on the platform at Station Prime, but Renla wasn't ready to give them that much credit. Sure, things were calm, and the platform didn't normally get much use, but the moonie squatters were a hazard to health and good order.

Renla set her stylus down next to the handheld compiler on the registration table. She sighed into her hygiene mask, then turned to the healer sitting next to her and raised an eyebrow. The healer's young eyes assumed a brave front. More and more moonies flowed into Station Prime every day, most with the same symptoms, and all destitute, but Renla didn't have enough people to keep the moon's life support systems running and improve the defensive works and deal with refugees and provide security across the moon and solve all their petty little problems. The Fighting 11th were diggers, not peace forces or health inspectors.

And half of the moonies that shuffled into Station Prime had lived their lives completely off the grid, as algae farmers, small-time miners, or smugglers, so the official records Renla had were useless. Renla had to use every available bit of womanpower in the Fighting 11th, including herself, to register the moon's population onto the local compiler system by hand. It was the only way to get a handle on the mass of people arriving at Station

Prime every day, and eventually figure out who had left the moon and who hadn't.

The healer nodded to Renla. "I can do both the registration and the health screening, ma'am."

Renla stepped off the platform with Lyn and into her office, resolving the door behind them. Silence enveloped them. She removed her mask and waved on the lights. They couldn't afford to waste resources by leaving the lights on all the time. Renla tinted the windows so they could see out but no one could see in. "What's up, two?"

"Ma'am, comms with gravside just went dark."

Renla cocked her head and stroked her chin. "Strange. Our end, or theirs?"

"Doubt it's us, ma'am. The system up here is rickety, but all the diagnostics checked out this morning."

Renla plopped into her hoverchair and rubbed her temples. She didn't like what this portended. The refugees, the sickness, and now this. She arched an eyebrow at her two. "The next shuttle from gravside is scheduled to arrive tomorrow, right?"

"Check, ma'am."

"Keep working on the connection gravside, but if that shuttle is late, even by a nanosecond, I want to know."

"Check, ma'am."

The worry melted from Lyn's face, but the hint of frustration remained. Even when Renla stood and made a move toward the door, Lyn didn't move, much less salute to signal that she knew their conversation was at an end.

"What is it, Lyn?" asked Renla.

Lyn gestured around her, arms sweeping to take in all of the moon. "Aren't the defensive works a waste, ma'am? We're spread pretty thin already, but we're still building strong points and launch tubes and even a rail gun. The civilians . . ."

"Moonies."

". . . are getting restless, too. They think we're protecting ourselves against them . . ."

"The thought occurred to me."

". . . but the war is over, and every subcommander in the Fighting 11th is asking, 'What for?'"

Renla leaned against her desk and folded her arms across her chest. She turned up a corner of her mouth. "Call it a hunch, Lyn. An insurance policy." She nodded toward the moonies massed on the platform outside her office. "That sickness they have? It can't be a coincidence. Someone's trying to depopulate this rock, and we don't know why."

Now Lyn settled her hands on her hips. "You think Moon is prepping for a fight?"

"Our comms just went dark, didn't they?"

Lyn set her jaw. "Maybe someone gravside had something to do with both the sickness and the comms blackout."

The name "Nayr" sprang to Renla's mind, but she bit it back. He was old enough now to insert himself into palace politics, but she needed proof before she could cast her gaze to the palace. Renla narrowed her eyes in a challenge to Lyn. "The sickness. The exodus. The comms blackout." Renla shook her head. "Something's up. Keep building."

Lyn frowned. "Those are refugees out there, and they're sick. Why aren't they the immediate priority?"

"Look, you and I both know I have no great love for moonies, but the comms blackout is unsettling." Renla turned to the window and shrugged. "The sickness isn't bacterial or viral, Lyn. It's biotech, or I'm not a combat engineer. We need to figure out a way to scrub it out of our air. Only the moonies born up here seem to come down with it. The troubling question is, who would have the will and the know-how to make a biotech agent like that? Did this come from the moon, or from Dom? Someone thinks the last war isn't over, and I'm not going to sit around and let that someone get a jump on me. I don't care where they come from."

Lyn cocked her head and looked at Renla askance. "If it were up to you, wouldn't we just abandon Moon?"

"Absolutely not. There's an interdimensional portal to the White Planet trailing in the moon's gravity well, and it's my job to know who goes in and who goes out." Renla crossed her arms. "Speaking of which, is that derelict space station on the far side of the moon up and running yet?"

"Harkov? Not yet . . . but it was just a research station. I'm not sure—"

"Strip it. Arm it. Upgrade the boson drive, power core, and mag shields."

Lyn sighed and jotted something down on her handheld compiler. "Yes, ma'am."

Renla gave a conciliatory gesture. "Okay, I'll think about slowing down the defensive works and the Harkov refurbish, but I remember the last war, Lyn. My first obligation is to serve the Queen, then protect my diggers, and then, and only then, worry about a bunch of dirty, coughing moonies."

Lyn paced in a circle and gesticulated with her hands, as if she'd won a small victory from her boss. "If you have no love for these people, then why register them by the thousands? She gave Renla a quizzical look, calmer now than before. "They're going gravside anyway, ma'am. After they leave, they won't be our problem."

Renla rose, patted her aide's shoulder, and moved toward the door, signaling that their conversation was at an end. "Trust me on this one, Lyn. If this turns into a shooting war, we'll want precise records of every nook and cranny on this rock. We'll want to know who's here and who's not." She peered out the window and onto the platform. "The next war will make a lot of criminals, and a lot of victi—"

She froze, her gaze riveted on the moonies outside, in particular on one man, standing at the table with the healer doing the registration and health screening by himself. The blood drained from Renla's face.

Lyn eased aside. "What's wrong, ma'am? You look like you've seen a ghost."

Renla dared not divert her gaze from the man at the table, a little girl in his arms. "I have," said Renla, blinking once. "Seen a ghost, I mean." Renla pointed to her distiller racked on the wall, then reached out a hand to dissolve the door. "Get that distiller ready. Just in case he's dangerous."

The murmur and hum of the platform broke on them like a wave when the door opened. Renla eased toward the man and his daughter, crept almost, unwilling to believe what she saw. As she neared, she overheard his conversation with the frazzled healer.

"... her name is Sera," said the man.

His voice was unmistakable. It was him, she was sure of it.

"And her mother? Where is she?" asked the healer.

"On Home ... er ... gravside." His eyes softened at the mention of the girl's mother, and he leaned forward with heartfelt earnestness. "We need to—"

He saw Renla. Their eyes locked, and recognition washed over him. His face grew as white as a sheet. His eyes darted this way and that, as if contemplating flight. He pulled Sera closer to him and bent his knees, ready to dash off.

Renla held up a hand in a plea for calm. "Shahl."

Lyn powered up the distiller with a hum, and the man's eyes grew wide with fear. "My name ..." His eyes darted between Renla and the distiller. "My name is Anda."

"Healer," said Renla, "mark both 'Shahl Jeber-li' and 'Anda' down for his name." She focused her attention on the man who called himself Anda, but whom she knew as Shahl. "I thought you were dead."

"Shahl is dead. I am Anda now."

"I . . . I have to arrest you. I can't ignore a palace warrant. I'd be cashiered in a heartbeat."

Shahl's lips trembled. "If someone else were here instead of you, someone who didn't know me, would I be under arrest?"

Renla shrugged. "I'm here."

Lyn slid around behind Shahl, the distiller trained on his back, but Renla shook her head to call off her aide. Renla took a step toward Shahl. His daughter clutched his neck, her back to Renla. Her long auburn hair was odd, out of place. Every other moonie child she'd seen had a close-cropped or shaved head.

The girl coughed quietly. She had the illness, too. She was born here, then. She looked to be about six or seven. Shahl had been hiding out on the moon for a long time.

Renla was almost close enough to grasp Shahl's sleeve. "Shahl, the Queen almost chose you to be her husband, then you disappeared. Zharla will be very, very interested to know you're alive."

Shahl winced, as if at a painful memory. "I need to find my wife, Renla. She left Moon to go to Home, but I haven't heard from her." His eyebrows softened in a plea. "Please help me."

Renla bit her lip and forced down the emotion rising in her throat. She knew Shahl Jeber-li well. He was a good man, at heart, but she couldn't defy her best friend, the Queen. "You're under arrest, Shahl Jeber-li, by order of the Queen. Right now, she's the only person that can help you."

He sighed and looked down at his child, in resignation. "Don't hurt Sera."

Sera coughed and looked at Renla with red-rimmed eyes, her face hollow, but fearless and utterly trusting of her father.

Renla took another step forward, careful not to touch the girl. Her father might not be a moonie, but she was. "You two are going gravside on the next shuttle."

Sera perked up and smiled. "To Home?"

Renla's lip curled at the smell of algae on the girl's breath. "Yes, to Ho . . . Dom."

Sera squeezed her father's neck again. Her face brimmed with childish joy as she peered into his face. "See, Abbi. I knew we were going to Home."

Renla's heart twinged at the girl's innocence, but kept her distance nonetheless. Shahl's face pled with Renla to keep his daughter safe. Renla narrowed her eyes and considered the girl and her father for a moment.

Shahl Jeber-li had a moonie daughter, and Renla would have to send them both gravside to face the Queen's justice. Maybe Renla would get some answers about the comms blackout when that shuttle showed up tomorrow. If it showed up tomorrow.

She turned to Lyn and removed all tenor of compassion from her face. "Take them to the brig. I need you to give tomorrow's shuttle pilot a personal message for the palace. They need to know an old friend is coming to visit the Queen." Renla grunted at her two. "I bet the shuttle's electromag comms will work just fine."

4 | Moral Force

A QUEEN WAS NEVER TO SHOW emotion in public, but how Zharla wanted to. The urge to scream at the world and its weighty expectations, at her weak and distant husband, at her manipulative son, built like a pressure cooker left on the heat too long. An anxious wind wandered over the platform at Meran's intercity transporter station, bringing the taste and crispness of fall to the air. But Zharla boiled inside.

The platform was clear of passengers. She'd sent all her people away, so she could have a moment's peace, a chance to consider her plight, to wallow in the pity of her life. This small consolation, this bit of solace, away from the palace and its politics, was a perquisite of being Queen.

When the message had arrived from the moon shuttle yesterday, saying that an old friend was coming to visit, Zharla pounced on the chance to escape from the palace. Maybe Renla was on the shuttle. Zharla had no older friend than Renla. She yearned to see Renla again.

She needed love, without strings attached. She wondered, for the millionth time, how her life might have been different if she'd chosen Shahl instead of Ahrik. Her mother wouldn't really have killed Shahl, like she'd threatened. And Zharla wouldn't have won the burden of rule, this yoke, without Ahrik. Once light, this burden now chafed and pinched and tightened at her neck.

Away in the distance, a speck of light grew in the burgeoning dawn. The shuttle flickered on the horizon.

Maybe Zharla could have raised a natural son or daughter, or many of them, in love and harmony, if she'd chosen Shahl instead. She loved Nayr, but he didn't deserve to be burdened with circumstances beyond his control, like she had been at such a young age. Power was ruining him, she could tell. The unflinching loyalty of 100,000 clones had stoked his ambition until it burned like a swirling bonfire, a vortex whose only reason for being was expansion.

She felt herself being sucked into his need for power and violence, against her will. Maybe Ahrik was right to want to stand up to Nayr, to force him to wait to hold power, but a piece of her begged to give Nayr his chance. She had to encourage her son's decency and goodness by giving him the opportunity to fail.

The shuttle drew closer, bearing Renla on her impromptu visit from the Emerald Moon. At least Zharla would be able to enjoy the loving company of her closest friend for a few days.

Pangs of regret needled at Zharla's breast. Nayr had declared himself free of Zharla and Ahrik, then stayed at the palace. Her relationship with Nayr now resided in a tenuous netherworld, where he wanted her political confidence but not her maternal concern. A tear formed in the corner of her eye at this thought, but she fought it back with a determined sniff, asking herself where she had failed as a mother.

The bosonic hum grew as the shuttle closed with the platform. It settled to a stop before her. The basso wash from the engine flowed over her, rippling her robes and tickling her ears. She drew in a cleansing breath to suppress the vestiges of emotion, to steel herself for yet another encounter with circumstance, a reminder of what love her life lacked.

The main hatch hissed open, and Zharla sucked in her breath in shock. A ghost stood before her, a specter blown in on the dusty wind of times past, a little girl resting on his hip, her long auburn hair flowing over her shoulders and framing a face full of insight and peace, and wonder at the brightness and splendor of a new world.

Zharla couldn't bear to look at the father, that ghoul, but she didn't need to. Her knowledge of him pulsated from every receptacle of her memory, unforgettable hope and pleasure wrapped in layer upon layer of the regret she'd built up over a life without him. It had been long enough that she'd stopped looking for him, long enough that she'd lost hope of seeing him again. Last week, she'd finally given in to Ahrik's protests to stop living in the past and entertaining impossible thoughts.

And yet here he stood, Ahrik's brother, Shahl, eyes as placid and kind as the day he left, fifteen years ago, now with a child whose face carried his incisive wisdom and guileless peace.

The little girl squeezed her father's neck, and he rubbed her back with a tenderness that pricked at Zharla's heart. Oh, to be that little girl, wrapped in arms of love and compassion, held close by that man, standing there.

Shahl looked up and down the platform with a nervous air. He bit his lip. "Your Majesty . . . I thought we were under arrest."

Zharla thought those impossible thoughts, forbidden ones. Did she err in her wish? Did she really have an obligation to bind her heart unflinchingly to Ahrik and their stillborn and stilldead marriage? Her yearning for slivers of love, even the precious scraps that fell from someone else's table, begged her to forget every promise she'd ever made.

If she were not the Queen, she would not feel so bound by others' expectations. She forced herself to look only at the girl, for fear of what she would find in that other face. After all, if he had a daughter, then he probably had a wife, too, or at least some other woman that held his fancy.

Almost imperceptibly, she shook her head, then whispered, "Did Renla tell you to say that?"

The man stepped off the shuttle and onto the platform, the soles of his moonie boots clomping on the rough stone. "Zhar . . . Your Majesty," he said, nodding at the girl, "this is Sera."

Zharla gave a curt smile, her gaze focused on the middle distance. She searched her soul for the strength even to utter his name. The wraith of what could have been would haunt their every shared look, their every conversation.

She had always called him "my Shahl," back when she thought he'd be her husband, but she dared not utter that now, after all this time. In the overripe silence that followed his introducing the girl, Zharla knew she had to say something. Admitting that he might care for someone else now would brook too much pain, would be an admission that their feelings, all those years ago, had somehow been misplaced.

She worked up the courage to glance at his face one more time. Tears wickered into the corners of her eyes, and all her political power, won with Ahrik at her side, the laudations of an entire planet stroking her ambition, faded into meaningless oblivion, a wisping memory on some distant thread of time.

She smiled then, like she hadn't smiled in an age. She loved her husband, and her son, but they were flawed, irascible. And gone. Her Shahl, even after all these years, was as perfect as the day they first fell in love.

He smiled back, and something beautiful bloomed within Zharla's breast. This hope within her, what she felt, it could grow. At that moment, she was sure that hope held no limit at all. "Thank you for coming back to me, Shahl."

His face fell, stabbing and twisting like a knife slipped, with too much ease, into the hope that she'd so briefly known. Anger and sadness seeped in, to make their counterattack on the hope that had dared to show its face.

Love couldn't be that easy.

"Oh," he said, trying to smile once again, but the corners of his mouth turned in a slightly different direction this time. "I guess Your Majesty didn't hear. My name is Anda now."

Zharla kept her face as immovable as stone, while she did battle with the anger and disappointment within her. She refused to relent, though, despite the lack of caring that his words carried to her heart, refused to see this moment for anything other than the happy circumstance it was.

She smiled again. Her smile did not descend to the depths of her soul, but it was brave and strong and practiced over years of ruling a planet. "I don't care, Shahl." She gave him a pointed look. "All that matters now is that you're safe."

He gave a nervous look at Sera, as if unsure whether Zharla's words extended to his daughter. "Thank you . . . um . . . Your Majesty. We're grateful."

Zharla didn't care one bit for the girl or for her gawking at everything around them, but there was no need to let Shahl know that, at least not yet.

She would enjoy him for a while. Whether he wanted her to or not.

Anda burst into wakefulness. The knowledge of something amiss stabbed at his awareness. Light slithered through a tiny fissure in the blackout curtains, leaving the room musty and dark. He bolted upright, and his hand came down on the mattress next to him.

The empty mattress.

Sera. Gone.

He leaped out of the bed and into a fighting stance. The cold, hard stone sent shockwaves through his bare feet, and he widened his eyes to make out whatever shapes or movement he could in the dimness. Zharla had put him and Sera in Zharla's old chambers in the Tameri family estate, now a cold and lifeless building with few inhabitants. Whether being here was meant as captivity or warm reception, the empty bed compounded his anxiety. He'd stepped into Zharla's old chambers only once before last night, but he thought, bitterly, how this place had set his life on a path he never expected, as a participant in a war he neither wanted nor deserved.

Anda peered into the darkness. An unwelcome presence swirled in the room. "Who's there?" he growled. "Sera?"

"Abbi?"

There, near the door. In an instant, he saw the path he needed to take: over the bed, then across the rug to the doorway.

He moved, every muscle driven by the acutest fight reflex. His little girl was in danger.

They'd only been on Dom one night, and already his worst fears were realized.

"Abbi?" Her voice moved away as he flew toward it, and the rising terror in her voice filled his chest with dread. No, no, no. Zharla told him they would be safe.

He should not have believed her.

The door hissed open. He heard a grunt, like someone lifting a little girl and surging out into the corridor.

No!

He reached the rug and set himself to spring through the door before it closed, but in that moment, just before flight, shadows near the wall shifted. Something dark lurched toward him, a club or fist maybe, and it crashed into his chest with a burst of pain. The air went out of him, and the world spun as the force of the blow knocked him to the floor. His legs sprawled into the air as his body tried in vain to dissipate the kinetic energy from the fall.

He struck the floor and gasped for breath. Sharp pain blossomed in his head. He tried to raise himself up, but a boot on his chest forced him back down.

"It's probably best that you stay right there," said a voice, young and menacing and cold, not a voice he'd heard before, but one that dripped with the arrogance of always being obeyed.

He squeezed out a few breaths. "Who—"

"No, no, no," said the voice.

Anda could almost hear his finger wagging, and he was sure that the voice didn't belong to the boot. Anda was outnumbered.

Feet shuffled in his direction. "The better question is, are you my father?"

Anda squirmed against the boot on his chest. "If you hurt my daughter, I'll—"

"You'll what?" The young man chuckled, a hard and calculating sound. "Don't worry, your daughter is safe. I sent her to the palace healing center so my healers can take care of her."

Anda gritted his teeth and raised his palms in a sign of surrender. He was beaten, at least in the near term, and he didn't want to address this young man with some thug's boot on his chest.

"Let him up, 23," said the young man, with his air of presumed authority.

Who addresses other people with numbers instead of names?

The thug grunted, clearly reluctant to move, and released Anda, who pushed himself up and rested against the stone wall. He realized then who this must be.

Anda coughed. "You're Zharla's son, aren't you? Why—"

The young man cut him off with a scoff. "Answer my question. Are you my father?"

Painful memories flooded into Anda's mind, memories he'd long thought suppressed, and now this lunatic meant to dredge them up again. Anda examined his hands absently. "Leave the past in the past."

"I have your daughter."

Anda glowered. "The Queen gave her word that we would be safe."

Zharla's son merely folded his arms and curled his insolent upper lip.

Anda sighed and pushed himself to a standing position against the wall, to regain a speck of dignity. "The one who fathered you is dead, but there's more to being a father than genetics. Ahrik—"

"Don't use that name!" The young man's breath heaved in the stillness.

Anda couldn't help but think how seriously maladjusted this young man was. If he hadn't just kidnapped Anda's daughter, Anda might feel sorry for him.

The situation was delicate. Anda searched for boldness in the depths of his soul, then walked over to throw open the curtains. He wouldn't let this upstart win that easily. "Nayr, is it?"

The light that streamed into the room showed the young man stroking his chin, as if waiting to see where Anda was going with this.

"My name is Anda, or Shahl, as your mother calls me."

He grunted. "I've heard."

"Your conception was a crime that deserves to stay in the past." Anda gave a nervous glance toward the thug, who turned out, in the light of day, to be a clone of Nayr, albeit with a nastier aspect. The thug's scowl of unswerving devotion to Nayr unnerved Anda. "What do you want from me, Nayr?"

"The truth."

Anda was walking into a trap, he was sure of it. "Your mother—"

"She gives me half-truths. Tell me what happened."

"And you'll let my daughter go?"

Nayr nodded with an air of contemplation that Anda wanted to believe. He had no choice. "Tell me what happened," said Nayr, "and your daughter will go free."

Anda sighed and sat on the edge of the bed. He considered his options, which included nothing better than trusting his . . . well . . . nephew, he supposed. "Very well." Anda eyed the rug. "Your mother and I were almost married, once upon a time, but she chose Ahr—."

"The Usurper." Nayr gave a scowl like the taste of bitter milk.

Anda hesitated at the epithet, but continued. "The details aren't clear to me, but she was assaulted on her wedding night, here in these chambers, then Ahrik went off to war, and you were born. I . . ." Anda heaved a breath and rubbed his knees to hold back the emotions flooding into his chest. "I killed the rapist when . . . it's confusing . . . when there was a battle here, in this compound. That's when I realized that Sheresh was behind it all."

Confusion rushed into Nayr's expression. "Sheresh?"

"Sheresh Shehur-li, Ahrik's old military supervisor, and the first man to sit on the Council of Elders. He must be retired and out of the picture by now."

Nayr's look of confusion transformed into detachment, then into vivid hate.

"Wha . . . what's wrong?" asked Anda.

The clone moved toward his commander, face lined with concern.

Nayr fixed Anda with a poisonous glare, eyes drilling into him. Nayr's jaw flexed and rippled under the skin of his callow face. "You lie." He moved away. "Come, 23."

Anda leaped from the bed and grabbed Nayr's sleeve as he stepped toward the door. "I told you the truth, Nayr. We had a bargain."

Nayr stared at Anda's hand on his sleeve, then met Anda's expectant stare with indignance and disdain, like someone out for a stroll who is attacked by a swarm of pesky flies. He gave a slow shake of his head, a gesture full of finality and fury. "Sheresh would never do the things you accuse him of."

Nayr gripped Anda's hand, like pincers on a vice, and yanked back his sleeve. He said nothing more, but turned on his heel and burst through the door. Anda rushed to stop him, but the clone cocked back a fist and gave Anda a blow to the head that set his world to spin.

Anda collapsed onto the rug.

The door hissed closed, and even though he knew it would be locked from the outside now, Anda still crawled to the door, banging his knees, and slapped his hand to the reader. He slammed his palm onto it over and over again, each time yelling Sera's name, until his voice was sore and strength left him.

Grit and grime clung to every nook and cranny of in-mountain Meran, and Ahrik wanted only one thing more than to get back to the palace: to find Nayr and shake some sense into him. It was one thing to spurn one's own parents, especially one's mother, but it was quite another to shirk one's duty as a leader.

Years of training and molding Nayr into a worthy soldier, and for what? So he could fritter away an evening in whoring and drugging in Meran's warrens and tunnels with the very men he was meant to lead. What indignity.

Apparently, Zharla was put off by something else. She was pretty tight-lipped about it earlier, but Ahrik heard rumors of Nayr making a captive out of one of her guests that morning.

Ahrik had no patience for petty palace politics, and he certainly couldn't keep track of Zharla's guest book.

Ahrik's boot almost landed in a puddle of foul water, but he leaped aside at the last second, without disturbing the frothy scum. His evasive action sent him careening into a cluster of passersby.

One of them, a well-built man about a head taller than Ahrik, shoved him back. "Ho, friend"—by which he surely meant "enemy"—"watch it."

Ahrik jumped to a crouch and, on instinct, reached for Biriq, cloaked in the sheath at his hip. With his other hand, he reached out to grab the man's wrist, to squeeze the pressure point and pull him down to submission.

But he checked himself in the second before ruining the man's night in a spasm of steel and violence. He wanted to teach this thug a lesson, but he clenched back the invective that threatened to burst from his throat. He looked toward the ground to avoid being recognized.

Stay on mission.

"Sorry," he muttered. He hastened on, careful to deflect any more unwanted attention. He hugged shadows and peered into the occasional den of vice. He could handle a few common thugs if it came to it, but he didn't care to run into too many of Nayr's clones. He could disable one or two and make a hasty getaway, but any more than that would be a dicey proposition.

He knew. He'd trained them.

Ahrik sauntered into brothel after brothel and druggel after druggel. They became more frequent as he descended farther into the depths of the mountain. Darker and more vile. In one druggel, percussion thumped the air and dozens of bodies lounged in stupor, splayed over tattered couches and sprawled on ratty, mold-infested pillows. Some of them were Nayr's clones, but none of them had Nayr's rank insignia or unbridled arrogance. With every dribble of spit that Ahrik saw, and every squeak of flatulence he heard, he asked himself how deep Nayr's foolishness went.

He wrapped his scarf around his neck and mouth and walked out of the druggel. The belly of the mountain grew cold. Night fell and people left the public caverns and merchant warrens for a warm place to sleep, in the company of those they loved.

Ahrik would never enjoy such love again. Zharla had made sure of that, with her impertinent decision to try Nayr's mentor, then to push Ahrik away for her own reasons. Whatever those were. The Queen had grown as cold as the innards of Meran Mountain after their confrontation at the *birza*.

Like mother, like son. Nayr's selfish tantrums drove Ahrik and Zharla apart, like a steel wedge nestled into the smallest of fissures, then hammered into the crack in an orgy of pain. At the *birza*, Nayr had driven asunder the very circle of unbreakable trust between parent and child that he said he yearned for.

And just like that, everything Ahrik worked for, for years, was gone.

Ahrik didn't hate Nayr. He pitied him. Duty-forsaker. Family-breaker. Chaos-maker. Ahrik had ample cause for fury, but he chose instead to give his stepson one last chance to redeem himself. To show himself worthy of the honor accorded to him by birth.

He slipped into yet another stone corridor. This one was dank and vaguely green. Footsteps echoed. Ahrik's breath blew out in icy clouds through his scarf, now wrapped tighter over his mouth and nose like a mask. The footsteps rang up the corridor. They drew closer.

Two figures rounded a bend up ahead, and Ahrik knew at once he'd almost found Nayr. Ahrik edged toward the wall and eyed the two figures with an unobtrusive glance as they passed. Clones of Nayr. Higher ups, by the look of their number tapes in the low twenties and command designations on their collars. Ahrik tried to convince Nayr for months to use names and call signs instead of numbers, but Nayr ignored him.

That same cockiness extended to Nayr's command group, apparently. The two clones walked right by Ahrik, without noticing him, it seemed. If this mess devolved into the war that Nayr wanted, Nayr and his men would be in for a rude surprise when they operated in-mountain, in brutal and hostile terrain. In-mountainers had little patience for arrogant and ungenerous ways.

Ahrik hurried around the bend after the clones passed. A blast of hot air and percussion rushed over him when a door to his right dissolved and two more clones stumbled out, their eyes bloodshot and glazed. High thirties. They paused for a moment and gaped at Ahrik, as if they should recognize him but could not, through the drug-infused haze. They shrugged and continued on their way.

Ahrik palmed the door control so it would stay open. He narrowed his eyes at the sight of so many clones in one place and scrunched up his nose at the stench of sweaty human flesh, urine, and vomit, slathered with incense. A vain attempt at respectability.

As if this place could be respectable.

He stepped through the door. Out of nowhere it seemed two guards blocked his way. The new personal cloaking tech. He remembered being briefed on it, but hadn't seen it in action. Just like Nayr to use it for his personal security detail instead of pushing it down to his ketelis, where it would actually do some good.

In response to the guards' stony glares, Ahrik unwrapped his face.

They sucked in their breath and inclined their heads. "Your Highness."

Like wildfire gulping oxygen from the air as it raced over dry prairie grass, the attention of everyone in the room turned on him. The music stopped, as did ancillary murmurs. A few scantily clad women and men rushed from the room, and Ahrik saw clearly what kind of place this was.

He scanned the room for the cockiest pair of eyes he could find. It didn't take long.

"Well, well," said Nayr, off to the left, cuddling with a prostitute of uncertain gender. "Look who decided he missed me."

Ahrik glared at his stepson, weaving around legs and bodies to close the distance. "Come home, Nayr."

"What? It's not enough for you to embarrass me in public by arresting Sheresh on trumped up charges, and then murdering him in custody?" He scoffed. "Now you have to embarrass me in front of my men?"

Ahrik shook his head with vigor. "We did an investigation. Sheresh inflicted those wounds on himself."

"Liar." Nayr looked away.

"We gave you the world, Nayr, your mother and I. Don't throw it away."

Nayr's face grew dark. "Don't bring Mother into this. You have no right."

Ahrik bit back the retort to such an unjust implication. What was Ahrik's wrong in all this? Anger flared like sunfire in his breast, and he judged the final distance between them. An unconscious clone lay at Nayr's feet, but Nayr still had his arm around the prostitute.

Ahrik leaped over the unconscious clone and landed right in front of Nayr, but before he could clutch his stepson by the collar and rattle his head back and forth, a dozen distillers surrounded Ahrik with their menacing hum.

Nayr just smiled up at Ahrik and squeezed the person next to him closer. He wagged a finger on his free hand at Ahrik and shook his head. "Na, ah, ah, Ahrik. You don't mind if I call you Ahrik, right?" He stood up, now chest-to-chest and eye-to-eye with his stepfather. "No violence outside the training room. Isn't that the rule?"

Ahrik groaned in his throat. The corner of his mouth curled toward a snarl. "Do you really think you can beat me?"

Nayr stood and brushed a piece of lint from Ahrik's shoulder, or at least pretended to. He gave Ahrik a look of false pity. "I already have. Can't you see that? I'd press my advantage, but I'm not in the mood for regicide."

"I can see what you're in the mood for." Ahrik looked around the room and shook his head with disgust.

"Just blowing off a little steam before the whole ketel goes on exercise tomorrow." He motioned to his men, and the distillers stowed once again.

Ahrik pursed his lips and pushed down his frustration. "Answer me this, Nayr. What else could I have done? I taught you everything I knew, but you never learned to recognize wisdom."

Nayr shrugged and motioned toward a game of *chartak* laid out on a table nearby. "Who says I didn't? I'm winning, aren't I?"

"You're not coming home, then?"

"Are you my father?"

Ahrik stared at him for a beat, and found nothing, no emotion, no shred of human feeling in those vacant, blue eyes. He turned on his heel and deftly avoided contact with Nayr's men, retreating toward the exit.

When he got to the door, Nayr cleared his throat, and Ahrik stopped to listen, but did not do him the courtesy of turning around to face him.

"You know what your problem is, Ahrik?" asked Nayr. "You lied to me my whole life, you robbed me of the freedom to make my own choices. You thought you were helping me." Nayr gave a short laugh, then cut it off with a tone of warning. "But now I'm free, Ahrik, free from you and your tyranny of lies."

Ahrik pulled his scarf onto his head and dissolved the door, but he couldn't help himself. He turned back toward Nayr on the threshold and nodded toward the game of *chartak*. "In *chartak*, you can lose all your pieces, but you still have a chance to win if you have the Queen." Ahrik smiled with feigned confidence. "And I have the Queen."

With that, Ahrik set off up the corridor, before Nayr could suss out Ahrik's bluff. Ahrik knew what the Queen had told him, that she wouldn't seriously challenge Nayr if he rose against her, but at least the lie would buy Ahrik time to prepare for what came next, to run, to trade space for time.

Nayr's fury vented into the corridor before the door resolved once again behind Ahrik. He smiled and reached out to Hawk over the tendril link: *I need you to prepare a secret order.*

Sir?

We need to dissolve the Ketel of Nayr.

They will resist, sir.

What do you suggest?

Dissolve all the ketela, sir.

Including mine? Ahrik breathed in the chilly in-mountain air as he walked back up the corridor toward Shtera Umqi. *Do it. Execute the order tomorrow, while the Ketel of Nayr is on exercise.*

Yes, sir.

5 | Danger in War

RENLA LEANED BACK on her chair and balanced her heels on the stone desk in her office, waiting for Lyn to give the morning update. Renla looked up in exasperation at the ceiling, carved out of dull, lifeless rock, like the rest of this forsaken moon. She didn't want to screw up her first stint at command, and she knew her religion taught her to revere the Emerald Moon, but life here was austere and thankless, even by army standards. The only thing worse than the algae-based food was recycled moonie air.

Lyn entered, and Renla motioned for her two to sit. "Did our guests get on that shuttle the other day?"

"Check, ma'am, and the shuttle pilot passed on the message to the palace."

"Good. I have enough problems with these people camping out on my station platform."

"I noticed you didn't call them 'moonies,' ma'am."

Renla cocked an eyebrow. "That doesn't mean I like them."

"Except maybe the two that left on that shuttle. Anyone can tell that the girl is special, ma'am, and her father seemed to be an old friend of yours."

Renla shrugged, unwilling to concede the point. "Call it a feeling, but those two might turn out to be pretty important, Lyn." Renla took her feet from her desk and sighed with exhaustion. "The morning update? I saw that the comms with gravside flickered on and off last night."

Lyn's spry face reflected none of Renla's fatigue. She waved a data capsule in her hand. "Still nothing much from Home, ma'am, but I read through the Convention on the Emerald Moon. You may not like those refugees . . ."

"Squatters." And probably rebels, still.

". . . but the treaty is clear: anyone on Station Prime needs to be treated humanely."

A dull, age-old anger simmered up in Renla's chest. Who were these squatters, to think they had a right to anything Renla had? How many of Renla's friends had the people on this rock killed? Renla hadn't fought them for fifteen years to turn around and, because of some treaty, just start liking them. Some of these squatters had blood on their hands, she was sure of it.

Renla gave a helpless expression. "Without comms, we don't know if they're processing refugee applications gravside, Lyn. Nothing I can do. This is a transit station, not a hotel."

"They're sick, ma'am."

"It's not a hospital, either." Why didn't Lyn get it? These squatters could all be rebels, just waiting to go down and make more trouble gravside. Renla's career would be over if she sent them down on shuttles without permission, even if she was pretty sure they were clean, which she wasn't.

Lyn frowned, but Renla had learned in their short time together that this didn't mean Lyn had given up. Lyn shrugged brightly, as was her wont, jumped up, and tossed the data capsule in the air. She smiled when she caught it again. "Ma'am. I'll take care of it."

Before Lyn could leave, that characteristic spring in her step, Renla cleared her throat. "Lyn, wait." Renla sighed and leaned forward on her desk. "What are you planning?"

Lyn cocked her head, a wry smile on her face. "Ma'am, it didn't seem you wanted them to be your problem, so I figured I'd make it mine."

Renla took her turn to frown. She still hadn't figured out what to do with this subordinate of hers who mocked her with plaintive obedience. She needed Lyn to run the Fighting 11th, and Lyn knew it. The diggers trusted Lyn, especially after she prevailed on Renla to scale back the pace of building defensive works and refurbishing Harkov Station. Renla turned up her hands in mock defeat. "All right, but I want the platform clear, and figure out those comms. No one squats on the platform without an approved refugee application and a ticket gravside."

Lyn smiled and saluted, a distinct air of triumph in the action.

After Lyn left, Renla leaned back on her chair again. She knew, in her heart of hearts, that hundreds of sick people stranded on the platform at Station Prime were actually her problem. But she didn't want to admit it to Lyn, because admitting it meant having to do something about it, and doing something about it meant asking gravside for more resources and people, because the 2,000 diggers in the Fighting 11th were not enough to manage the rapid influx of refugees on the moon. Or, rather, squatters on the moon.

People with means, those who didn't need to apply for refugee status, were leaving in droves. Those without means parked themselves at Station Prime, grasping at the hope that Dom would approve their applications. They thought that Station Prime was a clean zone, free of the illness, which was far from certain, especially with so many sick people in one place. Renla knew the immigration quota. She'd read the treaty too, and they'd already met their obligations. Dom had already given the moon all the resources it would get.

No point asking gravside a question you already knew the answer to.

Of course, since this wasn't a Fighting 11th problem or an Emerald Moon problem, but instead a gravside problem, Renla would have to solve it up here, on the moon. This was the Law of Military Bureaucracy: all problems roll downhill. She had to solve this with nothing but her wits and her diggers' resolve. No help was coming.

But if she didn't like Lyn's solution, she'd better have a backup plan.

She cursed and sent a quick message to a local contact, the *pir'e* who ran the temple at Station Prime, a moonie she met once on Dom. Renla didn't like doing what she was about to do, but it was an opportunity to stick it to the moon once again, for old times' sake.

She donned her hygiene mask before going out on the platform. As she exited her office and crossed toward her quarters, she spied Lyn and a clutch of diggers fanning out among the squatters, passing out notices. The squatters kept their distance when they could, wary of the diggers' battle gear and their masks. At least someone was doing something.

The hundreds of people huddled on the platform were a pitiful lot, their meager possessions gathered around them in ragged piles. The squatters' illness pocked the air with the staccato, hollow sound of coughing. The Fighting 11th's healers were certain it wasn't viral or bacterial, but Renla wasn't taking any chances. Every digger in the 11th wore a hygiene mask in public spaces. Always.

Moonies respected people in masks. They weren't too high on intelligence.

Renla skirted the main mass of squatters on the platform, and one of their children, a dirty little urchin of about five, brushed up against Renla's leg in her scrambling play. Renla recoiled and tried to determine if it was a boy or girl. With the short haircut it was hard to tell, and this one clearly hadn't bathed in some time.

The child froze and stared back, eyes red-rimmed and wide with fear. For a moment, Renla and the child held the stare, until Renla saw tears form in the corners of those big, red-rimmed eyes. Something raw in the child's face touched a chord. This kid hadn't even been born when Renla began fighting rebels over moon and Dom, during the last war. Renla reached out a hand. "Hey, kid . . ."

The child sprang back and released a shriek of blood-curdling terror. It ran back to its mother, continuing its keening wail. The mother, some twenty meters down the platform, gathered the child in her arms and scowled at Renla, a helpless fury in her eyes. That mother was about the right age to have fought against Renla, back in the day. Renla stared right back and rested a hand on the qasfin at her hip, as a warning, then turned and walked off.

Back at her quarters, Renla doffed her uniform and chose her best go-to-town outfit—well, her *only* go-to-town outfit—and coaxed her short red curls into a full-bodied blossom on top of her head. She looked at herself in the mirror. She looked nothing like the commander of the Fighting 11th Combat Engineers. Just a girl on the town. She already felt dirty about what she was going to do, but she also harbored a guilty glee at getting back at some former rebels and solving the squatter problem at the same time.

Before stepping out the door to meet the *pir'e*, she grabbed her wrist compiler and set it to record, then briefly considered letting Lyn know what she was up to, at least in general terms. She bit her lip and shook her head. No need to get Lyn involved.

Renla stepped onto the public transporter headed toward the innards of Prime. Looking around, she could tell no one recognized her. If they had, she would be on the wrong end of nasty stares and withering scowls. She nestled herself into a corner of the transporter and waited for the last stop, where there would be fewer prying eyes for her rendezvous.

Renla exited the transporter when it reached the end of the line, then set off down the deepest, darkest tunnel branching off the platform. She kept one hand near the slit sewn into her billowy skirt, so she could access the *qasfin* strapped to her thigh with the slightest provocation.

She reached a dive bar at the end of the tunnel and found a seat near the back wall. Her wrist compiler chimed, but she ignored it, because at that moment the *pir'e* sauntered in, and she didn't want to draw attention to it. She should have silenced it earlier.

Renla noted with satisfaction that the *pir'e*, like her, had doffed his official garb. Instead of red clerical robes, he wore a rather fetching pale blue suit with a garnet choker about his neck. The suit brought out the color of his piercing eyes, and he knew it.

She could tell.

Ordinarily, seducing and blackmailing a *pir'e* involved two principal challenges. The lesser challenge was the vow of celibacy they took when they committed to their religious order. It was easy enough to discern which *pira* were truly committed to this vow and which Renla might be able to turn. This *pir'e* was of the less committed variety. She could tell by the glint in his smile when he walked through the door and spied her sitting there. Renla tucked a wayward curl behind her ear. She had what it took in the looks and wits department, and this *pir'e* was ready for escape.

Men were so easy to fool.

She ordered a *hender*, a tamarind-flavored sweet water, and he ordered a *mligh* sandwich, flatbread wrapped around spicy meat and roasted vegetables. Very popular with the working classes gravside, but not as much here, apparently, based on the look the server gave the *pir'e* when he ordered. The dive was dank and grimy, but packed. Easy to get lost, blend in.

Renla beamed hello with her eyes. Seduction aside, the greater challenge in Renla's plan was blackmail. *Pira* owned so little of value that coercion rarely worked, unless, of course, they valued staying in the clergy more than getting caught in an illicit dalliance. And this *pir'e* liked the idea of being listened to. He was very, very good at being a *pir'e*. She'd heard his sermon last week. It sizzled with fervor, and the temple was packed. Renla saw in his eyes that he had plenty of the conceit she was about to use against him.

"You're not hungry?" he asked, after their orders came.

She shook her head. Stay mysterious. "It takes a while to get my mind off work."

Her wrist compiler chimed again. She blushed a bit, and was glad for the dim light.

"You can check that, if you like."

"No, no. I'm here with you." She sipped her drink and made sure the *hender* glass hid her wrist compiler from his view. It recorded everything, from their conversation and wardrobe to his heartbeat and blood pressure.

He took in her dress, his eyes just lustful enough to encourage her. "I almost didn't recognize you," he said. "Impressive."

She looked around the little dive. "The moonies around here probably don't care about our day jobs, but I'm not taking any chances."

He smiled, definitely not his least attractive feature. "You're right. We *pira* don't make much headway down here, either." Ah, there it was. He liked the idea of being a *pir'e*, but was willing to justify a little escape now and then. He worked another bite out of his sandwich.

She embraced the silence and waited for him to make his move.

He obliged soon enough, smiling again. "How're things, Renla?"

She shrugged, as if the squatter influx was an everyday headache instead of a crisis waiting to burst. "We need to find a new home for a few hundred people."

Maybe a few thousand.

He furrowed his brow and fixed his eyes on his half-eaten sandwich, signaling that he didn't want any part of Renla's problem. When he wiped his hands and folded them on the table, though, Renla reached out and inserted her fingers into his. The look on his face made clear that he would agree to anything she said in that moment.

She squeezed his hand. "Can't the temple help accommodate them?"

"Well, maybe . . . I could ask." He bit the inside of his cheek, but didn't squeeze her hand in return quite as hard as she hoped he would.

The *pir'e* might be out of practice after a long period of celibacy, or he might be having second thoughts. She had to move quickly. She stood without letting go of his hand. "I know a place not far from here. Follow me."

Her wrist compiler buzzed yet again. She'd have a thing or two to say if Lyn was flooding her with messages. She shrugged and gave a timid smile. He glanced at his sandwich, as if considering whether to take it with him. *Pira* were not rich.

"Don't worry," said Renla. "When we're done I'll buy you another."

"Where are you taking me?" he asked, wiping his mouth. He voiced the question, but the crook of his smile told her he would go wherever she led. Her wits and looks were working just fine. She had time to wear him down on the squatter thing. She almost had enough on her compiler for a tidy little blackmail, too. Even if he didn't want to help her with the squatters, he would after she was done with him.

She led him by the hand, out of the dive and around the corner. The foot traffic was sparse in the tunnel, and the light dim, which was why she'd chosen this place to begin with. She continued down the tight stone corridor, looking for just the right place. "You're too uptight," she said. "You need to live a little."

"Oh?" He laughed. "I suppose a strait-laced military officer is the one to show me how?"

She stopped and looked at him in mock affront, at a bend in the corridor where his back faced a small niche nestled into the wall. She took his hand and slipped it behind her waist, then cradled the back of his neck in her hand and kissed him. Hard. Passionate.

He kissed her back.

A couple of passersby chuckled behind her, but they had no idea what was really going on. The whole time, her wrist compiler was recording his every bodily function. As she pressed him between the wall and herself, she could tell she had enough for blackmail, to force him to help her with the squatters.

She kept at it, moving her lips from his mouth to his neck. He put both arms around her and squeezed her even closer. "Yes," he said, "I knew the military wasn't as strait-laced as all that." He rubbed her back and ran a hand through her curly hair. "You can't even control your own commanders."

Renla pulled back. She didn't let people insult the army unless they were in the army. "What's that supposed to mean?"

"I . . . I'm sorry. Haven't you heard?"

She narrowed her eyes and shook her head.

He shrugged. "Right before I met you, I checked the caller networks. They're back on now, finally. Your man Ahrik ordered the trial of one of his top commanders."

"What?"

"Then he died in prison."

"What?!"

Her wrist compiler chimed, and this time she looked down to see a caller headline: "Military Commander Dies in Custody." As she called up the personal messages on her wrist compiler, she asked absently, "Who?" she asked. "What was the charge?"

And how did he die?

"Hmmm . . . he supposedly attacked the Emerald Moon, but we haven't been attacked, so I didn't get it. I don't remember the name."

The sickness was an attack, after all. She scanned Lyn's messages, but they only asked Renla to contact her, so Renla scanned the caller headlines instead. Her mouth dropped open. "Sheresh?"

"That's the one," the *pir'e* said, giving his winning but naive smile.

Renla's mouth quivered as she read the caller story. "Oh, Sweet Lady of the Emerald Moon, they charged him with crimes against the race."

The *pir'e* stroked his chin. "That sounds right."

"There was no investigation into how he died?" Renla asked, fighting off a sense of growing consternation.

"The palace initially denied he died in custody, then claimed it was suicide. Someone leaked something."

Realization hit her like a ton of regolith. She turned and sprinted off toward the transporter station, seduction and blackmail forgotten. The squatters were the least of her worries now. From down the corridor, the *pir'e* called out, "Where are you going?"

She ignored him. All she could think about was the danger they were in now, all of them. Not just the Fighting 11th, or the population of the Emerald Moon, but the millions of people gravside. This meant war, or a resumption of the last war. It was too early to tell which. A pit of despair and worry opened up in Renla's stomach as she ran.

What were Ahrik and Zharla thinking, arresting Sheresh? He was Nayr's mentor, and Nayr commanded 100,000 clones, the last ketel of clones ever grown. And they had just reached fighting age. Surely Ahrik would know the danger of arresting Sheresh. Nayr was unstable, and he had 100,000 supersoldiers at his beck and call. He wouldn't just stand aside while his mother and the king consort had his mentor's blood on their hands.

Unless Queen Zharla had nothing to do with this, and Ahrik had intentionally picked a fight with Nayr. Renla knew that Ahrik had little patience for his stepson's impertinence. Worry stabbed at her. Did her old friends, Ahrik and Zharla, have a falling out over this trial? Everything was, suddenly, uncertain.

The transporter ride back to the transit station was interminable. *Where are you?* she messaged Lyn.

The old enlisted barracks, came the response.

When Renla got to the station she found the platform empty, as she'd expected she would. Not a squatter in sight. She barely even slowed down, though, on her way to the old enlisted barracks, originally built for a time when the garrison numbered above ten thousand. Now, the barracks stood empty, barely habitable, with decrepit infrastructure and dank walls.

Just before she palmed open the door to the old barracks, the door dissolved and the five-year-old child from earlier scurried out and careened off of Renla's leg, then skittered onto the floor.

"Oh, dear," said Renla, and helped the child up.

Then Renla noticed that she was clean, and that she was a girl. The girl squinted at Renla, as if trying to place a face she knew she was supposed to recognize. The child reached up and grabbed Renla's hand. "Thank you."

Renla stared in surprise. The girl wasn't scared, and Renla wasn't revolted, but Renla shook the thought from her mind. The girl was still a moonie urchin. Even a moonie could get scrubbed clean with enough effort.

A voice rang out from inside the barracks. "Hey, come back he— Oh." Lyn saluted. "Hello, ma'am."

Renla returned the salute. "You moved them to the old barracks?"

Lyn nodded. "I hope you don't mind, ma'am. They were empty."

Renla scowled. "Does that mean I have to feed them as well as house them?" Renla didn't like this solution, but she also didn't want to undermine her two's initiative.

"No, ma'am," said Lyn. "I've already put most of them to work at Prime's algae farms. So many people have left that the farms are short of labor."

Renla sighed and motioned Lyn closer, for a more private conversation. "The squatters are the least of our worries now. We need to establish martial law in Prime and the rest of the moon's settlements. And we need to recruit some of these refugees into the force. The Fighting 11th is about to live up to its name once again."

Lyn gave a confused look. "Martial law? The news confirmed your suspicions about an attack. They're putting the perpetrator on trial. What's the problem?"

Renla gave a violent shake of her head and grasped Lyn's shoulders to drive home her point. "It's Sheresh Shehur-li, the member of the Council of Elders. He ran half the planet, and he started the last war."

The color drained from Lyn's face at this information. She was barely old enough to read when the last war began, but a measure of recognition registered in her eyes. "Which side are we on, ma'am?"

Renla stared into the middle distance, at a loss. "I . . . I don't know." She bit her lip. "Prepare my shuttle. I need to go gravside."

Nayr brimmed with excitement. Dawn broke on his ketel's training exercise. Nayr couldn't have asked for a more perfect morning. His atmospheric engineers nanoseeded clouds for months in preparation. They tripped the nanos yesterday, and now the fog rolled in deep and thick.

The dawn light shone dull through the fog as Nayr's command shuttle settled onto the floor of the valley. This valley, just north of Meran, seat of the planet's power, had once been the domain of Ahrik.

Ahrik. The Usurper. Nayr simmered at the two minders from the Usurper's ketel, loitering a few meters from where Nayr landed, listening to the decoy briefing from 4, Nayr's intel chief. Nayr's sons swirled around them in preparation for the most important moment in his ketel's young history.

Nayr shook his head with pity for the Usurper's delusions. Nayr learned that morning about the Usurper's secret order to dissolve the ketela, including the 100,000 of Nayr. In a few hours, the Usurper's arrogance would be moot.

He chuckled. The Usurper. The would-be king. The man that Nayr once called father, before Ahrik showed his true colors. With the dissolution order, he finally slipped up. Now Nayr had the excuse he needed to do what he was about to do.

Nayr leaped down from the shuttle. After the murder of Sheresh while in detention, the Usurper and Mother had scrambled to salvage the meager scraps of their legitimacy. Yesterday, two of the Usurper's men showed up to shadow his ketel, presumably to make sure Nayr and his sons didn't step out of line before the Usurper published the dissolution order.

Today's exercise came just in time to stop Ahrik's tyranny. If the dissolution order came into effect, Nayr would be forced to watch his 100,000 sons scattered throughout the army, to languish under strange commands, while His Highness, the mighty Ahrik, the Usurper, could make his own clones his closest advisors. Breathing out in fury, Nayr lifted his combat gear from the deck of the shuttle. He glanced at 2, who prepared for combat next to him.

Nayr shivered at Ahrik's hypocrisy. Soldier for soldier, Ahrik's forces were still the best, even if his units mixed clones and *hayla*, women and men. But the 100,000 of Nayr would own the day today. As physical specimens, Nayr's sons were far superior to any other soldiers, and they were now on the cusp of greatness, finally old enough to fight for themselves.

Nayr peered through the fog rolling over the valley. Twenty thousand of his best assault troops awaited his command, while another ten thousand waited in reserve. Most of them he could sense over the tendril link but not see. They waited in shuttles, transporters, and interceptors of their own. Their qasfina were honed and sharpened to draw first blood. No longer would Mother serve as Ahrik's puppet.

Nayr gave the order over the tendril link, so Ahrik's minders a few meters away wouldn't hear: *Launch*.

The sound of five hundred vehicles priming their boson drives filled Nayr with an anticipation he'd never felt before. This was no simple training exercise. This was the real thing. His ketel would put an end to Ahrik's tyranny today. The Usurper had no clue what was coming.

Nayr nudged 2 once the boson drives got too loud for the minders to overhear. "I live for danger, 2. Only those who face danger win in the end."

2 nodded and strapped on his distiller pack and qasfin, tightening the straps. "We face danger all the time, Father."

Nayr grinned. "And all we do is win."

The boson drive on his command shuttle hummed with eagerness. Nayr checked his systems. Distiller arming and diagnostics. All-terrain cloaking. Recon and targeting. "All systems go, 2," he said. "Visual check."

They checked each other's combat equipment. Distiller. Qasfin. Extra *kall* packs. Boson bombs. Survival gear.

Through the fog, Nayr heard a flight of interceptors lift into the morning gloom with their characteristic high-pitched whine. They were bound for the far-flung outposts of Ahrik's vaunted empire, where they would create a host of diversions for the Usurper to deal with.

One of the minders sauntered over, and Nayr narrowed his eyes. The minder was a clone of Ahrik. He only had two thousand or so remaining after the war Ahrik had started to usurp women's rule seventeen years earlier. The minder's uniform bore patches from a dozen campaigns. He was just over thirty-five years old, but slivers of gray flecked his temples. His cold, hard stare told of the eight thousand of his fellow clones who'd preceded him to the grave.

Nayr couldn't wait to help this minder find a grave of his own.

Nayr turned from the approaching minder and nodded at 2. "Tendril check." *Ketel of Nayr,* he cast over the network to his 100,000, where only he and his clones could listen in. *We are one. No matter the danger, and no matter who opposes us, we win. Do your job. Win.*

The minder stopped about two meters away and saluted, but looked down on Nayr. Nayr saluted back, but he hid his anger at the minder's airs. When Nayr was fully grown, he would be taller than the Usurper and his clones. Assuming any were left alive after Nayr was done with them.

For now, Nayr couldn't let on that danger lurked, so he asked, "Report, keteli?" To 23, head of his security detail, he cast, *The moment he senses danger, do it.*

Check, Father.

"Sir," the minder said, "just confirming the plan. Airborne insertion south of Meran via the ocean, with supporting elements hitting points across the contin—"

Nayr threw his hand up. "I got the briefing already." He pointed to the back of his skull, where his internal compiler was implanted. "Tendril network. The King Consort may use aural comms with his mixed ketel, but I don't." Nayr smiled. "Lift off in three."

The minder pursed his lips, turned on his heel, and melted into the rush of men to confer with his fellow minder once again.

4 hurried through the bustle and saluted. Nayr's ten-member personal security detail followed close behind.

4 looked about with an uneasy eye and shifted his weight. *Father,* he cast, *target is on the move.*

"Speak." Nayr prided himself on knowing when his men had something on their minds.

"Father, I can arrange a larger security detail for you."

Nayr frowned. "No. We're the main effort, but small and fast is better. You create enough diversions, there's no way we can fail."

"There's danger in war, Father," said 4. He adjusted his distiller harness.

"That's why you're my intel chief, 4. Your pessimism keeps me honest." Nayr glanced at 2 and held a hand out in expectation. "But only those who face danger . . ."

2 smiled. " . . . win in the end."

"Now," said Nayr, double checking that his qasfin was secure and accessing his internal compiler, "patch me through the target feed. You two do your jobs. My detail and I will deal with the Usurper."

"Check, Father," 2 and 4 said in unison.

Nayr raised an eyebrow in 4's direction. "And make sure I get both minders in my rig."

4 nodded and hurried over to the minders. He looked back and frowned at Nayr. *One of them insists he stay with me.*

You know what needs to happen, 4. Nayr suppressed the worry that flashed into his mind. Would his bookish intel chief be up to the task?

The minder came back and gave Nayr a cautious look. "Sir, my colleague will stay with your intel chief to monitor the operation from here." He gestured toward the electromag in his hand and clicked the switch, as if bragging that his comm system could possibly be better than Nayr's tendril network. "We'll be in constant contact," the minder said.

Nayr gave a sage nod. "A wise choice. Her Majesty will want to know the outcome of the exercise." He cast to his security detail lead, *Be ready on my mark, 23.*

23 gave an almost imperceptible nod, then Nayr grinned at the minder and stepped through the shuttle's starboard hatch. As Nayr planted his feet on the shuttle deck, he gave the "move out" sign with his hand. His security detail filed into the shuttle behind him, followed by the minder.

Nayr leaned out as the shuttle pulled away. *Ahrik will never know what hit him, 2 and 4.* Then he whooped. "Win!"

The hum of boson drives filled the valley. Through the mist, Nayr saw shuttles and interceptors form into pods and break off for different targets in Meran and across the Eshel, everywhere Ahrik had a major concentration of forces.

Nayr had reclassified the exercise as a rapid reaction exercise after the Healer had tipped him off to the order to disband the ketela. Nayr checked his internal compiler. The target was on route to Meran's port area.

The seekerbot feed also told him that the Usurper and Mother were alone. Nayr sniffed with distrust. Ahrik might have a trick or two up his sleeve. He always did, but Nayr had the ultimate insurance policy: Mother. Ahrik would do anything to control Mother. That was how he ruled.

Knowing your enemy's weakness reduced danger in war.

Nayr's command shuttle peeled off from the main pod making for Meran and headed out over the ocean. At a raised eyebrow from the minder, Nayr shouted over the boson drive's hum, "We need some separation for our delayed approach to the landing zone."

Nayr gave a reassuring smile, then watched the minder with care. The minder toggled on his electromag and said something unintelligible to his comrade on the other end.

Nayr cast to 4: *Get ready.* To 23: *As soon as he toggles off the electromag.*

The minder cut the line, and 23 moved like quicksilver. His qasfin slashed into the minder's cortex, disabling the minder's internal compiler, just in case his tendril comms had enough range out here to reach his base. 23's distiller primed and gave a brief and intense crackle, then the minder gasped, and his head lolled forward. He lost his grip on the handhold. The minder's legs buckled and the distiller opened up a crisp hole in the minder's chest, spitting elemental slurry out the open bay door.

Nayr heard a thump, and 23's boot appeared where the minder's back used to be. As the minder fell out the door, his body turned and Nayr saw his eyes. Wide with surprise. Laced with hate.

The tang of human flesh turned to carbon slime reached Nayr's nostrils. 4, he cast, *Now.*

No response. Nayr shivered.

4? Nayr cast again, brow furrowed.

"Father?" asked 23.

Nayr gripped the handhold a bit tighter. "I—"

Dan . . . ger . . .

4's tendril link winked out in Nayr's mind.

Nayr gave 23 a grim look. His heart pounded. This was his only chance. There was nothing for it now, even if 4 blew their surprise. "Proceed to the objective."

Nayr paused, to calm his breathing, then cast: 2, *we need to go in hot.*

Confirmed, Father, cast 2. *Instructing all units to engage post-haste.*

23 sidled over and gripped the handhold next to Nayr. *Will this work, Father?*

Nayr fixed him with a fierce glare, an act that took a force of will that was only possible on the brink of first combat. Adrenaline swilled in his veins, and he forgot about his little pills for a while.

"We win, 23. We always win. Remember that." He surprised himself with the steadiness in his voice. He checked the seekerbot feed. To the pilot, he cast: *Go in fast. The Tameri estate.* To his security detail: *Trust your comrades. Follow my lead. Win.*

2: *Father, units have engaged across the western Eshel, but resistance is stiff.*

I don't need you to defeat the Usurper everywhere, just pin his forces down so I can deal with him in person.

As the command shuttle approached the Tameri estate from the direction of the port, Nayr checked the seekerbot feed. Ahrik and Mother were still alone. The shuttle touched down, fluttering the trees and bushes with subatomic wash. Nayr jumped out and headed toward the main building. *23,* he cast, *on me.*

The rest of the security detail fanned out to secure the compound, padding over the soft, green turf to take positions at the main gate and along the walls. Nayr launched himself up the steps to the main building, then turned to 23. This was the most delicate piece of the whole operation, and it would play out between him, Ahrik, and Mother. "Wait for me in the entryway, 23. Intervene only if they make a move on me."

"Check, Father."

Nayr turned to the door, then froze. It stood ajar, like the maw of a crocodile waiting for some unsuspecting creature to alight. Nayr reached out, as if to touch the darkness, then saw his hand shake. He reached for his qasfin, flexing his fingers on the grip and wiping his other hand on the trouser leg of his uniform. Even though the cloud cover was thick that morning, and the light dimmer than usual outside, the mansion stood dark. The air hung silent and still.

He crept forward. The stale air wafting from the doorway suggested a house little lived in, which he knew to be untrue. Air and dust settled into a space much larger than it needed to be. The building itself was a mausoleum to past lives, as if it knew the work of death that Nayr's sons sowed across the Eshel.

As his eyes adjusted to the crepuscular entryway, he made out the grand staircase ahead of him and the hollow darkness of the ballroom to the left. He stopped short. Two figures stood at the base of the staircase, wrapped in darkness. By the way she stood, he could tell which one was Mother. The outline of a qasfin and distiller on the other figure were just visible in the murk. The Usurper.

Mother cleared her throat. "I'm so glad you came alone, son. Less messy that way."

"I—" Nayr's voice shook, and he paused to take a breath. "Mother, his tyranny. It's over."

The Usurper chuckled, but a motion from Mother cut him off. "Choose carefully your next words, son," she said. "I don't take kindly to threats."

Nayr took a cautious step forward. "Mother—"

The hum of a distiller charging cut Nayr off. "Stop, Nayr," said the Usurper.

23's distiller primed in answer, threatening a standoff, but Nayr waved 23 down. He gestured at the Usurper. "Mother, don't let this madman deceive you anymore."

The Usurper gave a threatening grumble, but Mother cut Ahrik off once again. The Usurper's distiller died down as well.

Mother sighed. "This is about you, son, not him."

"He is finished, Mother."

"You think you can replace him?"

Nayr took another step forward. If he could just get close enough to Mother, then he could turn the odds in his favor. "Mother, he has deceived you for all these years, as much as it pains me to say it."

The Usurper hissed. "Enough of these games, Nayr."

"Ah'ke," said Mother, warning in her voice.

"No, Zhe'le." The Usurper took a step toward Nayr. "You're wrong about him. He doesn't care about the people of the Eshel, much less about women's rule. Even now, his 100,000 are spreading out over the globe like a virus. He has the blood of two of my best men on his hands, and who knows how many more across the Eshel."

Nayr scoffed. So, 4 killed his minder, after all. "If you knew me so well," said Nayr, "why didn't you see this coming?"

The Usurper cried out in anger and leaped toward Nayr, but whether to intimidate or attack, Nayr didn't care. He crouched into his stance. 23 gasped behind him, and two distillers primed and went off. Pain lanced up Nayr's arm, but he bit it back. Behind him, 23's body fell to the ground with a thud, followed by the clatter of his distiller on the polished stone floor. Danger in war.

"Ah'ke!" screamed Mother. Nayr looked up to see Mother restraining the Usurper. "Don't make this worse."

The Usurper wrenched himself free of her grasp and stepped back. "How many good women and men must die for his little charade, Zhe'le?"

Nayr rubbed his arm gingerly. Surface wound. Barely even grazed him. "Well now, Usurper," he said. "That depends on you, doesn't it?"

Mother planted herself between them. "Enough, both of you." She fixed Nayr with an icy glare. "We know why you're here, and we know you'll get what you want in the end. The question is, what price will you exact from those who love you?"

Mother's look transformed from aloofness to pity. The corners of her eyes sagged and her shoulders slumped. Her look cut Nayr to his core. It sparked a tinder of long-suppressed brimstone in his heart. A pure, animal hate surged inside him. He sprang to Mother and whipped his qasfin from its leather sheath.

In an instant, he had Mother's neck pinned between his left forearm and his blade. He meant her no ill, but he had to make his point. He put his mouth next to her ear so she could hear his demand with perfect clarity.

He smelled the lavender in her hair and felt the tension and fury in her neck. He reveled in his power. "Mother," he said. "Tell me it's mine. The Eshel. Dom. The ocean, the sky, the moon. Say it's mine, all of—"

The demand stilled in his throat. He peered around in the dark. "Where's the Usurper?"

Mother took a long, slow breath, utterly fearless. Powerful. "He's gone. You won't find him."

Nayr released his grip and huffed. He had to find the Usurper. He checked the seekerbot feed. Nothing. Target lost. He began pacing back and forth in front of the staircase, peeling off his gear: boson bombs, survival gear, *kall* packs.

He couldn't win until the Usurper was dead. He had Mother captive, and he could declare victory, but everything rode now on finding the Usurper, on killing him. The Usurper threatened Nayr's rule. As long as he lived, Nayr's peace would not be safe. Nayr's breathing became shallow and vapid, and he stopped to rest his hands on his knees, head down.

Then an even more sickening realization flooded over him. "I . . . I'm sorry, Mother, I don't know what came over me. I could have killed you."

He realized his qasfin was still in his hand. The grip slipped in his sweaty palm, and his forearm ached from the pressure. His eyes grew wide. He flung the qasfin away. It clattered against the staircase.

Mother placed a reassuring hand on his back. "There, there, son. I knew you wouldn't hurt me. You love me."

Mother crouched down and held his chin, their eyes on a level. She squeezed a bit harder than she should have, but he didn't care about that now. Wracking remorse began to take hold. To sink its claws into his heart. Tears welled in his eyes at what he had almost done. The tension of combat exhausted him.

"Look at me, Nayr," said Mother. "Remember this."

Confusion took hold on his face. "Remember what?"

She released her grip on his chin and smiled with a tenderness that only a wise mother could. "This is what winning feels like."

Nayr's anger flooded back. The Usurper made her believe lies like that. Bent over, head hung, Nayr examined his hands. They shook. Where were his pills?

Mother stepped onto the first stair, then turned with her haughty grace and shook her head slowly. "Nayr, Nayr, Nayr."

His face shook with fury at the lies that the Usurper used to twist Mother's mind. "What?" he asked. Spittle leaked from the corner of his mouth.

She clenched her jaw. "If you ever touch me again, I'll kill you myself."

He rose and stormed out of the main building. He accessed the Revenge file in his internal compiler and overwrote the file's contents: "Kill Ahrik. Protect Mother."

2, he cast over the tendril link as he strode back to his shuttle.

Father?

We need to get the ketel out of this place.

Retreat from our positions, Father?

No, no. Nayr fumed. *We need to get the ketel out of Meran. I hate this place. I want to build a new headquarters by Mekele Eshel, where the capital was before the Usurper moved everything to dirty, stinking Meran.*

Yes, Father. We'll start on it right away.

Nayr and his team loaded onto the shuttle and pulled away.

"Father," asked one. "Whure's 23?"

Nayr glowered at the main building receding below them. "He didn't make it. Send a team for the body."

Renla sat on the floor, building a house out of blocks, a blessed respite from thoughts of war and hate. The antechamber to the *birza* stood empty except for her and Shahl's daughter, Sera, who was a competent architect, at least with blocks.

The gray, stone-paneled antechamber was a vast monument to glories lost, a testament to the stale power that Ahrik and Zharla had built, then frittered away. They had built the palace back when their power was unrivaled, but now they clung to remembered legitimacy.

Renla had been here at the palace for a week. Soon after arriving, Shahl was taken somewhere else, probably at the old Tameri place, and Renla had seen very little of him or the Queen. Then Ahrik went missing. Nayr's clones were everywhere, and the petulant teenager sat by his mother's throne, a prince consort of sorts. The moonie girl was the Queen's ward. That was worth a measure of respect.

"No, no," said Sera, shifting some of the blocks that Renla had set down. "We have to keep the rooms small or we won't be able to keep the air in." She coughed and looked at Renla. "My Abbi always says, 'Extra spaces make blue faces'."

Renla gave the girl a quizzical look. "Were you born on Dom, or on the moon?"

Sera peered up at her, a puzzled look on her face. "I am a daughter of Moon, but my parents were forced to leave Home." She coughed into her sleeve once again, leaving specks of red on her white cotton dress. "Where do *you* think I belong?"

Anyone who knew Shahl and his sharp, inquisitive nature would know that this was his daughter. For that matter, few who met her could resist her charm, and Renla found it harder and harder to think of her as moonie filth. She patted Sera's shoulder and made to stand, unwilling to give the impression that she cared too much.

A throat cleared behind them, and Renla turned to find the austere steward staring down her nose at Renla. "You will be seen now."

Renla checked her wrist compiler. Twenty minutes remained before her appointment with the Queen. "Already?"

The steward just shrugged and nodded toward the throne room, as if that ended the discussion.

They had forgotten what she was to Zharla. Renla nodded at Sera. "You keep building, okay?"

Sera cocked her head as Renla stepped away. "Will Auntie Queen make me better?"

Renla sighed in frustration and glared at the ceiling before turning back to the girl and plastering a fake smile on her face. "Sera, the Queen can do anything. Are you taking your medicine?"

"You can call me Serit." She beamed, guileless and without malice for the disdain with which Renla obviously regarded her. "They don't give me medicine."

Renla stifled the disbelief that threatened to burst forth. The girl was blood to the Queen and her son, regardless of where she was born, on the moon or on Dom. She deserved to be treated, to be healed. Such a surfeit of injustice, even against a moonie.

Renla couldn't do anything about that. She gave the moonie girl a curt nod. "The Lady keep you, Serit."

The steward dissolved the door to the *birza* and rapped her staff on the stone floor. Renla stole a glance back at Sera before the door resolved behind them. *If anything happens to that girl, a lot of people will be out for blood.*

Renla's combat boots squeaked on the polished stone floor. A decade ago, a thousand workers toiled a year to build this palace on the outskirts of Meran, shipping stone from the four corners of the globe on the new global transporter system that Ahrik and Zharla constructed after the War for the Emerald Moon. The palace project, along with a planet-wide communications infrastructure and a massive bureaucracy, jumpstarted global trade and reinforced the treaties ending the war.

Zharla and Ahrik gave the planet peace and prosperity with their centralized bureaucracy and trade-favorable policies, but they also made it easier for one individual, Nayr, to control the planet with his 100,000 clones. They should have seen their folly. Now Ahrik was missing, and there was no check on Nayr's ambition.

Renla scanned the throne room. Was Zharla missing, too? How quickly the whole of planet Dom had slipped into tyranny. Zharla's throne was empty, and Nayr sat on the consort chair next to it, one hand draped over the headrest, like a snake.

Behind Renla, the steward called out in her commanding voice, "Commander Renla *mebood* Tamer-li, of the 11th Hand, Combat Engineers."

Renla put a fist over her heart in the common salute. They'd told her to use the fealty salute in the throne room, but she refused to show obeisance to a slipshod youth of seventeen with no combat experience. Still, he outranked her by birth, if not by experience.

Nayr waved a hand with an air of supercilious detachment. "If we share a family name, of sorts, do we really have to salute each other?"

Renla held the salute, waiting for him to return it. The bitter taste of disdain slid into her mouth. She wanted to spit at his insolence and throw his petulance back at him, but she resisted the urge. That time would come.

"Fine," he said after a moment, then brushed his chest with his fist. He shifted his body and draped a leg over one of the armrests.

"Comfortable, sir?" Renla asked on her approach to the throne.

He scoffed. "I never believed the stories about you. My mother's former slave, freed to enter military service. A rising star, given command of the unit founded by the Usurper's father. And yet here you are. The legend lives."

Renla straightened her back. *Arrogant pig*. "I was your mother's bond-servant, not her slave. There's a big difference, sir." She looked around. "Where is she, may I ask?"

"What? No 'Your Highness'?"

She glared at him. "Titles are earned, sir, not given."

"Oh, this is rich." He leaned forward and rested his elbows on his knees, then gave her an insolent look. "You think you haven't been given anything in life?"

As a matter of fact, she hadn't. She'd started from nothing, fought in the trenches during the War for the Emerald Moon. Lied about her age to get in, in fact. Everything she'd gotten, she paid for dearly in blood and sweat. Ire bubbled up her throat. She clenched her jaw to keep calm. "I'm here to earn my unit's respect, sir."

Nayr grimaced and muttered, "At least you remember that I outrank you."

How did anyone take this seventeen-year-old lump of flesh seriously? "Sir, the Emerald Moon has been attacked with a bioweapon, and Sera, the Queen's niece, needs medical attention. A lot of moonies will be pretty peeved if she dies down here."

Nayr raised his eyebrows in mock alarm. "My best healers have seen to her, and I've gotten no reports of an attack." He stroked his chin. "The moon, you say? Has Station Prime been damaged?"

"I didn't make the trip down here to bandy words." She closed her eyes. "Sir."

"Insubordination doesn't fit the legend, Renla."

"I want answers, sir."

"I've given them."

Renla folded her arms across her chest. "Where is the Queen?"

As if on cue, a door whooshed open in the back corner of the room and Queen Zharla stormed out of the shadows. She glared at Nayr and made a beeline for Renla, heels clicking her characteristic, impatient beat on the floor.

"Re'le, my dear." She wrapped Renla in an embrace of oldest friendship. "My son's men kept me tied up in a meeting, then I heard that your appointment was moved up . . . I'm sorry for not being here earlier."

Zharla pulled out of the embrace and held her friend at shoulder length.

Something was off in the Queen's look.

Renla searched for any hint that Zharla believed Nayr's lies. Finding none, Renla smiled and let her friend's love course through her. "You're here now, Your Majesty."

Zharla took her by the hand and, their backs to Nayr, walked with Renla toward the main entrance to the *birza*, toward the haughty steward, and Sera beyond. "Now," said Zharla, "What do you need?"

Renla almost stuttered her step, because at the moment that Zharla asked the question, she squeezed Renla's hand using the simple code they'd developed in their youth, when they'd grown up as playmates, one of them a bondservant, the other the scioness of a powerful mining clan. The sign was clear: pressure at the pinky, then at the thumb. A warning.

Renla squeezed the sign back, to show that she'd understood, and that she knew that they were being watched and listened to. A dozen thoughts rushed to her mind. Concern for her friend. A rough plan for how to proceed. A list of commanders she could trust. "As I told the prince consort," said Renla, "the moon has been attacked, and I'm concerned for Sera's health."

Zharla stopped and turned toward her, but kept their hands locked. "An attack? First I've heard." She squeezed Renla's hand in the sign for a lie.

Renla focused all her attention on keeping an even face, on showing no hint of the righteous indignation she felt.

"As for Sera," said Zharla, with a smile, obviously for Nayr's benefit, "we're doing all we can." Another squeeze. Another lie.

"Thank you, my Queen." Renla squeezed out the letters *A-H-R-I-K*, with a question.

Zharla smiled, but worry flashed into her eyes. *F-L-E-D*, she spelled out, revealing that Ahrik was now gone. Her smile returned, forced. "For you, Re'le, I would do anything."

In his consort's chair, Nayr scoffed and slapped his armrests. "Oh, please." He stood. "Mother, why don't you send her on her w—"

Zharla froze him with a glare. "Son," she said, not even deigning to turn all the way around to face him, "you will learn your place."

Renla narrowed her eyes at the exchange, and at the currents that ran underneath it. Shahl was a prisoner of Nayr, then, and not the Queen. She must be trying to help him escape, too. Renla stepped back and knelt, head bowed, fists to the floor in the fealty salute. "I serve Mother Eshel, and Queen Zharla, with my life."

Then a thought struck Renla, like a dagger of ice. Nayr had the Queen captive, somehow, and was holding Sera as ransom, or bait.

Zharla crouched down and lifted Renla up. "Come, Re'le, I'll walk you out."

"I'll come with you," Nayr said, trotting up behind them.

As they strode toward the exit, hand in hand, Renla felt Nayr's eyes on the back of her head, watching them like a hawk. She squeezed out *C-E-R-A*, with a question.

Zharla squeezed no response, but as they embraced, Renla saw a single tear glisten in the crease of the Queen's eye.

As soon as Renla left the palace, she headed straight for the officer's club. In her mind, she scrolled through the names of hand commanders she knew, selecting the few women and men she'd trust with her life. More often than not she scratched a name off the list as not quite trustworthy enough, but by the time she got to the officer's club she had five names on her mental list.

Standing before the vaulted entrance to the officer's club, she buried the list deep in her thoughts. Secrets are dangerous in a civil war.

She prayed that at least one of the hand commanders on her list was inside, then palmed open the door and entered the bustle and din. She scanned the officers socializing there, struck by the artificiality of it all. Either it was all an act, or the battle lines hadn't yet been drawn. She was certain, though, that the ones on her list would be loyal to the Queen instead of Nayr.

She worked the room, inserting herself into the false role of loyal army officer. In a civil war, loyalty was in short supply. Before the fighting started, everyone wanted everyone else to believe they'd be fighting on the same side.

After an hour of slimy glad-handing and vacuous conversation, she finally found one of the officers she was looking for, the hand commander of an interceptor unit based on one of the twenty-four elevator stations. When she finally got him alone, she leaned in. "We need to talk."

The hand commander peered at her, his stare like cold flint. He'd guessed Renla's intent. "I don't want to know what about."

She nodded. "You don't." Renla looked through the floor-to-ceiling windows at the fading light of day over Meran Bay and wondered if she would regret her next move. "I need pilots, and I need interceptors."

The other commander's flinty stare did not waver, like his mind was waging a battle against itself. After what seemed an eternal pause, he scanned his surroundings with his peripheral vision. "There are others we should speak to."

6 Strategic Reserve

Zharla rose early enough that she could achieve a semblance of solitude. In the three weeks since the coup, which Nayr called a "re-alignment," his clones had watched her like hawks. She was too valuable, apparently, to be let out of their sight, even for a moment.

And her niece, the maddening little urchin called Sera, was sick, and not getting any better. Nayr mostly kept her at the palace healing complex, but when she was here, at the Tameri family estate, she coughed all the time. Nayr could do more to help her. He just didn't. Zharla resented the unrequited love the girl represented, the family that Zharla should have had with Shahl, but it didn't seem quite right for Nayr to pretend to make Sera better without really doing so.

Zharla gave a contented smile. She had Shahl near her again, oh intoxicating nectar, the threads of her hope slowly weaving themselves into a tapestry of love within her breast. Such a balm could salve a thousand ills, cure a thousand injustices.

Zharla drank in the early morning stillness as she padded down the back hallway on the second floor, the stone chilling her bare feet. She thought what good reason Nayr's clones had to worry about losing track of her. She heard what Nayr did to those who failed him. He had one hundred thousand clones. What did it matter if one or two went missing here or there, never to be heard from again?

He needed to learn a lesson or two on how to rule. She mulled thoughts of escape, but she would endanger her link to her son if she went missing. At heart, he was a good boy. She would get through to him, some day. This feud with Ahrik couldn't last forever.

She tiptoed to the servants' stairwell, so she could exit the back way. At this hour, not even the servants were up to make breakfast. So far, she hadn't seen any clones, either.

She crept down the spiral staircase and placed one hand next to the stone jamb of the kitchen door, which always stood open. Her training shoes hung from her other hand, and her running pouch was strapped to her waist. She stopped to listen. Hearing no sound in the kitchen, she jerked her head around the jamb to scan the room, then settled back into her hiding spot. The kitchen was empty.

A feeling of guarded optimism crept into her heart, like the first spring stroll after a winter of storm and discontent. She might actually make it, not to freedom, of course, but to a morning of solitude.

It would be a test of whether she could escape, if it came to that.

Someone yawned on the stairs behind her. "Auntie Queen?"

Zharla jumped with panic, but it passed when she realized who it was. Only Sera called her that.

Zharla gave a wan smile. How did she not hear the pesky girl descend the stairs behind her? "You're up early, dear."

Sera cleared her throat, then squinted into Zharla's eyes and asked, "What's wrong, Auntie Queen?"

The girl's deep reservoir of empathy irked Zharla, reminding her so vividly of Shahl and what she'd given up by choosing Ahrik all those years ago. Zharla reached over and patted down a wayward strand of Sera's long, silken hair. "I thought moonie children had their heads shaved."

Zharla shuddered when Sera reached up and squeezed her hand. The sooner Sera was gone, the better. The girl smiled, though, without guile, as if believing Zharla's affections were real. Almost, Zharla wanted to like her.

"Abbi says my hair is to remind me that I belong to Home, not Moon." Sera coughed, a rasping hack more suited to a person fifty years her senior. She coughed again, then again. Eyes watering, she looked at Zharla and smiled with no sense of irony at all, then wiped her mouth with her sleeve. "I'm okay," she whispered, as if Zharla had asked, "but I worry about Abbi."

Zharla shook her head in disbelief. Every day brought Sera closer to death, it seemed, yet still she had the capacity to feel for others. Zharla knew, deep down, that the girl deserved better, but also knew that intervening would strain her ability to reach Nayr, would make it harder to avoid a bloodbath.

There was no telling what Nayr would do if Zharla vexed him. Ruling meant making hard choices.

Zharla leaned over and kissed Sera on the forehead. Better to keep the girl in line with false hope than to cause her more worry. "You'll both be okay." Guilt stabbed at Zharla's core. "Just listen to your cousin Nayr."

Sera nodded, as if she too believed it, or wanted to. "Cousin Nayr said that bad people would hurt me if I went outside." Sera took one more step down and took in Zharla's clothes and the training shoes in her hand. "You're going outside. Won't they hurt you, too?"

Zharla's mouth grew thick. The guilt of lying to such an innocent creature almost broke Zharla's voice, but she thought of all the hopes she'd vested in Nayr over the years. "I'll be careful," said Zharla, caressing the girl's cheek. "Now, try to go back to sleep."

As if reminded that it was too early to be up, Sera yawned, turned, and made her way up the stairs, her little stuffed animal dangling from one hand. When she'd almost rounded the turn of the spiral staircase, she turned with inimitable matter-of-factness and said, "I'll go outside soon. I'm going to help Abbi find Imma."

Zharla darkened at the thought of Shahl's wife, how that should have been her, happy and in love. Zharla shuddered to think how Shahl's wife could leave him. She shut her eyes to squeeze out the pain of what could have been. She'd give up all the power she'd built with Ahrik for a quiet, secluded life with Shahl. She opened her eyes and smiled in Sera's general direction, but found that the girl had already gone.

A muttered curse of good riddance passed her lips, and she bent down to slip on her training shoes, pressing her fingers against the tongue to seal them. She adjusted the running pouch at her waist and sliced through the stillness of the kitchen, steeped with anticipation for the cooking that lay before it. The darkness melted into the dull predawn as she slipped out the rear doorway of the Tameri mansion, accompanied by the knowledge that, at some future point, she might have to abandon Sera to the tenuous grace of Nayr.

He was a good boy, just a bit too hard on others.

She buried the guilt she felt over Nayr's behavior under the weight of duty to her people, then dashed across the soft green lawn, careful to step on the fullest tufts, to cushion her passing. How could she think of one little girl when millions depended on her to stop this war?

She pressed herself against the spur of Meran Mountain that abutted the rear of the compound, then caressed the cool rock face and pulled in a long draught of the fecund aroma of dew-moistened stone, at once strong and gentle. She would have to be strong and gentle, like her dear mountain home.

Like Sera.

Zharla saw it clearly: a storm of fury and hate brewed within her household, within her son, and she did not know if she could keep the storm at bay unless she sacrificed a solitary, innocent life. She might have to, though, for the good of the whole.

Maybe the storm wouldn't break. Maybe Nayr would reconcile himself to the reality of his parentage, to Ahrik, and be content with a different sort of rule, one wholly subordinate to Zharla's authority. Of course, if it meant avoiding an all-out war between Ahrik and Nayr, she would give Nayr her throne, with all its power.

In the dimness, Zharla ran her fingers along the cool, craggled rock and felt lines of worry crease her face. Ahrik was gone now, and she did not know whether he intended to fight Nayr or not. Nayr and his 100,000 were insinuating themselves into every nook of her bureaucracy. She had to let it happen, to avoid war.

She didn't like it, not one bit.

After a few moments of searching by feel along the rock, she found what she sought, a slim, hand-sized outcropping at eye-level, a palm-scanner disguised as rock, put there by one of her clan's founding mothers to give access to an escape route in times of distress. Generations of Tameri women had kept the secret of the passageway through the mountain. She hoped that her son's overweening eye had not yet discovered this secret, too, because she might have to use it to escape, sooner rather than later.

She paused before pressing her palm to the reader. Was the risk of Nayr finding out worth it? She pursed her lips, but she couldn't get thoughts of choosing Ahrik and working with Nayr all those years, in vain, out of her head. Where had she gone wrong?

The time had come to do something right.

She pressed her hand to the reader. Better to find out now if Nayr knew about this secret passageway, when her designs were innocent, than when she fled for real.

She entered the passageway. The lights flickered on and the door re-formed with a hiss behind her. How long had it been since she'd been in here? Since she came with Ahrik's men during the last war, during the battle for this compound. A pang of regret stabbed at her heart. They'd fought for this compound to make sure that they were the ones who would raise Nayr and his 100,000, the way he should be raised, with an unflinching faith in women's rule and committed to the principle of freedom.

She sighed. They'd won the battle, but lost so much since. Could she bear to leave Nayr, if it came to it? Would it do any good?

She hurried through the tunnel at a brisk walk. When she got to the end, she looked through the spy hole, then listened for sound on the other side. All clear. She pressed her palm to the reader and slipped through. The door reformed behind her in the shape and character of the mountainside.

In a dark, secluded alley of out-mountain Meran, two old stone houses almost met, forming an even darker, more secluded corner. Into this darkness, now fading into morning, Zharla crept, the Queen over all the planet, leaning into shadow like a thief. She touched her slender running pouch. A small fortune rested there, plumb against her waist.

She took a deep breath and burst through the gap between the houses and into the morning, setting aside her worries for a run in the clear air.

The brisk morning quickened her pace, but movement in her peripheral vision froze her heart in a rush of adrenaline. She kept running. It might have been nothing.

Her feet flew over the stone pavement, rupturing the morning and echoing off the stone walls around her. She startled a street sweeper as she rounded a corner in this, Meran's wealthiest neighborhood.

But her goal lay deeper within Meran, where the city's poorest citizens wallowed in a mire of hopelessness.

She caught it again, movement off to her left, on the next street over. She was sure of it this time, because dawn had just broken over the Bay of Meran, and the light silhouetted a figure, slinking in the next lane. The figure's head turned in her direction.

She picked up her pace, which already would have punished those who didn't run as much as she did. If she could just make it to in-mountain Meran, she could lose her pursuers in the warrens and narrow alleys.

At the next corner, she didn't see the figure off to her left. Maybe she'd lost him. She ducked into the next street to her right and made a quick jog down an alley to her left.

But it wasn't enough. Just as she ducked into the alley, she saw another figure down a side street, from the opposite direction of the first.

She huffed and increased her pace once again. She flew down the rough stone pavement with a vigor born of frustration, at her son's insolence and the string of events that had led her, and others, to be captive in her own home.

As she neared the entrance to in-mountain Meran, the pavement became less even, the street more grimy with accumulated detritus, refuse, and caked urine. She slowed down to compensate, and to her chagrin she saw both the figures she'd seen before, and then a third. They kept their distance, but they abandoned the fiction that they just happened to be out for a run in the wee hours, like her.

When she saw Nayr sidled up against the grand stone archway at the western entrance to in-mountain Meran, picking his nails, one foot propped up in a gesture of nonchalance, verging on disdain, she knew the game was almost up.

Almost. Nayr knew about the secret passageway, but at least he had the grace not to use it himself. The hidden palm reader outside the passageway would only let women through. Perhaps something was still sacred to him, after all.

She slowed down as she passed him, but only just, and said, "Keep up if you want."

He had the good sense not to lay hands on the Queen. That was sacred, too, after that little breakdown when Nayr put his blade to her neck. She was safe, for now.

Nayr caught up to her as they descended into the murk of in-mountain Meran, the rising light of a new dawn squeezing through the entrance behind them. His breathing came light and easy, as effortless as hers. "You can run," he said, smiling, "but you can't hide from the Ketel of Nayr, Mother."

Zharla ignored him. Let him think he was winning.

The in-mountain dimness always surprised Zharla, even though she came here often. The palid, artificial light was a poor substitute for the sun, yet years of housing and relocation projects had failed to move Meran's poorest out-mountain. Old habits died hard. When families lived underground for two thousand years, they found the mountain hard to give up.

The path led down, the way gnarled and twisted. She had to slow. Then Zharla finally saw what, or who, she was looking for, a huddled form nestled into a carved niche along the pathway. She slowed to a walk and reached for the pouch at her waist. She squeezed out two coins and knelt down beside the form.

The person started, and Zharla saw that it was an old man, his pale, sunken face registering alarm at being woken. Recognition quickly overcame his surprise, though, and he made to rise.

"Mother," Nayr began behind her, then grunted in frustration and kicked at the gravel pathway.

"No, no, don't rise," said Zharla to the old man, ignoring Nayr once more and resting a hand on his arm. She pressed the two coins into his hand. "Grace of the Lady attend you," she said.

"And you," the old man croaked, then added, "Your Majesty."

The footsteps of three or four clones crunched on the path as they caught up. Zharla didn't care to acknowledge their existence, either. What would it cost to avert war, with an entire ketel of 100,000 bent in obeisance to Nayr's will?

"Keep up," said Zharla, her breath billowing out in clouds of angry condensation. She dashed off again, in search of the next person who'd had to pass the night on the street.

A dozen times she handed out coins, then a dozen times more. Every time she saw a glimmer of hope in the eyes of her beloved people, if but for a moment, peeking through a life of disadvantage, hunger, or pain. To one bedraggled young woman, two filthy children snuggled up beside her, Zharla gave six coins, enough to feed them for months, perhaps even change their fortunes forever.

But then one of the children, a girl about Sera's age, coughed and drew a tattered stuffed animal up to her chin, one of its limbs nearly detached from its body. Stuffing bled out from the tear. Her cough was completely different from Sera's, just a normal morning throat-clearing, but like a wave all of Zharla's guilt rushed back. She was using random acts of charity to suppress the guilt of doing nothing to help Sera and Shahl. Zharla could certainly help them, if she wanted to.

Nayr started to protest at this latest largesse, like he had every time before, but Zharla cut him off with an icy look. She saw it in his eyes: he was content to simply let Sera die. And he felt not an iota of guilt about it.

Zharla's pouch was empty now. She turned away in disgust, as much at Nayr's cold heart as at her own. She thought, bitterly, how close the seed falls by the bush.

Was Zharla just as willing to let Sera die?

Zharla set her jaw and trotted back up the pathway, through the warrens and alleys of in-mountain Meran, and to the grand stone entrance. All the while she worked out how to salve her conscience.

When she arrived at the grand entrance, the rising sunlight streaming in from over the bay, she slowed to a walk and gave Nayr a maternal smile. "Tell me, Son, what got you up so early?"

He pursed his lips and flared his nostrils after jogging up beside her. "It's not safe—"

"Oh stop, Nayr," said Zharla. "I gave you more sense than that."

He shrugged, then grew as distant as the stars. The grand entrance loomed overhead. He reached out and almost brushed her arm. Almost. "Mother, stop."

She stopped, but looked down at where he'd nearly touched her, then challenged him with a stare. She waited, he beside her, until he lowered his gaze in submission. She could tell he hated it, being kept in his place.

She walked through the entrance, then stopped to take in the rising sun over the bay, a brilliant orange light commanding out-mountain Meran like a king consort, shining with deadly splendor, but not nearly as graceful, wise, and powerful as the moon, which controlled the life-giving waters of the planet.

"Nayr," said Zharla, the smiling image of Sera vivid in her mind, "someday you will learn that to rule is not to control. The sun sees everything, and powers everything, but controls nothing."

He chuckled, a more nefarious sound than she'd heard him make before. With this sound, another portion of hope for peace died within her. Would she have to do what she most feared? Could she abandon her son? What would make him see reason?

"No," he said, shaking his head, "I am not the moon or the sun." He swept his arm over the horizon. "But I will control all I see, one day."

She suppressed a snarl, then began to jog off.

He spoke again, and this time his voice was cold, as emotionless as she feared he'd become. He sniffed. "She's dying, Mother."

She paused, then thought of the grief that Shahl would feel if Sera died. Her death would crush him. Zharla knew what she had to do. "If you harm my niece . . ."

Nayr paced to her side. "Mother, the man you call Shahl is dangerous." He looked out over the bay. "I don't want him near you anymore."

The exertion of her run glistened on her proud brow. "He's harmle . . . they're both harmless."

"No, Mother. Your longing eyes betray you. Shahl controls you, and controlling you is . . . is . . . is controlling the moon."

Zharla looked at her son, stunned. She had made him, but had she made him like this? Guilt haunted her mind like the shadow of death. Had she taught him this immoral disregard for life, with her selective charity and her willingness to sacrifice the few for the many? But what else could she have done? To rule is to make hard choices.

He looked up at her with mock concern, his face harboring more hatred than a seventeen-year-old face should. "Mother," he said, "you need to choose between them, between Shahl and Sera. You can't save them both."

Ice shivered down her spine. "You want to separate Shahl and me?" She narrowed her eyes at him. "Careful what you wish for, son."

Vision cloudy, Zharla turned and dashed toward home. As she fled, her breath came in ragged gulps. Waves of emotion coursed through her: anger, disbelief, bewilderment. She had thought she still had a chance to influence him, but no, he would force her to choose between two lives, of the man she loved and his innocent daughter.

The look in his eyes flashed into her mind over and over as she ran, the cold, lifeless look that said that life had become cheap. How power consumed the soul.

Power had consumed him so fast, even faster than for her, in less than a month. She had to make this right. Somehow, she had to get Nayr's attention, to make him see the light.

Ahrik looked into his bag and wondered how long it would be until he had to beg or steal food. In the five weeks since the coup, his rations had dwindled quickly. All his regular supply points would be watched. Using thumb credit was out of the question, since Nayr would follow the bioscan straight to him.

He refused to endanger his women and men by drawing them into the open on his account. By now, most of those still in the Ketel of Ahrik would have gone to ground, or to the Emerald Moon, where Nayr would not have consolidated his power yet. At least, that's what Ahrik hoped by sending Renla there with his last order before he fled Nayr's tyranny.

And so he waited, out in the open but in perfect hiding. With a bandage wrapped around his head and his arm in a sling, he could pass as a clone discharged from service, now indigent and unemployed. Soon enough, one of his old clones living in in-mountain Meran would come along and take him in.

Problem was, he had told himself that for five weeks, and now he'd begun to believe that none of his clones would ever walk by this spot. The clones still serving in the force had fled the Eshel and Nayr, but those already wounded and discharged back into civilian life? There were three or four hundred of them still scattered throughout the Eshel. Surely one of those old soldiers would amble by eventually and see a brother in need.

Surely.

His stomach growled a need for something more than a few nibbles of ration bar. His cracked lips begged for something more refreshing than a few drops of water. But he kept a sharp eye on his three-sixty.

He overheard rumors that the Queen had come into the mountain depths that morning. This news gave him comfort, if not hope.

A scuffle of activity broke out in the cavern of Shtera Umqi, Meran's central market. A child darted from the cavern and up the thinly-lit stone corridor where Ahrik parked himself during the busiest part of the day, just off the cavern. The boy's flowing hair danced and billowed behind him as he ran.

"*Nayra! Nayra! Nayra!*" he shouted, using the in-mountain slang for Nayr's clones. His voice rang as he flew up the corridor and around the bend into one of Meran's many in-mountain warrens.

The boy's shouts cut off, mid-word. Ahrik felt the back of his neck prickle. Danger. A woman screamed from the direction the boy had fled. Ahrik leaped to his feet. People ran in every direction. Pandemonium coursed like adrenaline through the veins of the mountain.

But through the uproar, Ahrik heard the unmistakable, soul-crushing tromp of military boots. They came from the cavern, and from the corridor.

Ahrik's pulse spiked. He didn't know if they were coming for him, but he felt just as trapped. He knew he had fewer options in the corridor, so he grabbed his bag and slipped into the angry currents of humanity swirling through the cavern.

He walked and pushed toward one of the other exits from Shtera Umqi. He saw a uniform. He spun and weaved through the chaos. He saw another uniform.

He planted his foot to turn again, but his foot kept going. Where his toe was supposed to meet traction, it met only the slick black grime accumulated over years in the depths of the mountain. His knee hit the ground first. Pain shot up his leg and back, but out of instinct he curled and rolled out of the way of trampling feet.

There was no way was he going to survive years of combat only to be trampled to death by a senseless, screaming mass of innocents riled up by a few overconfident clones with not even a shred of real combat under their belts.

If they wanted real combat experience, he would teach them a thing or two.

He wiped his fingers over the black grime and rubbed it onto his face, recoiling at the smell. If they had face recognition tech, he didn't want to make it easy for them. He ditched the bandages that now hung loosely from his arm and head and strapped on his qasfin, Biriq. He worked his distiller out of his bag and slipped the distiller pack onto his shoulders and his hand into the weapon, then wriggled himself into a crouch and crawled over to a sturdy-looking market stall, dragging the bag behind.

He jumped and pulled himself up by the corner post of the stall, pushing against the wall of the cavern to keep himself stable. He scanned the cavern, about two hundred meters in diameter, and counted uniforms.

Three or four uniforms covered each of the six main exits from the cavern, but there were two dozen or so smaller tunnels, at various levels of the cavern, that had one or no uniforms posted. He didn't know where all the tunnels led, or if Nayr's thugs waited in the shadows just inside the unguarded ones, but he had to chance it.

He leaped down from the stall and threw the bag over his shoulder, balancing its weight. His recon took less than a second, but he saw a tunnel he could get to without being seen, about forty degrees along the arc of the cavern wall. He only had to engage his bioflauge combat suit's cloak without tripping the *nayra's* sensors.

That would be tricky.

He grinned as a thought occurred to him. He gauged the distance to the opposite side of the cavern. With his fingers inside the distiller, he ramped up the weapon to maximum power. The hum that blossomed out drew a few worried looks from people rushing by, but he gave them a confident nod from his crouched position, smiled, and sprang to a standing position.

The people around him scattered.

He squeezed off a distiller charge—*thunk*—and at once engaged his bioflauge suit's cloak. He bolted toward the tunnel, and none too soon, since two of the *nayra's* charges slammed into the wall of the cavern where he'd just been crouching.

He laughed inside, because he knew they couldn't see him. The charges flying around ruined the sensors that should have allowed them to see him even when cloaked. He smiled at his old soldier's combat wiles.

As the two charges splashed into the wall behind him, a faint sizzle and crack sounded from across the cavern. With glee, Ahrik also heard a scramble of voices, soldiers rushing out from under falling debris. He knew all the in-mountainers had the sense to stay away from the *nayra* during a surprise raid, when there was a chance for violence.

And nowadays, in-mountain, there was always a chance for violence when *nayra* showed up.

Four more strides along the cavern wall, and he lurched into the tunnel. Pain pulsed from his knee. He jammed to a stop against the stone wall. He had his weapons ready against the danger the tunnel might hold. He needed a moment for his eyes to adjust to the poor light.

A shadow stood two meters away from where Ahrik crouched. The shadow materialized into a man as Ahrik's eyes adjusted. The man held something squirming, at arm's length, pinned against the tunnel wall and gasping for breath. A child.

But Ahrik didn't strike. Was this man a soldier, or a man corralling a recalcitrant son? In the chaos, it could be anything. Was the boy gasping for breath, or whining? Ahrik saw locks of hair flail in the darkness. Was this the same boy who'd sounded the alarm about the *nayra*?

If the man holding the struggling boy was a soldier, he'd be trained how to fight a cloaked opponent at close quarters. Ahrik tensed like a cat ready to spring.

The man turned his head toward Ahrik. He assessed for a beat. The man could probably make out shadows and the dust that Ahrik kicked up, even if he was cloaked. Ahrik's advantage wouldn't last.

The man sucked in his breath in a sure sign of recognition, but Ahrik saw the outline of a distiller pack and qasfin before the soldier could react. Ahrik couldn't shoot his distiller, for fear of hitting the boy, so he pushed off the tunnel floor with his legs and shoved his distiller into an uppercut aimed at the soldier's chin.

But the man was a clone of Nayr, and he was quick. Ahrik's sudden thrust negated his cloaking mechanism for an instant. His distiller was visible flying at this speed, and Ahrik was weak from weeks of malnourishment. The clone dodged. He took most of the uppercut on his shoulder. He grunted, then released the child and swung his gloved fist at Ahrik's head.

The child coughed and gasped for air. Ahrik didn't see what happened next. The exertion of the last few moments caught up with him and he parried the punch poorly. Poorly indeed. Light flashed in Ahrik's vision as the clone's fist met Ahrik's temple. Pain seared from the blow. Next thing Ahrik knew, his back slammed against the wall and the clone came at him with blood in his eye.

Ahrik felt the cloaking mechanism shudder and flicker off. On instinct, Ahrik lashed out with Biriq. He tried to get his legs underneath himself again, but he didn't know if he'd be able to. Would he die like this, bloodied, in some nameless alley?

The soldier cocked back his own qasfin, ready to strike with the killing point. Ahrik raised his own blade to parry, but saw, in agonizing clarity, that he was still too slow. He was going to get poked by some green clone's shiny new blade, and leave his blood all over the place, and there wasn't a thing he could do about it.

Curse his fragile body.

Curse Nayr and his bloodlust.

His own blade moved in slow motion. He waited for the clone's inevitable blow. It didn't come. The clone's arm wavered. The arc of his strike wobbled and Ahrik's blade met his with the ethereal, teeth-tingling ring of steel on steel.

What?

The rush of cheating death surged through his body, and Ahrik saw what happened. The child who raised the alarm, with the flowing locks, rammed his shoulder into the clone's knee. For a split second, the clone's fury turned on the boy.

The opening was small, but it was enough. The clone realized his mistake too late. Ahrik's blade flew, and this time Ahrik balanced himself and compensated for his feeble strength. He threw his hips forward even more than usual.

Biriq flew. Ahrik had never seen it flash like it did in that gritty tunnel. His strength and bioflauge suit threatened to fail him, and the thin hope of womankind's freedom hung by a thread, but oh how Biriq flew.

The blade caught the soldier in the jugular and exited through the windpipe with a swish of red. The clone's head whipped back, then lolled forward in shock and incomprehension. His body crumpled to the ground.

Something inside Ahrik wanted to feel sorry, but he didn't have time. All ketelis were trained to transmit their location over the tendril link before they died. Ahrik couldn't take any chances.

He flipped the blade over to the killing point and cocked it one final time before jamming it into the compiler implanted at the base of the clone's neck, cutting off his tendril link.

Shouting rang out in the cavern. They were coming. The boy eyed Ahrik with a look that said he should follow and dashed down the tunnel. They weaved and slithered through the press of people, running ever down, down, deeper into the belly of the mountain.

Ahrik lost track of the turns they made. His lungs burned with the effort. Unbridled need drove him on. The surge of his small victory convinced him that he would not die cornered, like a rat. Maybe he was invincible, after all.

They stopped, finally. Ahrik bent over his knees and gulped in the stale air of the mountain depths. His heart pounded, and he looked up, elated at cheating death once more, to take in his surroundings. Check his three-sixty. Nothing looked familiar. Pale faces stared at him, but greeted the boy with recognition.

The boy nodded at Ahrik and handed him a cloth to wipe his blade. "Thum *nayra* wasn't nuver gonna cutch us."

The boy had a thick in-mountain accent. Ahrik nodded his thanks and began wiping down Biriq. "Where . . . are . . . we?" he asked between gulps of air.

The boy chuckled. "'Bout thurty meters from where yuh always suttin'."

Ahrik stood up and narrowed his eyes. "Thirty . . . ? How . . . ?"

A woman sauntered up and tousled the boy's hair. "Thunk you fur saving 'im, Yur Highness." At Ahrik's look of shock, she gave a sheepish grin. "Wu've always knuwn who yuh wuz, but it seemed like yuh didn't wanna be . . . public 'bout it."

"Th . . . thank you."

She pulled back a thick blanket hanging over a rough-hewn opening and waved him into their small hovel. She gave an apologetic smile. "Come un out u'th'tunnel."

Ahrik crouched and stepped into a dank outer room, lit with antiquated wax candles. The air carried the sting of disinfectant and stale human. Like lives left to erode in a slow, never-ending pattern of decay. The walls bore sparse ornamentation, a small square rug hanging off-kilter on its frame, a religious icon to the Emerald Moon, and a flickering holo of the boy and his mother shading their eyes from an overbright sun. By the look of their skin, Ahrik guessed that the boy and his mother didn't go out-mountain too often. Like the picture was taken on a rare vacation.

The woman shrugged. "Ut's not much, Yur Highness, but ut's safe, at least fur a luttle while."

To Ahrik it felt like a palace, a home warmed with loves given and hopes gained. How long could he evade the *nayra* down here?

More heads poked into the little hovel, peered around, and disappeared. The whole neighborhood knew who he was and what was going on.

Ahrik was glad to be among friends for a bit. He pursed his lips. It couldn't last. Nayr was ruthless. He would turn one of these good people in short order. It would not be pretty.

He'd have to move on soon.

"Mother?" The boy raised an expectant eyebrow at his mother.

The woman turned an animated look on Ahrik. "I ulmost furgot. Yur Highness, wu've recorded sumthin' for you. Figured yuh wuz off th'grid."

The woman tapped a holobox and a recording flickered on. Ahrik cocked his head in wonder at how they could afford a holobox when it barely looked like they could afford food, but the recording quickly captured his attention. The Council of Elders, minus one, sat in Meran's largest courtroom. Nayr's clones lined the walls.

"Looks like a sham trial," said Ahrik. "Who's the defendant?"

The woman scratched at the floor with her toe before answering. "Yuh are, Yur Highness."

Ahrik let the thought sink in for a beat, not quite willing to believe what his eyes and ears witnessed. He sighed. "That would explain why they came down in such force today." He gave her a grave look. "Nayr wants my head. It's not enough for him just to take power."

"We're yur friends. We cun keep yuh safe"—she sniffed—"until yuh need t'leave."

Ahrik nodded slowly. Leave. The realization that he might have to concede defeat to Nayr stabbed at the pit of his stomach. The life drained from his legs. He reached for the frayed arm of the couch and slumped down into it. He didn't know how to fight Nayr with no army. Had Renla had better luck on the moon? He stroked his chin. He could he leave Dom behind, trade space for time, and make a stand on the moon. Maybe.

He studied the fierce and hopeful gazes that these worthy in-mountainers gave him, sitting, exhausted, in the warmth of their hovel. He could not abandon them to Nayr's predations.

Ahrik didn't want to concede defeat, but he knew that insurgency would go only so far before Nayr simply started killing everyone. Ahrik knew what hate Nayr could conjure. He'd felt it once himself, before conquering that demon within his own breast. "I can stay here for a time," Ahrik told his host. "Not long. Nayr is too powerful."

The woman nodded at the boy, who left and came back with a bowl of gray but steaming gruel. The woman pursed her lips, then attempted a smile, like she knew what this gesture would cost them. "Jus' regain strength, Yur Mujesty."

Ahrik pulled open his bag and stuffed in his distiller and Biriq, now sheathed. He frowned at all the empty space inside, then scanned the humble dwelling and blushed. Staying here would be asking many to die, and for what?

The boy held out the bowl to Ahrik, with a wide and gentle smile. "Everythung w'have is yurs, Yur Highnuss."

"Thank you. The Lady has no limit to Her generosity," he said, using the traditional show of gratitude. In that moment, though, Ahrik knew that he could no longer bear to face these good people. He smiled at them all the same, with what he hoped was reassurance. "I will stay a few days," he lied, "to recover."

He thought of Hawk, and wondered if he was still alive. He thought of all those whose lips would no longer utter the sacred Oath of the Keteli Soldier. Ahrik glanced once more around the room as he ate.

He would leave tonight, under cover of darkness, so that these good people's faces would not haunt his dreams. Their looming deaths felt all too familiar. Maybe, he told himself, he could draw Nayr off, away from here.

But he did not know if he could still fight. Ahrik swirled the question in his heart, and found that he could not answer it.

Anda shifted his feet and scanned the courtyard of the Tameri family estate, for the millionth time, for any movement in the wee morning light. Fog began to descend, to nestle over the vast expanse of close-cropped grass, bordered by flower beds. The fog filtered the light of the full moon into an even duller shade of green.

He reached for the vanilla charm at his breast and slid open the lid just a crack. He breathed in the redolence and let it fill his consciousness with the sweet memories he made, once, with his little family.

He trembled at what he had to do now. For Esh'a. For Sera.

Anda rapped his toe against the oversized potted fern he hid behind. The sound, and his frustration, reverberated through the vaulted entrance of the mansion reception house, a building set off from the main mansion and built in the time since that fateful day, seventeen years earlier, when Zharla snubbed him in favor of his brother, Ahrik.

The reception house was no less ornate or grand in its scope and design than the main mansion. This was where Zharla had told him to wait, in the loneliest hours of that morning, with little hope that he would achieve his design.

Doubt clawed at his chest, and yearned to show him the error of trusting her once again. He ignored this doubt. The situation gave him no good choices.

He had to trust the woman he once loved, a woman that better sense told him he should not trust.

A hunched form, probably an elderly woman, emerged from the eerie mist at the corner of the mansion. Anda was surprised to see her carrying a load, something unheard of in the old days, a woman bearing a burden. She moved from the mansion toward the main gate, the only way out of the compound on foot. Her path led right by the reception house where Anda hid.

Anda cocked his head at the odd sight. Was he supposed to stop her and ask for the way to find Esh'a? Was this the help that Zharla had promised after she came back from her run the other morning?

The figure's muffled footfalls tapped against stone pavers. She passed not two arm's lengths away from Anda, right under the vaulted awning covering the entryway to the reception house. She shifted the burden on her back, but gave nary a nod in his direction, much less a "good morning." Of course, he kept well into the shadows created by the potted fern and the alcove in which it sat, as he wanted as few people as possible to acknowledge his morning, good or otherwise.

Nayr would be very displeased with his plan.

Two bulbous stone pillars supported the entryway awning. The dark figure made for one, then set down the bundle. Anda perceived now that she definitely moved like a woman, where before he'd only guessed such. Her flowing cloak and hood disguised the obvious markers of her gender, but she walked, hunched, like a woman twice his age.

She straightened as much as an elderly woman might, then looked straight at him, or at the shadows that concealed him, at any rate. She hobbled in his direction. His blood pumped faster through his veins, and he gained an acute and sudden awareness of his surroundings. He scanned the courtyard once again, then cast a nervous glance through the translucent doors of the reception house. Was someone else waiting here, one of Nayr's thugs, ready to pounce, to decry his faithlessness?

The crone beat an inexorable yet ponderous path toward his hiding spot. If the guards found him out here, at this time of morning, they would ask questions, and questions had a tendency to result in bodily pain and reduced visiting privileges with Sera, whom Nayr had moved permanently to the healing complex in the palace, across the leeward valley from Meran. That move had happened the same morning that Zharla ran through in-mountain Meran, with Nayr on her heels.

Anda didn't know what Zharla's run had to do with him and Sera, but Sera's removal was worse than torture.

The old woman shuffled to a stop on the other side of the potted fern and made as if to poke around in the lumpy, black lumen. Only then did Anda realized that the stone pillar where she'd set the bundle hid both of them from the view of the guardhouse at the main gate. Even if the guards happened to look this way, they would see nothing out of the ordinary.

She tossed a small packet onto his side of the fern. It rustled through a few leaves and landed in the damp soil. He looked up in surprise, for she hadn't given any indication that she'd even seen him, besides looking in his direction earlier, which he chalked up to happenstance, since she made no move of recognition thereafter.

He picked up the packet and gulped back the dryness that assaulted his mouth. "Wha—?"

"Shhhh! Voices carry well in the morning stillness, even with the fog."

He recognized the voice. "Zhar . . . Your Majesty?"

She sighed and threw back her hood, but made as if to tend the plant. "I told you someone would be here to help," she whispered.

"I didn't think you'd come yourself."

Her gaze softened, and he saw her eyes clearly for the first time. She looked away and wiped her nose.

"You've been crying." He reached through the fern, to grasp her hand, maybe, or a wrist.

She pulled back and clenched back tears. "I had to see you one last time."

"Your Majesty—"

Zharla choked on a sob and Anda froze, even more unsure of himself. She took a deep breath and glared at him through the fern. "Don't touch me unless you mean it." She fumed, as if locked in a battle with her conscience, then rubbed one of the spidery leaves between her fingers. "What I wouldn't give to hear you call me Zhe'le just one last time."

The words hung in the air like a wraith, a twisted and painful vision of what might have been. Storms of passion and guilt surged in Anda's breast, and he very nearly did reach for her then, for she never looked more beautiful or powerful or vulnerable than she did in that moment, but Sera's face sprang to his mind, and Esh'a's, and he knew what betrayal would cost, and he stayed his hand, clenching his jaw and his fist until the nails nearly broke the skin of his palm and his teeth ground out the last vestiges of temptation.

He dared say nothing.

She undid the clasp on her flowing cloak and whipped it off her shoulders with frightening terseness. "Open the packet. Drink the solution."

"What will it do?" Part of him wanted it to strike him dead then and there, but a greater part of him wanted it to transport him far away, to wherever Esh'a was, to safety, away from here, so they could be together again, to work through their mutual doubts as he knew they always would when they decided to marry.

"It'll make you want to throw up," said Zharla, "but it'll also suppress the nanobots that Nayr is using to keep track of you."

"Nanobots? How did he . . . ?"

"I don't know." She pursed her lips and considered his gaze. "Probably in your food," she said, then shook her head and gave him a rueful look. "The men in my life are not what I thought."

"Your Majesty, I never meant—"

"No." She waved off his explanation. "You have nothing to answer for compared to Nayr and Ahrik. Their pride grows like a virus, to fill the whole world." She shoved the cloak in his direction. "The nanos are with you forever now. It'll be two or three days before they grow back, but that should be enough time to find your wife and get away."

"And . . . and Sera?"

"Meet me at Shtera Umqi at midnight after tomorrow's sunset, on the shortest night of the year." She nodded toward the bundle behind her, by the pillar. "That bundle contains most of what you'll need to save your daughter."

He nodded and opened the packet, then held the vial between his thumb and forefinger. He looked at the cloak and then at the bundle she'd left by the pillar, sussing out how the next few moments would go. His gaze fell once again on Zharla. "I can't change what happened, Zhe'le."

Tears of joy sprang to her eyes when he used her familiar name. "Thank you, She'le."

He held her gaze and made his eyes wary. "This is goodbye?"

"My world is destroyed, She'le, and you ask me this?" She cast him a look of pain and dismay.

Again, words escaped him.

She gripped the edge of the pot, near her waist, her knuckles as white as the marble the pot was carved from. "My advice is that you look only forward. The world is changing, Shahl. Not just for me, but for everyone. Find your wife in the refugee camps. Find Sera. Then go. Leave Dom forever."

A sudden fear gripped Anda's heart, and he doubted once more. Maybe he should stay, make a life here, with Zharla, his first love. But Sera's young and eager face sprang to his mind once again. "I need to know." His shoulders slumped. "Will Sera be okay till then?"

Zharla stomped her foot in frustration and pounded her chest. "On my heart, Shahl, which has never for a moment stopped beating for you, your daughter will be safe. She is my charge."

Anda opened his mouth and drained the vial into his throat, grimacing at the foul taste. He took the cloak from her and wrapped it around his shoulders. Fighting delirium and violent cramps, he pulled the hood low over his face and hobbled to the bundle lying next to the pillar, then threw it on his back, as he'd seen Zharla carry it earlier.

His feet tapped the stone pavers, the dull metronome of a tainted future. He turned around before he stepped out from the vaulted awning. Zharla was already striding back to the palace, the past already forgotten, her head erect and her back determined and straight. He hunched a little deeper and passed through the gate and into the fog gathering in the city beyond. No movement of *nayra* stirred in the guardhouse. How the underclass moved under a veil of invisibility.

Doubt about this plan still ate at his convictions, but he once again had no choice. He might find Esh'a once again, but he had lost Zharla forever.

His stomach churned, and not only from the solution he'd drunk.

Zharla woke to gentle nudges from small fingers.

"Auntie Queen," said Sera in her ear, too loudly, "you fell asleep."

Zharla fumed a sigh and sat up on the floor of the makeshift playroom that Nayr had installed in the south wing of the healing complex. Did it occur to the moonie girl that Zharla would rather be doing something, anything, than playing dolls on the floor? Zharla hadn't liked playing dolls as a girl, much less as an adult.

She plastered a fake smile onto her face, but behind her smile lurked worry, worry for Renla, worry for Nayr, and worry for Shahl. "Cerit," she said, "Auntie Queen has a lot on her mind."

Sera sighed and pretended that two dolls were engaged in a conversation, just like Sera and Zharla. Sera scrunched one doll's head to the side and slumped its shoulders. "Do you miss Abbi, too?"

The question stabbed at Zharla's heart. Shahl's departure had left a wandering blackness within her, had turned time into an agony of patience, with Sera's every flit and tumble about the palace healing complex a reminder of what Zharla could have had. The love between Shahl and his daughter made Zharla and Nayr's relationship seem saccharine by comparison.

"Yes, child." Zharla couldn't resist tousling Sera's long, auburn hair. She rued what the girl represented, but she had to admit that Sera spoke truth.

The girl could suss out the crux of any problem with a carefree question and doe eyes full of empathy.

Sera smiled and offered up the other doll. "Abbi will find Imma, and then we'll be together, and we'll be happy."

Zharla twinged with guilt. She wanted Shahl to fail, not to find his wife, so Zharla and he could marry and set things right, set things back to how they should have been all those years ago, when she'd chosen Ahrik instead of Shahl for a husband.

The regret chewed away at her like a cancer. Shahl's return had rekindled dormant passions, and now a dam of frustration strained against a sudden flood of longing. Shahl was supposed to meet her tomorrow night in the Meran central market, as they'd planned, then he'd whisk Sera away.

But Zharla couldn't bring herself to go through with it. What would Nayr think if Sera disappeared, and his own mother had something to do with it? After all, if she kept the girl here with her, Shahl would have to come back to her eventually. She quickly suppressed the thought, guilt sweeping over her. What would Shahl think of her if she manipulated him so?

But she had no stomach to choose between Nayr and Shahl.

She accepted the doll from Sera and made it ask, "Why does being with someone make you happy?"

Sera bobbed her doll's head up and down, then chuckled. "Silly. Being with people doesn't make you happy. Loving them does." Sera turned to Zharla and took on a conspiratorial tone. "That's what my Abbi always says."

"Your Abbi is a wise and beautiful man," Zharla responded, leaning back toward the little girl. Her regret and envy aside, Zharla actually had begun to enjoy having the girl around. Her time with Sera had transformed from a thankless and bitter chore into a welcome burden, despite the impertinent questions and the loss she represented.

Zharla set down the doll and rubbed Sera's cheek. Zharla needed to be nice to Sera. That was her way into Shahl's heart.

Zharla was about to work herself off the floor when Sera cocked her head. "Do you love Cousin Nayr?"

"Well, y . . . yes," Zharla stammered, "he's my son."

Sera furrowed her brow in deepest puzzlement. "You smile around me, but not around him. Why?"

Zharla suppressed a flaring anger with pursed lips and a haughty brow. Her voice grew cold. "That's a grown up question."

Zharla couldn't hide from the truth. Did she really love her son? Was this little girl right, that her relationship with her son was a figment, a mere ghost of what it should be? Zharla knew what she wanted. She wanted what Shahl and his daughter had, those unbreakable ligaments of purity that bound child and parent in emotion and thought. She wanted Nayr to hang on her every word, to recall her life lessons at the most opportune times, like Sera did for Shahl.

Sera shrugged and picked up the doll that Zharla had set on the floor. "I don't like Cousin Nayr," she said. "He's not happy."

Zharla stood and looked away from the girl. "I will teach him to be happy. You'll see."

Zharla loved Nayr. Nayr loved her. If she left him, for just a bit, maybe he would realize how much he loved her, how much he still needed to learn about ruling with wisdom.

Then realization flashed into Zharla's mind. Maybe that was it. Maybe Shahl just needed to see what a great mother she was, and then he'd give up on his silly quest to find his wife. His wife was probably dead anyway, laying in some muddy ditch or floating in the cold vacuum of space.

Zharla gave the girl a supercilious smile. "You'll see. Nayr loves me. He'll remember what I taught him. You'll see."

A plan coalesced in Zharla's mind, a seed of excitement, then a sprout of hope. She would teach Nayr a lesson he would never forget. Tomorrow. A lesson of love. A lesson on how to abandon his hate.

Then Shahl would love her.

She stroked Sera's hair once again. "It's getting late, dear. Go bring a book from your room." She squeezed Sera's shoulder and leaned toward her with a conspiratorial air. "You can sleep in my room tonight. Would you like that?"

Sera grinned and bobbed her head, then grabbed her *dubbi* and sprang for the door. The girl's eagerness almost made Zharla feel guilty for the minor deception.

Almost.

As soon as the girl was gone, Zharla padded over to her wardrobe and took out her bioflauge suit and combat boots, along with her ready bag, with all the essentials for an emergency. She checked Nayr's training schedule on her handheld, then punched in a command for two of Ahrik's soldiers to meet her the next morning.

Shahl would see. He would see what a good mother she was. She didn't need Ahrik. She would keep Nayr from starting this war, and then Shahl, her Flame of Peace, would come running to her, like she always hoped he would.

7 Friction in War

Nayr finally felt like he was getting somewhere. They were close to finding Ahrik, he was sure of it, and his little plan with the Healer to get his Uncle Shahl away from Mother was working. The pesky Renla was back on the Emerald Moon now, where she couldn't meddle with Mother. Nayr's devoted sons were implanted in all the most important parts of the bureaucracy. Not to run the bureaucracy, of course, but to ensure that it didn't run contrary to Nayr's will.

Winning was what he did.

He drew in a deep breath of contentment and set off down the corridor toward Mother's chambers, as he did every morning. He had no way to displace her from power. The Queen was far too entrenched in the minds of the people for that. Better to curry her favor and rule under the auspices of her legitimacy, like Ahrik had.

Nor would he want to displace her if he could. She was much too dear to him for that.

His heels clicked on the polished stone floor as he walked. He nodded to the palace guards who saluted him as he passed. Half of them were his sons, and the rest were either loyal or were kept quiescent by the leverage he had over them. As long as he controlled the palace he controlled the Queen, and as long as he controlled the Queen he controlled the world.

Nayr rounded the final corner before the outer door to the Queen's chambers. Two stately stone pillars framed a recessed entryway. Old-fashioned wooden doors rested on massive metal casters, so that they opened by sliding into the walls. Mother had doors like these on the entrance to her chambers at the Tameri estate when she was young, and she'd wanted doors like these when she built this palace. Just bigger. A sentry stood in front of each pillar, one a clone of Nayr's and the other a *hayel* non-clone, a holdover from Ahrik's regime of spreading power to the common people.

The two sentries snapped to attention and gave sharp salutes as he approached, fists to chests. He returned the salute and nodded to his clone. "Report."

"No movement, Father," said the clone. "She didn't enter or exit after lights out."

"Excellent," said Nayr, with a sly grin. He tugged on the silver chain to chime the bell to his mother's quarters. No one answered. He furrowed his brow. Usually he heard a "come in" or "enter" when he called on Mother in the morning.

He tugged again. No response. Nayr scowled and pulled on the finely-linked chain yet again. Still no response came, so he pounded on the wooden doors, rattling the metal casters in their grooves at the top and bottom edges.

The *hayel* sentry gave him a nervous glance and turned his head as if he wanted to say something, but snapped his attention back to the front when he saw the look on Nayr's face.

Nayr ignored the *hayel*. Embarrassment flushed into Nayr's face instead. At that moment, he thought that he had no way to get into Mother's chambers if the door was locked. No easy way, at least.

He yanked one final time at the silver chain, but the result was the same. Suspicion crept into his mind. Mother never missed a morning meeting like this. She was always there for him. Always.

He could not govern without the Queen behind him.

Nayr narrowed his eyes at the sentries. "You heard nothing last night?"

The *hayel* acted as if he wanted to say something again, but again kept his mouth shut. Out of the corner of his eye, Nayr saw the clone furrow his brow almost imperceptibly at his counterpart.

They were hiding something.

The *hayel* sentry looked straight ahead. "Nothing to report, sir."

"Okay, then. Break down the doors."

"Father, I—" began the clone.

"Sir—" said the other.

Nayr slammed his heel onto the stone floor. The shock echoed down the hall, then died with a chill that would freeze water. A servant rounded a corner, read the situation, then focused his eyes on the ground as he passed by, mouth quivering with disquiet. The two sentries stared, startled.

"I said, break down the doors."

"But . . ." said the clone, eyes searching the heavy wooden door, with its thick metal locking mechanism. "How?"

"We don't know how this door works, sir," said the *hayel*.

Nayr sighed, rolled his eyes, and held out his hand for the clone's distiller. "See those metal balls at the top and bottom of the doors?" Nayr didn't even bother to take the clone's distiller pack, just jammed his hand into the distiller, still connected to the pack on the clone's back, and discharged at the rows of bulky casters. *Thu-thu-thunk. Thu-thu-thunk.* The matter scramblers made short work of the casters, leaving a series of ragged holes, molten rock sizzling around the edges.

The doors settled with a thud, but did not fall. Nayr handed back the distiller. "Push."

The sentries looked at each other, shrugged, and leaned into the doors. It didn't take much. The doors creaked, tottered, then fell into the Queen's chambers with such force that the stone floor buckled under Nayr's feet. Splinters of stone exploded out from the impact zone. In the corner of the wide open room, where the furnishings were thickest, a small body darted behind a divan. It cowered under a shower of stone fragments. The racket rippled out from the doors.

Nayr accessed his internal compiler and scanned the room for traps and weapons. He strode in and made sure to keep the figure huddled behind the divan in sight. His boots crunched over the ruined floor before he came to a stop in front of the divan, plump and purple and at odds with the recent, lively destruction. Nayr grunted a question at the little figure. "She's not here, is she?"

The two sentries crunched up behind him. They shifted their weight at the tension in Nayr's voice, but Nayr kept his focus on the little form behind the divan. He stabbed a finger in the direction of the ground. "Here. Now."

Eyes wary, the little moonie girl's head rose up from behind the divan, followed by her body. The little brat fixed her cunning face in that lying rictus that Nayr had endured since she dropped out of the sky to torment him.

The girl's voice cracked with guile when she spoke. "I'm scared."

Nayr saw right through her. He centered his thoughts and cast to his new intel chief. *6, Queen's chambers. Now.* Then, he gave his best impersonation of a smile and bent his head in the girl's direction. He spoke with deliberate care, to be sure her little moonie mind understood. "Where. Is. She?"

Sera's lower lip began to tremble. "I . . . um . . ." She took a deep breath, then shivered. "She's not . . . here."

Nayr stroked his chin and nodded. The girl's puddling fear was probably an act. He wondered just how important this girl was to his plans, or if she was expendable. "Yes," he said, "I can see she's not here."

Without taking his eyes off Sera, he beckoned to his clone sentry, one hand held out, expectant. "Distiller."

The rustle behind him said that the clone was withdrawing his arm from his weapon to turn it over, but then the clone cleared his throat. "Father, the girl is under the Queen's protection. Her Majesty told us so herself."

Nayr turned an impatient gaze on his clone, then slipped his hand into the clone's distiller and felt for the trigger grip. The weapon primed to his touch, and he aimed. "Yes, I know."

Nayr squeezed the trigger. The weapon sprang to life. *Thu-thu-thunk.* Three beautiful holes blossomed open in the clone. Chest, throat, face. No blood, just a sizzle and a gasp, cut off by instant death. The perforated cadaver fell back and twisted, since the distiller on Nayr's arm was attached to the backpack still strapped to the clone's back. The clone's arms hung limp, reaching for the floor.

Nayr yanked on the distiller cord to give himself some slack, then retrieved his arm from the weapon's casing. He let go of the cord and distiller with a flourish, and the cadaver crashed to the floor. Blood began to leak from where his head struck the cockled stone.

The *hayel* sentry looked around the room with a nervous gulp, but did not look at Nayr or the fresh body lying on the ground. 6 entered the Queen's chambers. He huffed. His lips parted, as if to speak, but then he surveyed the scene and pressed his lips together with an air of detached assessment.

The moonie girl stepped forward and put her fists on her hips. "You killed that man." Tears of anger welled up in her eyes. "He was nice to me."

Nayr chuckled and planted his feet in front of the girl. He crouched down until their eyes were level, then moved his hand toward her shoulder. She slapped it away.

Nayr laughed off the girl's insolence. "Sera, is it?" He gave his head a shake of regret. "Some things can't be helped. He was good, but I love my mother very much, and I have to be sure she's kept very safe." Nayr cast to 6: *Where is the Queen?*

"Auntie Queen thinks you're a bad man," said Sera.

After an annoying hesitation, 6 responded: *We don't know, Father.*

Nayr snarled at yet another lie from the moonie girl, then leaned his head into an impatient smile. "Do you know where she is?"

The girl fixed him with a glare and crossed her arms. "If I knew, why would I tell *you?*"

Nayr stood up and threw his head back in a laugh, then fixed the girl with a glare of his own. The laughter died on his lips. "You are fortunate that we share blood. Increases life expectancy."

Steam simmered behind the girl's eyes. She studied his mouth, as if weighing his words but not understanding them fully. She gritted her teeth. "She sent me to my room to find a bedtime story. When I came back she was gone."

Nayr glanced at the *hayel* sentry to confirm the girl's story. The sentry nodded, perspiring. "That's what I was about to . . . ah . . . say earlier, sir." He stole a glance at 6, as if he could help. "Didn't hear a thing after the girl left."

Nayr threw up his hands. "When was this? Eight hours ago? And you didn't report it?"

The sentry shuddered and stole a glance at his dead comrade's body before he looked Nayr in the eye. "No, sir . . . I . . . uh . . ."

"Quiet, keteli," said Nayr. *Any idea how she got out, 6?* Nayr turned to the girl. "Did my mother leave with you?"

Sera scrunched up her face and put her hands on her hips with a defiant, silent glare. She said nothing.

Nayr leveled his gaze at 6.

6 gulped. *Father,* he cast, *the Queen must have slipped out with the girl.*

Nayr pursed his lips and glared at the *hayel* sentry. *Her bioflauge suit,* Nayr cast. *The sentries couldn't see her in the dim light.*

If Mother was gone, then pesky Renla probably had something to do with it. Nayr could tell that some unspoken message had passed between them when she was here. Uncle Shahl, Sera's father, probably had something to do with it, as well. He was an enigma, ever since he arrived. Then he disappeared yesterday.

Renla and Shahl needed to be found. No one mocked Nayr's power like this.

Father, cast 6, *we picked up a heat signature in the corridors at about that time, but we thought it was a house cat.*

Nayr's fury increased by degrees at this new tale of incompetence. *A cat? What?*

The Ketel of Nayr could never rule the world with misadventures such as this. Nayr took two paces toward 6, who took a reflexive step back.

"Father, I . . ." 6 put up two hands in a plea for understanding.

Nayr closed to within whispering distance. "Silence," said Nayr, his voice low. He stuck his face close to 6's. "I only use my real voice because I'm too furious to cast over the tendril network."

Nayr looked around the empty room. The space taunted him. It told him he was weak. Powerless even. Nayr put a hand on 6's shoulder. The clone didn't flinch, but Nayr could see in his eyes that he wanted to. "6," said Nayr, "think of this as an opportunity."

"Opp . . . opportunity, Father?"

Nayr gave the clone a paternal squeeze on the shoulder, and nodded toward the dead sentry. "Yes, an opportunity." Nayr smiled. "Are those seekerbots ready?"

6 nodded.

"How many?"

6 shrugged. "About a hundred."

"Good. Send those out. Make more. Make a thousand more. Send those out. Find the Queen. Find the king consort."

"Yes, Father." 6 frowned. "What about the operations slated to use the seekerbots? The interdiction patrols against smugglers? The search for rebels?"

"Perhaps I didn't make myself clear," said Nayr, teeth clenched. "This is the new priority."

6 nodded. "Yes, Father."

"And 6?"

"Yes, Father?"

"Did you send that old compiler to the Healer in the refugee camp?"

"Yes, Father."

"Tell the Healer he is not to harm my uncle, just get him away from here."

"Check, Father."

"Speaking of getting away from here, how is my new headquarters coming along in Mekele? The smell of disloyalty in Meran eats at me."

"Construction is nearly complete, Father. We've had three thousand workers on it for almost a month."

Nayr smiled a dismissal at 6.

As his intel chief loped off, Nayr accessed his internal compiler. He brought up the file named Revenge and overwrote it: "Kill Ahrik. Find Shahl. Watch Renla. Rescue Mother."

He turned and gave the moonie girl a placid smile, then held out his hand. "Come along, now. Let's get you to the healing complex, so we can make you better."

Zharla crouched in a dark alley, watched, and bit into a piece of fruit. The cavernous Shtera Umqi of in-mountain Meran still bustled with the last of the evening shoppers and the beginnings of night-life. In-mountain Meran never slept, but as the cavern's lights shifted from day mode to night mode she wiped the last of the fruit's succulent drizzle from her chin and sucked her fingers clean for good measure.

The hardest part of running away from Nayr was the perception. People would think that the Queen was finally standing up to her son. She would become a rallying cry for the budding rebellion against the rule of the one the people now called the Tyrant. But it was a lie.

He was still her son. She would prove to them that he was a good boy, just deceived by those around him. Her gravest mistake was letting that traitor, Sheresh, get too close to Nayr. If not for that, she would still be Queen in fact, Nayr would be earnest and kind, and Ahrik would love her with a fervent passion, like he used to. She just had to do something to make Nayr recognize his lack of judgment, that he still had so much to learn.

She stood and listened to the in-mountain night murmurs, the bubbling lovers' quarrels and trysts, the chirping tones of in-mountain music, the staccato calls of night vendors selling cheap food, easy love, and everything in between.

Nayr sometimes sent patrols down here, and they often came to Shtera Umqi, mostly because the rest of in-mountain Meran was a hostile, no-go zone for them. In-mountainers had a fitful relationship with authority, so even Zharla had to keep her senses sharp and her bioflauge ready, especially in dark warrens like this, where not everyone would recognize the Queen, a distant sovereign from an out-mountain palace.

But she had to risk the danger, on this night of nights. She told Shahl she'd meet him here, in the market, on midsummer's night.

This was not a rendezvous she would miss. Ever since he'd dropped back into her life, she wanted nothing more than to be with him, to drink in the elixir of his presence and breathe in his intoxicating goodness, a goodness to which she could only aspire. She yearned for him to hold her like he used to, when they were young, before her mother forced her to marry his brother, Ahrik.

She shuddered at the thought of Ahrik. Long ago, their mutual disdain had grown into tolerance, then into respect, and even love. At some point they'd even had passion, but she realized in the moment that Shahl walked back into her life that what Ahrik gave her was a cheap copy of what she could have had if she'd been brave, if she'd stood up to her mother and chosen Shahl all those years ago. Now, the regret of years lost and the torment her life had become mixed together in a potent cocktail of desire and longing for what should have been.

Shahl would see the love she had for him, she was sure of it. The way he held her gaze, held her prisoner to the thought of him. Just by being near her, Shahl would make so many things right.

"Your Majesty."

She started at the voice behind her. Had she let her thoughts drift so far from the present that she allowed someone to sneak up on her? No one should recognize her down here, where the throne of power was a mere figment, a distant idea in a place where gangs and cutthroats ruled.

She turned and slid away from the voice, giving herself space and time to strike, if she had to. Her hands and feet were enough to dispatch common criminals, but Nayr's clones were a different story.

Bouncing into her fighting stance, testing her balance on the balls of her feet, fists and elbows ready to lash out, she peered in the direction of the voice. A deep hood obscured a man's face, and the light from the market silhouetted his figure.

She scowled. "I'm not—"

The man looked over his shoulder, then threw back his hood and moved into a shaft of light. "Zharla."

Tension poured out of her, and a thousand happinesses flowed into her soul at once. She sprang, carried on wings of joy, and wrapped him in her arms. "Shahl! I knew you'd come."

He was a miracle come true.

"Zharla, I . . ."

"Why don't you hold me?"

His body stood as rigid as stone. He worked his shoulders into the embrace and put separation between them. "It's midsummer's night. Do you know what that means?"

She didn't want to let go, not after what seemed so long. The last day without him nearby was a torment at the limits of her ability to bear, but now the wait of years was finally lifted from her mind. Ahrik was gone and not coming back, and Shahl was here, with her, away from the prying eyes and scheming minds of the palace, the two of them finally alone together. "Wha . . . what does it mean, She'le?"

He breathed with discomfort, squirmed a little. "My name . . ."

She reached for her handkerchief, tried to look away from him, but could not.

"My name is Anda."

She shook her head as only a loving Queen could, then caressed his face with her eyes. "You will always be my Shahl. I can think of you in no other way."

"You chose Ahrik over me seventeen years ago today. Do you remember?" He sighed and looked back into the bustle and din of Shtera Umqi, then drew just a bit closer to her and lowered his voice to a whisper. "I am married to another woman."

"She's dead, Shahl." Zharla squeezed his hands. She would convince him of her love, soon. She beamed into his face. "We can be amazing together, Shahl. We can save Sera from Nayr. We can show Nayr the error of his ways."

He placed his hands on her wrists and guided her hands down to her sides, then let go. He avoided her gaze. "I need to find my wife."

The words sliced through her bioflauge, to her heart within. But she couldn't just give in. His return had reminded her of everything she'd missed, of every touch unfelt and every word unheard. To give that up a second time was death.

She snuck one hand into his. His fingers were cold, flaccid, but he did not pull away. The commotion out in the market died to nothingness in her mind as she studied his face, looking for any sign that he recognized what they could have.

Finally, he raised his eyes, almost met her gaze.

She smiled, as if he saw her for the first time, in love, like they once were. "Keep your wife, Shahl," she said. "Have your family. I only want that small piece of you that you're willing to give me."

She stole his gaze then. His eyes bore a storm of fury and passion, an elemental struggle between love and self-loathing. She could swim in that turbulent sea for an eternity and never tire, cast about and bobbed by waves of heartache and lust.

His hand, still in hers, showed signs of life. His mouth quivered and his fingers twitched to the beat of her pulse. Nothing else mattered, nothing else in the universe at all, except the answer to her proposition of love and attachment and presence. To whatever piece of himself he would give.

Beats passed into moments, and moments into seconds, and still their gaze of indecision and passion and regret held. For hours it could have held, until the sun rose over the bay out-mountain and insects buzzed their song in the heat of the morning sun. She couldn't say how long their gaze endured, only that she was winning this unspoken battle with an unseen enemy, fear and loss.

He squeezed her hand, then released it and stared into the middle distance, between them. "Zharla, I—"

"Shhhh." She rested her hand on his chest. If he would speak rejection, she didn't want to hear it, and if forbidden passion, she did not want him to utter words that would cause him guilt. "Just hold me in your heart, my Shahl, my She'le."

He looked down at her hand on his chest, as if realizing for the first time that they were so close, as if waking from a trance. "Zharla, I . . . I need your help."

"Anything."

"Protect my daughter. Just one more day."

A knife twisted in her breast. She fought down the disappointment with quivering lip. "You're still looking for your wife, aren't you?"

"How can I choose which piece of myself to give you, Zharla?"

She willed him to say no more, but hung on his every word. "That doesn't matter, She'le."

"You're the only person I can trust to protect her right now."

"Of course," she said, herself battling the turbulence between love and self-loathing. Her voice trembled. "I . . . I'll protect her."

"I need to go, Zharla."

Zharla refused to relinquish her hope. One day. "You have the bag I gave you?"

He gave a thankful nod. "I'll come for Sera tomorrow night."

He made to pull away, but she clutched his arm. "She'le," she said, "I love you."

He pulled his hood down over his eyes with his other hand, but the blank space under the hood stayed fixed on her. He sighed, and Zharla heard the longing and pain leave his lungs. "Yes," he said, "I've always known, deep down, that you never stopped loving me."

Then he was gone, and, against the blackness in her heart, and against the market vibrance that did not care, she said, "I will protect Sera with my life."

Movement caught her eye a few meters away. A scuffle.

Someone cried out, "Ho, there!"

She fought to focus through the haze of what Shahl had just said, and a realization of what she saw fell upon her, then threatened to overcome her. Two of Nayr's clones had Shahl by the arms. His hood dangled from his shoulders, torn. He hung his head and avoided their gaze.

Had they recognized him? She didn't consider the answer to that question, but sprang into action. Doubt attacked her resolve. What would Nayr think if his men caught her? Would he think his own mother didn't love him?

That didn't matter, she realized in midstride, on her way to intervene with the clones. If she didn't save Shahl now, Nayr would probably kill him or torture him or lock him away, or all of those, and Shahl would forever wonder if he could have found his wife if he'd struggled just a little more, fought a little harder.

And he was about to fight. She saw it in his stance and in how he flexed his fist. But gone were the days when peace forces in-mountain would just rough a person up and drag him in. These were clones, Nayr's clones, and if Shahl resisted they'd just plunge a distiller charge into his chest and ask questions later.

Her conscience could carry a lot, but not that. Never that.

In that moment, she made a choice, a choice founded upon years of regret and unrequited love. She loved Shahl's life more than she wanted the people of in-mountain Meran to love her son. Nayr could recover from a little popular discontent, but seeing her Shahl struck down by Nayr's brutes would devastate her.

Nayr was still a good boy, but Shahl had to live.

She removed her cloak and let it hang from one hand, then stepped into the light of Shtera Umqi. People stopped and gawked, at the powerful woman who'd just appeared out of the alley, and at the man about to get a beating from the Tyrant's thugs.

She strode up to the putative combatants and announced, "I'm right here."

One of the clones sneered and lashed out to shove her away. "Hus Mujesty wunts—"

Zharla dodged the shove, grabbed the clone's wrist, and pulled him in the direction of his own momentum. He squealed in surprise as she twisted his body and sent him crashing over her knee. He writhed on the ground, and a few of the bystanders gave swift kicks to the more sensitive parts of his body.

"Ho, leave uff!" The other clone's distiller panned on the crowd, its hum menacing, and then stopped at Zharla. He fingered his qasfin sheath with his other hand and fixed her with a glare. "Buck. Off."

Zharla cocked her head, insolent, and in the movement made the briefest of eye contact with Shahl, a signal for him to run.

"You fool," she said to the clone, patting down her hair. "I know I don't look my best, but don't you recognize the Queen?"

Shahl wrested himself free and dashed into the crowd, briefly drawing the clone's attention, but Zharla pressed on.

"If you shoot me, you'll have to answer to 'Hus Mujesty'." She held up air quotes to tell the clone what she thought of her son's new title, prompting murmurs of laughter from the gathering crowd. Everyone there knew that the Queen was the only one with majesty, that Nayr's title was hardly earned.

The first clone rose from the ground slowly, and the one with the distiller scanned his surroundings, lowered his weapon. "Uh, Yur Mujesty . . ." He looked to his comrade, then back to Zharla. "Our urders are tuh find yuh und the king cunsort und a mun with hus duscriptio—"

"Enough," said Zharla, pulling the clone's attention back to her. "You found me."

From the other side of the market cavern, she saw Shahl turn and give her one last, longing look, then disappear into a tunnel.

"Yur Mujesty?" One of the clones held out wrist restraints. "We have urders."

She smiled, but lowered her voice to a snarl. "Try to put those on me, and I'll clamp them around your neck." She turned to the crowd and raised her voice. "Remember this night, this midsummer's night, when the prince consort tried to detain the Queen."

She paused as a fearsome thought occurred to her. Midsummer's night also marked Nayr's coming of age day. She still had so much work to do, to mold and shape her son.

He had lessons to learn.

She activated her bioflauge and disappeared. The clones froze. Zharla slipped into the crowd.

From a tunnel onto Shtera Umqi, a patrol of reinforcements pushed through the crowd, which erupted with jeers and taunts for the clones. Zharla caught pleasing grumbles of "Hail the Queen" and "Fail the Tyrant," and she wondered if this would be enough to teach Nayr not to be so heavy handed.

After a last glance at Zharla, Anda shouldered his bag and ran. The dark warrens of Meran enveloped him, sheltering him from the prying eyes of his pursuers and the searching gaze of the woman who begged for his affections. Had they been alone, in the moment she caressed him with her eyes, instead of surrounded by masses of people pumping in and out of Meran's central market, he probably would have given in. Esh'a would have drifted out of his life, and he would have made a new life with Sera and Zharla at the palace.

Anda had almost tried to tell himself that Esh'a would be happier that way, without the burden of Anda's past and the friction it created, but a seed of doubt lingered in Anda's breast. Sure, she would be free to make a new life, wherever she was, free of a fugitive husband and a sick child, and Sera would receive care from the best healers on Home.

He entertained these thoughts as he fled, Zharla's telling gaze burning into his back in that dark tunnel, and he knew that these were weak excuses for dishonor. Some piece of him, a dwindling piece, wanted to know where his wife was. Did Esh'a come to Home to provide for Sera and him, or to escape Moon and her life there, to be free of him and Sera? The answer to that question would tell Anda whether he was free to follow the currents of passion to Zharla's open harbor, or whether something deeper obligated him to stay true to promises he'd made to an absent wife.

Anda dashed and wound through the mountain's tunnels, always upwards. He had to know whether Esh'a wanted the life he offered or not, so he made his way to the out-mountain refugee camps. Doubt scratched at his mind; he had heard nothing from her for weeks. Frankly, he wouldn't blame her if she just wanted to get away. A life of exile on Moon is no one's dream, and she'd gone into exile for him. That would wear on anyone.

But Esh'a was a fighter, and now, with another war brewing, the fight would sound its siren call once again, and draw Esh'a back into the fray. Anda didn't have it in him to fight. Not this time. Not in this war. Sera needed him, but Esh'a would pick up a distiller and blade at the slightest provocation. She could be anywhere, in a militia in some muggy corner of the globe, or even melting into some refugee work gang, the perfect cover for an insurgent.

When his thighs burned and his lungs ached, Anda burst out of the mountain's eastern entrance and into the chill of early morning. The half-moon, threatening to set, sent its green light over Meran's leeward slopes. Anda crept out of the lush moonlight, into the shadows, and stilled his breathing to listen for the whine of seekerbots, the new tech the Tyrant had unleashed. The high speed bots couldn't operate in-mountain, but they were a constant danger for fugitives out here, in the open, with their facial recognition tech.

When he was sure he didn't hear the telltale whine of a seekerbot's microdrive, he cast his gaze ahead, to pick his path. On the outskirts of town, at the edge of the free-standing buildings, sprawled the camps. He'd visited all the camps except one the day before, his one day of freedom, but had found no trace of his wife. The last camp was run by the gangs of working class Meran, so he'd left that one for last.

He hoped Esh'a wasn't there.

Anda ran down the mountain and saw the last camp ahead of him, forbidding ochre lights trimming its fence, lined with opaque biomesh. Beyond the camp, on the next rise, stood the palace. Anda squinted. On the top floor of the southern wing, he just made out the room in the palace healing complex where the Tyrant kept Sera captive. After he found Esh'a, the two of them would go there and free their daughter, then they'd all be together again, and all would be well.

Anda tried to look normal as he walked toward the camp, passing those out on morning errands. On the richer, windward side of Meran, the streets would be deserted, but here, in the working class out-mountain neighborhoods of leeward Meran, the sights and sounds of human life met him on all sides. The smell of *mligh* roasting on a spit wafted on the breeze, from somewhere near. The meat's telltale sizzle meant that day drew nigh, that soon the working classes would be out and ready to purchase simple meals.

He suppressed his natural inclination to make eye contact and greet those that happened by, in twos and threes, perfect strangers all, and focused on the ground about two meters ahead. He had to process every unfamiliar sound, to be sure a seekerbot wasn't about to sweep down on him. By the time he reached the camp, both his body and his mind ached with fatigue and longing for his family.

Anda noticed that green moonlight no longer hung on the air. He looked back and saw the dim blue of pre-dawn hugging the rim of Meran Mountain. Then a high-pitched whine pierced the morning air.

His blood turned to ice.

He made for the gate with renewed vigor, shifting his bag to his front to obscure his profile. He kept his head down against the seekerbot's facial recognition tech. A dark-shrouded guard emerged from a makeshift hut just inside the gate. Anda didn't see a distiller, but the guard hefted a wicked-looking halberd, and a look that said she knew how and when to use it. The halberd's blade flew down to block his way, and his heartbeat ticked up. A cloud of hot breath hung over his head in the chilly air.

Anda waited for the guard to say something. The seekerbot drew closer, then the whine went deeper as it passed. Anda half-expected it to turn around and veer down on him, but it didn't. He said a prayer of thanks for the dim light, which probably made it difficult for the seekerbot to recognize him.

Anda eyed the guard and nodded toward the camp. "I need to find someone."

The guard gave a hiss that sounded like hot oil poured over ice. "No one goes in or out between dusk and dawn."

Anda fidgeted and pointed his thumb at the light coming over the mountain behind him. "Dawn is here."

The whine from the seekerbot grew closer once again, making another pass. Anda looked down and away from the sound as best he could, without drawing undue attention.

The guard took a threatening step forward. "We don't want people like you here."

"People like . . . ?" Anda looked at the guard with mock affront, then froze as the whine zipped by and lowered once again. "I'm from Moon," he said through gritted teeth. "These are my people."

Anda cringed inwardly at the lie, but he was just as much from Moon as he was from Meran, even though he was born here, before the war. The guard lowered her shoulders and raised the halberd a few centimeters, not enough to show that danger had passed, but enough to show that Anda had made an impression.

The guard thought for a moment, then shoved the halberd closer to his face. "Prove it," she said.

Anda shrugged. "Did you fight in the rebellion?"

Her eyes grew wary. "Maybe."

Anda held up his palm. It shook. The seekerbot turned for another pass. "Scan it. I'm Anda. If you fought for the rebellion, you know my story."

"You're *the* Anda?" She drew her halberd back to parade rest, unaware of the danger that the whining seekerbot presented. "They said you died."

"Hiding."

The guard beckoned him closer and held out a scanner. "You're the king consort's brother, and he can't help you find the person you're looking for?"

Anda drew as close to the guard as he dared, to hide in her shadow as the seekerbot's whine crescendoed. He cleared his throat and held out his palm to the guard. "Former king consort, and, no, I can't ask him for help." He breathed against the tightening in his chest and averted his eyes as the seekerbot passed. "It's complicated," he whispered.

The guard gave him a pitiful look, then grunted when his biometric scan came up. "You're really him." The guard's eyes shifted nervously. "There's someone you need to see."

"Yes, I need to find my—" Anda's body tensed at a shadow moving from the guard hut. "What's going on?"

Another guard circled around behind him. Anda made as if to run, but the guard with the halberd grabbed his arm. Her vice-like grip surprised him.

Her eyes bore a look of apology. "I believe you, but the Healer is hard to please." She gave him a guarded smile. "I'm sure you understand."

The two guards relieved him of his bag, but the renewed crescendo of the seekerbot's keen told him he needed to get indoors, and fast. Pain twinged through Anda's shoulders as the two guards yanked him farther into the camp.

The seekerbot's whine dissipated, but Anda realized that it didn't matter anymore. Defeat, that familiar companion, reminded him of its presence.

8 Methods of Resistance

AHRIK CLOAKED AND CROUCHED. He kept to the long shadows of dawn in one of Meran's out-mountain parks. He couldn't be too careful. Not after Nayr's goons had gotten so close in Shtera Umqi two days before.

It might be easier just to give in. Let Nayr try him in absentia and convict him in a sham trial. Ahrik could gather his forces once again, to fight another day, in another place, and still lose. Even if Hawk was still alive, stockpiling weapons and mustering fighters to Ahrik's banner, it offered no guarantee of victory

Ahrik was desperate. Nayr's spies were everywhere, as if he had eyes floating in the very air itself. In the two days since he fled in-mountain Meran, Ahrik had seen dozens of Nayr's clones, but none of his own. Ahrik could almost feel Nayr's noose tightening.

The loneliness was the worst part. An age ago, his wife and stepson loved him, and the women and men he led enveloped him in the embrace of loyalty. Now, he distrusted human interaction altogether. His stomach growled with hunger. Every day, new dangers lurked.

No appetite was sated, physical, emotional, or social. Even Zharla, when they were together last, would not caress him like she once did. He wandered now in a wasteland, devoid of love, hope, and human touch. The sad, disconsonant horizon in his mind extended to the limit of his understanding.

He needed money, fighters, and weapons if he was truly going to fight. And he needed sleep. He almost used thumb credit the other day, but caught himself at the last moment. He cursed his weak mental state. He had to find a way to get himself and his fighters out of the Eshel, to fight another day, or at least to distract the Tyrant here, closer to home. He was better to his women and men alive and hungry than dead and fed. His needs dwarfed his assets by at least ten-to-one, and he would have to even that ratio before he could begin thinking of retribution and revenge for all of Nayr's injustices.

And so Ahrik cowered in the shadows on a rumor and a hunch. A promise of a drop of water in a desert where all he tasted was dust. An anonymous message yesterday told him that someone he could trust would be at the Meran central park at dawn, on Meran's windward slope. He had little choice but to trust that hope.

He looked at the burgeoning light on the horizon and realized what night had just passed. Midsummer's night. The anniversary of Zharla wedding him, and changing the course of his life in so many ways he did not expect. How many years was it now? He did not even have the will or energy to figure it out.

The danger all around him made such memories trivial nothings.

He fingered his distiller. He'd used it to escape from Shtera Umqi, but he didn't know how much more he had in him. If this anonymous rendezvous turned out to be a betrayal, if Nayr got closer, he did not know if he could continue the fight.

No parkgoers ambled through the crisp dawn air. Only strolling lanes, not people, wandered vacant and hollow through the desolation that Nayr had made of this place. Even the birds and the ground squirrels sensed the terror that the Tyrant sowed in the heart of the Eshel.

Somewhere far off, on the leeward side of Meran, a seekerbot whined. Ahrik frowned. The seekerbot tech was meant for military use abroad, not in local law enforcement.

The shadows of night threatened to melt into day. The moon set. Ahrik grew wary. He could move with relative ease at night, but Nayr owned the day.

As sunrise threatened over the bay, Ahrik caught movement in a stand of trees at the lip of a rise some hundred meters away. Someone was being just as careful as him. The person used the shadows and advanced a bit at a time. She or he only stayed in the dawning silhouette for short periods.

Ahrik eased his distiller up to a shooting position and rested his elbow on one knee. The weapon's round bulk settled in his palm. He slowed his breathing and waited. He swiveled his head this way and that to listen for movement on his flanks, to keep the area where he saw the person move in his peripheral vision.

More movement. A figure slunk and tacked from shadow to shadow. A woman.

How long had it been?

He shook the thought from his fuzzy mind. He feared to trust such animal instincts when greater dangers lay in wait. He examined the approaching figure. She was well-armed, her movements not quite sly enough to hide the outline of a distiller and qasfin. A digger or gunner, perhaps, but probably not infantry. Ahrik kept his peripheral senses alert, in case this was a diversion or a trap. He adjusted his grip on the trigger inside his distiller.

His hand trembled. His aim wavered.

The woman stopped under a tree, then brought some sort of optical device to her face and scanned the area. She slowed as she panned past his position. Ahrik's stomach churned, but he had no idea why. He had nothing left to lose.

The woman slipped the optical device into a carrier at her hip, then made an obvious show of stowing her distiller and securing her qasfin in its sheath. She held up her hands in conciliation, then crept forward to within range of a stage whisper. "Ahrik," she whispered, "First to the fight."

Ahrik narrowed his eyes. This could be a trap. Did he recognize the voice? Could it be? He frowned back the possibility, then raised his weapon and whispered back, "Butcher."

The woman didn't give the response to the challenge. Ahrik aimed his distiller, then gave a menacing growl. "Give the response, or I shoot."

The woman raised her arms in a frantic motion. "Ahrik, they didn't give me a challenge or response," she hissed. "It's me, Renla."

"Three seconds." He took a deep breath to make sure of his aim. "Three."

"Ahrik, when Zharla almost died, she said . . ."

Ahrik's distiller thrummed to life. His stomach churned with more than hunger. "Two."

". . . that she would have borne your children."

Ahrik tightened his grip on the trigger, to that familiar point just before the mechanism made contact, that delicate moment of memory between life and death. "One."

The woman who said she was Renla sucked in her breath and winced. If she moved, Ahrik would slime her, then deal with the consequences.

But he knew it was Renla. She didn't give the response, "Kafron," but he knew, in his heart of hearts, that he shouldn't squeeze her into an elemental mess.

He lowered his weapon but didn't power it down, even though he knew it was a pretense. A bluff at resolve and iron will. "Lift your combat blouse, so I know that no one's forced you to wear explosives on your waist." He grimaced. "He got some of my best men like that, Nayr did, in the coup."

She lifted her combat blouse to reveal her skin-tight tactical liner underneath, then turned to show that she had no explosives strapped to her back, either.

Ahrik powered down his distiller and rose from cover behind the bush, then stepped forward. He uncloaked and stowed his own distiller. "Sorry about that, Renla. I . . . Nayr . . ."

Renla moved forward and hugged him, an embrace of oldest friends, of mentor and trainee made, at last, into colleagues. An unslaked desire sparked in Ahrik's chest when Renla drew him close, and he lingered in her embrace longer than he should have, but not as long as he wanted.

Renla broke the embrace and held him at arm's length, eyeing him. "You know I'd do anything for you, sir."

Ahrik saw the look she gave him, in spite of the faint light. Did she feel more in the embrace than mere friendship, or was she making a point of keeping her distance? Ahrik mulled the possibility. The implications.

Ahrik regained his composure, barely, and motioned for the optical device that Renla had attached to her hip. She turned it over, but he couldn't discern how it worked. He looked a question at her.

"It detects infrared rays like body heat. I could tell that no one else was around this morning." She shrugged. "Keep it if you want. My research techs are producing them by the hundreds now, in case Nayr attacks Moon and we need to go completely dark."

Renla handed him the carrier, and Ahrik strapped it to his combat belt. "How long are you going to be on Dom?"

Renla glanced around her, as if preparing to reveal a secret. "This one's quick. I have an errand at Nayr's . . . at the old command center, then it's back to prepare the defense of the moon."

Ahrik clenched his teeth. "I built that command center, not Nayr."

Renla reached for Ahrik's hand. The thrill of human touch sprang back as her fingers reached his. Another signal? But then she stuffed a wad of cash into his palm and locked eyes with him, and he couldn't interpret the look.

"We need to free Shahl's daughter."

Ahrik narrowed his eyes. "Shahl is alive?"

Her face blanched. "How long have you been off the grid, sir?"

He shrugged. "Catch me up."

"Shahl was out by Kalevo, on the moon, but I caught him when he came to Prime. He said he had to find his wife, so I sent him here. I don't know what happened after that, but now he's gone and Nayr is using his sick daughter as bait, to lure him back, or something." She grimaced. "That part's not clear. No one really knows what he's thinking."

Ahrik grunted in as noncommital a way as he could. "I'm trying to stay alive, not get in deeper."

She gave a dark chuckle and patted his shoulder. “Sir, we're in deeper than you can imagine, and Nayr gets stronger with every second we do nothing.”

He grunted again. “Where is the girl, if I decide to do something?”

She handed him a slip of paper with a map. “South wing, palace healing complex, top floor. If you can free her, great. If not, give Nayr something to worry about. Tie down his forces for a bit, then get to Peshron. That's far enough away that you can make a stand.” She looked away, as if to leave, then pointed at the slip of paper. “There are frequency codes on the other side of that. Hail me if you run into trouble.”

He threw caution to the wind and gripped her hand so she wouldn't let go. “Come with me. Let's fight together, like before.”

Her eyes drilled into him. Renla squeezed Ahrik's hand with a sense of finality, then released her grip, closing his fist around the money as she did so. “Those days are gone. She loves you, Ahrik. She always has.”

Ahrik stuffed the money into a breast pocket. He made a frustrated click with his mouth. “If she loves me, she hates being with me.”

The lights went off around the park, casting the grounds into sudden darkness. The lights should still be on, this soon after dawn. Nayr's tyranny couldn't even keep the lights on. Soon, day would be as dark as night. “I . . . I don't know how much more fight I have left, Renla.”

She fixed him with a stare as steady as the moon. “The Queen needs you, sir.”

He gave a brave smile, unwilling to disabuse her of that vain notion, then patted the money in his breast pocket. “Thanks for this.”

“We need you in this fight, sir.”

He could not bear to answer her, not with the despair thrashing his breast. But in that same instant, he knew what he should do. He thought of Hawk, and the old base outside Meran.

Renla reached a hand to his shoulder and squeezed, an utterly maternal act. “Gather what forces you can,” she hissed through clenched teeth, as if fighting a battle of her own. Her eyes locked on his with a mix of pity, passion, and pleading. “First.”

Ahrik lowered his eyes in doubt, utterly without conviction in the response: “To the fight.”

With that, Ahrik cloaked and shuffled off, thinking of what might have been and tasting the regret of having been spurned yet again. He simmered with a desire to make Nayr pay for the lives he had ruined, but how was Ahrik, a has-been, supposed to exact the required price?

He knew where he needed to go to answer that question, but he did not want to go there. He looked up at Meran Mountain and wondered how long it would take him that day to get around to the leeward side on foot, through side streets and alleyways.

Anda narrowed his eyes when the so-called Healer ambled in, clutching Anda's bag. A desire to leap across the room and strangle him assaulted every part of Anda's being, but the halberd-wielding guard gripping his arm and thoughts of family gave him pause.

Anda struggled briefly against the guard's grip. "The Healer?" he asked. "Is that what you're going by now?"

At the man's basso chuckle, a rumble, really, all the pain and torture of Anda's early life came flooding back to him. This man had robbed him of his innocence at the bud of youth, then forced him to fight in the rebellion against women's rule during the War for the Emerald Moon.

Anda shuddered in his core. The suppressed horror of that time recalled within him an inexorable thirst for revenge. He clenched and unclenched his fists, struggling to remind himself of all the good memories he'd made since.

The Healer narrowed his eyes at Anda and leaned forward with a baleful hum. "I may remember you. I may not." He tore open Anda's bag and set it on the desk, the one piece of furniture in the makeshift room. He rummaged through it and pulled out the distiller pistol that Zharla had put into the bag. It looked and sounded like a real weapon, but the microcore was spent, so it wouldn't actually hurt anyone.

But the Healer didn't know that. He chuckled and waved the distiller around, as if he'd found something humorous amongst Anda's meager worldly possessions, then shrugged at Anda. "If you're carrying around one of these, then you're just another moonie on his way to the grave."

Anda drew in a long draught of air. Nothing would change the past. Even revenge, he told himself, would not cleanse him of the trauma of a too-early introduction to violence and pain.

After all, he met his wife because he was forced into the rebellion, the price of the conspiracy that led to Zharla's rape and the uprooting of women's rule. Anda tried to catch a whiff of the vanilla charm at his chest, under his tunic. He smiled despite it all, his daughter's illness, their ruined farm, Esh'a's disappearance, and his renewed captivity at the hands of his old nemesis.

He forced himself to smile, if nothing for his family. Fate had a way of turning ill into gain. He hoped this would be no different.

He had no choice but to hope.

He tucked his tongue into his cheek and scowled, to show he wasn't intimidated by this bulbous man's pompous air. "You know exactly who I am. I saw it in your eyes the moment you walked in here."

At this odd exchange between seemingly old acquaintances, the guard's grip slackened, and Anda shook his arm free. The guard took a half-step back, looking a question at the Healer.

The Healer just smiled with inflated confidence. The guard stood down, but her piercing eyes still missed nothing, the edge of her halberd glinting with what little light the hut provided.

Anda dared to hope he was winning.

A grating sound tore Anda's attention back to the Healer. He laid the distiller pistol on the desk, then fondled it with surpassing overstatement. "Maybe I remind you of someone you used to know."

"Why do they call you the Healer?"

The Healer grumbled deep within his substantial chest, then gave his characteristically fake, condescending smile. "I make things better."

A chill swept through Anda, but he sucked in a slow breath, for strength. "Maybe people would be interested to know that a former *pir'e* and secret leader of the rebellion is now in charge of a refugee camp," he said. He nodded toward the guard. "Can we settle this without the halberd?"

"Settle what?"

"Why am I really here?"

"I had the same question." The Healer picked up the pistol and raised it toward Anda.

Anda shuffled forward, but the guard did not react. Anda crossed his arms to cover his fluttering belly. Even if the pistol wouldn't kill him, that guard and her halberd would. "I need to live."

The Healer laughed as if a butterfly had just landed on his nose, then his visage took on a forbidding air, the pistol trained on Anda's chest. "If you die, no one will know we met."

Anda searched the Healer's face. The boss was toying with him. Anda read mirth and hatred in the large man's face, but also fear, just a little.

It wasn't much of an opening, but it was an opening.

Anda scoffed away the Healer's off-handed disdain, then assumed an air of false bravado, which he hoped was convincing. He chanced a lie. "If I don't return to the palace, powerful people will start looking for me."

This was, of course, partially true.

The distiller dipped as the boss considered this, but Anda couldn't tell if he was stalling for effect or genuinely pensive. After a beat, the Healer gave his basso chuckle once more and nodded away the guard, who slipped out through the rug over the entryway with nary a word of protest.

They were alone, which Anda, upon consideration, did not find entirely comforting. The Healer raised the pistol and leaned in again, this time with a grudging respect. "Did the palace send you?"

Anda saw the Healer's fear ratchet up ever so slightly, and let the implication sink in: the palace had left a few scores unsettled after the war, just in case, and the Healer never knew when the palace might want to settle accounts. Anda smiled and rubbed his chin, as if it stored some hidden reserve of knowledge. "Tell me where my wife is."

The Healer leaned against the side of the desk, waving the distiller with typical disdain, and threw a hand up in mock defeat. "Sorry. Can't say that I know her."

"You know her. She is probably the only woman from Moon with long hair."

The Healer nodded with false sagacity, then averted his gaze, his body language displaying a studied carelessness. "Moonies' hair often grows out in the time they're here."

Anda shook his head with incredulity. "I'll give you one more chance, before I walk out of here. You forced her to train me for your little rebellion all those years ago."

The Healer pursed his lips and raised an eyebrow in challenge, then trued his aim once again. "You walk, you die."

Anda glanced at the rug over the doorway with a grunt, or rather a monstrous bluff, because he had no wherewithal to believe that he would not be dead in nine seconds. Not from the fake distiller pistol, of course, but from the halberd. How loyal was the guard to the Healer? Anda suppressed these doubts. Family came first. He had no options left.

He couldn't bear the thought of giving up on finding Esh'a. He couldn't look Sera in the eyes without knowing he'd tried, really tried. Better to die trying than to face Sera knowing he could have done more.

He would die anyway, at some point.

So, he gambled with his life and prayed that Sera would understand, that someone would look out for her, protect her from the mess that his generation had made of humanity.

He gave the Healer an inquisitive stare while, behind a carapace of grim resolution, he worked up the courage to do what had to be done, to take that fateful step toward the outside, after which he would either live or he would die.

Everything about the Healer's smug body language and the waving distiller pistol told Anda it was his move.

He stepped toward the door and grasped the edge of the rug. Life offered no prize for the timid. The sheen of subtle surprise on the Healer's face as Anda turned away, and the fact that the Healer didn't immediately try to discharge the weapon, told Anda that, at the very least, he had seized the initiative.

Then the Healer clicked the trigger, and nothing happened. "Wha—?"

Anda pressed his advantage. With utterly false confidence, he turned and flung the rug to one side. The morning air cooled his cheek as he half-turned and glared at the Healer. "If you can't help me find my wife, then I'll be on my way."

Anda pushed through the door. Outside, the morning light framed the hefty bulk of the guard, her face marked by genuine surprise at the sight of Anda, alive. The guard's fingers tightened around her weapon, and Anda counted the seconds till his doom, till the Healer gave the order for the guard to strike.

"Wait," came the Healer's voice from behind. "Against my better judgment, I'm going to let you live."

Silence followed. Confused, the guard crept her hand down the weapon's carbon fiber shaft, but everything else in her body said that she was ready to kill.

Anda eased himself back around and let out a slow sigh of relief. He grinned at the Healer, that vile man. "I see," said Anda, "that you are ready to deal."

"I don't want the attention of the palace."

"I want my wife back."

"I don't have her."

He narrowed his eyes. "You know where she is." Anda cocked his head. "What's your game? You smuggle refugees from Moon to Home, then sell them off to the most wretched places in the world, to do work that no one else will do?" Anda searched for any sign that he was close to the mark, a twitch of the upper lip, a quick eye movement, anything. "Where do they go, hmmm? The upper Eshel? The Kereu?" Anda studied the Healer's face and crept forward, his jaw set with determination. "Off-planet?"

There. An involuntary wince. Anda's heart sank. Could his wife be back on Moon, after they'd come all the way here to find her? Or . . .

His mouth went as dry as the vast, irradiated ice at Dom's north pole. His head swam, and he fought to maintain his steely composure. His voice withered to a whisper, barely a croak. "You sent her to the White Planet." Anda set his teeth against the vertigo. "Where?"

The Healer eyed him with grudging respect. "I knew you'd figure it out eventually." His thin, inscrutable smile faded. "I can't promise she's still alive."

Anda stepped toward him, fists clenched.

"Okay, okay," said the Healer, chuckling again, but with a little less smugness than before. He held up Anda's bag with one hand and a beat-up handheld compiler with the other. He handed the bag to Anda, then shook the compiler to wake it up. He pushed it toward Anda. "This terrain map will show you her last known location."

An old-fashioned sand model emerged from the compiler display, a rotating topographical map of a planet, with what looked like coordinates marked at one location.

He looked at the Healer. "This is the White Planet?"

The Healer nodded, then notched his head to one side. "Inertial navigation will zoom in automatically as you get closer. Are we done?"

Anda grunted in the negative. "Why should I trust you?"

The Healer gave a flourish with one hand. "My life is forfeit if you tell anyone I've given you these coordinates."

Anda narrowed his eyes, his distrust unslaked. "How do I get to the White Planet?"

"There's a refugee ship leaving from Shtera Umqi tomorrow evening. Make sure you and your girl are on it."

Anda offered a curt nod. All he had to do now was rescue Sera and get to that ship. He looked through the bag, to make sure that everything Zharla gave him, everything he'd need to save Sera, was still there. "Where's the distiller pistol?"

The Healer leaned toward him. His face regained its customary, menacing vigor. "If you're not on that ship tomorrow night, I'll find you."

Anda set his jaw against the anxiety swirling in his gut.

The Healer whipped out the pistol from some hidden pocket at his back and waved it in Anda's face. "I don't like loose ends." He gave a chilling smile and handed him the pistol. "Of all people, Shahl Jeber-li, you should know that."

Anda's anxiety spiked. The Healer did know him, after all. Thoughts of revenge flooded Anda's consciousness, but so did the image of Sera and her loving, intelligent eyes. He tapped his temple and stuffed the fake pistol into his bag, then gave a conspiratorial wink to the Healer. "Your secret's going with us to the White Planet."

The Healer raised one eyebrow in mock relief, then nodded at Anda, as if to say he was free to leave.

As Anda exited the camp, examining the sand model on the old compiler, he thought he noticed a clone of Nayr loitering in the shadows of the guardhouse, but he wasn't sure. Could Nayr's reach already be so long that the gangs were beholden to him?

When he was out of sight of the refugee camp, he placed the aged compiler into his bag, unsure whether it would ever be of use, or even if he should use it at all.

Then he noticed that the seekerbot no longer loitered overhead, but it gave little comfort to his harried soul.

Nayr's thighs burned, despite the pre-dawn nip. He was glad for this run, to get his mind off Mother's disappearance yesterday.

He ran at the head of the command company, now swelled to 500-strong, in a formation running up Meran Mountain. The sound of footfalls and water sloshing in hip packs gave rhythm to the morning, and the sticky breeze off the ocean carried the stench of 500 sweaty men to Nayr's nostrils. About a third of the way back in the formation, 3 called out a new cadence:

Up in the morning before the sun!

The response erupted from the first third of the formation:

The Ketel of Nayr is gonna have some fun!

The run wasn't fast, but Nayr had to keep from twisting an ankle on the uneven ground while maintaining an even pace. He didn't want those at the back to accordion mercilessly fast, then painfully slow.

3 called out again:

While you're sleepin' in your bed!

The formation responded:

We're figurin' out how to make you dead!

Once the sun broke the horizon over Meran Bay behind them, they would be able to see the top. For now, all he saw up ahead was gloom. Nayr worked hard to be in better shape than his sons. They had the benefit of enhanced genes to get them up the mountain. At last, nearly to the summit, he began to hear hard breathing around him. The challenge of leading his men gave Nayr a rush as dizzy, almost, as a drug. Almost.

Way back in the dawn of time!

In a secret cave where the sun don't shine!

Nayr focused his mind and called up his closest advisors over the tendril link. They were running in the formation behind him: 3, leading the cadence, but also 2 and 5. *What do we do about the the Usurper and his brother?* he cast to them.

3 responded first: *Kill 'em.* 3 was bitter about Ahrik's men killing 4, one of 3's closest friends. Nayr wouldn't soon forget that treachery.

2 shot back: *Shahl isn't a threat, but the Ketel of Ahrik has to be neutralized.*

5: *Agree. Shahl has no claim to rule.*

3 sang out the cadence once more:

We were grown in genetic swill!

So we could learn to kill, kill, kill!

3 cast anger through his thoughts: *Shahl has the Queen's affection, which is as much claim as the Usurper has.*

Nayr looked up. He could see the peak. Sunrise had begun. He considered the danger of destroying the Ketel of Ahrik. Others had tried before him, but failed. They'd paid dearly for the attempt. It was one thing to eliminate the odd retired keteli and make it look like an accident, or to disappear one of Ahrik's hobbled clones and make it look like the peace forces simply keeping the peace. It was another thing entirely to go after an active, fully-armed force of experienced clones. He cast to his principals: *Can we destroy Ahrik's clones?*

We get up early and train late!

To introduce you to your fate!

2: *It'll take half the ketel—50,000 men—a year to track down and eliminate the last 2,000 of Ahrik's ketel.*

3: *No, 2, you're wrong. Have you seen what's coming out of the research division?*

5: *The nanobios? They're experimental. If we get the genetic signature wrong, they could kill millions.*

The peak of Meran Mountain rose within sight. Sunrise glanced off its crest. Nayr could sense his sons' fatigue now, but the hard part was almost over. Going down would be easy by comparison.

We'll find you where you hide and snooze!

Then turn you into toxic ooze!

Nayr called out the response along with the rest of the formation, which helped take his mind off the burn in his legs. Nayr looked to the peak. Only fifty meters to go. The steepest part of the run.

Just a few more deep breaths to grind out, snatched in between cadence responses. Nayr's legs tingled with pain. All he could think about was the top, and reaching it without showing weakness in front of his sons.

Primed distiller, sharp qasfin!

I'm a gene-spliced killin' machine!

Twenty more meters. Heads down, breathing heavy all around him. Nayr smiled at the satisfaction of driving his sons to exhaustion. The more they sweated, the less they bled.

Creepin' in the dark, after the sun!

Nayr trotted to a stop as 3 made the final cadence call. Nayr yelled out the response at the top of his lungs. His weary body flooded with mental energy:

The Ketel of Nayr is gonna have some fun!

Nayr forced himself to remain upright after he reached the summit. He breathed in through his nose and out through his mouth. He had to be the last to drink water. Around him, his sons whipped out hip packs as they reached the top. He turned to take in the view of the bay and out-mountain Meran sparkling under a new sun. Even if he hated the memories he had of this place, he was still master of all he could see.

An uncomfortable hush drew Nayr's attention back to his sons. Some still huffed up the mountain, and others milled about, but a substantial number focused their attention on something toward the back side of the peak, which daylight was only just beginning to illuminate. Nayr couldn't see what was going on, but commotion rippled through the milling men, and some of his sons cast awkward looks in his direction. Those closest gave him a wide berth.

2 pushed through the press of men, and Nayr frowned. He cast to 2: *Will no one dare bring me bad news?*

"Father," said 2, eyes shifting with nervousness, "there's a woman up here who says she wants to see you."

Nayr swilled some water and followed 2 to the back side of the mountain. His men parted. They spurned him like a magnet whose polarity had switched.

Nayr and 2 came to the woman. Nayr noted with chagrin that his sons gave an even wider berth to her than they gave him.

The figure wore a form-fitting outfit. Black combat bioflauge by the looks of it. Very expensive. The suit wasn't activated, so the woman obviously wanted to be seen. She sat stock still, gazing out over the gloom of leeward Meran. He couldn't see her face.

"Ma'am," said 2.

The woman did not acknowledge him. Nayr scratched his jaw. His sons were trained to treat all women with deference, but this level of aloofness from a woman was rare.

"Ma'am," said 2 again. "This is a closed military zo—"

Realization dawned for Nayr. He rested a hand on 2's shoulder and eased him back. Nayr paced toward the woman, against 2's grunted protest.

Nayr stood next to her. He crossed his arms and took in the gloom over the leeward valley. In the back of his mind, he wondered how long it would take for the shaking in his hand to restart. "How'd you get up here, Mother?" He glanced over the rugged, leeward face of Meran Mountain. "Where did you disappear to yesterday?"

She raised an eyebrow in his direction. "You think I don't train as hard as you? I've been waiting here for some time."

"We didn't see you set out ahead of us." Nayr motioned with his head for his sons to give them more privacy.

"Nayr, your father and I are—"

Nayr hissed. "He's not my father, and you know it. He killed my best friend."

Mother pursed her lips and looked out over the valley. It began to take form as the sun crept over the bay behind them. She stood and looked back toward the ocean. The rising sun now bathed it in rising light. Her eyes pretended that 500 of his sons weren't even there. She cast him a sideways glance, as if fighting some inner battle between the light, on one side of the mountain, and darkness on the other.

She turned and nodded toward the gloom receding from the leeward valley. "When making your choices, do not think that dark will always be dark and light always light. There is a pathway through the gloom. Even if you do not see it, it is there, and time will show that it is a better way."

He turned on her, feigning a look of admiration. "You came up the far side of the mountain? In the dark?"

"Send your men back down the easy way. I'll show you a better way." She stood and darted toward the darkness. She leaped onto one boulder, then another.

"What are you plan—" Nayr scowled at Mother's retreating form. He looked in his sons' direction. 2, Nayr cast, *lead the men back down.*

Father, cast 2, *you need a security detail.*

He eyed his leaping mother and responded, *No.*

A shuttle on overwatch?

Nayr shook his head, then scanned the rocks on the darker, more barren side of the mountain. Fifteen meters down the mountainside, Mother crouched on a boulder. She looked back at him with impatience. Her body coiled, ready to spring.

She leaped to yet another boulder. "Follow me!"

Nayr leapt down the mountain after her. Mother's agility and strength surprised him. As they descended, the leeward valley before them lightened by degrees. It made the going easier, and Nayr didn't have to pause as often and wait to see whether the boulder his mother had just launched from moved or not. The descent took so much cognitive effort that, even if he wanted to, he couldn't center his thoughts to call for help from 2 over the tendril link.

As the sky lightened, the descent became less steep, the leaps from boulder to boulder less harrowing. The vegetation became more substantial, and the ground less rocky. Still his mother careened down the mountain, as confident and sure on the treacherous terrain as any mountain creature. The burn moved from Nayr's thighs to his calves and shins.

His mother stopped at a ledge and looked out over the valley. Nayr forced his breathing to slow and deepen, so as not to reveal his fatigue. The way she stood, hands on her hips and eyes expectant, told Nayr she had some lesson to teach him. Instinctively, he started to center his thoughts to reach out to 2.

She smiled at him, but it was fake. Was this more of Ahrik's and Shahl's treachery coming through? He smiled back, just as fake. How did she learn to navigate the mountain like that?

As if reading his thoughts, she said, "When you were a young boy and I was recovering from my coma, I would come out here to think." She peered at him. "I know this mountain like the back of my hand."

"Impressive, Mother." He drew in a deep breath through his nose, and the hair rose on the back of his neck. Danger. Finally his thoughts were centered enough to reach out to 2: *Need exfil.* "What's the point of all this?" he asked Mother.

"You are taking the easy path, Nayr, the path of violence and hate. Your men will kill and die for you, without hesitation."

"Magnificent, isn't it?" *2, where are you?* Did Mother know how to jam tendril comms?

"No!" Mother swept her hand over the mountain and the valley. "Unseen dangers lie all all round."

Shuttle dispatched, Father. ETA four minutes.

Nayr sighed with relief, but at that moment he heard a rustle of leaves behind him. Alarm flooded his system as he whirled to face the threat. He was unarmed, but ready to fight.

Two of the Usurper's clones emerged from the underbrush. They weren't armed either, at least not that Nayr could see, but the fight would be precarious. He was quicker, but they were more experienced. He widened his stance and cursed his stupidity for trusting the situation so fully. Ahrik and Shahl deceived Mother too well.

Mother's hand pressed upon his shoulder. He tried to shift out from under her grasp, but she gripped tighter. Somehow, she managed to make her hold feel gentle. "Nayr," she said. "This is a teaching moment, not an attack."

Nayr narrowed his eyes and half-turned, keeping both Mother and the Usurper's clones in sight. The first rays of sunshine peeked over the crest of the mountain, and his ire rose as he realized the effort that Mother had gone through to put him here. "The Usurper and Shahl have twisted your mind, Mother."

She nodded to the two men, who rustled back into the brush. To Nayr's surprise, they decloaked a shuttle twenty yards down the mountain. That must have been how she did it, how she got up here.

As if reading his thoughts once again, she said, "I ran up the mountain from the bottom." She gave a little laugh. "The best things in life are hard to come by."

Nayr's anger returned at Mother's insouiscance, and at the subterfuge she used to get him here. The Usurper and Shahl put her up to this. Probably to frighten Nayr. He saw no lesson they could teach him.

He clenched his jaw. "You think I haven't done anything hard?" He swept his hands out. "You think all this has been easy?"

This time, her laugh was a full-throated guffaw. She threw her head back. The mockery stoked his anger even more, knowing how much The Usurper and Shahl twisted Mother's perception of him. His hands shook and his vision blurred for a moment, and he wondered if he could sneak in a pill without Mother seeing. Probably too risky.

She sauntered over and, as her laughter subsided, slapped both hands on his shoulders in jest. "I was seventeen once, too. Trust me, all of your hard choices are in front of you, not behind you."

He sneered, his fury feverish now. "What has The Usurper done to y—"

Her hand lashed out, and she struck him across the face. Nayr was stunned, but in the split second after she hit him but before she composed her face with mock anger, genuine regret flashed across her face. It was the first time she'd struck him, but also the first time he'd seen such weakness and vulnerability in her.

He kept his face as stony as the mountain, but made careful note of how he might turn this weakness into an advantage in the future. The Usurper's and Shahl's lies could only go so far.

He stared at her, focusing all his effort on controlling his shaking hands and tremulous breathing. He waited for her to make the next move. The moment that followed violence always showed truest intention.

She sighed, and when she spoke her voice dripped with false remorse. "I shouldn't have done that." She looked at the ground, as if at a place in the deep past, somewhere in-mountain. She peered back into his eyes. "I can't let you make the mistakes I made."

Nayr stuffed a hand into his pocket to finger the comforting little bag of pills nestled there.

Mother reached into a pocket of her own and extracted her handkerchief, which she always did when she was anxious. "Nayr, killing Shahl and Ahrik would not solve your problems," she said. "It would just create new ones."

He smiled, no hint of pain on his face or hurt in his voice. "Mother, I know what's really going on here."

"I'm going back to my estate, to take your cousin to the palace healing center, where she can receive the care she needs." She nodded sagely, but with an air of regret. "Time will help you see things more clearly."

With that, Mother spun and leaped off the ledge, onto the next boulder, and on down the mountain. The Usurper's men pulled off in their shuttle and faded into the distance. The shuttle 2 sent for him appeared on the eastern horizon, and Nayr looked down to consider Mother, flitting over rock and crag.

He pinched a pill from his pocket and plopped it under his tongue, then closed his eyes as the ecstasy calmed his body.

The Usurper and Shahl deceived Mother, and now she underestimated him. For that, The Usurper and Shahl would pay. But he also had to keep a close eye on Mother, to make sure she didn't interfere with his plans. He had to save her from their treachery, and he had to figure out how Renla was wrapped up in all this. Nayr accessed his internal compiler and scrolled his mind to the file called Revenge. He overwrote its contents once again: "Kill Ahrik. Destroy Shahl. Question Renla. Save Mother."

Mother was now dangerous, the product of The Usurper's and Shahl's deceptions. He'd have to be extra careful with her, but his priorities were still clear. 2, he cast, *get those nanobios ready. The Ketel of Nayr is going hunting.*

Renla checked her wrist compiler. Still nothing. Her eyes darted this way and that, searching for all the ways this could go wrong. Rebellion was an unforgiving business.

Leaving Ahrik at the park that morning was one of the hardest things she'd ever done, but what she was about to do would set her on a path of fear and violence she had never expected she would travel. Seeing the Queen torn between her son and her people needled her with doubt. The Queen refused to break openly with her son, for fear it would worsen the brewing conflict, so to everyone besides the Queen, Renla was about to look like a traitor.

Only she knew what was really going on, that the Queen was as much a captive of Nayr as the girl Sera was. The Queen, her dear friend, needed someone to fight for her, so Renla sauntered with false confidence across the main parade of the old Global Command Center, where the Ketel of Nayr was based until the new headquarters was finished in Mekele. Renla's stated objective was a supply requisition for the Fighting 11th, a cover for her deeper, darker intent. She focused on the dazzling blue sky and gentle breeze rising off the ocean to the west of Meran, and on the hundreds of menial tasks that make a headquarters run, anything to keep from thinking about the millions of people depending on her. At any moment, one of the thousands of soldiers she passed could challenge her, could melt her down to elemental slime.

In an instant, the tyrant Nayr could simply decide she should die, and his clones would kill her, no questions asked.

The afternoon sun shone over the vivid, green grass and sparkling polished stone buildings of the complex, for now the nerve center of Nayr's power. His 100,000 clones guarded all the critical points in the complex, although less sensitive areas were left to the ill-trained conscripts that Nayr began to recruit almost immediately after overthrowing Ahrik. She would rather deal with the conscripts than with Nayr's ruthless, calculating clones, connected to Nayr's tendril communications network by compilers embedded in their necks.

But she couldn't avoid the sensitive areas today. She had very little margin for error.

Renla arrived at the healing facility and scanned her palm to the reader at the security gate. The clone guarding the gate drummed his fingers and looked back and forth between his compiler display and her, his blood red beret bobbing up and down. His stony glare told her, *You're one of Ahrik's protégés. You might be tainted, like him.*

Loyalty is always in short supply during a civil war, even though she'd done nothing to raise suspicion about where her loyalties lay. Yet.

Renla hid her gulp with a smile, as if this were just another trip gravside to ensure that her hand's supply requisition went through. "Is there a problem, keteli?" she asked.

He eyed her. "Here to collect supplies, ma'am? Odd for a hand commander to fill a healing supply requisition herself."

She clasped her hands behind her back, unsure where she mustered the bravado. "All sorts of strange things happening nowadays." She shrugged and looked up to the sky. "My unit's up on the Emerald Moon, at the end of a long supply chain. I can't be too sure."

He narrowed his eyes, then waved her into the healing facility. His motion felt more like a concession than Renla wanted, but she smiled and nodded to him, a gesture that, she hoped, was as noncommittal as his had been.

She checked her wrist compiler, as if checking the weather forecast, but it still hadn't picked up the dead drop location.

She wound through sterile stone hallways, devoid of happiness and, almost, of people. She stopped and tapped at her wrist compiler, to be sure that the passive comm link was still scanning for the dead drop location. She had to reach the dead drop within the specified window, or her contact would retrieve the list, and this whole trip, with all its risks, would be for naught. If she failed, she would probably die.

The plan she'd made with the other hand commander, the one she found at the officer's club, would also be for naught. She had to get the list today, or, when the fighting really started, they'd stand no chance against the military force of an entire planet.

Her boots squeaked to a stop at an entrance labeled "Supply." The wizened clerk behind the counter looked up from her handheld compiler display.

The clerk tossed her head in Renla's direction. "I don't get too many hand commanders in here. What've you got?"

The clerk seemed unlikely to betray Renla, if given the opportunity, but Renla took no chances. One hand on her qasfin, she fished the requisition form out of her thigh pocket and handed it to the clerk.

The clerk reached for it, underarm fat jiggling, a look of surprise on her face. "A paper form? I haven't seen one of these in . . ."

"Since the war?"

The clerk brought the form close to her face, then looked over the top of the paper at Renla, then back at the form. "Let's see. 11th Hand, Combat Engineers. Emerald Moon. Looks complete." The clerk set the form down on the counter and eyed Renla's name tape. "I'm not going to ask if you're *that* Renla."

Renla judged silence, under the clerk's conspicuous glare, to be the better part of valor.

The clerk shook her head and brushed her fingers over the compiler display to fill the order. "I shouldn't do this, but I've been around long enough to know that we need people like you to help us stand on the right side of history." She handed a receipt slip over the counter and leaned toward Renla. "A bit of advice: whatever you're doing here, do it quick."

Renla narrowed her eyes, the unsolicited comment making her suddenly unsure she should trust the clerk. "How do you—"

The clerk cut her off with a motion that beckoned her even closer, then whispered, "I'm a supply clerk." She smirked. "I know everything."

Renla glanced at the receipt slip. "Okay then . . . um . . . do you know how I can get this item right now? I need to carry it back on my person instead of putting it in the elevator queue."

"Item five-two-seven-nineteen? NewSkin?" The clerk cocked her head, her wrinkled eyes now wary. "You get lots of surface wounds on the Emerald Moon, do you?"

"Let's just say I might need it sooner rather than later."

The clerk bit the inside of her cheek for a beat, then grunted and passed through a door in the back wall. Her absence passed from seconds to minutes.

Renla fingered the latch securing her qasfin on her right thigh and wondered if the game was up. She did an electromag sweep with her wrist compiler, to see if the supply clerk had any listening devices trained on her. Renla fidgeted with the receipt slip, then stuffed it into a thigh pocket.

Footsteps sounded behind her. She whirled and unlatched her qasfin, ready for battle. Two supply orderlies stood planted to the floor, eyes wide with fear. They weren't clones of Nayr, but a young woman and man, neither more than eighteen. Probably conscripts. Their eyes told Renla that they'd never felt the killing fury of battle.

Renla relaxed, but cursed her clumsiness. Not everyone was on the wrong side of this war. "Sorry. I dig at the Emerald Moon." She shrugged. "Pretty tense up there."

"Um, that's okay," said the young woman. She handed Renla a package, colored staid military brown, rimmed with putrid green, "NewSkin" prominently displayed, along with the words, "Six individually wrapped, sterile skin regeneration packets, four centimeters square."

"Thanks," muttered Renla, and rushed out. No need to make more of an impression than she already had. When she turned a corner, on the way to the exit, she half expected alarms to sound. Her boots made a ferocious racket in the halls of the healing facility, at least to her own ears. She turned the NewSkin package over in her hands to read the instructions, then stopped, her blood cold.

They'd given her the wrong package. In bold black letters, the instructions said: "For use only on fresh wounds."

This must have been the only way the clerk could get her the NewSkin right away, without raising suspicion. The NewSkin she wanted could be slapped onto old wounds, or even on healthy skin. Instead, she'd gotten NewSkin that could only be used on fresh wounds. She took in a deep breath and steeled herself for what she would have to do.

Her wrist compiler chimed. The dead drop. She puzzled through the location on the tiny map, but didn't know the Global Command Center well enough to picture the place in her head. She'd just have to work her way toward the beacon, and look natural doing it.

She set off again, tearing open the package to remove two individual packets, which she slipped into a breast pocket. One was primary, the other backup. The other packets she stuffed into a hallway trash bin marked with "incinerator," along with the receipt slip. She wanted as little evidence as possible of this trip.

When she emerged from the healing complex, sunset threatened. The sky over the ocean had turned a husky azure, and the breeze off the water had picked up. She shivered as she walked across the massive parade ground, anxious to be done and on her way. She grew conscious of curious stares as she walked. She should have removed her hand commander insignia. Curse her military habit.

She glanced down at her wrist compiler, then looked up at where it led her. *Sweet Lady of the Emerald Moon.* Every soldier in the army knew the military intelligence building, by reputation if not by sight. Since Nayr came to power, more people went in than came out. Loyalty was in short supply during a civil war.

Her breath grew brittle. Had she walked into a trap?

She strode up to the end of the line to gain entrance to the military intelligence building and muttered a prayer to the Lady of the Emerald Moon. Every detail counted.

She unlatched her qasfin and handed it to the guard, who scanned her right hand and left iris, then took her weapon into the guardhouse for cataloging. Renla checked the dead drop location one last time, then unlatched her wrist compiler too. She looked inside the waist-high, wrought iron fence and located the dead drop, on the far side of a trash bin, next to a tree in a pitiful little park. Only an insidious strain of tyrant would put green space inside the most hated symbol of his repression.

"Any other devices, ma'am?" said another guard, with the same stony glare as the other clone guards she'd seen that afternoon. All clones of Nayr wore those blood red berets, and they could transmit fearsome amounts of information over their tendril network, instantaneously. She had to assume they were keeping a close eye on her, and that they knew where she'd been.

"No other devices," said Renla.

He waved her on. "Take your turn in the scanner, then register your appointment up ahead."

Appointment? She didn't have an appointment. A bead of perspiration formed at the small of her back. Renla moved into the body scanner and drew in a deep breath, an effort to keep the color in her face.

As the scanner searched for tech and biotech devices, Renla strained to look through the deepening gloom at the registration desk up ahead.

The guard waved her through. Her heartbeat quickened. The obsidian-faced building loomed over her and the rest of the gelatinous mass of uniformed women and men shuffling toward the entrance. Diggers in the army called military intelligence types "eyes," so this building was known as the Black Eye, a name whose meaning had gone from comical to forbidding in the course of only one month, since Nayr's coup.

Renla scanned her surroundings. The small park with the dead drop lay to the right, beyond the wrought-iron fence, a smaller rendition of the larger perimeter fence, complete with tips sharpened to nasty points.

She bit her lip and furrowed her brow as she shuffled to her right through the river of people that meandered toward the building. How was she supposed to get to the park? Hopping the fence was out of the question, and she couldn't just walk up and examine the park fence, looking for the gate. If she didn't already know where it was, someone would question her for sure.

She remembered her training. *Observe. Move. Secure.* She continued shuffling to the right, toward the park, but kept her eyes and ears open, her demeanor matching that of the glob of people entering the building. She was fortunate to have come now, at sunset. With so many eyes waiting in line, she had more time to observe and move.

She heard the clue she was waiting for. Someone sighed in frustration nearby and used the word "park." She craned her head from left to right, eyes on the building entrance, but used her peripheral vision to identify anyone moving on a vector toward the park. There. A woman and man together.

She followed the couple into the park, through the well-hidden gate, and found the trash bin she was looking for, right next to a bench. Perhaps it made sense to put the dead drop in plain sight, but she shook her head at the cliché. Obvious could also be inconspicuous.

Renla sat down and rested her elbows on her knees, head down, as if relaxing after a long day. The success of her mission and of their incipient rebellion, this insane gambit, rested on one little cog: the list containing the coordinates of every one of Nayr's bases, outposts, warehouses, and control centers. This Global Command Center, his healing facilities, and secret bunkers. Every bit of infrastructure he used to run his insipid bureaucracy of hate and deception, even the new headquarters he was building in the central Eshel.

Renla looked up at the Black Eye, gleaming even in the dull light, then down at the precisely manicured grass, whose very cut and sway seemed to bear witness to Nayr's articulate malice.

Not a blade out of place. The grass wouldn't dare.

Renla knew which building she'd put at the top of the target list when she got back to the moon.

She scanned the ground and found what she sought, a slip of paper stuck to the inside of a bench leg, where no one would think to look. She eased the paper away from the metal leg, careful not to tear it. Every scrap of information on there was vital, and could be the means to keeping Nayr's hatred from reaching its tentacles to the Emerald Moon and beyond, through the portal, to the unsuspecting alien civilization on the White Planet. That piece of paper was also the key to saving the Queen from Nayr.

Renla made as if to toss the paper into the trash bin, but palmed it instead, glancing around, to see if anyone had noticed. Everyone seemed to be going about their business.

Renla opened the scrap of paper inside her palm, verified it contained coordinates in miniscule font, then slipped it into her pocket, beside the NewSkin packet. As instructed, the paper with the coordinates was reinforced to resist wear and moisture. She stood, stretched, and thought about how to get away from the Black Eye.

An explosion echoed from across the parade. She froze. The ground shook. Waves of uncertainty and adrenaline washed over her. A thousand mouths gasped in unison, and two thousand eyes fixed on the healing facility across the parade, one wing now a flaming ruin, a column of dust and fire rising into the dusk. One woman, sitting on the next bench, brought her hand to her mouth and said, "Explosives." A man stood up from leaning against a tree and remarked, "We haven't seen a weapon like that since the war."

Renla smiled, but rushed to hide it. The supply clerk was a confederate, after all.

As if with one accord, hundreds of people waiting to enter the Black Eye surged forward, and hundreds making their exit found new urgency, creating a mass that surged toward the exits in the wicked fence surrounding the midnight building.

The small gate leading out of the park jammed up with a small crowd, and Renla saw her chance. She took a deep breath and recalled the words on the NewSkin packet: "For use only on fresh wounds." She gritted her teeth and threw a leg over the fence, as if to straddle it, but instead of lifting her weight carefully the rest of the way over, she slammed the inside of her trailing thigh on one of its wicked points, raking her leg as she fell the rest of the way over, careful to avoid the artery.

She grunted away the pain and examined the wound. It bled more than she expected it would. Someone asked if she was okay, but she waved him off. She whipped out the NewSkin packet and hid the target list in the palm of her hand. She tore open the rip in her uniform trousers to gain better access to the wound, then nestled the target list inside the NewSkin packet and slapped it on her thigh. Her hand smeared with blood. She bit her lip at the pain as the NewSkin wove nanofibers into her skin, around the wound and the list.

She bit her lip and forced herself to breath as blackness crept into the borders of her vision. But a little pain, or even a lot of it, was better than letting Nayr's clones catch her with that kind of information. She tugged on the edges of the torn biomesh trousers, but there was no resealing the trouser material when it was soaked in blood.

Renla looked to the exits from the fence around the Black Eye. People paused to be scanned. Renla knew the clones were checking for differences from the entry scans. She hoped her gamble would work, the last scene in today's intricate dance of rebellion. The clones would definitely notice a loose scrap of paper that hadn't been there before, but reinforced paper hidden under attached NewSkin? Their search would have to be pretty thorough to find that.

She took her turn in the exit scanner, and was about to step through to freedom when one of the gate guards wearing a red beret waved her down, his face a stony replica of the Tyrant. "Ma'am, please come here."

Renla's heart pounded a rhythm of imminent doom, for her and for the others she could have helped. Did the guard see her palm the scrap of paper in the park? She clenched her fists as she moved toward him. She had no weapons aside from her hands, but she would go down fighting.

To her surprise, the guard handed her a rolled biomesh bandage and nodded at her leg. "Do you need a healer?"

She grabbed the bandage and wound it around her leg. She wasn't bleeding anymore, but the bandage would win her sympathy from anyone else who stopped her. She kept the wrap tight, then tucked in the loose end.

When she looked up at the guard to express thanks, she realized that his stony stare was not calculating or incisive at all. Up close, this clone looked disinterested, overloaded with processing so much information in such a short time. She brightened, but wrapped the emotion deep within her hatred for the system that the guard represented, a system of omnipresent fear. If Nayr's clones focused this little attention on the moment, on the day-to-day, then their rebellion had a chance. A small chance, but a chance.

She thanked the guard, then walked away from the Black Eye, toward freedom. Now, to even the odds.

Rebellion was dangerous work, but revenge would be sweet.

9 Night Fighting

A NERVOUS WIND STUTTERED through the shallow valley north of Meran. The pale moon of midsummer cast its greenish hue over two solitary pines, just over the lip of the ridge. The ghosts of Ahrik's dead sons haunted this place, his secret underground base outside Meran.

The base that was so old even Nayr didn't know about it. At least, that was his hope. Two days earlier, he never would have thought he'd have to fight for his life against Nayr's clones, or hide like a rat in a park, waiting for a secret meeting with Renla, of all people. He thought of how much he would change about these last two days, if he could.

Ahrik sat on the ground and worked the soreness out of his legs after his long walk around Meran that day. He examined the palm reader on top of a waist-high stone pillar between the two pines. The reader was caked with grime, and the Oath of the Keteli Soldier carved into the side of the pillar was weather-beaten and barely readable. He ran his fingers over the oath. How much its meaning had changed over the years.

When he rose to the top of the world after the last war, Ahrik built his Global Command Center at the other end of the valley, between here and Meran. Now it lay in the hands of Nayr. The first casualty of Nayr's coup. The Black Eye at its center now watched over all. The nerve center of Nayr's tyranny.

As Ahrik had crossed the valley outside leeward Meran that afternoon, he saw smoke rising from the direction of the Black Eye. He wondered if that omen bore good or ill.

He peered into the quiet night. The tatters of his legacy lay in the valley and underneath this ridge, the original home of the Ketel of Ahrik.

He hoped to find more than shattered dreams here. He hoped to find solace, and maybe a place to die while the tourniquets of fate squeezed the final residue from his suppurated life.

He pressed his palm to the reader and held his breath, unsure if it would work after all this time. He hoped Hawk had been able to make this base ready, unless he was dead too, like so many of the rest.

The wind changed. A cool night breeze blew off the ocean. Ahrik welcomed the tinge of salt and algae on the air. After what seemed like an eternity, the ground beyond the stone pillar growled and shimmered, then dissolved to reveal a ramp. The dark, dank slope led down to wasted dreams and crypts of bygone glories.

Ahrik unsheathed Biriq and gripped his distiller a bit tighter. He couldn't be too sure. Nayr might have discovered even this hiding place, like he had discovered Ahrik's hideout in Shtera Umqi two days before. He stepped onto the worn stone ramp. His footfalls echoed down into the darkness. He stopped and listened, to see what foulness his intrusion stirred up. He slid to the wall and stepped farther down the ramp. As he did so, the earthen door behind him grumbled back into resolution.

The lights flickered on. He gave a rueful grin in the pale blue light. Military grade microcores lasted for a long time, even if the lives of the women and men who wore the uniform did not.

He crouched down and put his face close to the floor. He squinted to detect any disturbance in the dust, any errant ripple in the sea of grime. He frowned. If anyone entered this way, they didn't leave footsteps.

Hawk was probably dead.

Nayr might try to send seekerbots down here, though. Ahrik set his wrist compiler to scan.

No bots. So far.

He breathed a sigh of relief, and then his stomach growled. Being on the run for so long made him forget how famished he was until he got someplace safe.

He couldn't be too careful. He didn't mind dying, but he didn't want to be killed. Nayr would have to dig deep into the archives to find a record of this place, but he had 100,000 clones at his command, and all it would take is one clone to ask the right question. To find the right document. For Nayr to guess where Ahrik might go for a measure of safety.

He tromped his way through deserted training rooms, and then the old barracks. In the healing hall, where so many of his 10,000 had lain and never risen, during the last war, he paused and sat on a creaking metal cot. The dust settled once more at his feet. The stale air stung his nostrils. The pain of what he should have done differently swirled in his chest.

He wept, like he'd never wept before.

He used to be a good man. His people once trusted him. His wife loved him once, she truly did. His clones, his dear sons, once saw in him a leader, a man worth following.

And now? The flickering light in the healing hall struggled to fill the space. Shadows of regret leaped at Ahrik from every spidered corner. He was no one to lead 10,000 clones, or to lead a planet, when he couldn't even lead one young man, a boy, to respect the use of power. In all his years of rule, Nayr's upbringing was the only objective that truly mattered, and Ahrik had failed.

He had failed Zharla. He had failed his sons. He had failed Dom.

He leaned his elbows on his knees. Tears dripped from his face to form muddy puddles on the floor. He saw no end to this river of remorse.

A sound rang out behind him, and he whirled. His survival instinct flared in the time it took for the sound to register in his brain. Something tapped a metal cot. The soundwaves still reverberated off the smooth, stone walls.

Crouching down, he raised his distiller and scanned his surroundings using the optical device Renla had given him. Nothing. "Who's there?" he hissed into the murk.

His distiller crackled with life, and he squeezed a charge off. He didn't know why he did. Maybe to have something to listen to besides the eerie silence.

The charge sizzled and shot through the air, then slammed into a wall some fifty meters away. A gob of basic elements slid down the smooth rock face as the blue phosphorescence of the distiller charge wore off.

He might have imagined the sound. He could be delusional, his fears pinging in the vast caverns of a hope-starved mind. He shrugged his pack farther onto his shoulders, then continued his advance. Only puffs of dust and the delicate outline of his soles on the floor marked his passage.

After the healing hall came his old quarters, along with his office and the corridor that led to the cavernous assembly hall, the only space in this base once large enough to hold all 10,000 of his sons. How often he had rallied his sons here. How often he had inspired them. Mourned with them. Mostly mourned. He no longer knew how many remained, after the coup.

Ahrik ran his fingers over the names of the deceased from long ago, carved into the cavern wall like sentinels guarding a forgotten fortress. A wall no grateful civilian would ever see. Keteli names were earned from their comrades, not given at birth, so their names didn't sound like normal names. Ahrik searched for some he knew best: Brain, Risen, Goggles. Others, like Hack, Edge, and Shift, he knew nothing of at all.

More often than he liked, he found "No Name" and the date of death inscribed into the cavern wall, along with a unit name like "3–3 Marauders" or "4–2 Soul Crushers." They had died before earning a name, the grief doubly difficult to bear.

He rested his head against the wall and bit back even more tears. Seven thousand names, their bodies scattered across the vilest places of moon and earth, would haunt his days and nights till the sun rose on his life no more. For each, he asked if he had done enough.

A short distance away, a throat cleared.

Ahrik didn't care. The fight drained from him. When would war end? When would its demons be banished?

"Sir," said the man, in a voice Ahrik recognized.

Ahrik sighed in relief that he still had someone to lead, but also at regret that it wasn't yet over. He turned to face Hawk, his chief reconnaissance pilot once upon a time, and now his closest advisor.

Ahrik sniffed away the tears. "You're alive, at least."

Hawk looked at the ground. "Only barely. One of my men pretended to be me so I could escape."

"The *nayra* got him?"

Hawk fixed him with a determined glance. "There's a fight yet, sir."

Movement rustled in the darkness behind Hawk. About thirty of Ahrik's clones, his dear sons, shuffled closer. Some hobbled up on prosthetic legs, and one or two wore prosthetic arms. Some carried a little more weight in the middle than they used to, but each face shone with the fervor that Ahrik remembered from yesteryear.

Ahrik grimaced. Nothing surprised him anymore, even seeing his former ketelis in a derelict base. He scanned the small crowd. "How long has it been since you were wounded and discharged?"

Clones had once been a closely-guarded secret, but after they were discovered and integrated into society during the War for the Emerald Moon, many of his wounded sons took up civilian lives, with jobs and families and peaceful days and as natural a death as old war wounds allowed.

The men shifted their feet at Ahrik's question. "Not too long," said one. "We can still fight," said another.

Hawk stood rigid, his combat decorations and other patches dull in the dim light. His distiller, though, gleamed with menace where it hung on his back, well-cleaned and ready for combat. Hawk fingered the clasp on his qasfin sheath. He was primed to fight at any moment.

Ahrik stepped closer to Hawk and shook his head. "This is madness," he whispered. "Half of them will be dead in a week." Ahrik inclined his head toward them, as if they couldn't hear what he was saying. He pursed his lips with finality. "Send them home, Hawk."

Hawk bit the inside of his lip, like a *chartak* player weighing his hand. "I can't," he said after a beat. "They volunteered."

"I won't ask more men to die for me," Ahrik hissed. "Accept the new reality. Nayr won."

"With respect, sir," said one of the men as he hobbled closer on a bad leg. "We may die anyway."

Hawk furrowed his brow at Ahrik. "How long have you been off the grid, sir?"

Ahrik stroked his chin, and only then realized how scraggly his beard was. Did he look as gaunt as these men looked well-fed? "I'm hungry," he said to Hawk.

"Sir? Oh . . ." Hawk reached into a thigh pocket and produced a ration bar.

Ahrik tore open the seal and began to wolf it down, then froze when he saw the dismay on the faces of his former soldiers. Some averted their eyes, to avoid the image of their commander reduced to such depths. Ahrik stared at them, mid-chew, unsure of how to proceed. Through a mouthful of food, he asked, "What happened after I went off the grid?"

Hawk cleared his throat again, but with a distinct timbre of discomfort this time. "Sir, we are at war. Nayr has started to hunt your clones." Hawk's eyes flicked from Ahrik to the men. "These men had comrades with simple, peaceful lives, but we've heard nothing from them since the *nayra* came for them in the dark of night. There are rumors of officers preparing to rebel, that the attack at the healing complex by the Black Eye was part of something bigger. No one has had news from the Emerald Moon for over a week."

Ahrik narrowed his eyes and began to chew again, a thoughtful expression on his face. That would explain why he hadn't seen any of his discharged clones for almost a month in Meran, and why Renla was evasive about her plans. "What am I supposed to do?" he asked with a shrug. Crumbs clung to his beard. "I'm lucky to be alive myself."

The man with the bad leg leaned closer, unsteady. "We're here to fight, sir, not because we want to, but because we have to."

Ahrik looked at the empty wrapper in his hand and wondered where the ration bar had gone. He tossed the wrapper on the ground, ignoring the gasps of surprise at this act of indifference.

He stuck his hands out to the sides, palms up, as if considering two weighty options. "He has 100,000 clones, each one a supersoldier, a global command-and-control network, and enough tectonics and atmospherics to turn every mountain on Dom into a barren and flat wasteland." He gestured at his other hand. "We have only us."

"The old armory in this base has enough weapons to arm an entire hand," said Hawk, "and we know others who are willing to fight for you."

Ahrik harrumphed. "Do the weapons still work, after all this time?"

The clone shuffled nearer on his bad leg. "We have the element of surprise, sir. We can degrade Nayr's command-and-control before he realizes what's happening."

Ahrik frowned. "He'll just build it up again."

"If we don't fight, sir, we'll die anyway," said another clone. "But we'll die alone and afraid, and cowering in the dark."

Ahrik stared at the wrapper on the ground, and silence descended on their little gathering like a shroud. Perhaps a life of fear was better than an early grave.

For a long while, the foul winds of his despair beat upon the seedlings of his men's hope, a mere sprig of feeling within Ahrik's breast. Who was he to decide their fate? Blast the odds, the insufferably long odds, to sunfire and damnation.

He reached down and twisted the wrapper in his fingers, then crumpled it into a tight little ball with newfound strength in his hands.

He peered into his men's eyes and faith kindled in his heart, a flickering flame that he knew could one day blaze. "First."

"To the fight," they responded as one.

Nayr glared at his staff principals. Silence reigned. Their faces showed the utmost respect for his authority, but Nayr sensed deception just beneath the surface. He trembled with ire. "You are not doing your jobs . . . you are not fulfilling your sacred oaths to me . . . if you do not find out who is doing this."

"Father," said 2, eyes cast down, "there is still a possibility that these events were not caused by rebels . . ." 2 trailed off and stole a nervous glance at the others, who looked at 2 to speak for them when Nayr crossed blades with his staff. 2 gulped, seeing that Nayr would let him continue. "Father, the Usurper neglected communications and other infrastructure for years while he was at the helm—"

"Enough," said Nayr, voice as still as a mountain lake. He counted off on his fingers. "The rebuilt transporter terminal at Hof Chelek. The water processing plant in Peshron. The mining facilities at Meran. The communications link with the Emerald Moon. The transporter station at Mekele serving the southern districts." He cocked his head and furrowed his brow. "And now an explosion yesterday at the healing complex of the old Global Command Center in Meran, right at the fulcrum of my military authority. Not two hundred meters from the Black Eye. This damage will require millions of *keina* to repair, and you're telling me, 2, that this might just be bad luck?"

2 sighed. "It's just, Father, that our intelligence services aren't certain there's actually a rebellion."

"Look at the transit logs," said Nayr, a challenge in his voice. "Did Commander Renla from the 11th Hand enter the Black Eye or the healing complex yesterday?"

2 squirmed in his seat. "Father, I . . ."

Nayr glared.

"I'll look into it, Father." 2's shoulders sank.

Nayr pushed his hoverchair back and stood, eyes of meticulous, paternal care fixed on 2. He walked around his desk to where his five principals stood and panned his gaze from one to the other. "No one has this much bad luck. There's a rebellion." He sneered. "You just have to find it."

Nayr let the silence emphasize his point. They had failed him. Of course, he couldn't undermine their confidence, so he added, "I'll grant that it's not easy to root out rebels and conspirators, but you're up to it." He nodded toward the door. "Dismissed."

They saluted and left. The room stood empty, a reminder of the cavern of loneliness and desire in his chest. He felt the weight of power it would take to clamber out of this pit of solitude. He ambled back to his hoverchair and let out a tired sigh.

He looked out his picture window and took in the expanse of his domain. His new headquarters was coming along nicely. The languid summer breeze washed over the gentle hills of prairie grass that radiated from here, at his new headquarters base, at the geographic center of the Esheli continent, and so at the center of the world. The central tower, with his office nearest the pinnacle, served as one of two hundred high-power tendril relay stations that linked the thoughts of his sons and him together in a global network of command and control.

Nayr could think an order, and in an instant one of his sons, even half a world away, would execute it without hesitation. Any news of import came directly to Nayr from his staff principals. Information in, orders out. With such power, he must find and destroy the perpetrators of this sabotage.

The only gap in his enhanced tendril network was the Emerald Moon. His thoughts couldn't reach there. Yet. But he would find a way to exercise command and control over Renla on the moon. Soon, the reign of the Usurper would be a dingy memory in the minds of the people.

His new headquarters in Mekele Eshel stood at the center of his power, but the Usurper and his old Global Command Center back in Meran still housed most of the military decision making apparatus. They would all move here to Mekele Eshel eventually, but there hadn't been time since the realignment from the Usurper to him. Soon enough Nayr would truly be in control of the world, with his new capital in Mekele Eshel, away from the smelly, algae-filled wind off the ocean and all the mindless supporters of the Usurper.

He stroked his chin. He would have to do something about those supporters at some point.

He looked down. Something was in his hand. A little pill. For the anxiety? When had he put his hand in the storage compartment of his desk? No matter. He slipped the pill under his tongue and let the gentle currents of anoesis melt his worries away.

A tendril ping intruded on his bliss. He frowned and wondered what could be so important that they would disturb his reverie.

Father, cast 2, *Renla was at the old Global Command Center yesterday . . .*

As I thought.

. . . and one of the Usurper's clones is in custody.

Nayr brightened at the possibilities. *Where?*

Here, Father. Just processed.

Excellent. Bring him to me.

Yes, Father.

Nayr narrowed his eyes in thought and leaned back in his chair. He searched deep in the recesses of the tendril network. When he found the clone he was looking for, he cast a thought to him: *Is it ready?*

Nayr tapped his foot. Why did his clone not answer immediately?

After too long a delay, clone 4378 answered. Nayr sensed the clone's surprise at the commander reaching out to him directly, once again, over the tendril network. *Yes, Father,* he cast, *you want it now?*

Bring it yourself.

Yes, Father. Right away, Father. Joy pulsed over the tendril link. The clone was ecstatic to have some face time with the boss.

Nayr smiled. The Usurper said leading men was hard. Maybe for him. Now all Nayr had to do was wait to see which one showed up first, 2 or the clone buried deep in his research department.

After a few minutes of pacing alternated with finger-drumming, the office door chimed. Nayr rushed to pick up a reading compiler and lean on the side of his desk, so it looked like he had better things to do that wait for an underling to arrive. "Enter," he said.

Clone 4378 poked his head into the room. His face brimmed with eagerness, but his body language was timid and deferential. He eased himself the rest of the way into Nayr's office, gasped a few breaths, and gave a bright salute. He slipped the pack off his shoulders and held it to his chest as he peered around in wonder at his surroundings.

"You made good time," said Nayr.

"Thank you, Father." He grinned and bobbed his head up and down. "Want to see it?"

Nayr rolled his hand forward, to show that 4378 should get on with it. The clone nodded and ripped open his pack. The biomesh seam rustled and slurped. The clone reached in and brought forth a small black box with a leather strap affixed. He looked obsequious eyes at Nayr and asked, "What do you think?"

Nayr cocked his head and grunted. "I thought it would be more . . . something."

The clone gave a shrewd look. "Ah, but it works like the Lady's charm."

"There are many ways to interpret that." Nayr stepped toward him and reached out to cradle the object in his own hands. "You've tested it?"

4378 nodded.

Nayr's excitement grew by degrees as he turned the small black box over with his fingers. Finally. This was supposed to have been impossible. The Usurper certainly would never expect it.

A warning note sounded in the back of his mind. He looked at the clone with a face devoid of emotion. "You're the only one who knows about this?"

4378 nodded again. "Just like you said." The clone added another eager smile, then took on a conspiratorial air. "Shall I show you how it works?"

Nayr nodded, and the clone drew close to show his commander a small button on the side of the box. "This button codes the box to the nearest tendril receiver." He held up a small, black cylinder with a switch on top. "Whoever switches on this transmitter can speak or cast whatever he likes, and it will access the tendril network as if he's the one wearing the box."

Nayr narrowed his eyes. He wondered if someone else could hack his own tendril network. "How did you test it?"

"I copied my tendril profile onto my external compiler and sent a message to myself." He strapped the box onto his own neck and pressed the coding button on the side. "Father, it needs to be placed at the base of the neck, as close as possible to the internal compiler." He handed the transmitter to Nayr. "Here, Father, you try."

Nayr relieved 4378 of the transmitter, then looked at him askance. "Did you cast or speak your test message?"

"I spoke, Father." 4378 grinned with satisfaction, perhaps unaware that casting thoughts might require more effort than sending speech.

"And how do I direct the tendril cast to a particular individual?" asked Nayr, closing his eyes and focusing his thoughts.

"Just like norm—"

The clone's face contorted with pain. He clutched his head. He emitted a dull groan, then staggered toward the nearest wall.

Presently, almost instantly, Nayr received the message he'd cast to himself, via the box at the clone's neck: *Win.*

The clone groveled in the direction of the wall, and Nayr sighed with impatience. "Range?"

"With the new repeaters"—the clone winced, a sign of weakness, then gritted his teeth—"it has global reach." He took a deep breath and worked himself back into a standing position, a bit wobbly in the knees.

"But not to the moon?" Nayr shook his head with disapproval. "That's what I really need, to extend the tendril link to the Emerald Moon."

The sorry clone cast down his eyes, but drew himself up in a semblance of standing at attention.

Nayr gave the clone credit. He had pluck. "Let's see if we can send a more complicated message, shall we?" He accessed his internal compiler to check the time. 2 should be here with the prisoner soon. Oh, well. 4378 would do.

Nayr switched on the transmitter and focused his thoughts once again, reaching out to 2 over the tendril link: *Bring in the prisoner as soon as you arrive.*

The clone standing before him buckled and cried out in pain. He crumpled to the ground and tore at his hair with clenched fists, ending up in a whimpering, fetal mess of a human.

Nayr grunted. "That's interesting."

He leaned down and released the clasp that fastened the black box to the clone's neck, then stood to examine the black box up close. His door chimed, and without waiting to be called 2 strode in, trailed by two prison guards from the ketel, a prisoner clutched between them.

"Ah," said Nayr, "the Usurper's weevil."

The prisoner glanced at the quivering clone on the floor. Fear glossed over his face, but he quickly replaced it with a sheen of supercilious hate.

The Usurper and his clones always had an unnatural disdain for their genetic betters in the Ketel of Nayr.

Nayr decided to start out with persuasion. He gave the prisoner a smile. "Tell me, where are your rank markings? What unit are you with?"

The prisoner gave a perfect military salute. "Sir, my unit and rank are classified. Request permission to speak to my ketel commander."

Nayr paced toward the prisoner. The law of the ketel was clear. A keteli could only be interrogated by his ketel commander. But this was a special case: treason. "Well, we're in a bit of a quandary, aren't we?" asked Nayr. "You see, we're looking for your ketel commander now. The Usurper seems to have . . . disappeared."

The prisoner didn't hesitate. "Sir, request permi—"

"I know, I know. You said that already." Nayr waved his hand in front of the prisoner's face, then stopped as if to consider a gentler option. "What is your name, keteli?"

The prisoner simply stared into the middle distance.

Nayr stroked his chin. "Aren't you the one that the Usurper calls Hawk, his old pilot?"

Still the prisoner ignored Nayr.

"Well then," said Nayr, looking at the guards with purpose, "perhaps you could help us find him." He cast to the guards: *Hold him.*

Understanding sprang to the prisoner's face and he struggled to break free, but the guards were strong, and as ready as Nayr expected them to be. Nayr brought the black box and its strap to the prisoner's neck, who whipped his head back and forth. 2 reached out and grabbed the prisoner's hair. With the prisoner's head stabilized, Nayr had no trouble strapping on the box and placing it just at the nape of the neck, like the research clone had demonstrated. He pressed the coding button to link the box to the prisoner's internal compiler, and thus the Usurper's tendril network.

4378 gave a gasp from his curled position on the floor. The life slipped from his body, like a transporter cutting into a morning mist, with naught but a sigh to mark its passing.

"That's a shame," said Nayr. "He was good."

The prisoner saw this and his breath sped up. His eyes narrowed with smoldering hate.

Nayr flipped the switch on the transmitter and challenged the prisoner with a look, pouring all his disdain for the Usurper into his cast: *Usurper, Nayr will find you.*

The prisoner squealed in anger and pain, like a gutted swine. "No!"

Turn yourself in, Usurper. Answer the charges against you. The Usurper had turned Mother against him. Even when Nayr tried to protect Mother from the Usurper's intrigues, she still tried to convince Nayr to trust his stepfather. Nayr snarled. How could she trust the peace of the world to the Usurper, a source of such evil?

The prisoner's body convulsed. His legs gave way. Blood shot into his eyes. The guards held him up as limpness crept up his body, from his toes to his head.

"Are you Hawk?" Nayr asked.

The prisoner hung his head, his breathing labored. "I. Am. Hawk."

Nayr nodded with approval, then pressed on: *If you turn yourself in, Nayr will spare your clones.*

The prisoner's head lolled, and his body lost all vigor. Nayr, grim, nodded. The guards released the prisoner, and he crumpled in a heap. His body shuddered, then went as still as a lake after a storm.

Nayr hummed in approval. "Hawk's better off this way. He was strong. There's no telling what it would have taken to extract something useful from him using traditional methods." He bent down and unstrapped the black box from Hawk's lifeless neck, then looked at the guards. "Dispose of the bodies."

After they'd dragged out the two corpses, 2 gave Nayr a measured look. "What just happened, Father?"

Nayr placed a hand on 2's shoulder. "Let this be a lesson on how to suss out a rebellion."

"But Father, we know exactly what he was doing when we captured him. He wa—"

"No, no. None of that matters now." He sighed. "I told you to find a rebellion, and now I've found it for you. The prisoner was caught in an act of sabotage against the peace of the planet, using banned technology"—Nayr held up the black box—"just like the sabotage that we've seen with alarming frequency of late." He paused, considering options. "I have reason to believe that my uncle Shahl is in league with the rebels, and even aiding and abetting them."

"I . . . ah . . . yes Father, of course."

Nayr placed the black box into 2's hand. "Figure out how it works. Close hold."

2 saluted. "Yes, Father."

Nayr nodded his dismissal, then watched as his most trusted aide exited the room. Nayr patted the transmitter in his pocket. A bit of insurance.

Just in case the rebellion spread. He accessed the file called Revenge and wrote: "Kill Ahrik. Make Shahl disappear. Detain Renla. Rescue Mother."

The antiquated ventilation system of Ahrik's old base wheezed a rhythm of doom. He gazed into the eyes of his women and men and saw fate reflected back, like a sea of glass catching the failing rays of one last sunset. Many of them would die. He knew it. They knew it. But they followed nonetheless. Loyal to the bitter end. To write the final chapter in the story of the Ketel of Ahrik.

"When last we gathered here"—his voice bounced off the rough-cut stone walls of his old subterranean base—"our numbers were not so meager, nor our prospects so dim."

His hodge-podge force drew closer as he opened up to them with his fear and pain. They numbered less than two hundred, a company of his active ketel stationed in Meran, swelled by two dozen of his retired and wounded clones and a few volunteers that Ahrik and Hawk had gathered by ones and twos over the course of the last day. Ahrik's call to muster spread strictly by word of mouth, and they'd come on foot. This mission would be one of stealth and deception, of slicing into the night to deliver death and confusion to a much stronger enemy.

Well-worn weapons dangled against bodies unused to their heft. Women and men adjusted the straps on their distiller packs. The unfamiliar creak of steel prosthetics mingled with the familiar redolence of determination and human sweat.

Ahrik took in their penetrating gazes and felt the full cost of their gambit. "Many of you have families now. They'll have priority on the refugee ships. We will keep them safe."

Ahrik did not know if he could deliver on that promise, but he had to believe he had given them something to hope for. "The old healing complex was attacked the other day, and something is in the works for the elevator stations," he said. "The odd tendril message we all received today means that the Tyrant is close. Now is the time to strike."

He looked at those on his right, led by Hawk. "Hawk, take my shuttle. Before you move to the Emerald Moon, go to the other cities of the Eshel and find our old comrades-in-arms. Inspire them with the fervent duty that dwells in our hearts. Send some to make a stand at Peshron, then take what soldiers you can spare to the moon." Ahrik paused as thoughts of his own mortality encroached upon his mind. "Commander Renla of the Fighting 11th. You won't find a better commander than Renla to stand against the Tyrant."

Hawk and the rest of his team saluted. "Check, sir."

Ahrik rested a hand on the hilt of Biriq and replanted his feet to face those on his left. "Those of you fighting in Meran tonight, find your sector and cloak in place. If the Tyrant has found a way to hack tendril communications, we need to keep chatter to a minimum. Then give him everything he can handle as soon as my signal goes up."

Ahrik looked at the four men on his own insertion team, four of his most experienced clones. Some of the few clones still in his active force. "Our intelligence says that the Tyrant is away in Mekele, overseeing the construction of his new headquarters," said Ahrik, "so now is our best chance to get Sera and the Queen out and away from here."

He looked over them all once again. "We fight for freedom, and for a better life for the ones we love."

Ahrik slipped Biriq out of its sheath. The walls of the cavern whispered with the echo of his women and men drawing their own blades. Ahrik tapped Biriq to the main housing of his distiller. One ping. He passed to them all the hope and confidence he could in one final look. "First."

They pinged back. "To the fight."

They trudged and lumbered up the ramp to the main exit. Ahrik pressed the control, and the door hissed open. The oranges and reds of sunset brimmed the eastern sky. In twos and threes, his beloved keteli soldiers melted into the dusking light, faces slathered in black and gear softened with cloth to suppress the errant clink.

One last fight for the Ketel of Ahrik.

Longing tugged at Ahrik's heart. He wanted, more than anything, to reach out over the tendril network and give his soldiers the hope they deserved, but he couldn't, not if Nayr might intercept or hack his comms.

After the last of the diversion and recruitment parties had disappeared into the brush of leeward Meran, Ahrik turned to the four who would go with him to the palace. "The girl is in the south wing, on the top floor of the healing center." He nodded. "You know what to do."

Ahrik turned to one of the men. "Did you find the pills?"

"Yes . . . Father," he said, handing him a small leather packet.

"Just 'sir'," said Ahrik. He turned the small packet of pills over in his hand, then slipped them into a thigh pocket. "Thank you."

Ahrik squinted across the valley at the palace and set off into the fading light, armed now with vivid hope for success. The stickers in the long grass clung to his bioflauge suit with more urgency than normal, begging him to turn back from this manic quest to free Zharla and his niece, Sera. Each step on the rolling, gloomy slopes counted the cost that this night augured.

He glanced at the men trudging along beside him. They too wore bioflauge suits, but theirs were antiquated and glitchy, the last ones they found in the old base stores. Dusk made chilling, floating wraiths out of their moving forms. The swish and bump of their gear and weapons provided the only accompaniment to the stillness.

Stealth was their greatest ally now. The longer they went without being noticed, the better chance they had to release Zharla and Sera from Nayr's clutches. He hoped the victory would justify the lives that would be stilled this night.

They avoided the sentry patrols at the palace easily enough. They were mere conscripts, not Nayr's supersoldiers. Forty meters from the main gate, the men who crossed the vale with Ahrik peeled off in the direction of the south wing and the healing center. They hugged the vegetation for concealment.

As Ahrik expected, the palace environs were flooded with light, so Ahrik waited on the fringe, in the shadow of a cedar bush. So his men would be out of the way when things got hot.

He unhitched his distiller from his pack, made sure it was set to shoot tracers, and twisted his hand into the casing. He took a deep breath and let it out with with a soft hiss. "First to the fight."

Ahrik pointed the weapon into the air and gave the trigger a long squeeze. *Thu-thu-thu-thu-thunk*. Five red tracers shot up into the sky. It took less than half-a-second for the verbal challenge to go up from the gate. So, Nayr had his clones at the main gate, not green conscripts. A distiller coughed and sang, but Ahrik had already scurried to the other side of the cedar when the matter scrambler charges chewed up the ground behind him.

He found a depression in the ground and crawled in. He waited, and drank in the delicious sound of explosive charges going off all over out-mountain Meran, in response to his signal. Then, in the distance, fighting, and at the palace gate a flurry of activity. A volley of orders marked by conflicting voices and tones. A shuffle of feet told Ahrik that a patrol had left the palace gate to investigate the source of the tracers.

After a few moments, he gathered his legs underneath him and crouch-walked back to his original position. The patrol approached, their sweep taking them on a wide arc from the gate.

Ahrik brushed off twigs and dirt and switched off his bioflauge cloak. He stowed his distiller and pretended to clean his nails with the killing point of Biriq.

The patrol had about five men, by the sound of their steps padding over the grass. When they noticed Ahrik in the shadow of the cedar, they stopped short and fanned out, weapons at the ready.

Ahrik ignored them.

"Ho, there," said one.

Ahrik looked up and raised an eyebrow at the soldiers. Definitely *nayra*. The presumed leader bore a striking resemblance to Nayr, which would mean that he was higher up the chain of command, possibly the captain of the gate guard. He had only two digits on his number tape.

Ahrik rose and made a calming motion with his hands. "Okay, okay. Shine your light on me, if you want, so you can tell I'm the king consort."

A distiller pointed in his direction and light flashed over his face. "Right . . . uh . . . sir. You're under arrest."

Ahrik sheathed Biriq, then sauntered over to the leader and gently pressed the casing of his distiller downwards. "Put that thing away. I'm no threat to you."

Another clone cleared his throat. "Sir, did you discharge a distiller just now?"

Ahrik chuckled, with as much apology as he could fake. "Yeah, sorry. Accidental discharge. I was cleaning the casing." He shrugged. "It just went off."

Mumbles of disbelief rippled through the patrol, but the leader nodded his head with sagacity at this explanation. One of his subordinates came forward with wrist restraints, but the leader sent him back with a violent, curt shake of the head.

Explosions and the distant grumble and burp of distiller exchanges echoed over the city behind Ahrik. The *nayra* looked out over Meran and squirmed in their gear.

Ahrik scratched his chin and nodded toward the palace. "Meeting you like this has been wonderful, but I'd like to see my wife, the Queen."

The clone leader cleared his throat. "Yes, sir. Of course, sir."

Before the patrol leader could lead the way, Ahrik set off toward the main gate. He nodded to the gate guards like he owned the place. In a sense he did, so he strode on through. His feet crunched over the gravel pathway.

The fading light beat with the sound of his fighters creating diversions around Meran. Ahrik estimated that the four men tasked to free Sera were scaling the wall to her room now, melting into the dusky sandstone in their bioflauge. He stole a glance in the direction they'd be, but he couldn't see their telltale shimmer on the wall.

When he was a few meters from the steps leading to the main entryway, two squads of *nayra* dashed out of a lower side door and made their way to shuttles waiting in the main courtyard. The insignia of the Palace Guard glinted on their shoulders. Their leader barked instructions in what Ahrik recognized as a hasty battle brief: "Squad Four to reinforce Sector 5. Squad Three to Sector 2. Multiple engagements."

Their faces bore the uncertainty that seeped into every soldier's heart before combat. These men ran to the sound of the guns, yet they had no idea what to expect. Some would not live through the night, but such was the soldier's lot. All did their duty. Some died. Some lived.

Thoughts of his own women and men stirred in Ahrik's breast. If the four here at the palace got to Sera's room and she wasn't there, or if she was guarded well, his men would have to fight it out. If his soldiers down in Meran couldn't break contact before these reinforcements arrived, they would almost certainly die.

Ahrik had to work quickly. Once Nayr figured out what was going on, even from far away, he would come looking for them in all his fury.

The patrol leader caught up to Ahrik. Perhaps he wanted to give the impression that he was in control instead of Ahrik leading the way. Ahrik suppressed a grin and quickened his pace.

"Sir—"

The patrol leader's protest faltered. The main palace door hissed open. The Queen stood at the top of the stairs, glowering at the *nayra* below her. The patrol leader gulped, then averted his eyes in deference.

Ahrik gave a flourish with his arm and bowed until his distiller pack nearly slid up his back and onto the ground. "Your Majesty," he said, "I have returned."

The patrol leader cleared his throat. His face was red, and his eyes were still averted. "Your Majesty, we had orders to arrest the former king consort on sight."

"Former?" asked Ahrik.

Zharla laughed. "Orders from whom? My son?"

The patrol leader gave a sheepish nod.

Zharla scoffed. "I'll discuss this with the prince consort." Zharla reached a hand toward Ahrik, but kept her gaze fixed on the clones. "Now, if you'll let us be, my husband and I have business to attend to."

Putting on an air of confidence, Ahrik ascended the stairs, two at a time, his back pillar straight.

Ahrik studied Zharla's face as he approached. Would today be a day she was happy to see him, or not? Her smile at the clones was bright, but he saw the strain on her face. He already sensed the wan embrace she would give him, if she embraced him at all.

The door hissed to resolution behind him, leaving them alone. Ahrik opened his mouth to speak, but Zharla's hand flew up and caught him on the jaw with a vivid slap.

Ahrik rubbed his chin and gave her a stunned look. "I was wondering about that."

She clutched his shoulders. "I was worried sick about you."

She kissed him, hard.

Ahrik didn't believe it. He felt the space between them, even as she pressed herself to him. He pulled back and did a quick scan of their surroundings. Was she in league with Nayr? Was this a trap? Did that ceramic vase on the side table hold some sort of bioweapon? Nayr must want Ahrik dead, if he was trying to hack his tendril comms. Ahrik wouldn't put it past him to make his own mother a pawn in his quest for power.

He narrowed his eyes at Zharla. "Where's Sera?"

"Are you here to take her?"

"She's one of the few innocents in all this."

She gave him an offended look. "She's safe. Nayr is taking good care of her."

Ahrik's breath caught in his throat, and the worry that their intelligence was wrong writhed in his mind. "Is he here?"

Zharla looked at him askance, betraying nothing. "He's a good boy, Ahrik."

Eyes darting, Ahrik reached back and unhitched his distiller. Silken tentacles of helplessness wound around his heart and shortened his breath. The lives of his men outside, scaling the wall, would be for naught if their intelligence was wrong, and Nayr was here but Sera was not. Nayr could have laid a trap so neat, to draw Ahrik out into the open and destroy his faithful cadre all at once.

There was only one way to find out.

He grabbed Zharla's hand. "He's using you. Come with me."

She yanked her hand back. A snarl formed on her lips. "I see light in him, Ahrik."

Ahrik stepped back and flexed his fingers inside his distiller. His vision blurred with rage, and he felt an irrepressible urge to destroy. The ceramic vase on the stone side table edged into his vision. Instinct took over. It was the vase or Zharla. Something had to break.

He lashed out with his distiller. The vase shattered, and the silence between them accentuated the pitter and scrape of ceramic shards skittering across the polished stone floor of the entryway. Ahrik half-expected a cloud of greenish murk to rise from the ruins of the vase and whisk him away from this mortal coil, but fate gave him a few more minutes of life, at least. He couldn't look at his wife, but he felt her eyes bore into him. He would not free her tonight. He saw it in her eyes, in the set of her mouth and feet.

But he wasn't ready to die, not when others depended on him. His sons. The volunteer women and men who followed him now. Renla and her Fighting 11th. Everyone who still clung to a shred of hope.

He turned toward the exit. He cleared his mind for battle, but paused when Zharla sniffed with an air of pretension.

"So, you're just going to leave me again?"

Ahrik was about to press his palm to the door control, distiller primed, body poised, but he whirled, unable to let this insult go unanswered. He stabbed a finger on his free right hand at her. "Don't you dare make this about me. We wouldn't be in this mess if you hadn't told me to stand aside and let Nayr take over."

She shook her head, a glazed look on her face. "I'll get through to him."

Ahrik curled his lip in a sneer of his own. "Congratulations, Your Majesty. You avoided a civil war, only to reap the terror of your maniac son."

"The planet is at peace."

"Every tyranny has humble beginnings, Zharla. Nobody misses a few old clones, here and there, when they disappear in the dead of night." Ahrik shook his head. "But he won't stop there. He'll never be satisfied."

"Stay, Ahrik. We can make him better."

"I'd as soon shape stone with my hands."

"Have you lost faith in me?" She snorted with disdain. "The people, at least *they* still follow me."

"Soon they won't have a choice." Ahrik threw up his free hand. His heart sank at how futile his efforts were. Her devotion to Nayr blinded her. "They love you, Zharla. They'll do anything for you. Come with me. We'll take Sera away from here. We'll make a new start."

"So that's it? You're giving up on Nayr? On us?"

"No." Ahrik reached into his thigh pocket and yanked out the small packet of pills. He foisted them into Zharla's hand. "When the time comes, you'll know how to give these to him."

"What are these? Where are you going?"

"To live, I hope. To fight another day." He checked his distiller, to make sure the tracers were off, and the live charges on. His weapon hummed with a fury that echoed his own. "Come find me in Peshron when you're ready to answer for the lives of the women and men who will die tonight, trying to free you and the girl from the Tyrant."

He spat the last word.

Zharla snatched at his arm. "Ahrik, wait."

"Goodbye, Your Majesty, and stand back, if you know what's good for you." He tore his arm back, and she shifted away, eyes wide with alarm. He set his face against the fury he foresaw, brought his weapons to the ready, and palmed open the door.

The night and a dozen distiller charges rushed toward him as he sprang over the sidewall of the stairs and onto the greenery, his mouth open against the explosion he knew would come. He gave no thought to the danger. If he died, he would die trying to save his soldiers.

He cloaked mid-air, ducked, and rolled into the greenery. The steps exploded where they had hoped to fix him in their ambush. Stone fragments showered down, and the concussion washed over his head and shoulders. The sidewall of the stairs took the brunt of the blast.

He used the roiling dust cloud as concealment. He knew exactly where they'd be. He'd trained most of them, or at least his men had. He ignored the pain in his ears and stomach and forced his sluggish legs to the attack. He dashed along the side of the building until he made out the end of one leg of their L-shaped ambush, then he launched toward them with all his hate and anger. At the betrayal Nayr's clones represented. At the terror they had brought to the world.

Most of the clones still had their distillers trained on the steps. Some sent speculative charges in that direction, waiting to see what would emerge from the dust. Ahrik got most of the clones in the first leg of the L with only three distiller bursts. Those on the other leg barely got two charges off before they too lay still.

He saw the insignia of the Palace Guard on one shoulder patch and knew that they were one of the patrols that had exited the palace as he entered. That was part of their ruse, apparently. A feint to make him think his plan was working.

Ahrik heard a shuttle's boson drive spring to life, twenty meters away. He didn't hesitate. He sprinted toward it and leapt into the open bay as it was lifting off. A poorly-aimed distiller charge zipped by his shoulder and into the evening.

Ahrik aimed and squeezed, then braced for impact as the pilot slumped forward. The shuttle jerked as it glanced against something, probably the two-meter palace wall, telling him that the internal stabilizers were turned off or broken. He braced for impact. The shuttle slammed into the ground, and Ahrik flew against the bulkhead next to the hatch leading into the cockpit.

After impact, he took a deep breath and checked his extremities. No permanent damage. As he grabbed the pilot's body and flung him to the floor, he searched for his clones over the tendril link. He sensed nothing from the four that came with him to the palace. Maybe some were still alive in Meran. Those sent to rally forces from other cities were too far away by now to make contact over his tendril link.

He wanted to go to Meran to save his women and men fighting there, but he had to know if Sera was safe. He slammed up on the controls. The shuttle jerked under his ill-practiced hands. The controls and navigation systems were intuitive for those who had spent years in such craft, but his pilot training was basic. He nudged the wounded shuttle into the air and wobbled around the palace, to where the four men in the extraction team should have already been scaling down the wall with Sera.

Four bodies lay on the ground by the wall of the south wing of the palace. He shoved the shuttle down to the ground. He found no signs of life and dragged all four bodies on board, then looked up the sheer wall of the healing facility. He read the distiller scoring. His men hadn't even gotten up to Sera's floor.

The desire to make good on his losses boiled inside him, but he could not scale these walls like his men could. He did not have the genetic modifications that made it possible for them.

The sounds of fighting throughout Meran slowly died on the dusky air. He was losing, and his hope wisped away with every distiller silenced behind him in out-mountain Meran.

A pebble fell next to him, and someone called from up above, near Sera's room. He looked up, and a roiling ire replaced his hopelessness.

Nayr, or one of his clones, waved from the roof. "Slow going, Usurper?"

Ahrik took hasty aim and squeezed the trigger in his distiller. Charges sizzled through the night breeze, but struck nothing. The figure on the roof had already ducked behind cover.

Distiller charges churned into the ground in response. Laughter echoed from the roof as he fled.

Ahrik leaped back into the safety of the shuttle's energy shield and screamed a curse into the cockpit. He would concede defeat tonight, but he refused to give Nayr the satisfaction of seeing him humiliated.

Helpless and fuming, he flew toward Meran, and tried to hail his soldiers, both on the electromag and over the tendril link. No response. He set down at a spot where one squad was assigned, in the port warehouse district. Nayr's clones had done their work and fled by the time Ahrik arrived. He found blackened, smoking remains, and nearly tripped on a twisted, half-melted metal prosthetic leg when he debarked. The stench of burned flesh and oozing stone attacked his nostrils and sat bitter on his tongue. He kicked at the ground in frustration and cursed the Lady of the Emerald Moon. There wasn't even enough here to bury.

He could bear no more, having failed so many. He set a grim course for Peshron.

That ambush at the palace was too easy for him to escape. His women and men followed his orders into the real ambush.

A light rain began to fall over Meran. It feathered over the transluced hull, as if Nature wept for those fallen that night. Ahrik opaqued the hull and flew by instrumentation. He could not bear the sad image of rainfall now.

So much death. Nayr would never be satisfied. Not for the first time, Ahrik considered simply giving up.

10 Boldness

ANDA REMEMBERED A TIME when he was meant to live out his days in peace, in the sweet embrace of family, enjoying a quiet life in the remotest part of the Emerald Moon. He never meant to relive his days as a soldier, a dragooned blade in someone else's war.

And yet here he was, shrouded in the thickening night shadow of the palace, sneaking through the wet moonlight on an impossible errand, an impostor in a stolen uniform. After he and Sera and Esh'a came through to the other side of this madness, he promised himself he'd grow fat and lazy in some forsaken corner of the universe, a place where war could not extend its insipid tentacles and twist his peace into an infinity of little horrors.

His boots sank into the soft ground in the creeping night. Chirping crickets and the smell of recent rain were all that accompanied him on his mad errand to free Sera from her imprisonment in the healing center, in the south wing of the palace.

He came to the two-meter wall surrounding the outer courtyard of the palace. A chunk of the stone wall was missing, as if a monstrous animal had rammed it, scattering rock, then wandered off, wounded. Anda slipped through the ragged gap, bathed in shadow and guilt. Anda hoped that, with Nayr's attention diverted to the incipient rebellion and the Emerald Moon, only a skeleton garrison would remain at the palace.

Anda crept along the wall of the building, eyes shifting here and there, searching for movement, until he realized that a soldier who was supposed to be there would walk straight across the courtyard. He pushed off the wall and made a beeline for the main entrance.

Then he saw the bodies. At least a dozen of them. All young clones of Nayr. All shot through the head, in a neat L-shaped formation surrounding the entrance. A pair of specialists, working in grim, eerie silence, prepared the bodies for removal.

Anda's eyes darted to the shattered and slurried steps, obviously destroyed by a barrage of distillers and explosive weapons. An ominous dust hung on the air. The tang of explosives on the night breeze harrowed his mind with the memory of being caught in a bomb blast on his *qer'ish*, seventeen years earlier, before this mad descent into war. All of a sudden, his forehead felt cool with sweat and he searched the night for something to explain this carnage, knowing he would find none, at least none that would give him comfort on this cruel night.

He remembered why he hated war so much.

A soldier emerged from the guardhouse next to the ruined stairs, the uncertain light suggesting that he too was one of Nayr's clones, his eyes deadened to awareness and to the effects of the massacre that lay before them. Anda's stomach clenched. Not because he feared getting by this soldier and into the healing complex—with the uniform and false palm prints Zharla had put in Anda's bag, he would get through—but because of the trauma that seeing the clone and his callousness dredged up.

In an effort to suppress his anxiety, Anda motioned behind him as he strode up to the crumbled stairway. "What happened here?"

Anda's stomach churned. During the War of Independence, as they called the last war on Moon, the man now called the Healer had kidnapped Anda and forced him to train as if he were a clone so he could infiltrate his brother's ketel, then kill him. The only reason Anda had gone along with it was to escape the captivity, torture, and lies that the Healer had heaped upon him, day after day, week after week. To Anda's everlasting regret, the Healer had made him betray his principles of kindness and peace, and he had wondered ever since what he could have done differently.

The clone fingered his qasfin and curled his lip in a challenge. "Yuh gut a lotta nerve, shuwin' up 'ere."

Anda hadn't tried to kill Ahrik, but he did kill a man, accidentally, and that man was just as dead as if it had been on purpose. Everything Anda had thought about himself turned out to be false.

He was no pacifist, as he'd thought, no paragon of nonviolence, and he spent the next three years fighting in a war he couldn't stomach. He had blood on his hands now; they were thick with the stuff. Only Esh'a had saved him from wasting away in ignominy and self-doubt. No torture matched that of a pacifist being forced to fight a war.

And here he was, risking war and killing again, to save his daughter.

Anda adjusted the bag on his back. Something in there poked into his shoulder blade, but he ignored it. He was supposed to be tough, a keteli soldier, a lifelong veteran, not some green recruit.

Anda knew the clone would think he was from the Ketel of Ahrik. After all, he and Ahrik were fraternal twins, so they looked similar. Anda was ready for the clone's challenge. He held his hands up, palms out, in a conciliatory gesture. "I'm one of the good ones. See." He pointed to the scar at the base of his neck. "We rebelled against the Usurper during the war."

The guard narrowed his eyes further. Nayr's clones had certainly inherited his skepticism. The guard scratched his chin and held out a retinal scanner, but he took his hand off the qasfin at his waist to do it. "Scan," he said.

Anda suppressed a sigh of relief. Scanning his palm might have given him away, since he had little faith in the false palm prints he'd found in the bag Zharla gave him. The ketelis often used retinal scanners instead. They were less invasive and quicker, and Anda's retina was scanned, all those years back, into the Ketel of Ahrik.

The guard examined Anda's neck and read the scan. "Huh." He looked at Anda in a new light. "I 'eard 'bout people rubellin' ag'inst th'Usurper buck in th'day, but I thought it wuz a hoax. Yuh really cut th'inturnal cumpilers out of yur necks so th'Usurper couldn't track yuh?"

Anda nodded, suppressing the guilt of the lie, and the guard whistled in awe. "What unit were yuh with?"

"The 3–3 Marauders. Here's the battle ribbon." Anda pointed at his chest and thought how much trouble this uniform must have been for Zharla to assemble. Such an elaborate lie, deep as night. Maybe Zharla's help was genuine, after all.

"Yuh're one'f Ahrik's clones, so I shuld ask more questions . . ." The guard scanned the night, as if someone might see him ignore procedure. "Go un in. Visitin' one'f yur mates?"

Anda nodded, but made no verbal reply. He wasn't about to give the guard a chance to second-guess himself. Better to rely on that tried and true human characteristic, true even in clones bred and raised with a twisted notion of subservience, to believe what they wanted to believe.

Anda had trouble plumbing the depths of that lie as he made his way, full of false confidence, to the room where Sera lay captive. He passed a few healers on the night shift, and occasionally a member of the cleaning staff.

He waited for just the right moment. A healer strolled down the hallway toward him, engrossed in her handheld. He scanned up and down the hallway to make sure they were alone, then Anda snatched her handheld and stuck his fake distiller pistol into her back. She started to turn and protest.

"Quiet," he hissed. "Face the front, or I'll melt a hole in your back." Anda flooded his mind with thoughts of Sera and Esh'a and what he still had to do to see them again and live that fat and happy life in beautiful exile. This was the only way he could make the lie work.

"Think hard about your next move, soldier," said the healer, her voice venom. "Assaulting a woman is still a capital offense."

"I said quiet." Anda pressed the distiller deeper into her back.

The woman stiffened, but Anda sighed. "Look, I don't want to hurt you."

"Give me back my handheld."

"I can't have you raising an alarm."

"Let me see your face."

"Face to the front, for the love of the Lady. I don't want to hurt you, but I will if I have to."

Sera. Esh'a.

The healer put her hands up. "Okay, okay. Take it easy."

"Into that closet." When she didn't move immediately, Anda shoved her in that direction, but regret soon tugged at him.

When they were in the closet he waved off the lights and said, "Lie down."

The healer's voice trembled. "I thought you weren't going to hurt me."

"On your front, hands behind your back." He didn't want to scare her. *What if this were Sera, and some other man was just trying to save his daughter?*

She started to sob softly when he slipped bindings out of his bag and fastened her wrists together. Then he fastened her ankles together. As he set down his bag, he said, "Stop crying. Please."

Her sobbing transformed into a pitiful whimper.

"I'm sorry about this," he said, removing his boots and uniform blouse. He hoped his clothing underneath wasn't too rumpled. "Where's your badge?"

"What?" The whimpers subsided into sniffles. "I use my"—sniff—"palm for access."

Anda touched her head, in what he hoped was a fraternal gesture, but which probably frightened her, coming from a stranger she thought was armed, in the dark. "Someone I love is in grave danger," he said, removing a gag from his other thigh pocket. "I need your badge."

Sniff. "Left breast pocket." Sniff. "Don't try anyth—"

Anda stuffed the gag in her mouth, then tied it down behind her head. He turned the healer over, and her muffled screams crescendoed in alarm.

Anda sighed, then eased open her left breast pocket.

She writhed, and Anda had to pin her legs with his own to stabilize her. Against her screams, he reached into her pocket and liberated her badge.

Her nostrils flared with anger and fear, but her eyes bore surprise that he hadn't gone further.

He pulled off her slippers and put them on his own feet, wiggling his toes at the snug fit. Then he stuffed his combat blouse, trousers, and boots into a clothes hamper. He crouched and gave her what he hoped was a filial pat on the shoulder. "I'm not good at this. You'll be fine here till morning, but for the love of the Lady of the Emerald Moon, please keep quiet."

He emerged from the closet, the healer's screams having transformed once again, thankfully, into sniffling. He saw himself in the full light of the corridor, then tried in vain to smooth down his healer's tunic. He tried in vain to calm his breathing.

Almost there. Save Sera.

On his approach to Sera's room, Anda saw the guard outside Sera's room drift in and out of sleep. Either all of Nayr's clones were playing fast and loose with the rules while the commander was away, or reality didn't match Nayr's myth of martial invincibility.

Maybe the Ketel of Nayr was like any organization, with a wide range of competence. Anda thanked the Lady that Nayr kept the most competent clones with him and left the ones that slept on guard duty back here at the palace.

Anda surveyed his surroundings. Just as he remembered from when he was here the previous week, there was a service corridor about twenty meters beyond Sera's door, and around that corner, the laundry chute, and freedom.

Anda waved the healer's badge in front of the palm scanner, and it chimed a warning that startled the guard into consciousness.

"Sorry," said Anda before the guard could gather his wits, "looks like the palm reader system's acting up again. The door didn't open."

The guard shook the sleep from his head, then shrugged, stood, and put his own palm on the reader. Life at the center of Nayr's demesne must be comfortable indeed if guards could be this lax.

Anda smiled as the door dissolved open. "Thanks."

"Don't be too long," the guard grumbled.

Inside, Anda's heart melted. Sera breathed deep and sound, her *dubbi* clutched close, the light in the room as soft as a cloudy moon. He went to her bed and took her in for a bit, reminded at long last why he'd taken on so much risk, why he'd left the Emerald Moon at all. To reunite his family.

He reached down and uncorked the pendant with the vanilla, in order to wake her with pleasing smells of home.

"Shahl."

Zharla. He whirled and whipped his eyes around the dark room. "Where are you . . . um . . . Your Majesty?"

A shadow moved from the corner, where the light didn't quite reach, and the Queen began to take shape. "To you I am Zharla," she said, "not the Queen."

His mind raced. The scent of vanilla reminded him of family, of love. How could he escape with Sera now? He plastered a smile of pleasant surprise on his face. "It's the middle of the night."

"I knew you'd come eventually." She took another pace forward. "I slipped in while the guard slept."

"Zharla, I . . . What are you wear . . . Oh, I see."

She emerged into the light wearing a sheer nightgown, muscles perfectly defined underneath, the female form statuesque in its perfection.

Anda looked away, at Sera, anywhere but at Zharla, his first love of so many years before. Like a dam bursting, he remembered with perfect clarity the intensity of passion he'd felt yesteryear. "I . . . I can't. Esh'a."

Her breath warmed his neck, and her fingers stroked his cheek, gently guiding his gaze back to her. "I made a mistake when I chose your brother over you."

Her fine features and powerful eyes still captured his attention, even all these years later. Anda closed his eyes. "We've all made choices, Your Majes . . . Zharla."

He tried to look away again, but her hold was fast. Beautiful and strong.

"Don't leave your wife. Just give me the love we could have had."

Her mouth was so close to his now that he could smell the sweetness of her breath, feel the desire of her hand clenching his back. "Zharla," he implored.

"Zhe'le," she said, with a hint of reprimand, urging him with his eyes to use her familiar name.

"Zharla, I—"

"Abbi?"

Salvation. Sera. Zharla squeezed his hand, but retreated to the shadows and threw a cloak around her body.

"Cerit," said Anda, leaning down to gather his daughter in an embrace. "We have to go."

She smiled. "I smell Imma."

"Where's your *dubbi*?"

Sera pulled her *dubbi* close and coughed, a raspy, hollow convulsion that shook her little body. "Will they make me better somewhere else, Abbi?" She gasped, as if finding a long lost toy, then whispered, "Are we going to find Imma?"

Anda closed his eyes and squeezed out another lie. "Yes."

"Where are you going?" asked Zharla from behind, leaning closer, an uncomfortable menace in her voice.

Anda turned and faced her, wary of where her loyalties lay. "Zharla, if you ever loved me, you'd know you should help us leave."

Zharla's nostrils flared. "You spurn me, then plead for help?"

"I never could lie to you, Zhe'le." His eyes searched the dark corners of the room for his next words. "We cannot live under the Tyrant's thumb." He shifted Sera's weight on his hip and wrapped her in a blanket. "Are you ready, Cerit?"

She nodded, eyes wide with uncertainty, and showed him her stuffed animal.

Zharla moved behind him. "So that's what you call my son now? The Tyrant?"

Anda ignored her. His errand would not wait. The healer in the closet would be found soon, and the guard at the door would realize his mistake. "Cerit," he said, "I need you to be quiet and very still. Climb into this laundry basket. I'm going to put some other blankets on top of you, so people can't tell I'm carrying you."

Sera pulled her *dubbi* close. "I'm scared, Abbi."

Anda kissed her cheek. "You have nothing to fear."

Zharla's hand graced his shoulder, and a forbidden thrill jolted through him. "She'le, you won't get past the guards."

He twisted his shoulder away. "Turn me in if you must, Your Majesty, but if you had any sense at all you'd flee with us. Our refugee ship leaves from Shtera Umqi tomorrow."

Zharla choked on a sob, and a wave of guilt washed over Anda. "Zharla, I'm sorry—"

"I'm trying to"—she cleared her throat—"help you."

Anda's eyes softened, then he sighed. "I can't give up my family, Zharla. What you and I had, what we could have had, that's gone."

Tears flowed down Zharla's face. Anda gritted his teeth at the pain he'd caused, but told himself over and over that it was worth it. He loved Esh'a, even if they hadn't parted on good terms, even if their love wasn't was what it had been.

Sera popped her head out from the laundry basket. "Like this, Abbi?"

He nodded at his daughter and shushed her with a soft caress.

Zharla lifted some extra blankets out of a nearby closet. "I can't change the way I feel about you, She'le. You will always be my Shahl, my Flame of Peace."

She set the blankets into the basket with Sera and raised her arm, revealing the pendant he'd given her many years earlier, before she'd chosen his twin brother over him, before Shahl had died and he'd become Anda at the hands of rebel torturers. The pendant gleamed as brightly on her wrist as the day he'd given it to her.

A very different kind of regret washed over him then, a pain at the pit of his stomach that intimated what could have been. He took a deep breath. Oh, how he wanted to give in to the tenderness and passion that Zharla offered him.

"When I love," he said, "it is an action, Zharla, not something that just happens to me."

Zharla covered her face with a hand. Her body racked with a sob as violent as Sera's cough had been. Anda could not bear to watch. Sera sniffled in the basket, then ducked under the blankets.

Zharla let loose one more sob, then pulled in a deep breath, which she released with exquisite grace. Her composure regained, she looked him straight in the eye. "Go to the White Planet. Find your love."

He looked at her for a beat. "Nayr may count your life forfeit if you let us go."

She shook her head vigorously, a refusal to believe those words. "No. He still loves his mother."

Anda looked away again, suddenly unsure of what he'd just done, of what fate he'd sealed for the woman he first loved. "Where will you go? What will you do?" he asked.

Zharla wrapped her arm around his shoulder, enveloping him in a gesture of consummate sisterly care. Despite his high-minded words of love for Esh'a, his heart still pounded a little more fervently against his chest.

"Me?" she asked. "I'll go to die with the man I call husband." She escorted them to the door. "Think of me often, She'le. Favor me with kind memories. Grant me that."

She spun to the door. It whooshed open, and the guard scrambled to attention upon seeing the Queen.

Zharla led Anda, the basket hovering ahead of them, toward the back of the building, to a darkened stairwell. Anda pulled Sera out of the basket. They descended the stairs and arrived at the servants' entrance at the back of the palace healing center. Zharla paused to let them pass out into the midnight air, then gripped the doorjamb. The night breeze ruffled the cloak wrapped around her shoulders, and she shivered. Her eyes bore the tenor of battle. She cast a wistful glance toward the mountain behind them. "She'le," she said, "remember."

The words stabbed at his chest and twisted at the sinews of his heart. He could not look her in the eye. A thousand years ago, it seemed, she had used those same words when she ripped out his heart and chose his brother over him for a husband. He thought he'd forgotten that pain, buried that memory, but it clawed at his mind.

Sera, beside him, reached up and squeezed his hand. Looking down, he saw his own fear mirrored in her sweet face. She had begun to understand the pain he felt, and it pained him even more.

Then her face transformed into a smile that reached from her eyes to her soul. "Abbi," she said, "will we find Imma now?"

How he wanted to give in to that childlike optimism.

Instead, he avoided Sera's gaze and glared at Zharla's feet, his eyes cold. "Sometimes, Your Majesty, it is better to forget."

Zharla choked back a sob, as if absorbing a blow. The door to the palace healing center hissed back to resolution, and naught but the breeze whispered through the green moonlight.

She was gone.

Renla gripped the armrests of her command seat to keep her hands from shaking. They were about to relinquish those heights that, once abandoned, could never be regained. A rebellion unleashed would not be forgotten. A shiver began in her core and traveled up her spine. Three weeks had passed since Renla found loyal officers to conspire with, after her encounter with the Queen at the *birza*. Ahrik, Shahl, and the Queen went missing. After their disappearances, Renla and her confederates put their planning into high gear, culminating in this moment.

"Shuttle 11-Two-Zero-Five," crackled a voice over the electromag. "Provide mission clearance number, over."

Lyn, seated in the navigator's chair forward of Renla, let out a desperate breath and stole a glance back at her commander. Lyn flipped open the electromag comm channel. "Elevator Station 22 Control, we request berth for urgent repairs. We sustained damage in a training accident, over."

In the fraught pause that followed, the pilot, seated next to Lyn, flexed his grip on the flight controls. He was no combat pilot, just a transport driver in an engineering unit, and Renla had asked him to fly into the teeth of the enemy. He came from one of the other hands, stationed gravside, and was so wet behind the ears that he hadn't even lost that civilian softness that all newbies come with.

Renla leaned forward and patted his shoulder. "You're doing fine, pilot. Maintain current bearing and speed, but don't use the starboard inertials. We want to look like we're limping in."

The pilot wiped his brow with his sleeve. "Check, ma'am."

"Ma'am," said Lyn, "they're not biting."

Renla had no choice but to press on, despite the uncertainty. She had to take the fight to the Tyrant, and she had to do it now. The Tyrant was on a manhunt for Ahrik, and if he was fair game, then everyone was. Nayr had also made a hostage of Shahl's little girl, Sera, presumably as leverage to get back at Shahl for whatever sin he had committed. Renla had to strike now, while Nayr's attention was focused gravside instead of on the moon. Open another front against the enemy. Ahrik and Zharla needed a fighting chance, which was usually all they needed.

Renla and the Fighting 11th had one thing going for them: surprise. Renla puckered her lips as if weighing the odds. "They'll take the bait, Lyn. Don't worry."

Renla wasn't so certain. Another shiver ran up her spine.

The electromag sizzled to life. "Shuttle 11-Two-Zero-Five, access denied. Proceed to Station 23 for processing."

Lyn turned panicked eyes toward Renla. They had to dock here, on Station 22. The diversion and the secondary attack were timed to them docking at 22. In the next five minutes.

Renla's knuckles turned white on her armrest.

"It was too dangerous for you to come, ma'am," said Lyn.

"We're starting a war, Lyn. Danger is what we do." Renla wondered if Lyn and the pilot actually believed her false confidence. "We're combat engineers. Insert, destroy something, exfil. We've got this."

Renla opened up the internal channel to the rear cabin, where her strike team readied themselves for the space drop. "Seal up," she ordered. "Blow the hull."

Renla, Lyn, and the pilot slapped on their helmets and sealed them home with a slurp. Lyn flipped the switch to depressurize the cabin. The shuttle lurched to port as the strike team blasted a hole in the rear starboard hull.

"Pass me the comm, Lyn," said Renla.

"Over to you, ma'am." Lyn's voice sounded tinny inside Renla's helmet.

"Station 22 Control, we have a hull breach, and we're leaking atmosphere. We won't make it to 23. Request immediate berth, over."

Another pause, then the controller's voice crackled on once again. "Ma'am . . . uh . . . we are in force protection condition 2. Only verified, mission-essential berths allowed."

Renla pursed her lips in annoyance. She didn't want to pull rank, and possibly give away her identity, but she had to. The mission required it. "I'm a hand commander. If you don't tell us which berth you want us in, we'll choose our own, over."

"Uh, check, ma'am . . . I'll . . . uh . . . run your request up the chain."

Renla cut the channel, then chuckled. Nayr had created a massive bureaucracy, one run mostly by his clones. They had the ability to think independently. They just didn't. Everyone in the clone-controlled bureaucracy was so busy worrying about what higher-ups thought that they couldn't handle deviations from very well-defined scripts. As Renla had expected, this controller was so risk averse that he wasn't about to go head-to-head with a hand commander.

Her Fighting 11th called them "drones."

Renla flipped open the internal channel. "Strike team, prepare for debark. Target essential infrastructure. Tendril link repeaters, access points to the hangar bays, comm network nodes. Ignore defensive positions. We're not coming back. We just need to get their attention, and make it harder for them to attack the moon or Dom."

The team leader's voice buzzed in her helmet. "Check, ma'am."

Lyn unstrapped and rose to gear up for the debark, grabbing her distiller pack and adjusting her qasfin. Renla motioned for her to switch to their private channel. "Lyn," said Renla. "Get in, get out. Do *not* stand and fight."

Lyn looked at Renla and nodded, but Renla could tell that her aide didn't like the idea of backing down from a fight.

Lyn gave her a warning look of her own. "Just make the rendezvous, ma'am," she said. "This plan is crazy enough without you improvising and . . . you know . . . The 11th needs you."

Renla smiled and shrugged, a nonchalant gesture to hide her jitters. "I'm just a diversion, Lyn. Victory goes to the bold, and sometimes that means improvising." She stood and saluted. "The Lady keep you."

Lyn frowned as she returned the salute, then primed her distiller. It shuddered as the microcore thrummed to life. Their equipment was worn, as were their spirits after a month of isolation on the moon. They needed a win here.

"The Lady keep you too, ma'am," said Lyn. "Dig on."

"Dig on." Renla watched as her aide sprang to the rear of the shuttle, then launched herself out the rear hatch with the strike team, toward Station 22. Through the transluced hull, Renla saw the strike team fire up the explosive-drive thrusters that her research department had developed that month. The members of the strike team fanned out toward their targets all over Station 22.

They shot through space on a monstrous bet. Their most recent intelligence said that Nayr's drones didn't have sensors on the elevator stations precise enough to identify a human-sized object approaching a station. The strike team should be invisible. But they couldn't be sure.

Renla froze when the electromag in her helmet burst with static. "Shuttle 11-Two-Zero-Five, this is Station 22 Control," said the controller, a tone of challenge and alarm in his voice. "Confirm objects exiting your craft, over."

Renla exchanged a nervous look with the young pilot. She sat down in her command seat and clicked open the channel using the controls on her helmet. "Check, Station 22 Control." Renla took a deep breath, hoping he'd buy her lie. "That was debris from our hull breach."

Seconds ticked by. Renla's palms grew sweaty. If the station's sensors could track the strike team's trajectories after all, they were done for.

"Ma'am?" asked the pilot.

Renla held out her hand, palm down, in a calming gesture, once again with false confidence. The pilot nodded, eyes as wide as the moon on a clear night.

"Proceed to Bay 2," said the controller. "Berth Three-Nine-Seven."

Renla let out her breath. "Check, Station Control. Three-Nine-Seven. Thank you, over and out."

Renla had to maintain the illusion of normality as long as possible. Make them think it's a normal day, then blow up their world. Renla grimaced. Nayr would regret taking over the government and undermining her friend, the Queen. He would regret attacking innocents on the Emerald

Moon and taking his cousin hostage. Renla moistened her dry mouth, the taste of indignation and sweet revenge on the tip of her tongue.

Renla's jaw dropped when they entered Bay 2. A pair of hulking carriers occupied much of the space in the bay, making it difficult to maneuver. Rack after rack of interceptors were arrayed along the bay walls, too, waiting to be loaded onto the carriers. A steady stream of tugbots loaded container upon container into the carriers.

The pilot latched the shuttle onto a waiting tugbot and whistled over the shuttle comm. "I see why they didn't want us to berth here."

"Whatever they're preparing, it's big," said Renla. She shook her head. "Question is, are they going up to the moon, or down to Dom? There are twenty-four elevator stations orbiting the planet, each with two bays like this. If even half of them are occupied with this kind of force . . ."

Renla trailed off, unwilling to verbalize the thought. Lyn's admonition prised its way into her mind: *Don't go improvising and getting yourself killed.* She nodded in the pilot's direction. "You ready for some crazy?"

The pilot heaved a sigh and avoided her gaze, his helmet pointed at the shuttle control panel. Renla couldn't tell if he'd heard or not. "Ma'am," he said after an uncomfortable pause, "I volunteered for this mission." He muted his channel for as long as it would take a sigh to dissipate. "We all did."

"Good, because this just turned into more than a blow-and-go. Do you know how to deactivate the microcore safeties on a distiller?"

The pilot looked back at her, his face even more nervous than before. He looked toward the rear, as if someone else might hear them speak such madness. "Ma'am . . . uh . . . I tinkered with this stuff as a kid, but only in controlled stasis fields. I *can* disable all four safeties, but if we did that here we might . . ." Recognition dawned. "Oh."

Renla tapped her helmet in a knowing gesture. "We just need to be off this station before the microcore melts."

The pilot slumped in his chair, the reality of combat settling onto his visage. "I . . . uh . . . how're we supposed to get off the station if our little atomic is on this rig?"

Renla rose. She lifted her distiller from its rack and handed it to him. "We'll figure it out. Rig a trip switch to melt down the microcore when the drones break in here. If we play it right, we'll be long gone before they crack open the shuttle."

The pilot's face blanched. He opened his mouth as if to say something, but reconsidered. He shook his head and blew out a breath, fogging his helmet. "That's crazy alright, ma'am."

"You can do it, right?"

"I wouldn't be a combat engineer if I couldn't, ma'am." He hefted Renla's distiller. "Rendezvous at the airlock in twenty?"

Renla nodded, then extracted a data capsule from her breast pocket. "I've got a present of my own to leave them. Dig on."

"Dig on," said the pilot.

The tugbot reversed them into Berth 397. Renla left the pilot to finish the makeshift atomic, then exited the rear hatch and walked to the nearest access point to the station. As the airlock cycled, she latched her helmet onto her back. Standard protocol in a space station. Always ready for vacuum.

A maintenance tech saluted her on the other side of the airlock. A drone. The corridor was full of them, walking this way and that, their faces full of devotion and youthful folly, but Renla knew how dangerous they were. To a man, they were stronger, faster, and better trained than any other soldiers in the army, unswerving in their devotion to Nayr, and utterly devoid of creativity. Or empathy, for that matter.

The tech tapped on an external compiler in his hand. "What's the problem, ma'am?"

His blank stare told her he had no idea who she was. She'd put on false insignia for this mission. His stare confirmed to her that Nayr's precious tendril network hadn't processed that she, commander of the Fighting 11th, might be the one doing this, that this attack was coming from the moon, not from Dom. She gave the tech a curt smile, to establish the power hierarchy. "Rear starboard hull breach. Check the starboard inertials, too. They jammed. Nothing internal to the rig, just do enough external repairs to get us on our way. My techs will take care of the rest when I get back."

"Check, ma'am," said the tech.

Renla could tell he was only too happy to make superficial repairs on an add-on job. Mounting an invasion was a lot of work for techs like him.

The tech tapped away at his handheld, his face a study in concentration. "Berth Three-Nine-Seven, right ma'am?" he asked, not looking up.

"That's right." Renla put a hand on her hip in a colloquial way and wondered why she thought this would work. "Say," she asked, stomach fluttering without mercy, "where's the nearest officer lounge?"

The tech looked up from his handheld and gave her a confused look. "Huh . . . what?"

She held up the data capsule. "I need to file the incident report."

"Oh, right. Officer lounge." The tech stroked his chin, then pointed to a lift down the passageway. "Up one deck, to port as you exit the lift."

"Thanks," said Renla, turning away. A twinge of guilt needled at Renla's gut. She was about to irradiate the station with an atomic. This drone would die, as would thousands of others. But she reminded herself of the system of which this drone was a part. He wasn't personally responsible for the Tyrant's atrocities, but he would carry out the Tyrant's orders if he received them. Nayr's killing machine demanded unthinking alacrity. Don't think. Just kill. One sanitized, bureaucratic step at a time. How else could she defeat evil like this, other than by breaking a few rules?

Renla's wrist compiler chimed. The strike team. Their explosives were in place. The attack on Station 24's elevator cable was under way, two elevator stations away. This was the most intricate part of the plan. Draw their attention away from Station 22 while Renla's own strike team set off its charges.

Renla didn't hear any alarms, which was good news. The Fighting 11th had declared war on Nayr's killing machine, and the drones on Station 22 hadn't figured it out yet. She bit her lip to contain her glee.

Renla went up in the lift, then sauntered into the officer lounge like she owned the place. She nodded to the attendant and sat down at a compiler. Without waiting for the attendant to challenge her, much less demand a palm scan, she inserted the data capsule into the compiler and wondered how long the hack would take to do its work. She didn't have much time if the hack was going to undermine the station's life support systems and allow Renla and her team to escape.

The lounge was empty except for her, the attendant, and ten compilers posted like sentinels along the walls. Plush hoverchairs and padded walls accented an unnaturally large space for a space station. Nayr must have spent a fortune to build these stations. He must not realize that all this empty space needed to be pressurized.

Renla scowled at the profligate waste.

The attendant, yet another drone, cleared his throat behind her. "Ma'am, you forgot to palm in."

Renla gave a look of mock surprise. It was too late to stop her. Too late to preserve network integrity, and too late to save the station. The Tyrant's drones still had their internal tendril network, using implanted compilers—tendril comms couldn't be hacked—but any secondary sensors relied on the electromag network that the external compilers in the lounge hooked into. Nayr's drones were about to find out how reliant they were on their electromags.

Renla smiled at the attendant in mock apology. "Oh, sorry." She reached her palm to the attendant's scanner and hoped that the alternate palm print her research team had stuck to her hand would work. Renla furrowed her brow at the attendant. "You know, I may not be in the system. My unit's based gravside."

The attendant examined his scanner and grunted. "So it would seem, ma'am."

Renla's hackles pricked up. Something was off. The attendant turned away like he knew something he wasn't telling her. He was trying to stay calm. Was he accessing his tendril link to call security?

Her heart beat through her temples. If the ruse was up, then she had to act fast if she was going to save the mission, but if the ruse was still intact then killing him now would blow it wide open.

The feeling that the op had just gone very, very bad flooded Renla's senses, like the smell of electricity before a lightning strike. The station alarms remained silent. She should have heard the explosions as her strike team's charges went off. Nothing. Something was wrong.

She leaped from her hoverchair and drew her qasfin, twisting her blade to expose the killing point as she lunged toward the attendant. He turned, Renla's blade plunging at his neck. He tried to dodge, but Renla was too skilled, too practiced. She expected him to move like that. Her blade pierced his neck at just the right point, where his internal compiler connected with his cortex, cutting off his link to the tendril network.

Without surprise on her side, the drone probably would have put up a nasty fight. Instead, his body slumped to the floor, twitching. She suppressed the pang of taking life, especially by subterfuge like this. His body convulsed, and he groaned while blood leaked out onto the metal deck.

She shuddered at how much more killing it would take to defeat the Tyrant's evil.

Renla burst out of the lounge, into an empty passageway. She regretted leaving the attendant to bleed out, not putting him out of his misery, but her diggers needed her now.

Her breath came more ragged than it should have as she ran. There should have been drones everywhere, but the passageway was completely empty. She cycled through possible explanations in her mind. The drones must be on alert, at battle posts. They'd sent the alarm quietly, over the tendril link, instead of using audible alarms. From far away, an explosion reverberated through the station. Out of ten members of the strike team, they only set off one charge? Another explosion, this one a bit closer. Two? Small consolation.

Lyn. Worry for her young aide jerked her mind into awareness. Renla skidded to a stop at the lift and returned to the deck she'd come in on.

When the lift door dissolved, Renla bit her lip and peeked around the jamb to see if the passageway was clear.

She promised herself that, if she got out of this, she'd never do something this crazy again.

The *thu-thu-thunk* of a distiller fight erupted from down the corridor. Steam leaked from distiller pockmarks in the walls. She glanced down. One of Nayr's drones lay on the ground, writhing in the final throes of agony, a chunk of his torso missing. Her shuttle's young pilot also lay on the ground, cold and still, head mostly missing after taking a distiller charge full in the face.

Renla's nostrils flared at what they'd done to him, this boy with so much promise. She slapped on her helmet and ripped the distiller and distiller pack off of the dying drone. She ran to the sound of the guns, pulling on the distiller pack as she went.

She rounded the last bend in the passageway before the airlock alcove leading into the hangar bay. She slid to the deck to avoid a barrage of distiller charges. She heard no shouting, which meant that the drones were communicating using their internal tendril link. Her electromag hack had done nothing to confuse the drones' response. She had failed. They'd fooled her, instead of the other way around.

Renla scrambled for cover behind a crate, then stole a glance out to assess the situation, unsure if they'd seen her. A team of maybe ten drones had someone, probably her diggers, trapped in the airlock alcove down the corridor, with no way to break contact. The drones had positions at both ends of the corridor, one right in front of Renla and another about twenty meters away. Her diggers couldn't shoot back in one direction without taking it in the rear. They couldn't even get to the airlock controls to seal the door, given the angles. Her diggers were outnumbered, outgunned, and outflanked.

She smelled pre-battle anticipation in the stuffy confines of her helmet. The drones at the other end of the corridor were also setting up a crew-served weapon, and they might have alerted the drones on this side of movement to their rear. She had only a fraction of a second to assess her options, the sliver of difference between life and death. So she jumped up from behind the crate and charged.

The drones on her end of the corridor were donning helmets. In the same moment that she squeezed the trigger of the distiller to pump charges into the backs of the drones closest to her, Renla's chest also surged with panicked realization. The drones with the crew-served weapon were going to blast through the hull to get a better angle at her diggers in the airlock alcove. That's why the drones were sealing their helmets.

Movement exploded everywhere as she charged. Her distiller vibrated with deadly energy. The drones by the crew-served weapon at the other end of the passageway traded frantic hand signals. The weapon crew and the drone security team must be from different units, far enough from each other in the tendril network that they couldn't communicate easily. On the near side, some of the drones had set down their weapons to affix helmets, but the ones covering the alcove from behind their barricade began to turn toward her, a new threat. Either they heard her, or the farther drones warned them.

Renla squeezed three bursts into the five drones on this side of the corridor. They crumpled under her distiller barrage, charges from their weapons spraying in every direction as their bodies flailed. A shout of alarm and pain cut off abruptly as one of her charges caught a drone in the throat.

She didn't have time to make sure they were dead, because the crew-served distiller at the other end was about to send death in her direction. She leaped over the barricade and squeezed more charges in the direction of the farther drones, who'd stopped donning helmets and were rotating the crew-served weapon to cut her down. She wondered if that crew-served weapon was already operational. If so, they they'd brought it online with lightning speed. Much faster than her diggers could have pulled it off.

These were not just mindless drones, after all.

As if in answer, the crew-served weapon's maw glowed a furious blue. The weapon crew had seen her before the other drones, then. Alarm pulsed through Renla. She planted her foot and slammed herself against the hull of the station. *Thu-wunk*. The air she'd just left sizzled with energy and death. The charge obliterated the barricade and slammed into a bulkhead, eating right through. She had about 1.5 seconds before they fired that crew-served weapon again, and she didn't have anywhere else to dive this time.

At least she could give her diggers in the airlock alcove a chance.

She launched herself from the wall, distiller alive. She would not die like a cowering animal. The angry hum of the drones' distillers filled the air. She rushed the drone position and counted the moments of vibrant life before her death.

In the corner of her vision, a figure darted out of the alcove, distiller likewise alive. One of her diggers. This new threat was enough to freeze the farther drones with indecision, for just a split second. Renla's stream of distiller charges plunged into the crew-served weapon and its crew. Her fellow digger's charges pinned down the drones who'd been trading hand signlas only seconds before.

A few charges came back at them. One grazed Renla's arm, and she cried out in pain, then stumbled and recovered, ready to press her attack.

But a hand yanked her back by the arm, inflaming the pain.

"No time!" Lyn yelled, her voice crackling over their private channel. Lyn pulled Renla back as she unloaded at the drones with her distiller. Wails of surprise and pain and confusion answered her barrage.

Lyn dragged Renla into the airlock, then tossed her commander to the ground and slammed home the airlock controls. The door hissed closed, shutting off the passageway. Lyn slapped sealant onto Renla's suit, where the distiller charge had grazed it. Renla's suit repressurized with a satisfying whoosh.

"Ma'am," crackled Lyn's voice over the electromag, "we are getting out. Now."

Renla clenched her teeth against the searing pain in her arm and looked at the airlock control. "The others?"

Lyn's face darkened. She shook her head.

Renla nodded. A weight pressed on her chest. She felt weak, whether because she had led eleven good women and men to their deaths, or because those mindless drones had outsmarted her, she did not know.

She would have time to learn lessons later. Now, they had to move fast, before the drones got the airlock open again. Lyn pushed Renla into the hangar bay, but stopped short at the sight of the carrier and rows of interceptors. "What's all this?" She turned to Renla. "Where's the shuttle, ma'am?"

Renla took a step toward the shuttle, then found her wits and clutched Lyn's arm. "We need to steal an interceptor."

"Ma'am, we can't both fit into an inter—"

All over the hangar bay, hundreds of interceptors unlatched from their berths and started to drift as the artigrav died. The ground lifted away from Renla's feet. The hack. It had worked, at least in part. Alarm lights flashed all over the bay. With any luck, the whole station would vent to vacuum within moments.

Renla pointed to the nearest interceptor, drifting just within reach. They wriggled through the rear hatch, into a space meant for one person. Renla shoved herself to one side while Lyn primed the interceptor's boson drive.

Lyn gripped the flight controls and the interceptor lunged forward, then yawed toward the hull of the nearest carrier. Renla winced as the interceptor caromed off the carrier's energy shield and tacked its way to the hangar exit. The interceptor bumped and dodged floating interceptors, Lyn sometimes using the forward distillers to blast a way through.

Distiller charges zipped by them. The drones were through the airlock and taking pot shots at them.

Then they got to open space and shot forward. Lyn said nothing. Renla couldn't bear to speak. The only subject it felt right to broach was the women and men they'd left behind. But Renla couldn't bear to bring them up.

Renla had almost forgotten what the pain of losing comrades was like, but even after all these years the sense of loss was still too familiar a companion. As they cut through space, she thought of all those whose deaths lay on her conscience. Those whose deaths she could have prevented, in hindsight. She pressed her eyes closed. She'd have many more deaths on her conscience before this was over.

Lyn pressurized the cockpit, and Renla removed her helmet. Lyn followed suit.

Lyn looked back in the direction they'd come. "May the Lady keep them always, close to her bosom."

Renla looked away, to keep from showing her tears. "Are we doing the right thing, Lyn?" she asked. Her voice cracked.

Lyn drew a deep breath and set them on a course to the moon, then shifted her weight to grip Renla's glove where it hid her tattoo. "Freedom, ma'am. *Cheret*. They did not die in vain, as long as we don't give up."

Renla kept her gaze on the middle distance, still unsure she could trust her emotions. "How much death can a rebellion withstand before it breaks?"

Lyn shook her head, as if struggling to acknowledge the question. "We're in it now, ma'am, whether we want to be or not."

"Yes—" Renla choked back a sob before gazing forward once again, to reflect on how many people she'd condemned to die. "That's what I'm afraid of, Lyn. I think I just started an atomic war in the name of *cheret*."

Nayr rubbed his temples, then set to cleaning his weapon once again. He lifted his distiller's casing out of its disinfectant bath and held it up to the late morning light that streamed in through his office window, to check for residual foreign matter.

He sighed and peered out the window. A bird settled on the stone sill and pecked at what it must have thought was food. To be so oblivious.

The calm light outside his window belied the torment swirling inside his head. He disconnected the distiller's barrel from the charge modulator and set it to the side. How could his five thousand sons scouring the western Eshel not find the Usurper? Nayr hadn't expected him to break out of the ambush, much less murder an entire squad, but to steal a shuttle and disappear? Unconscionable.

What was he doing wrong to allow such incompetence to creep into his beloved ketel?

Then disloyal soldiers attacked three of his elevator stations that week. Some of the evidence pointed to the moon, and Renla, but the evil conspiracy could go much deeper than that. How could this happen?

Not all the news was bad. His uncle snuck into the palace healing center last night in Meran to take the little brat away, just like Nayr planned him to. Mother departed yesterday on her shuttle, to lure the Usurper and his pesky soldiers out into the open, she said. She pretended Nayr was in Meran instead of Mekele, just like Nayr asked her to. Then she didn't come back. That wasn't part of the plan. Who was to blame for that?

He rested the barrel of his distiller in the disinfectant bath, the sharpness of the solution tickling his nostrils. He clicked open the modulator with his thumbs and examined its internal mechanism with his desk magnifying lamp. A displacer looked worn. He grasped it with a pair of tweezers and set it aside, then replaced it with a new displacer from his cleaning kit.

He removed the microcore from the kall pack and wiped it down with a biomesh cloth. He unlatched the feeder tube from the kall pack, then—

He exhaled in frustration and set everything down. A lack of sleep swelled his eyes. Chagrin lined his face. He stood and paced in front of the window that extended from one end of his office to the other and captured a commanding view of the plain between his new headquarters and Mekele. The wind swept over the plains with earnestness here.

He pursed his lips and reached out over the tendril link. *2, come.*

Almost immediately, 2 poked his head into Nayr's office. "Father?"

Nayr beckoned him in with a tilt of his head. "Sit."

Wordless and patient, 2 took the visitor's hoverchair.

"2," said Nayr, "I can't pretend anymore that things are going according to plan."

2 frowned and gave a fervent shake of his head. "Father, you always tell us that the plan is nothing. Planning is everything."

"We were supposed to be in complete control by now." Nayr stood and peered out the window, frowning as the bird took flight.

"These are not setbacks, Father. These are opportunities to show the power of the Ketel of Nayr."

He glared at 2 and clenched his jaw. "Renla is complicit in this little rebellion, and where is the Usurper? Where is my mother?" He lunged at 2 and threw up his hands. "Where are they?"

To his credit, 2 did not shrink from Nayr's frustration, but demonstrated absolute control and devotion. "We have doubled the size of the force looking for them." He made a calming motion with his hands. "We'll find them, Father."

Nayr scoffed and looked out the window again. "You'd better."

"Father, the gene-encoded nanobios are nearly ready."

"I pray that I am not disappointed by those, as we—" Nayr furrowed his brow. "What is that?"

"Father?"

In response, Nayr thrust out his chin at a crowd of people marching toward the main gate of the new headquarters, on the road from Mekele. He didn't need to hear them to know that their chants would offend him and threaten the peace and safety that he offered the world.

3, cast Nayr, *how could we let a rabble disturb peace and good order?*

On it, Father. A pause. *We estimate five thousand marchers. I was going to go out and settle them down, but—*

Kill them.

Kill them? Father, the Queen . . .

She's gone. If she wanted to rule, she should have stayed.

Another pause.

Yes, Father.

Nayr stared out the window at the scene unfolding below the bright light of the noonday sun. The light chased shadows from the undulating mid-continental hills. "Come, 2. You should watch."

2 nodded, gulped, and took his place next to Nayr. 2's crisp uniform whispered and creaked.

Nayr smiled and slapped his back. "Your face is whiter than I remember, 2. Do I keep you so busy that you can't get out to enjoy the sun every once in a while?"

"No, Father." A whisper. "I'm fine, Father."

Down below, his sons hemmed in the protesters on three sides, appropriately concealed by their bioflauge cloaking tech. Nayr nodded with approval at how effective the new bioflauge was. The protesters couldn't see them, but Nayr recognized the shimmer and movement of his men. He popped a pill in his mouth and let the medicine spread its contentment through his veins.

Beside him, 2 looked away from the scene unfolding below.

Nayr squeezed 2's shoulder and nodded toward the protesters. "Oh, no, don't look away now. We're about to teach them what happens to those who disturb the peace."

Distillers chirped and whumped down below. The protest descended into a panic. Limbs flailed. Order evaporated. Rabble-rousers fell.

3, cast Nayr, *let some of them get away. We have to get word back to Mekele somehow.*

Yes, Father.

After bodies stopped writhing on the ground, Nayr opaqued the window and turned back to the distiller still laid out on his desk.

He set about cleaning his weapon once more, humming the beat of his favorite running cadence. "See, 2," he said, "that wasn't so hard, was it?"

2 stood rigid, staring at the opaque window. "No. Father."

Father, cast 3, *just received word from units in the Kereu. We believe the Queen is en route to Peshron. We believe the Usurper will hold her there.*

Nayr smiled. *Well done, 3. Now it's time to teach the people of Peshron a lesson. We can't have people kidnapping the Queen, now can we?* Nayr set down his weapon and stroked his chin as he considered his options. *Deploy the atmospherics and tectonics. And send a unit that hasn't gotten a piece of the action yet. Spread the fun.*

Yes, Father.

Nayr hummed his cadence. He didn't blame Mother, really, for her behavior. The Usuper and Shahl coerced her somehow. She had abandoned Nayr, but it wasn't genuine. "You know what, 2?"

"Father?"

"We need to control the portal out by the moon."

"What of the Fight . . . the 11th, Father?"

"Renla? She is nothing. Besides, we have the nanobios if she gets out of hand."

"Nanobios on the moon? Father, the moon is full of civilians. The nanobios are experimental . . . to be used on the Ketel of Ahrik first."

Nayr shook his head. "2, 2, 2. The Ketel of Nayr is meant to bring peace to the world." He eyed his chief aide and confidante. "To this world and to every world."

2's gaze was impassive, but firm. "Yes, Father."

"Nothing goes in or out of the portal, understood? Not even civilians."

"Yes, Father. Of course, Father."

Nayr smiled. Things were looking up again. "2, ready my shuttle and my new bioflauge suit. I need to visit my uncle in Meran."

11 Criticism

THE SUN WAS JUST RISING on the other side of Meran Mountain, illuminating its leeward slope with dawn's reflection. It was still early, and the streets were mostly empty, as they were when Anda had come down a day earlier, in search of Esh'a in the camps. The disquiet of his encounter with Zharla squirmed in his breast, but something else gnawed at his peace, something he couldn't quite finger.

Anda stopped and grasped Sera's hand within sight of the eastern entrance to the mountain. He felt eyes on them. He peered into the receding darkness of early morning on the leeward side of Meran. A few stars still twinkled in the bluing sky. He shivered, in spite of the mild summer dawn.

They were being watched. He led Sera to the nearest shadows, a simple matter in the burgeoning light, and scanned their surroundings. The streets around the entrance were dead, but whether from slumber or fear of the Tyrant, he couldn't tell. The news of the elevator station attacks yesterday cast a pall over the street. War was imminent. He could almost smell it in the air. Shadows created in the growing light played morbid games over rough-hewn stone walls and lumpy cobblestones.

The *melmez* where he'd studied so long ago, in another age, lay nestled in a crook of the mountain, about five hundred meters farther up the street. Next to it the eastern entrance to in-mountain Meran yawned with blackness, its massive pillars of white marble glowing with the eerie menace of a new day.

He cast a nervous look around and stepped into the relative light of the cobbled street. He saw nothing, but felt the eye of fate peering into his core, so he crouched down next to his daughter, his face full of false confidence. "Serit, see those two stone pillars over there? We need to—"

Movement to his left cut him off. He sprang up and put himself between his daughter and this new danger. A soldier materialized out of the murky shadow on the opposite side of the street, as if out of the air. The soldier had his qasfin drawn, and flipped it over and back in the air, catching it each time, as if it were a toy. His boots crunched over the cobbles as he sauntered across the street toward them.

"Our cloaking tech has gotten good, hasn't it?" he asked, then spun his qasfin by the hilt and sheathed it in one fluid motion. He rubbed his hands together with glee. "Your brother will never know what hit him."

Anda cast his eyes about, to see if any more soldiers would conjure themselves up out of the fragile morning air. He gripped Sera's hand and retreated to put a wall at their back. "Are you a clone?"

The soldier didn't answer, only juked his shoulders, then leaped toward Anda and Sera.

Anda flinched, but lowered to a fighting stance. He cocked his fist back, ready to let fly.

The soldier landed precisely, with perfect balance, just out of range. He tilted his head in mock disappointment. "Come now, Uncle Shahl. Who am I? What kind of question is that?"

Sera coughed into her sleeve. "I don't like that man, Abbi."

"You're scaring my daughter, Nayr."

"I take it the healing care she received at the palace wasn't up to your standards? Why else would you reject my hospitality?"

Anda turned toward the entrance to Meran, and the refugee ship leaving from in-mountain later that day. "Let's go, Serit."

In a flash of atomic-sharpened steel, the qasfin emerged from its sheath. With a smooth hiss, the flat of the blade whipped in front of Anda's face, its gleaming edge held precisely at eye level. "Ah, ah, ah," clucked Nayr, holding the blade like a gatekeeper in front of Anda. "You made the right move back at the healing center, leaving my mother, but we're not done yet."

"Let. Us. Go."

Nayr didn't move the qasfin. "You're not going to ask why that was the right thing to do, with my mother?"

"I do the right thing because it's the right thing, not for any other reason."

Nayr chuckled. "How quaint." He tapped his toe once or twice, then fidgeted with false impatience.

Anda gave no response, just cast about for an escape, a path to freedom, to the White Planet, and to Esh'a.

"Okay, I'll tell you why," said Nayr. At this, he lowered his blade, but brought his face so close that Anda felt his thick, drug-suffused breath.

Nayr smiled. "That was the right thing to do because if you so much as look at my mother ever again"—he nodded to Sera—"then she dies."

"Wha—?"

"Oh, no need to worry now, unless you actually do have designs to corrupt my mother . . . you don't? Good."

Nayr grinned again.

Anger bubbled up in Anda's chest, like earthfire ready to erupt. "How dare you bring Sera into this."

Anda pushed his fury down. He grappled for control over his fierce protective instinct. Nayr's threats didn't matter. Soon they would be a million kilometers away, in another dimension, on another planet.

"Don't blame this on me, uncle." Nayr shrugged. "I'm the only one in all this with clean hands."

"You're a monster."

"I believe 'Tyrant' is the word they use now."

"So that's it, then? We can go?"

Nayr frowned and raised an eyebrow, as if to say, "Why not?"

Anda, unsettled, gripped Sera's hand and moved in the direction of the eastern entrance to in-mountain Meran, but they hadn't gone five steps before Nayr called out, with his addled voice, "Oh, I almost forgot."

He hopped up to them, laughed, and produced a small package. "I wanted to give this to you."

Anda gave the package a distrustful glance. It was flattish, cylindrical, and wrapped in paper, a profligate waste. Nayr turned it in his palm, and the paper made a happy, dissonant crackling sound.

"Oh, it's okay," said Nayr. "The paper has instructions on the inside, so it wasn't a total loss." He pushed the package toward Anda once again, with an encouraging nod.

Anda trusted his nephew's body language not one bit. "Instructions?"

Nayr grabbed Anda's wrist and plunked the package into his palm. The contents of the package rattled. "Yes, instructions for how to use them."

"What are they?"

Nayr shook his head in disapproval. "Silly, silly uncle. They keep the girl alive." He gripped Anda with a glare. "Go away, go far away, and if you ever come near my mother again, the nanos I put inside your body will tell me. Here on Dom. On the moon. On the White Planet. I'll know. And there will be consequences."

"You were never going to heal her, were you?" A shadow passed over Anda's heart, a cloud of enduring hate, seeds of revenge for which Anda had never before made a place.

"Go on then," said Nayr, "Go. Find your wife on the White Planet." He gave his wicked smile.

Anda sucked in his breath, and his visage hardened like deepest obsidian. "All this time, you knew. Did you send her there?"

"Imma?" asked Sera, her voice a whimper.

Nayr threw up his hands in mock apology. "It's a lot of work, running a planet. Must have skipped my mind."

Anda's veins pumped with fury. "Enjoy your sorry orgy of destruction and violence, Tyrant, because someday the people whose lives you ruin will hold you to account." Anda glowered and poked at his own chest. "I will make you pay."

Nayr laughed, a throaty, mocking guffaw. Then he spun and skipped to the other side of the street, his laughter trailing after him and his boots crunching over the cobblestones once again.

Anda held his daughter's hand, and Nayr disappeared into the air. From far away, it seemed, his cackle echoed through the empty streets: "I win! Ha, ha! I win!"

Sera squeezed Anda's hand, her eyes red and watery. Her lip quivered and she raised her elbow to her mouth, then her body convulsed with a cough, then another, and another. This was the worst fit she'd had, and they crumpled to the ground together, Anda helpless, unable to do more than cradle her shaking body.

Tears of rage and powerlessness burst down his cheeks.

Zharla hated abandoning her son and her fair city of Meran, but she had little left to give. She scrunched herself into a corner of floor between a seat and a bulkhead of a transporter en route to Mekele Eshel. She had on her black bioflauge combat suit, covered in a cloak and scarf ragged enough to convince anyone who saw her that she was no queen, but a destitute refugee in flight from danger. As Queen, she could never sit on the floor. Posing as a refugee, she had no other choice.

The intercity transporter system was packed nowadays, what with all the extraordinary security measures that Nayr took to keep the peace, after his fashion. Zharla understood why people were on the move. Some were even going to the moon. Some were fighting back. She'd heard the distiller exchanges across Meran the night before, before Ahrik showed up at the palace, and wondered if he had something to do with it.

Zharla had to move now. She couldn't be her son's captive any longer, and she couldn't be in Meran after the pain of Shahl's rejection. The eastbound transporter she rode was halfway between Meran and Mekele Eshel now, and her attention was fixed on the caller network display, scanning for some news about Ahrik or her son, news that he had chosen to make peace with the rebels that now faced him.

She knew her hope was vain, and the caller headlines showed only one story on a loop, about a terrorist attack on two of the twenty-four elevator stations. She did not believe it. After what she'd seen of Nayr's rule, she doubted anything on his networks. When she and Ahrik were in charge, at least the callers spoke with honesty about things that really mattered.

The transporter stopped at yet another small city, and even more people shuffled on. This was the first time Zharla had taken the local transporter from Meran to Mekele, and it took much longer than the ninety minutes she was used to on the express.

A man leading a young boy by the hand meandered in her direction and gave her a meaningful look. He motioned to the boy to sit beside her. Zharla scooted closer to the bulkhead, unaware that there was enough room on her speck of floor for another person, even if it was only a child.

She smiled at the boy and nodded at the man, taking in his foreign dress, more suited to the jungles around Peshron, across the sea. "Not from around here?" she asked.

His face took on a far-off look, sad with the memory of a life once lived. His shoulders slumped, and he stared at the floor by his son's feet. "Azrun."

Zharla cast her eyes down, then looked a question at the man. "Wha . . . what happened?"

His eyes narrowed with a glint of anger. "A few of us protested against the new security curfew. The *nayra* showed no mercy, nothing like when the Queen was still in charge." He choked up. "My wife and daughter were still inside our house when they demolished it, in retribution."

Zharla tried to smile. "I didn't mean to pry. I just—"

"And you?" He gave her a look that said he wanted to change the subject.

"Oh, me?" How much should she reveal? "I'm from Me—"

The transporter doors chimed and Zharla looked up. Just before the doors reformed, two of Nayr's clones slipped onto the transporter.

Everyone on the transporter went quiet. Zharla looked away, but she saw enough before she did. They were probably on patrol, armed with distillers, qasfina, extra kall packs, and various other implements of death and destruction. Their gear made them look older than their seventeen years, but their jocular tone revealed their true age. They weren't actively searching for anyone, but they'd recognize Zharla if they looked closely enough.

She couldn't afford to be caught. She had to get away.

If Nayr went off the deep end, she could rally her people as their Queen, but not if she was a captive to her son's ambition. If either of these two clones recognized her before she got away, she would be dead to her people, a useless figurehead. These clones probably already knew that she had escaped from their commander, their "father," as they called him.

The transporter set off again, and the man with the boy shuffled closer. "Where?" he whispered, as if the clones wouldn't hear.

Alarm flooded through Zharla. She frowned and gave an almost imperceptible shake of her head. What was he thinking? No one else would talk as long as those two clones stood near the door of the transporter.

Her alarm deepened when, out of the corner of her eye, she saw one of the clones glance in her general direction, then nudge his partner.

"Where did you say you were from?" the man asked again.

A few heads turned. The two soldiers pushed their way over. Zharla looked for a weapon, tried to get her feet under herself, to spring up and fight, if need be. If she could catch them unawares.

She was making a tremendous racket, shifting her legs like that. More heads turned. She felt eyes bore into her. The soldiers still made their way toward her spot near the middle of the transporter.

She pulled her scarf over her head in an old-fashioned sign of modesty. She hoped the man would take the hint and realize that she wasn't being rude, just quiet because of the clones.

"Mekele," she said, trying to give her voice a gruff, unroyal aspect.

She looked down to avoid the clones' gaze, and to her horror she saw a boot plant on the floor next to her own foot. The blood drained from her face. She felt lightheaded. As a matter of reflex, even though she recognized the insanity of doing so, she peeked up to see if the soldier had seen her.

He wasn't looking at her, but snarling at a woman and man sitting across the aisle from Zharla. The man had a sleeping child in his arms, and their dress marked them as clearly from Meran.

"You two," the soldier said, chuckling with his partner about something or other. He motioned at the couple with his distiller. "Up."

The woman began to protest, but the man nudged her and stood up, his face marked by fear. The child did not stir. The wife pursed her lips, but she stood as well, giving the clones an icy glare.

Zharla looked at the man from Azrun and realized what these clones were capable of. The couple might not be cognizant of the danger they faced, but she knew in her heart. She half-expected the clones to shoot them down right there, on the transporter, simply because the wife had looked at them wrong.

Zharla noticed one of the clones' qasfin clasp, dangling loose. His weapon was unsecured. She could reach out and draw it with no trouble at all, if she did it fast enough. But could she? She'd practiced many things, but not stealing the weapon of a clone with genetically-enhanced reflexes.

The couple jostled past, and the soldier's partner, muttering something to the couple about Merani trash, sat down in the seat the woman had just vacated. In the jostle for position, for a second or two, the clone's qasfin was right in front of Zharla's face. In one motion, she could whip it out, shove it into the soldier's hamstring, then leap up and hit the partner's jugular before coming back to finish the first soldier.

In those two seconds of fate, she closed her eyes and visualized how the engagement would unfold, just like she had learned to do before any fight. Her hand eased up toward the soldier's unsecured blade.

But then she felt a hand on her shoulder, the touch light but insistent. She froze, then looked up to see a young, maternal face peering into hers, full of recognition. Her weather-beaten cheeks and the black scarf with Merani tassels marked her as a working class out-mountainer from Zharla's hometown. She smiled, as if greeting an old friend. "We will help you."

The Merani woman raised her head and made purposeful eye contact with one, two, then three other passengers, all unassuming people who joined eyes with Zharla in that same spirit of recognition. Zharla felt equal parts elation and dismay, elation at discovering a hidden reserve force, dismay at realizing that her disguise was so thin.

The clone whose weapon she'd been about to steal shuffled away from her and sat down next to his partner. As he sat down, he nodded in the direction of the woman who'd just risen and said, without even trying to lower his voice, "Tuh bad she's taken, check?"

His partner chuckled, with the same brazen air. "Why should thut stop us?"

Both clones laughed. A pall of shocked disbelief fell over those within hearing distance. Many faces glowered at the open disrespect. Just a few weeks earlier, such a disrespectful comment about a woman would have been met with outrage by those in the transporter. But such was Nayr's reign of fear, where women could be trodden underfoot and no one could stop it for fear of being trundled off to the Black Eye, or worse, under suspicion of disloyalty.

Zharla, her blood simmering at the clones' insolence, narrowed her eyes and tried to think through the situation clearly. She surveyed the people around her. Those whose glances she'd exchanged earlier ignored her, for which she was grateful, but their faces had taken on a new sheen of discontent. She felt violence building on the air, but she had no way to communicate with them, no way to manage the conflict before it got out of hand and the two clones did something rash.

Would the clones hurt these passengers? She looked at the man from Azrun. Was his story true? Would her own sons' clones really bring a house down on innocents? If the passengers attacked the clones, out of hatred for acts like that, the clones would surely call for backup, which would make Zharla's escape even less likely. Zharla only had to get to Mekele, and from there stow away on an unregistered transporter bound for the Kereu, and Peshron. Ahrik could help her from there. He would know how to convince Nayr to back down, how to make him rethink his approach to ruling. It wouldn't take too much, maybe a battle or two.

The clones carried on, eyeing the people around them with a combination of disdain and hatred. Nayr's rule of fear was established enough that most people wouldn't dare challenge the clones' authority openly, but still young enough that a few people might just take the risk. Zharla wondered what her impromptu confederates had planned. After the clones' treatment of the young mother, the tension on the transporter was palpable.

She scanned the transporter again and looked at the confederates of the tassled Merani woman. Nayr's rule was about to be tested, at least in this transporter. She saw it in their faces, and worry settled in her gut like a large cat waiting to pounce, haunches tensed, gaze intent, foreboding. She gave the Merani woman an imploring look, hoping that the woman would see that Zharla didn't want violence on her account.

Then the transporter stopped. Zharla looked up in confusion. The transporter floated for a moment in its kall tube, then its auxiliary boson drive kicked in and it drifted toward the ground, some twenty meters below. As it descended, uncomfortable murmurs began to pervade the transporter, with the exception of the clones, whose jocularity did not abate. The Merani woman, her confederates, and everyone else in the transporter cast confused glances in all directions.

There was no station here, just open plain. Up ahead lay the main gate of Nayr's new headquarters, and beyond that the outskirts of Mekele.

The caller network feed went blank, and the driver of the transporter began to say something over the intercom, but it too cut off. Shortly, the passengers' attention focused on the clones. Something was up, and the clones knew what it was.

Zharla steeled herself. To fight, to run, to do whatever it took. Passengers began to whisper one to another, then to converse in louder voices. The Azruni man took hold of his boy's hand. He rose from his seat next to Zharla. The man's face grew pale as he cast his gaze toward the new headquarters, showing fear laced with determination, a disturbing mix.

Under the cover of the rising cacophony, the Merani woman leaned close, so close that her breath tickled the tiny hairs on Zharla's ear. The woman pretended to fasten her shoe. "There's a commotion at the main gate to the new base, up ahead. We'll give you a chance to get away."

Zharla motioned with her eyebrows to the clones then peered at the woman. "No violence."

The woman cast a knowing glance at her confederates, a look that said that fate would soon cast its dice. She shrugged, then leaned into Zharla again, as if fastening the other shoe. "We're not armed. They won't hurt us. Just get away."

Zharla felt as if a large cat sitting within her lifted off its haunches, beady eyes set on its prey, then took a baleful step forward. She reached for her handkerchief and tried to slow her breathing.

The conversations in the transporter neared a fervent level, no longer hushed. Zharla furrowed her brow and wondered if this was a cover for their attack on the clones. How many confederates were in league?

Zharla glanced through the translucent hull of the transporter. When the ground was three meters away, the door to the conductor's cabin opened and the conductor emerged, hand on his bald head, pudgy eyes wide with disbelief. The passengers hushed with unsettling suddenness, their breath bated on his next words, attention riveted on his every move. Even the clones quieted down.

"I . . . uh," the conductor said, but then simply shook his head in disbelief and looked at the passengers, then up at the ceiling, nothing but utter loss in his gaping mouth.

One of the clones cleared his throat. "We've stupped b'cause uv a dusturbance up ahead."

The transporter settled onto the wind-swept prairie grass. Its doors whooshed open. The breeze outside whipped by the openings, but Zharla still heard the gasps of shock and fright of those who looked out the doors, toward Mekele.

The young mother, the one whose husband held the sleeping child, put her hand to her mouth and clutched the door jamb, legs buckling. She looked at her husband. "No."

The conductor took a few more steps into the transporter's main cabin, stopped to listen, then pushed past passengers and out of the transporter door. The staccato chirp of distillers carried on the prairie breeze.

The cat within Zharla readied to spring. She craned her neck to see what was going on up ahead at the new headquarters, but the press was too thick. She looked through the hull of the transporter, toward Mekele Mountain.

The other clone clapped his hands together, and Zharla jumped. Everything felt sluggish, unreal.

"Wull, thut wuz fun," said the first clone, eyeing those around him and priming his distiller. Its threatening hum filled the terrified silence with a new, sinister sense of action.

"Everybudy out," said the other clone.

They knew. From their embedded compilers and their tendril link. They knew what horror transpired at the gate to the new headquarters, and they were going to kill everyone on this transporter to keep it secret.

The tassled Merani woman nudged Zharla with her knee and said, "Now."

The Merani woman nodded to her confederates and flung herself toward the clones, and the large cat inside Zharla leaped. The twisted horror of violence threatened to engulf her, but then instinct and muscle memory took over. She felt herself spring to her feet and hurdle the seat that the Merani woman had just vacated, pushing into the stream of passengers pulsing out of the transporter.

Hope burgeoned within her when her foot touched the windswept prairie grass outside the transporter, but then she looked in the direction that the transporter faced and something else entirely overcame her senses. Just at the next rise, where the road from Mekele met the main gate to Nayr's new headquarters, thousands of people screamed and scattered and ran for their lives. Red and orange tracers of fury and hate filled the air, emanating as if from nowhere. Her steps slowed. Her knees wobbled. Grief clutched her heart and tore it from its moorings. The other passengers ran from the violence up ahead, but Zharla stood with transfixed horror. The plains grew blurry in her eyes.

"Why, Nayr? Why?"

She fell to her knees and dug her fingers into the hard ground, ignoring the pain that lanced from her fingernails.

Then the shooting started behind her: *thu-thu-thunk, thu-thu-thunk*. The clones' distillers sounded hollow and distant inside the transporter, muffled by screaming passengers and the mass of bodies absorbing the deadly scrambler charges. Wails of pain leaked from the door behind her.

She slammed her fist into the ground. She could not leave them to die. But she had to. Their sacrifice would be in vain, otherwise. She leaped to her feet and ran, and hated every step, every divot she stepped in and every blade of long grass that whipped against her knees and shins. She hated herself for letting this happen, for letting her son become a maniac, for not protecting her people. She was responsible.

The *thu-thu-thunk* continued behind her. The wailing grew.

She oriented herself on the gate up ahead and flew on her feet, forcing down her regret and fear and anguish. Maybe she could save some of them. Tracers still streaked through the air, tempting her gaze like an evil lodestar, leading in the wrong direction. But she pressed on. Fear was nothing. Adrenaline fueled her flight, because she had no other source of strength or will except the desire to save her people. She screamed into the prairie wind, an inchoate, violent yearning for some other fate.

What more could she have done?

The shooting stopped, fore and aft, and wind and distance carried off the cries of the wounded and dying. When she got to the gate, lungs alive with fire, legs aflame, she fell to her knees and hammered the prairie grass with her fist, over and over. All around her, bodies lay, some writhing, most still, all unarmed, defenseless, a terrible monument to Nayr's tyranny. Her knuckles bled and her former self died a death for every person she should have saved, during all her years as Queen, and prior.

It was true. Nayr was the Tyrant.

A shuttle lifted off from the imposing needle tower at the center of the headquarters. She shivered, pulled her ragged cloak close about her. She recognized Nayr's shuttle. Zharla pined in her heart for the person she should have been, for the person she knew she no longer could be.

She remembered the small bag of pills that Ahrik gave her, and knew in an instant what she must do. If she could not convince Nayr of the error of his ways, at least she could send him a message. She engaged the cloaking mechanism on her bioflauge suit and set her steely gaze on the base of the needle tower at the center of Nayr's new headquarters, at the officers club where Nayr's most important clones congregated.

Nayr had brought some servants from the palace to serve there. They would help her. She knew it. Then she would find an unregistered transporter to Peshron, half a world away.

Anda took the carton of food handed to him and recoiled at the smell.

"Thut's the best you'll find 'round hure, luv," said the woman behind the counter, her voice thick with the in-mountain accent.

Sera tugged at his sleeve and coughed. "I'm hungry, Abbi."

Anda shuddered, then worked open the box to reveal a steaming hot mess of vegetables, pulse, and what must at one time have been meat. He smiled at Sera and made a hopeful gesture toward the box. "I got us some food."

They moved away from the food stand and found a spot of grimy ground to sit. Anda removed the disposable spoon from under the box and handed it to Sera, then reached into his pocket to extract the package that Nayr had given him. Sera had a coughing fit that afternoon, and he knew her little body couldn't take much more.

At least now people in bustling Shtera Umqi gave them a wide berth.

While Sera rooted around in the box for something edible, Anda unwrapped the package to reveal a small, cylindrical container made of dull, unassuming metal. Inside the wrapper, the instructions were vague: "One a day keeps the cough away."

Brow furrowed, Anda examined the container and pried open the lid with his thumbnail. It popped off easily, and inside Anda found a few pills, not many, only enough for about a week if Sera was to take one per day. His eyes frowned with worry. He wondered how long it took to get to the White Planet. Their refugee ship was leaving from a nearby launch tube in a couple of hours, but how long was the transit, and how long would it take to get healing care on the White Planet after they arrived?

"Abbi," said Sera, her voice raspy from coughing and her eyes red, "this doesn't taste good."

Anda scrunched his lips together in a gesture of evaluation. "Hmmm," he said, pinching a vegetable with his fingers and popping in his mouth, "that one didn't taste so bad."

He fought down the gag reflex and gave Sera an encouraging smile as he chewed with contrived gusto.

Sera smiled back, then coughed. Her eyes grew wide with the effort, as if another attack could be imminent.

He considered giving Sera a pill, but put the container back in his pocket, relieved, when she breathed deeply and picked up the spoon again. He would have to ration the pills, assuming they worked like Nayr claimed they did. Anda prayed to the Lady of the Emerald Moon that they would soon get Sera to the White Planet, and safety, where healers that truly cared could look after her.

That thin hope was all Anda could manage, with the scent of sweat and spice swirling around them in Shtera Umqi, the city's refugee transit center. People here passed from one moment of subsistence to another. The pain and loss pervading in-mountain Meran made it a threatening place for those loyal to Nayr. To the Tyrant.

Anda glanced around, as was his habit since fleeing captivity. No shiny distillers or glossy propaganda here. No boots and steel discipline, just filth and stench and the odd clutch of thugs enforcing what passed for law in the mountain depths, their rough-hewn truncheons dangling from their waists.

Sera wrinkled her nose at the food and handed him the box. Anda squeezed her shoulder, but didn't take the box. "You need to keep up your strength, Serit."

Her eyes fixed on Anda. She took another tentative bite and worked it around her mouth, like a dog working a bone.

"Serit, swallow." Anda dug the spoon into the opposite corner of the food and slipped a bite into his mouth, ignoring the unusual smell, chewing slowly. He needed to keep up his strength, too.

She took another bite, reluctant, but coughed after swallowing. A bit of food landed on Anda's bare arm, but he brushed it away quickly, before Sera could notice his disgust.

She wiped her mouth with the back of her sleeve. "Abbi, I'm not hungry anymore."

Anda pursed his lips. "You haven't eaten all day."

"Can you save it for later?"

Anda worried the food would be rotten later. He sighed in resignation, closed up the box, and stuffed it in his bag, where he knew it would only add weight. "Sure."

Anda hadn't eaten all day, either, but he suddenly had no appetite. He smiled at Sera, tried to be brave despite her rasping cough and tired, red-rimmed eyes. He needed to find Esh'a. She would know what to do.

He hugged Sera close, to keep her from seeing the worry lining his face. "Our ship leaves soon. I'm sure they'll have food there."

How many more lies would it take to keep her alive?

"Abbi, will we see Imma where we're going?" asked Sera, gathering up her *dubbi*, as if she could sense it was time to move yet again.

"Oh, yes," said Anda. "Imma will probably be waiting for us."

Another lie. If Esh'a were here with Sera, and he a captive on the White Planet instead, she would know how to handle this. She would know how to give Sera hope and the truth at the same time.

Sera beamed. "They'll have the *p'tera* flower on the new planet, won't they Abbi?"

And stroked his chin and hummed, as if he actually knew the answer to that question. He cocked his head. "Do you remember what it looks like?"

She squirmed with an excitement whose depths Anda could not fathom. "Oh yes, Abbi. Small groups of white or pink flowers on bushes up to my knees, just like you told me back on Moon."

He smiled at Sera once more, a gesture of deep pity. He had no idea what to expect when they arrived on the White Planet, or even if they would survive the trip. He shouldered his bag and held out his hand, eyes bright. "I think it's this way."

Just then, the lighting in the Shtera Umqi cavern changed, from the bright, bluish sheen of day to a faded puke green. Around them, people froze and looked up. "It never goes green," said one person. "Can *nayra* turn the lights green like that?" asked another.

Two thugs Anda had seen earlier ran past, truncheons at the ready. They also carried handheld explosive weapons, the kind that discharged slugs of metal using a chemical reaction, black and small enough to fit in the palm of one's hand. Anda had seen those weapons years ago, during the war. He'd even handled one once.

He didn't know those weapons still existed.

High above them, from the darkness of the gaping access tunnels, up near the roof of the cavern, came the hum of boson drives. Shuttles. And they were cloaked.

Anda guessed why they were here. His spine tingled.

"*Nayra!*" someone screamed.

Panic descended on the crowd. People rushed every which way, toward safety, toward loved ones, toward home. The market transformed from a sedate shopping district, packed with loitering refugees, into a chaos of human emotion. Fear. Uncertainty. Hate.

And battle.

From out of nowhere, shopkeepers and bystanders whipped out ancient weapons, long, black, and smelling of grease and sulfur. Like the bristles of a porcupine, the weapons of at least three dozen women and men trained on the roof of the massive cavern.

Under the bristles, the lesser fleas of humanity, those without weapons, scurried for cover. Anda almost wished he was armed. Almost.

Sera slipped her delicate hand into his. As if startled into action by the sudden movement of a predator, or of a shift in the wind, he sucked Sera up into his arms and ran toward the nearest tunnel. If the *nayra* had come for him and Sera, then it was bad, but if they'd come to slaughter those disloyal to the regime, then it was even worse.

As they crossed the thirty meters to the nearest tunnel, dodging discarded packs, scrambling bodies, and upended chairs, Anda saw, in his peripheral vision, weapons throughout the cavern easing back and forth in slow arcs, patient and disciplined. These were not mere civilians or thugs, then, but trained rebels. The shuttles up by the cavern roof were cloaked and shielded. The greenish light made the lurking shuttles very hard to see. If the Tyrant's clones didn't use tracers, it would be almost impossible to track them from the ground.

Only trained soldiers could last in such a deadly game of chicken. One wrong move, and it would turn into a massacre. The fighters on the ground crept toward the cover and concealment of abandoned shops and rocky overhangs. Neither side of the standoff could see the other well, but each knew the other was there, waiting, dangerous.

Anda and Sera reached the tunnel entrance, a haven compared to the threat of death swirling through the cavern. Anda felt the air close in. Whispers of panic and fear rippled up and down the frightened civilians huddled in the tunnel. Sera latched her arms and legs around Anda even tighter.

His eyes adjusted to the darkness. He patted her back. "It's okay, Serit."

Another lie.

A truncheon appeared in front of Anda's face, hovering over him like the shuttles in the cavern above. "Yuh. Stup here."

Anda didn't have a choice. The massive body attached to the truncheon blocked his way forward, and he wasn't about to go outside and play chicken with the Tyrant's clones. Sera started sobbing, and he rubbed her back. He scowled at the thug. "You're scaring my daughter."

The man narrowed his eyes, as if struggling to put a name to a face. "I know yuh."

Anda shifted Sera's weight to put his own body between the man and his daughter. He tried to make out the man's features in the darkness. "We need to get on the next refugee ship to the White Planet."

The man's face bloomed with disconcerting recognition. "Yur Shahl Jeber-li." He stroked his chin with one hand, but kept the truncheon raised with the other. "Thut makes yuh brother tuh Ahrik, th'king cunsort."

Anda froze at the sound of his birth name, and at his association with the palace. One more reason to go by Anda.

"Abbi—"

Anda shushed her.

"Ho, Blade," said the man to a companion, farther inside the tunnel. "Got us a catch. Shahl Jeber-li."

Blade whistled, then spoke into a bulky electromag in some sort of military code. Muffled chirps and squawks sounded back, too garbled for Anda to make out. "Hull," said Blade, raising an eyebrow. "One wunts 'em."

Hull smiled, revealing the missing teeth and withered gums common among in-mountainers. "Yuh two, fullow me."

Anda and Sera followed Hull deeper into the mountain, Blade trailing them, voices chattering out of his electromag the whole time. They wound through dim tunnels and switchbacks, doglegs and dips, until Anda was thoroughly lost.

"Ho, Blade," said Hull. "Whut news?"

"Stull circlin' utside. No shootin' yut."

They passed the rest of the journey in silence. They slowed as they approached another opening to the Shtera Umqi cavern. In the green light, Anda recognized that they were on the opposite side of the cavern from where they'd entered the tunnel.

Anda furrowed his brow with the calculations. They'd traveled roughly one kilometer through the tunnel labyrinth. A man, obviously a soldier, crouched near the entrance to Shtera Umqi, a grimy distiller trained up toward the cavern ceiling. Some sort of optical device was strapped to his forehead, the viewer down in front of his face. His well-worn bioflauge uniform would make him hard for the *nayra* to see without the benefit of silhouette, blending him into his surroundings.

"One," said Hull.

The soldier with the optical device snapped his attention toward them, then flipped up his viewer and smiled. "I'll be . . . Anda."

Anda cocked his head, then recognition hit him like a blast of wind. "Owin."

When Hull and Blade had said "One," Anda had thought it was a generic name for the commander, but this was Owin, the subcommander that Anda had fought under during the war. Owin was not only his *nom de guerre*, but the only name he'd ever had. That was how it went on Moon.

Like a flood, Anda remembered the pain and want and loss they had shared together, that special warrior bond that Anda thought he'd buried deep. But seeing Owin here didn't add up. He was from Moon, not Meran.

Owin moved toward Anda, one arm still stuffed inside his distiller. Always ready for battle. "Hill and Blade think you're the real Shahl Jeber-li, brother of Ahrik." He shifted the angle of his head warily. "I always figured you for a renegade clone."

Anda's conscience couldn't bear to face yet another lie. "My wife is on the White Planet. We need to get on the next refugee ship." Anda shifted Sera on his hip. "You could come with us, Owin. Moon is dying, and the Tyrant is killing Home."

Owin grimaced and stepped farther into the tunnel. He tugged up on a trouser leg to reveal a prosthetic limb. "I'm broken, Anda. I'm no good as a pioneer on a new planet, but I know evil when I see it." He dropped the trouser leg. "After the war, I made my life here in Meran, so when Ahrik started mustering forces to fight the Tyrant, I volunteered." He jammed his thumb in the direction of the shuttles circling like vultures in the cavern. "Ahrik sent me here to deal with them."

"You can take the man out of the army, but you can't take the army out of the man," said Anda.

Owin smiled and leaned close. "You said it." Owin waved a hand back toward the cavern and craned his head in Anda's direction. "Are they looking for you?"

Anda gulped. The question brooked truth, and Anda knew it. Anda's sense of mortality shivered up his legs. Only the thought of protecting Sera kept his legs from giving out. "I . . . uh . . . "

Owin grunted. "Don't answer that, but when things get dicey, and they're about to get dicey"—he pointed to the cavern—"you two get to the next tunnel and run like the sun itself is chasing you."

Anda nodded, his head suddenly light. Words escaped him. Battle loomed on the air, and in every one of Owin's fateful words.

Ragtag soldiers began to mull about near the mouth of the tunnel, just out of sight from the circling shuttles. Owin drew close to Anda, seemingly unsure of himself. "What happened to you after the war? You disappeared."

Anda looked past Owin, toward the cavern, as if it offered some sort of escape. "Look, I—"

Owin held up a hand and shifted his weight. "I don't want to pry. I was just killing time until"—his face brightened—"ah, here we are."

Anda realized how much of an interloper he must have seemed to his comrades during the war, all those years ago. Owin's calm was so effortless. Then again, maybe Owin didn't have a daughter to protect.

Owin motioned for them to move aside, and a woman and a man walked up the tunnel from the depths of the mountain, carrying a crate between them. They set it down, and immediately Hill, or "Hull" in the in-mountain dialect, jammed a tool into the top and pried it open. The lid clattered off, revealing long tubes, as thick as a man's calf, packed in wooden frames and sawdust. A wealth of wood, just to transport weapons.

Anda caught his breath. *These weapons are not from Home or Moon.*

The women and men around them split into teams of two, each with a tube between them, and slinked into the green dimness of the cavern. Blade and Hill looked on passively, awaiting orders.

"What're those, Abbi?" asked Sera.

Owin crouched down and grinned at her. "That's how we're going to keep you safe from the *nayra*." Owin looked at Anda as he rose to his full height. "With the *nayra* here, the folks on that refugee ship are antsy to launch"—he nodded at Hill—"but we'll send word that you're coming. They'll punch out as soon as you're on board."

"How can I ever thank you?"

Creases watered with fate formed at the corner of Owin's eye. "Just your being here gives us hope, Shahl Jeber-li. Hope for *cheret*."

Freedom. His courage was almost infectious. "I'm not—"

Owin offered his wrist. "I always knew you were more than you let on."

Anda touched the outside of Owin's wrist with his own. He knew what their escape would cost Owin and his women and men. A lump welled in his throat. He coughed it down. "Thank you."

Owin narrowed his eyes with confidence and lowered the viewer on his optical device. "Remember us."

Anda, with Sera clutched tightly in his arms, crouched next to the entrance to the cavern. The two-person teams snuck to their positions under deathly-still shop awnings and trembling wares. Owin crouched beside Anda, his distiller at the ready. "Surprise," he whispered, "is the best weapon."

Hill crouched in front of them and Blade behind, ready to spring. Owin nodded to someone in the cavern and trained his distiller on the roof of the cavern, or where, Anda presumed, one of the enemy shuttles floated through the air, like a vulture waiting to swoop.

From somewhere in the cavern, a red flare shot up. In the bright new glow, the shimmering outlines of three military shuttles glittered against the craggled roof. These weren't normal shuttles, though. Crew-served distillers poked from their hulls, and missile tubes lined the undercarriage. The only missiles Anda had heard of were armed with explosive weapons, the ancient, forbidden weapons. Sometimes atomics. His heart froze with terror. The *nayra* could bring down the entire mountain, on themselves if need be.

The shuttles answered the flare with their distillers—*thu-thu-thunk, thu-thu-thunk*—carpeting the cavern floor with matter scramblers, shredding stalls and filling the air with sizzling terror. The clones' charnel aim sparked cries of agony and shrieks of anger from below, but the fighters on the ground opened up with their own weapons, blasting light and fire.

The transporters' shields soaked up the fighters' puny projectiles. Anda's heart sank.

Then Owin pushed Anda out into the cavern. Anda took one last look, and Owin mouthed the word "*cheret*." As Anda launched himself toward the next tunnel, three of the long tubes spewed fire and three projectiles trailed flame on their way to their targets, up near the roof.

The sound was unlike anything Anda had heard before, like a giantess shredding rock with her hands. One of the projectiles found its mark, hitting the nose of a transporter. Anda yawned open his mouth against the impact, but the explosion still pounded on his eardrums and sent shockwaves down his spine. Sera shrieked and covered her ears. The other two projectiles glanced off their targets and careened away, harmless. Duds.

The transporters opened up with their missiles, just as Anda and Sera reached the tunnel. He heard three more tube projectiles screech toward the roof, but before they hit, the Tyrant's missiles thundered down. Anda and Sera flew down the tunnel and toward the waiting refugee ship, but all he heard was the din of a dozen explosions and even more shrieks cut short. A wave of heat overtook them. Behind them, Blade cried out, "Mera—"

Anda almost stopped, but Hill grabbed his tunic and yanked him forward. Sera shrieked on. The rumble of the cavern collapsing swarmed toward them from behind, like an earthquake waiting to suck them in. Up ahead, a refugee inside the hatch of the ship waved at them to hurry, his face wild and frantic. Dust billowed around Anda and Sera.

Hill must have heaved them aboard, because in an instant Anda felt themselves flung through one of the rear hatches on the refugee ship. The door, an old mechanical model, slid shut on its metal track, cutting off Hill's cry of agony. The sickening rumble of the cavern's collapse transformed into a backbreaking moan from Meran's bedrock.

Sera's shrieking died into silent fear at the otherworldly sound. Her look of utter helplessness tore at Anda's heart. He couldn't lie his way out of this one. They were going to die.

The ship's boson engine crescendoed to a furious hum and the transporter launched up through its tube. The boson field inside the transporter counteracted the acceleration, but the antiquated internal stabilizer system whined against the effort. Force pressed on Anda's chest, and he reached for Sera's hand.

With a *thunk*, they shot from the tunnel and into the open air above Meran Bay, but then a massive explosion filled the ship, or rather reverberations growled throughout its quivering structure. Silence filled the air and panic clutched his chest, as if these moments would be his last. But the ship's integrity held, and he didn't find himself plunging to his death in the water below.

Sera squeezed his hand. Her body shook. Through the surreal silence, she whispered, "Will we die before we see Imma?"

Anda chanced a look at the decrepit view display at one end of the cabin, the picture blurred and jerked, cycling between front view, rear view, and trip schematics. He gasped when the rear view flickered on. Meran Mountain, and the tens of thousands living there, was gone, replaced by a mushroom cloud clawing up toward the heavens.

12 Tension and Rest

INSIDE PESHRON MOUNTAIN, day blended into night, and night into day. Zharla felt the attack creep up on them like a beast of prey, salivating over the sweaty mass of refugees huddled in Peshron's central transporter station. Angry, earthborn thunder grumbled and pulsed from the belly of the mountain, *thu-wum thu-wum*, followed by a brief but agonizing silence. Then rock rippled under their feet, two tectonic waves of incomprehensible power, then utter silence turned every breath into a forbidding hell of anticipation.

The silence rattled in Zharla's mind. She dabbed her handkerchief to her brow and tried to take a deep breath, but the close air of hundreds of people huddled in the transporter station made breathing difficult. A collective hush settled over the mass of people each time a pair of tectonic waves passed. Zharla felt a powerlessness that no queen should ever feel, or any human, for that matter.

Her eyes wide with fear, she looked at Ahrik, next to her. He sat deep in concentration, directing the final preparations for the defense of the city. Heavy burdens lined his forehead, eyes shut tight against the pain his world held. His women and men, his paltry force, had scattered in-mountain and out-mountain in preparation for Nayr's onslaught. Could she apologize to her husband now, on the cusp of battle, beg his forgiveness for taking his brother back into her heart? She had failed to teach Nayr the way he needed to be taught. She had failed to avert war. She had failed to win Shahl back, and Ahrik's disdain was the cost.

"Ah'ke," she whispered. Her voice trembled, and she worried that those huddled around her would hear the terror in her voice, would thus succumb to their own worst fears. She realized, in those moments of sheer horror, just how insignificant she was, little more than a speck in the fabric of life. If her life ended now, its fabric ripped to shreds in some spasm of senseless violence, no one would take note.

Ahrik ignored her. He closed his eyes tighter still, held a finger on his earpiece, and whispered into his cupped hand.

She touched his arm and leaned close to whisper, so the refugees around them wouldn't hear. "Ah'ke, do we go further down, or up?"

He sighed from deep within his belly, like the last breeze of a once promising summer. He gazed at her, and his eyes said that he did not know where she should go, and did not care. He shook his head, a trapped beast coming to terms with a new reality. "Death lies in wait. Everywhere Nayr lays a trap."

Thu-wum thu-wum. Zharla clutched her handkerchief, looking up to see if the cavernous ceiling would hold, to see if these moments would be their last. The mountain rippled, but held, and she breathed once again.

Zharla gripped Ahrik's arm. With every part of her, she wanted to believe the words she was about to speak, to be braver than she felt. "We can do this."

Ahrik laughed, but cut off the laugh as his eyes gripped hers. "So brave? Let me tell you what your sadist of a son has prepared for us." A shadow passed across his face. "He will drive us up and out of the mountain with these tectonics, and when we're all out in the open he'll unleash the atmospherics. Very few will live, Zharla. Very few."

"Why is Nayr doing this?"

"Why not?" Ahrik shrugged. "He wants me dead, with all my clones. People bent on genocide don't stop to judge the rightness or wrongness of their cause, much less count the innocents who get in the way." He gave her a dead stare. "You set him on this path, Zharla. You told him who his father was. If you want to know why he's doing this, ask yourself why you did that." Accusation flashed into his eyes.

Zharla let her hand fall away from his arm and took a deep breath, in preparation for the fury that Nayr had in store. She closed her eyes and buried the guilt and pain that Ahrik's words bore. "We . . . I can do this. He won't hurt me, Ah'ke."

He stood and began to unhitch his distiller. "That's what I'm hoping for," he said, handing her his weapon. "You remember how to use this, right?"

She cocked an eyebrow at him. "I train, too, Ah'ke." She donned the distiller pack. "What's the plan?"

Ahrik nodded over Zharla's shoulder, and a patrol of Ahrik's soldiers appeared behind her. *Thu-wum thu-wum.* In the silence before the bedrock recoiled beneath them, he gestured to the two thousand or so people crouched in the transporter station, their nervous eyes darting back and forth. Ignoring the grumble that passed through the mountain, he said, "I can't keep them safe any more."

"Don't you dare give up," she said, standing up with an air of defiance.

Ahrik's shoulders slumped and he shook his head. "Someday I hope you'll understand me."

Zharla ran her eyes over Ahrik's soldiers, their eyes haggard and their faces hollow from fleeing the murderous Ketel of Nayr. She furrowed her brow. "Ahrik, where are your clones? Why do these soldiers have extra distillers?" She drew close to him, so only he could hear the hiss in her voice. "This is just like you, making decisions about us on your own."

Anger glinted across Ahrik's eyes. He pulled back and shrugged another distiller pack onto his shoulders, his glare fixed on her. "'Us', Zharla? 'Us' died when you told Nayr I wasn't his father. 'Us' died when you gave your heart to my brother, after I thought I didn't have to worry about that anymore." He looked away and sighed with frustration. "I'm not sure there ever was an 'us'."

Her throat grew thick and her vision blurred. Two decades of memories hit her like a wave of cold pain. Before she knew what was happening, her fist lashed out, but Ahrik dodged it and clamped a hand on her wrist. Guilt flushed up from her toes to her head, then anger, then pain as he squeezed. He narrowed his eyes at her in cold defiance.

The soldiers froze, eyes averted. A few people in the crowded transporter station gasped and exchanged furtive murmurs. A new, deafening silence rang in Zharla's mind. "Ah'ke," she said. "You're hurting me."

He released his grip. His face made clear that he thought she had tried to hit him for the last time. "Save your violence for those who deserve it, Your Majesty."

His words cut deep. They had a special love, once, but he'd just made clear that she was fully to blame for the state of their marriage. Anger mixed with her regret. He also bore some of the blame.

Ahrik adjusted his pack. "This is where I say either that I'm sorry, or that I wish you had chosen to marry my brother instead of me all those years ago." He shook his head with an air of pity and disdain. "Look at you. All you ever wanted was not to be like your mother, but here you are."

"I . . . I'm sor—" A sob broke off her apology.

Ahrik scoffed. "If you were really sorry, Zharla, you wouldn't have left a place in your heart for my brother." Ahrik looked away and his shoulders slumped with weariness. "My soldiers have melted an escape tunnel to the northwest. There's an old transit station about five kilometers from here. You'll see it once you get out-mountain. That's the rendezvous. I sent the distress call to Renla. She will extract any survivors." He gave a look that Zharla couldn't interpret, anger mixed with pity and determination. He nodded at the weapon he'd given her. "Keep that distiller primed. Goodbye, Zharla. Have a good life, maybe with my brother, maybe with the few minutes remaining to us."

He loped off, but instead of going toward the rendezvous point with Renla, he set off in the opposite direction, picking his way through the crowd. At the opposite end of the transporter platform, he turned and, over the heads of the frightened, huddled masses, he cast her a look of finality and utter pain, then melted into the gloom of Peshron's tunnel network. His departure was so sudden that it only just dawned on her how deeply she felt his absence. A cavity yawned open in her core and swallowed her heart. Was she really no better than her mother, scheming, controlling, violent?

A shuffle of feet yanked Zharla back to the present.

"Ma'am . . . er . . . Your Majesty?" A soldier stood with her feet planted shoulder width apart, her hand shafted into her distiller in a way that suggested she wasn't quite comfortable with the weapon yet. "Need help with that distiller, Your Majesty?"

Zharla pursed her lips in annoyance and shoved her arm all the way into Ahrik's distiller. She eyed the soldier. So young. Her insignia said she was the patrol commander. Zharla nodded toward the other woman's weapon. "How many people have you killed with that thing?"

Thu-wum thu-wum. Rumble.

"I . . . this is my first real action, Your Majesty. I just came from an immigration policing tour with the 11th—"

"Renla's Fighting 11th?" Zharla grimaced. "I want to see her again before I die, so get your patrol into that crowd and arm anyone with military or peace forces experience."

She spun toward the crowd and took a deep breath, intent on preserving as much of her dignity as she could. Now was the time for action. "People of Peshron, you've lost loved ones, and your home is crumbling beneath you. Be strong. If any of you have military or peace forces experience, take a distiller. When we get out-mountain, keep moving forward. No matter what you see, or what stands in your way, keep moving forward."

Thu-wum thu-wum. Rumble.

Another of Ahrik's motley patrols appeared at the other end of the platform. Zharla nodded to the two patrol commanders, one fore and one aft, then turned to the crowd. "Follow me."

Zharla's gut fluttered as they trudged out of in-mountain Peshron. Her legs felt weak, but not from the climb. When she thought no one else was looking at her, she took out her handkerchief and dabbed at her eyes. Guilt and abandonment and thoughts of what could have been coursed through her mind. She tried to suppress her emotions, to live in the present, but she couldn't.

At least at the front of the column, no one could see the tears stain her face.

The keening wind howling through the tunnel ahead said that they were almost out-mountain. Thunder rolled, far away, and Zharla knew that what waited for them outside the mountain was little better than what lay behind them. She stole a glance at the young patrol commander climbing the incline beside her. The commander's eyes were wide, her fear plain for all to see.

"Commander," said Zharla, sniffing, "don't let them see your fear."

Thu-wum thu-wum. Then, instead of the rumble they had grown to expect, a sickening, massive crack echoed throughout the mountain. Dust drifted down on them from the roof of the tunnel, and someone in the rear of the crowd began to scream. Then the whole mountain shook. Not a momentary shake, like before, but a sustained, demoralizing chain of convulsions that rose like an earthen seizure from the depths of rock below them.

Zharla and the patrol commander exchanged a frantic look. "Run," said Zharla.

She rounded the bend at a sprint and saw the mouth of the tunnel gape before them, a swirling gray-green gullet waiting to swallow them. Zharla fought down the urge to flee from the howling monster up ahead and sprinted forward and stopped at the tunnel mouth, its edges ragged as fangs, then turned to usher people out. "Move!"

Out-mountain, deep green storm clouds hovered above, emptying lashes of rain upon the world. A vortex of wind whipped over and around her bioflauge combat suit, drowning out her exhortations to keep the crowd moving forward. Lightning slashed and thunder roiled, within her breast it seemed. Static electricity menaced the air, the smell of ozone swirling.

The convulsions from the mountain grew stronger, the sound from Peshron's innards almost deafening. The faces of those passing her showed panic. Mothers and fathers gripped children and lifted them from the ground. They ran, faces slathered with fear. Even those holding distillers wore expressions of utter helplessness.

Zharla peered back down the tunnel to see how many were left to come out, and to her horror the roof of the tunnel began to flex and cave in. Dust billowed out of the darkness at the bend in the tunnel. A wave of liquefied rock crashed from the tunnel ceiling, engulfing the trailing patrol of Ahrik's soldiers and the refugees straggling just ahead of them, cutting off screams of panic and wails of children. Zharla's legs felt like they were made of gneiss and her mind of the same sludge that cascaded toward her from the ceiling. An instant passed in a lifetime, as if she had stepped out of time to witness horror and murder spawned in another reality. The inverted wave of rock flew at her, inexorable, ferocious, but all she could do was stare, helpless.

A hand gripped her arm and yanked her into the flailing storm. The jolt shook Zharla back to awareness. Pebbles pelted her legs and boots as she fell backwards, and a slurry of black basalt met her as she landed, hard, and slid down out-mountain Peshron's lower slopes.

Zharla came to rest on a pile of slag, riven with streams of ice water. Pain washed over her as the adrenaline wore off, then a shock of cold air tore into her lungs. Pebbles still rained over her body. A tinny whine rang in her ears, from the wind. In the greenish light, she could not tell if it was night or day.

She groaned away the ache in her body, then opened her eyes. The young patrol commander lay next to her. Blood streaked down the patrol commander's forehead, the blood driven by rain, and she gasped with pain. Around them dozens of people staggered down the slope through the driving rain. Rain. Pebbles weren't falling on her. They had escaped a crumbling mountain to face a brutal rain storm, driven by an unseasonably cold gale. Lightning and thunder snapped and cracked through the roiling storm, above and around and within them.

The once-solid mass of Peshron mountain quivered behind her, then collapsed from the inside out. Their world shook, and the earth itself groaned and gnashed. She wondered if Ahrik had made it out.

She shook the thought from her mind and focused on the present. Peshron was tropical. This winter storm was off by at least forty degrees latitude and four months. Nayr's atmospherics. After the rumble and tectonic agony behind them subsided, refugees from Peshron's transporter station began to slow and hunker down.

"Don't stop!" she shouted. She knew the storm would only get worse. She worked herself into a crouch and scanned the sky for interceptors, almost impossible to do with the wind and rain, now driving almost horizontally off the ocean. Nayr's men could attack at any moment from that thrashing sky. Zharla looked out to the northwest and shivered. Through the snarling storm, she thought she saw a clearing in the jungle. The rendezvous point.

"Your Majesty?"

Zharla looked down at the patrol commander, who stared at the ground two meters away. A darkened body lay half concealed by the black slag, a distiller hanging slack by its side.

Zharla slid down next to the body and examined the body's face and uniform markings. The skin was black, but not burned, the face frozen in a rictus of horror. "This is one of Ahrik's clones," she shouted against the storm. Zharla looked up at the patrol commander. "What happened to him?"

The commander wiped the blood from her forehead and crouched down, a sigh in her shoulders. She drew close, so Zharla could hear. "Commander Ahrik didn't tell you before he left, Your Majesty? Nayr deployed a gene-encoded nanoweapon that does this. We think it targets him and his clones." The patrol commander cast her gaze down. "He was worried about endangering you and the others, so he left by another way."

Zharla let this sink in, mixing regret with regret, then looked out toward the rendezvous point. Rain poured through Zharla's hair, and the cold air numbed her body to the bone. Keep moving. "Commander, organize these people into groups. We need to get to that rendezvous point."

The sudden crack of a sonic boom carried over the storm. At first Zharla thought it was thunder, then she looked up and saw an interceptor. As soon as it appeared, another boom whipped through the air and the interceptor was gone. Zharla looked to the side and to her horror saw the patrol commander slump forward with a sigh, half of her head missing from an interceptor's distiller charge.

A sense of imminent doom assaulted Zharla's awareness, and sadness at not being able to give the patrol commander a proper burial. "Groups of six, two distillers to a group! Move!"

She trudged through the wet slag and led her people into the jungle, every step harder than the last.

Renla's eyes grew wide with awe. Her shuttle raced low over the surface of Dom, on her way to answer the distress call from Ahrik. Since attacking the elevator station, Renla, Lyn, and the Fighting 11th had prepared their defenses for Nayr's inevitable reprisal.

The reprisal didn't happen, at least not in the way Renla had expected. Now she saw why.

The entire mountain of Peshron was under attack. Ahrik and Zharla were supposed to make a stand at Peshron, but the distress call said nothing about this. Renla felt it in her heart. Peshron was doomed, and the rebellion against the Tyrant fared little better.

"Two," Renla commed to Lyn in the other shuttle as they skimmed over the planet's surface, "confirm large cloud formation approaching Peshron, over."

Peshron was in a tropical area, its mountain of black basalt jutting out of dense green jungle. Since the cataclysm of The War, over two thousand years earlier, when humankind fled to the safety of the mountains, all Doman urban centers were situated under solid peaks like Peshron. The area had monsoons, but nothing like the wall of dense gray-green fury speeding off the ocean now. Lightning flashed through the slate murk, ominous tentacles of violence reminding all who beheld it of nature's power.

Of Nayr's power.

"Check, one," answered Lyn, the transmission warbling with interference from the storm. "It's moving fast." A burst of static filled the channel for a beat, then Lyn's voice returned: "...not natural."

It was easy enough for Renla and Lyn to slip two small shuttles, cloaked, through the planetary cordon, but it was quite another to find Zharla and Ahrik in this storm. This rescue wasn't going to be easy.

An interceptor screamed onto Renla's schematic from the west, paused for a moment near the base of Peshron, then screamed off to the east, right into the storm. Their transponders said they were Nayr's, probably hotshot pilots showing off how they weren't scared of the weather.

Renla was definitely scared of the weather. She just forced herself not to worry about it. "Two, that was the third interceptor we've seen on our scopes. Any indication they know we're here?"

"Negative, one. Each one... over the speed of sound . . . interval regular . . . every three minutes."

Renla's shuttle pilot approached and set down on one side of Peshron mountain. As planned, Lyn's shuttle made for the other side. Renla set the sensors to scan and opened the channel to her two. "Once the eye of that storm hits, we'll lose voice comms. Find Quarry Alpha and Quarry Beta. Meet at the rally point if anything goes wrong. Ping me every five minutes, one high energy burst if you haven't found them, two if you have. Confirm, over."

Only static answered her transmission. Rain lashed the shuttle's forward hull. A howling wind rocked the shuttle back and forth, and the pilot gave Renla a worried look. Renla ignored her pilot's worry and stood, checking her qasfin and gripping a handhold, one eye on the sensors scanning the exit from Peshron, searching for signs of human activity.

A basso hum reverberated through the mountain beneath them. The hum rattled the hull, then stopped, as suddenly as it had begun. Then it came again, a growl from deep inside the earth, gurgling up through Peshron mountain.

Renla bit her lip.

The pilot furrowed his young brow. "Tectonics?"

Renla nodded, slowly. The frequency of the tremors would tell them how long they had. Unease snaked into her chest, a fear that all the effort and all the life frittered away so far would be for naught. Renla knew atmospherics and tectonics only as rumor. How could her rebellion withstand such unbridled power?

Renla shuddered off her fear. They would keep fighting, no matter the odds. This war was about freedom and the human spirit, about living without regret. Whether in life or death, they would be free.

But death was coming. She felt it.

Yes, she'd used atomics first, before Nayr used them, but she'd done it to pull down tyranny, not prop it up. And against a purely military target. Her blood boiled at the thought of Nayr using her attack at the elevator station to justify the coming atrocity. These were his own people.

Or, they used to be, for the Lady's sake.

Pity for the lives that Nayr was about to snuff out clawed at Renla's chest. She rued her part in this infernal war and her helplessness to stop the violence. She had to keep fighting, though, even if the whole world died around her.

How war cheapened life.

The pilot turned to face Renla. "Ma'am, didn't they ban tectonics and atmospherics after what happened in the last war, at Hof Chelek?"

Renla scowled and nodded. The Tyrant was about to massacre thousands, maybe tens of thousands. For nothing.

Lightning flashed. Thunder echoed across the sky. The air around the shuttle sizzled with electric energy. Renla looked at the sensor readouts on her schematic. They were all over the place. Useless in this storm. They should at least have registered the soldiers defending the exterior of the mountain, most of them the straggled remnants of Ahrik's ketel, his few remaining clones and a collection of other soldiers from here and there. She locked her distiller into its rack near the bulkhead, then grunted. Distillers were dangerous in an electrical storm. "I'm going out."

"In this?" the pilot asked, making as if to follow. "I'll go with—"

"No," said Renla, cutting him off. Did the pilot realize how little time they had before Peshron became nothing more than a hole in the ground? She'd heard of tectonics and atmospherics, but she'd never witnessed what they were capable of. "Keep the boson drive primed. I'll be right back. Dig on."

"Dig on," answered the pilot.

A rush of cold air and waves of rain washed over Renla when she exited the rear hatch. In the time it took her combat suit to adjust to the unexpected elements, water ran down her back and numbness crept up from the end of her nose. The slate sky lent a forbidding, green hue to the terrain. Darkness descended as the storm thickened over the black basalt. She flexed her fingers inside her gloves and trudged over the loose volcanic soil of Peshron mountain, made looser by the driving rain. Pretty soon, none of this would matter, for Peshron lived on borrowed time.

Renla made her way down, toward one of Peshron's two main exits. Then another pair of tectonic grumbles rippled through the ground beneath her feet, as if to accentuate how little time remained. Renla tried to keep a clear mind as the questions mounted. Why hadn't the defenders hailed her, or at least challenged her? What did Nayr hope to achieve by leveling Peshron? Where were Ahrik and Zharla?

Through the wind and rain, Renla caught movement off to her right, not five meters distant. Visibility was so bad, she couldn't make out anything beyond that. A voice, young and afraid and male, challenged her through the whipping storm. "Halt."

Thunder clapped overhead, drowning out anything else the challenger may have said. Renla froze and waited for the challenge word, so she could give the response. Panic clutched her throat when she heard a distiller prime. Renla had no choice. She shouted the challenge word through the rain, hoping to avoid disaster. "Tunnel!"

"Rat," came the response, but the young soldier didn't power down his distiller.

Renla dove away, yelling, "Power dow—"

Lighting struck with an ear-splitting crack. The air buzzed with static electricity. The hair on Renla's neck stood up. She crawled toward the young soldier, hoping to find him alive, digging her elbows and knees forward over the slurried earth, frantic.

The mountain shook once again, an ominous *thrum-thrum*. Rain whipped and roiled. Renla got to the young soldier's foxhole to find a pair of boots melted to the ground, planted as if to convince any intruder that he was braver than he felt. Shards of carbon composite lay scattered in every direction. The remains of the young soldier's distiller. The distiller's microcore lay on the ground beside his left boot, thankfully intact. Not even a lightning strike could rupture a microcore.

Why hadn't the soldier kept his wits about him? Surely he knew the dangers of operating a distiller in an electrical storm. Her eyes wandered around the rough foxhole, a shallow cavity in the loose soil, about two meters in diameter.

Renla squinted into the rain. Twisted branches lay on the far side of the foxhole. She scrambled over, curious. There was no vegetation this high on Peshron mountain.

She stopped short. It was a person. She got close enough to recognize the facial features, blackened but intact. Despair opened in her stomach. Ahrik. She ripped off the blackened figure's gear to expose rank markings, and relief flooded her chest. One of his clones.

That would explain why the young soldier was rattled. His older buddy was fried to a crisp by . . . something. She examined the blackened form more closely. None of his clothing or gear were burned, just his visible skin. She tore open his uniform to reveal more blackened flesh, bubbled and knotted. The clone's face bore a look of horror. She brushed water from her eyes and cocked her head. He hadn't been burned, but eaten up from the inside. Renla's heart broke to think of the agony this man must have experienced upon his release from mortality.

She squeezed her eyes shut, then looked away. Her tears mixed with the rain. What could have done something like this, and why hadn't the young soldier fallen victim to the same fate?

The mountain rippled underneath her again, two more pulses of imminent violence. Helplessness washed over her as the ground shook, then receded as quickly as it had come, when she realized that the mountain would not collapse beneath her after all.

Lightning flashed once again, and she cast her eyes up the mountain, from where she'd come. The burst of lightning silhouetted the shuttle against the crest of the mountain. She checked the orientation of the foxhole. If she got back to the foxhole, she could get back to the shuttle.

Renla took another step down the bleak slope, then crouched in fear as a disembodied howl cut through the storm, a sound so unearthly that Renla thought, for a moment, that she'd imagined it. The howl pierced the artificial murk once more, and she knew it had to be real. Even through the swirling wind, she could tell that the sound came from downhill, closer to Peshron's eastern entrance.

She half-slid, half-trudged in the direction of the shriek, sending cascades of slimy basalt down the mountain with her. Where her feet stabbed the earth, rivulets of muddy water formed to memorialize her passing, if but for a moment.

The wail broke through the storm once again, just as the wind became fiercest. A mighty clap of thunder hammered down. Out of instinct, Renla crouched to the ground.

Through the thunder, the wailing continued. Either this man was wounded and fighting off death, or his soul had nothing left to give. She knew this pain, pain that could cause such loss, could drive a man to such agony.

The storm's fury began to lessen. Not die, but lessen, in a way that told Renla the eye was passing. The mountain convulsed with two more rippling tremors, these just slightly stronger than the last. Renla estimated that only five or six tremors remained before the end, a baleful prelude to holocaust. If she hurried, she could get back to the shuttle in the time it took for three tremors to pass.

She had to hurry.

Renla came upon the source of the wailing, a man staggering around the mountain, piling up something on the ground. As she drew close, through the wind and rain she saw what he carried, then fought the urge to vomit.

The blackened forms of some twelve men lay in a row. The man went from foxhole to foxhole lifting out the remains of soldiers and setting them down in one last formation, the bitter climax of duty. All the while, he screamed at the storm. She made out one word, over and over: "Nayr."

She knew who it was even before she saw his face, from the familiar way he moved and the pain in his voice. He carried his dead clones, the ones he used to call his sons, to their eternal repose in the Lady's embrace. He cared not for the physical danger he faced, for the storm, nor for the mountain about to crumble underneath him. He cared only for his sons.

Renla refused to see him die like this. She plunged toward him, her feet sinking into the shifting sludge. She slid to within two meters of him and screamed through the howling wind, "Ahrik!"

He set down the body he carried at the end of a long row, then turned and pulled up short, as if he were about to go out on some errand but was surprised instead by someone confronting him in the street, asking about the weather.

A sardonic smile broke on his face, then he sneered at Renla. "For *me*? Why have you come for *me*?"

He rushed at her and beat at her arms and chest, but his efforts produced little effect, after weeks of weary flight and malnourishment, chased by Nayr's drones.

The ground pulsed with tremors once again, but Ahrik ignored them. He staggered back and thrust a finger at the row of blackened bodies. "*They* are the ones that needed saving."

Renla reminded herself in which direction the shuttle lay, then widened her stance. "We have to go. Now!"

He sprang at her again, clothes whipping on his slight frame. Thunder clapped, stroking the sky with fury. Ahrik rammed his shoulder into her, but she had the advantage of higher ground and full meals. He bounced off and landed on his rump, stunned.

Then, as if nothing had happened and Renla had never appeared, a stony glaze overcame his face and he worked himself onto his feet, to continue his macabre errand.

Renla reached for her qasfin. "You'll thank me for this."

She slammed the hilt of her blade onto his temple. He crumpled in a heap of weathered clothes and bony limbs.

She sheathed her qasfin and clambered downhill of him, then heaved him onto her shoulder. For a while, they made good progress toward the shuttle, the mountain shuddering once more, but then the slope steepened. She leaned into the incline and attacked the loose basalt with her boots, pace quickening. Her thighs burned with a fiery ache, but she pressed on.

The mountain shook violently underneath them again, this time convulsing with new vehemence. Renla realized with a sudden rush of panic that she'd lost count of the tremors. How long before disaster struck?

Renla slashed the ground with each frantic step. Ahrik's weight burdened her, but the violence of the wind and rain lessened, so she felt like her pace had quickened. She looked up to find that the storm had passed enough for her to see the shuttle's silhouette against the mountain crest, without lightning. She clenched back the curse that made to burst from her chest. The shuttle rested twenty degrees to the right. She corrected course, assaulting the last fifty meters of ground.

The mountain groaned, and Renla heard a monstrous crack, like bones snapping deep within a behemoth.

Forty meters.

She screamed out against the panic and the pain in her legs. The mountain shuddered and quivered.

Thirty meters.

The pilot's head popped out of the rear hatch, a look of confusion and worry on his face. The ground rippled as deep, angry growls coursed through it. *Thrrrum. Thrrrum. Thrrrum.*

Twenty meters.

The pilot's head reentered the shuttle and, after what seemed an eternity, the rig began to hover just off the ground. Renla climbed with greater fury, ignoring how much the shifting ground slowed her progress.

Ten meters.

Far below her, something gave way, like a titan beast giving one last gasp of air. The ground dropped by about a meter, making the shuttle look like it had lifted. Renla screamed once more and threw Ahrik through the rear hatch. She leaped with all her might just as the ground fell away beneath her. One hand found a hold on the jamb of the hatch, but the other missed. Instead, it flailed in the storm behind her.

Renla didn't have to look down to feel yawning emptiness beneath her, where Peshron mountain had once been. They had to get away before the mountain impacted on itself. Who knew what kind of force the debris field would contain?

"Go, go, go!" she yelled at the pilot.

She heaved against the hatch jamb, but the force of upward acceleration kept her from grabbing on with her other hand. Panic stabbed at her chest as she realized that the inertial stabilizer field would only counteract acceleration if she were fully inside the shuttle.

With one hand whipping behind her, she struggled to maintain her grip. One, then two fingers came free of the hatch jamb. Renla pressed her eyes shut and prepared to meet fate. She had saved Ahrik. Perhaps that was enough. Dig on.

Her last fingers slipped away from the hatch jamb. She felt weightless for a split second, that elation just before the final flight to the everlasting realm.

But she did not fall. A hand gripped her wrist, fingers curling and tightening. She felt a yank, a life-giving tug of hope, and then new power in her limbs and heart. She heaved her flailing hand around to search for better purchase on the hatch jamb, with the feeling that she might just cheat death. A hand closed around that wrist, too, and a new, guiltier feeling overcame her, one of knowing that her perfidy against death was complete, that she was, for the time being at least, invincible.

The two hands pulled her up, and she came face-to-face with the pilot and Ahrik, their faces red and puffing from the effort of working against acceleration.

They dragged her the rest of the way into the rear cabin, and the hatch reformed with a hiss. Renla sucked down air for a few beats, grateful to be inside the inertial stabilizer field, grateful to be alive.

An ear-splitting screech keened through the shuttle. Adrenaline rushed into Renla's veins and her senses lurched to alertness. Confusion reigned for a moment, then silence, then comprehension as she understood what was happening. Lyn's ping. Every five minutes. One ping if she hadn't found them, and two if she had. Had the message gotten through before they were cut off, after all, or had Nayr and his drones found some new way to confuse and defeat them?

A disconcerting silence followed. Fully aware now, Renla sprang to her feet and rushed to the cockpit. She yanked open the electromag channel and said, "Two, do you copy? We have Quarry Beta, over."

She turned to the pilot. "Send two pings."

The pilot complied, then stabilized the shuttle's trajectory and maneuvered to a weaker part of the storm to improve the transmission. Ahrik plopped down in the navigator's seat, his gaze fixed on the electromag receiver. Renla bit her lip. After so much destruction and death, they could claim victory today. She shook her head. Only if they had the Queen.

For two hours they circled around the hole that was Peshron, looking in vain for survivors in the dense jungle and trying to hail Lyn. Then, as if out of the ether, the electromag sizzled to life. "One, this is two." Joy suffused Lyn's voice. "We have Quarry Alpha. Waiting at rendezvous point. One enemy interceptor is down. Expect enemy to reinforce. Hurry, over."

"Copy, two. ETA"—Renla glanced at the pilot, who held up one finger—"one minute." Renla beamed, her voice brimming with the swell of victory, but tinged with the pain of the thousands who lost their lives at Peshron. "Dig on."

"Dig on," crackled Lyn's voice in reply.

Renla closed the channel and slumped in her chair. If Peshron weren't a mass grave now, she would have pumped her fists in victory. Keep fighting. Dig on.

Ahrik sighed and turned to her, his head hung low, elbows on knees. He rubbed the side of his head, where Renla's qasfin had struck. "Thank you for saving me, Renla."

She nodded. "You would've done the same for me, sir." She eyed him with care. "Sorry about your head."

"Is that you say in the 11th? Dig on?"

Renla chuckled. "Dig on. Now to get you and the Queen to Moon, then to the White Planet. Somewhere you can fight back against the Tyrant on your own terms. Check, sir?"

"Check, Renla." Ahrik cast a longing look back toward his clones dead in the rubble of Peshron. "First," he said, weakly, using his own ketel's battle call.

Then Ahrik slumped in the navigator's seat, unconscious.

Renla gave a grim smile and propped up his head, her mood dark at the slaughter and destruction she'd witnessed, then uttered the response: "To the fight." Her eyes moist, she clicked on the electromag, "Two, as soon as we get back to Station Prime, we need to start charging that rail gun."

The voyage had begun in shock and silence. Anda had gazed at the other refugees and read only fear and sorrow in their faces. All eyes had stayed glued on the atomic mushroom cloud in the rear view display as the rickety refugee ship pulled away from Meran and Home.

Now Sera shivered beside him. Anda pulled her closer, as much to comfort the disquiet wracking his soul as to keep her warm.

They all had reason to fear. The ship they rode in was little more than a collection of metal boxes bolted together, with a boson drive slapped on the back and an automatic pilot to guide them. It didn't have a human crew, or energy shields, or defenses of any kind. If they met any of the Tyrant's forces between Home and the portal, they'd be space flotsam before they could say "White Planet."

When they were two hours out, the trip information view on the display in their deck of the rig began to show time to destination and distance travelled. They hadn't stopped accelerating since they launched, to hit the portal at maximum speed. An hour later, once the destructive cloud over Meran became indistinguishable from the rest of the planet's surface, most of the refugees lost interest and withdrew into quivering clusters of fright.

"I'm cold, Abbi," said Sera, with the same sense of fear that pervaded their cabin.

Anda put up a brave front. "Try to sleep, Serit. We'll be there soon."

Or we'll be dead. He'd heard the rumors, just like everyone else on Home confronted with the prospect of flight to the White Planet: the Tyrant's clones lurked in the space between the portal and Moon, hunting for unarmed, unsuspecting ships like theirs.

Then they were about to pass by Moon. Anda watched the display cycle to the trip information schematic. They'd reach the portal in five minutes, five long minutes that would decide if they'd be free, or dead.

The display cycled to the front view, and Anda's breath caught in his throat. The portal cleared Moon's horizon, showing a thousand scraps of metal caught in the eddies of the portal's weak gravity well, meandering among one another in uneasy vectors. Slanting sunlight danced over the space flotsam, like the glittering play of sunset on a rippled mountain lake.

"Look!" said a child on the other side of the cabin.

Anda's heart sank. The child didn't understand what this was.

"It's pretty," Sera whispered, from her place nestled against the bulkhead.

All around the cabin, parents shushed children, and soon enough the children gathered the unspoken message, that their parents' silence was not born of awe, but of reverence for the dead.

"Yes, Serit," said Anda. He didn't have the heart to disabuse her innocence. They likely had little time left anyway. Let these be moments of beauty, not fear. Anda squeezed his daughter's shoulders. "It's quite a sight, isn't it?"

With the rest of the adults in the cabin, Anda pegged his eyes to the display. Their death sentence would come as a small blip moving toward them at attack speed, missiles primed and target locked. None of them had exosuits, so a main hull breach would probably kill them all.

And Anda didn't trust anything on this death rig to work properly. He wondered why he'd brought Sera at all, asked himself if they'd have been better off staying on Home. Then he remembered the sweet aroma of Esh'a's hair and the warmth of her embrace, when it was warm, once, and reached for the small wooden canister hanging at his neck. He brought it close to his nose and cracked it open, breathing in the sweet pungence of vanilla. He pressed his eyes shut to swim in a sea of good memories, if but for a moment. It might be his last.

"Can I, Abbi?"

He held the canister up to Sera's nose and smiled. "What does it smell like?" he asked.

She beamed. "Like home."

Anda nodded. "And happiness."

Sera gave a sage nod and squeezed her father's hand. "We'll find Imma soon."

"I hope s—"

Something beeped. Anda whipped his eyes in the direction of the display and squinted through a rising panic. A new blip appeared ahead of them on the trip information schematic. Then the display cycled to the rear view, the dusty gray globe of Home, and, after an agonizing pause, to the forward view of the portal once again. A speck slid in front of a ruined, glistening hull out in the ship graveyard, and then its boson drive glowed blue. The speck began to grow as it sped toward them. Its silhouette revealed an interceptor. At attack speed.

The woman next to Anda huddled closer to her two children and began to mutter a prayer to the Lady of the Emerald Moon. A restless anxiety crept through the cabin, and Anda imagined a similar scene in the main cabins of the other two decks on this death rig. Word would travel quickly among the refugees jammed into the passages and compartments: Death drew near.

Then Sera began to cough, and Anda could tell right away that it was bad. *She can't die like this, full of pain and fear.*

Anda rifled through his shoulder bag for the cylindrical container, but kept one eye on the display. The rear view was useless, and the angle of the forward view made it hard to see how far away the approaching ship was, but the trip information schematic might show how much time they had. The forward view had just cycled on, so he had just enough time to get out the container that Nayr had given him, before the trip schematic cycled on.

Sera's little body convulsed with the coughing fit. Her cries, between coughs, squeezed his heart like a vise. She coughed and cried so much that she couldn't even say "Abbi." Those around them scooted away as best they could.

Dismay seized him when all but one of the pills spilled out of the metal container and onto the cabin floor. Anda pinched the one that remained and slid it into her mouth. She tried to clamp her mouth shut against the pill, her eyes wide with fear and misunderstanding, but it was too late. The pill was already under her tongue.

Her coughing subsided immediately. Sera's eyes went wide with surprise, and Anda began picking the pills off the cabin floor. He counted them, then, when he saw how effective they were. Only five.

The mother sitting next to them picked up a pill he'd missed and examined it, curious, then handed it to him with a tepid smile. Six. Nayr had given Anda's daughter a week's worth of life. Monster.

The mother next to them cleared her throat, her aspect uncertain. "Tha . . . that's a nano pill."

Anda furrowed his brow, trying to process her words, which were incongruous to the danger they faced. "A what?" he asked.

"It probably won't matter, now, but my son took a pill like that back in Meran. It has two colors and six sides. They told me that kind of pill has nanos to communicate with the healing equipment."

Another beep tore Anda's attention back to the display, just as the information schematic cycled on. A new line of information gav the estimated time to intercept: thirty seconds.

Death would come sooner if the interceptor had missiles.

He closed the metal container and turned it in his hands, the pills making a nervous rattle.

Anda glanced up again just as the display cycled from the rear view to the schematic. Twelve seconds to intercept, but still no missiles. Anda furrowed his brow. Was the interceptor toying with them?

Sera closed her eyes and rested back against a bulkhead, but whether out of exhaustion or calm Anda could not tell.

He examined the container, then cocked his head in confusion at a line of text engraved on the bottom, which he hadn't seen before: *A life for a life.*

Before he could suss out the meaning, the internal comm system crackled overhead. Anda jerked his head up, along with the other refugees in the cabin. Anticipation and fear curdled on their every jitter, their every eye movement.

"Refugees," a woman's voice said, "this is Pilot 27301 of the 11–2 Hellbats, Fighting 11th."

The refugees heaved a collective sigh of relief. "We're saved," whispered a man nearby. "Not so fast," said another.

The pilot continued, in a voice whose cheer was obviously forced, masking unutterable fatigue and trepidation. "My job is to escort you to the portal. Your ship can't make evasive maneuvers, but I'll keep the drones off until you're through."

Sudden silence. All eyes shifted to the display. Hot anxiety burst throughout the cabin, almost real enough for Anda to reach out and touch. The display showed the schematic for only a moment, before cycling to the rear view, but not before Anda noticed another blip on the display, approaching the Hellbat pilot at a fast clip from the direction of Home. *That* was attack speed.

The mother next to Anda gasped, and one of her children began to whimper. Mercifully, Sera slept, oblivious.

The front view cycled on, to show the two interceptors twisting and sliding around each other. Distiller charges lanced through space in a furious, deadly duel. Their boson drives glowed and dimmed in time with the shifting, bursting dogfight, an intricate dance of death.

The rear view cycled on. To Anda's horror, another point of bluish light appeared behind them. "Is that another interceptor?" someone asked, in a tremulous whisper. "Is it friend or foe?" asked another.

The schematic display showed one minute until they reached the portal.

Anda tore his eyes from the display. He couldn't affect their future now. He peered down at the container in his hand, then pulled off the lid to count the pills one more time. Still six. They could make it to the White Planet, and Sera might still die. Anda wanted to curse the Lady and the universe and this infernal war and everything.

Then something the mother next to him had said hit him like a load of rock: nano pills could communicate with remote equipment. The implications produced a hollow weakness in his gut. The nano pills must be related to the message. *A life for a life.* Nayr was capable of such a monstrosity, but how could he make this threat stick?

Despair, vivid and unyielding, clutched at his mind and heart. He could not judge the frailty of his hope in that moment of unfettered uncertainty, when all the things he had grasped so closely and for so long seemed ready to float away in a merciless explosion of debris, into the vacuum of space.

The cabin gasped, and Anda, out of reflex, glanced at the display, along with the other refugees. One of the interceptors had burst into a thousand pieces. Anda bit the inside of his cheek.

"Was that the escort?" the mother next to him asked.

Anda shrugged, and checked whether Sera slept. He could do nothing for their future now, but his gaze fell to the peaceful rise and fall of her chest and comfortable lay of her head in the crook of his arm. Did he really have an option besides hope?

The comm system crackled on again. "Hang on, refugees. There's another drone in your baffles."

The forward view showed the Hellbat racing toward them, and Anda got a good look at its markings: reflective silver trim and a ferocious red Hellbat logo blazoned on its lobes. Anda tore his attention away. They would live, or they would die, regardless of whether he watched that blasted display.

He closed his eyes and cleared his mind, thankful that Sera's death would be sudden, without the agony of knowing she was about to die in cold, heartless vacuum. It would be quick, at least.

The refugees around him gasped, but he forced his eyes to remain closed, to not incur more fear.

Then the refugees in the cabin cheered, and Anda couldn't resist looking at the display. In the rear view, an oncoming missile exploded in a stream of distiller charges. Two interceptors, the Hellbat and the enemy, sliced and slid around each other.

The schematic cycled on. Eighteen seconds to the portal.

In the front view, the portal leaped toward them, sunlight shimmering and gliding off its rippling surface, and off the graveyard of ships that floated there.

The ship jerked just as the rear view cycled on. A deep grumble rattled through the rig. Shouts of surprise erupted from the refugees, and Anda slammed into the bulkhead. He jammed his hand up and narrowly missed crushing Sera. Pain stabbed through his arm. He winced and looked up at the display to see an interceptor careening off toward Moon, out of control, its nose a fiery mess. Light from the sun behind them glinted off silver trim as it spun. With piercing agony, the interceptor began to break apart. The Hellbat logo flashed in the sunlight as the port lobe sloughed off the twisting wreckage.

Anda's shoulders slumped, glad that Sera did not witness his despair.

The enemy interceptor streaked toward them. Another missile emerged from one of its pods and blasted toward them. Women and men shrieked around the cabin.

The schematic cycled on, in its plodding, inexorable way, even though he knew their speed was breakneck. The ship seemed unaware of the destruction that bore down upon it.

This truly is a death rig.

The schematic gave two seconds before reaching the portal.

The ship lurched again, then shuddered like a giant absorbing a body blow. Alarms rang out all over the ship. Refugees huddled, breath stilled. Far away, doors hissed closed.

The front view cycled on again. Like an apparition, the White Planet loomed ahead, suddenly, peaceful and bluish against the black of space. The sunlight came from a different direction now, and it was brighter, yellower.

The rear view cycled on. It showed only stars, and a shimmer where they'd passed through the portal, but no interceptor gave chase.

Anda breathed a sigh of relief, but his throat seized with panic when the internal comm system burst to life.

Warning! announced the automatic pilot in a tinny voice. *Hull breach! Hull breach!*

The doors around them gave off weak hissing sounds, as if they closed only reluctantly. Refugees started pushing and shoving toward the main hatch in their cabin. Anda, blood pumping, looked down to collect their meager possessions, but there was very little to take, and he realized there was no point in moving anyway.

Space would kill them, no matter how close they were to the main hatch.

He took a deep breath—savoring the act—and assessed the situation. He only had six pills left, six pills to figure out a cure for Sera. He also had a mystery to solve: how could Nayr threaten their lives when they were on a different planet, maybe even in a different dimension? Nayr said the nanos he'd put inside Anda would communicate with him even if Anda were far away, on the White Planet. But how could Nayr maintain the link through a dimensional portal, especially when Zharla had given him a drink that suppressed the nanos for most of the time period of the transition?

Anda felt his face grow pale at two possibilities, both equally chilling: Zharla could have colluded with Nayr to give Anda fake medicine, with Nayr tracking him all along, or Nayr was lying outright about being able to communicate with the nanos inside Anda, and he had some other way of enforcing his threat. Could Anda trust Zharla's good will? Could he trust Nayr's threats?

Then Anda's blood ran cold. Nayr had threatened Sera too, not just Anda. *A life for a life.* He sensed the horrible truth of Nayr's threat the moment he considered it in this new light. Every quivering muscle in his body and every feeble ligament wanted this truth to be untrue, but Anda could not deny the terrible certainty in his gut: his and Sera's fates were somehow linked.

But how?

Anda's shoulders slumped, and he gulped back the dryness. If they lived to set foot on the White Planet, then they would be living on borrowed time.

A life for a life.

He gripped the canister of vanilla at his chest, partly to think of the comfort it would be to find Esh'a, but also because the sweet memories they made together, once, would make the next few days easier to bear. A part of him thought that maybe those memories would inspire him, would give him some insight to defeat Nayr's plot, to save them both and reunite the three of them once more, to live that fat and happy life he dreamed of, in some far-off corner of the universe.

Another part of Anda wished that the death rig would just fall apart right then. Being sucked into space would be so much cleaner. What a vagary was hope, that unforgiving taskmaster, for in that same moment Anda also thought of Esh'a not knowing what would become of them, and his chest burned with anguish. He steeled himself for what was coming.

He had no choice but hope.

Two hours more passed in their wild flight from one mortal danger to another, and still death restrained its hand. The White Planet filled the front view on the display.

Sera stirred and woke. "Are we there yet, Abbi?"

13 | Surprise

EVERY FEW MINUTES, another one of Nayr's interceptors swooped down, like a hawk toying with mice scurrying through a field, and picked off another one or two refugees. Zharla had done the math in her head. They could have covered the five kilometers from the ruins of Peshron to the extraction point in less than thirty minutes at top speed, as long as they carried the children, but instead Nayr's clones made the trek through the jungle a two-hour hell of carnage and fear as their sorry column picked through the underbrush for some measure of protection.

And she had no idea how much farther they had to go, the jungle was so dense. The storm began to subside, the wind howled less, and the rain fell in a steady drizzle. It was even light enough for Zharla to tell that it was late afternoon.

"Stay in your groups!" yelled Zharla, her voice hoarse from overuse. "Keep moving forward!" In the last hour, some had succumbed to the cold, and two were even struck by lightning, but the greatest danger by far was the interceptors.

Every stop they made was a death sentence for a member of the column. Each small group had a handful of children and three or four adults, two armed with distillers. They'd given up trying to shoot at Nayr's interceptors, though. The interceptors' shields were too strong and they swooped in from where the refugees least expected.

Once they heard the sonic boom over the dwindling storm, it was too late.

So, they sloshed from one patch of muggy, dense foliage to another, hoping that the old base where Renla would extract them was just around the next bend in the overgrown path.

A sonic boom ripped through the sky, and a shriek sounded from behind her. She turned, and her fury rose yet another notch. A young mother screamed, a limp baby in her arms, the side of its delicate little head missing, life oozing out.

Monsters. This was a game to them. She wanted to scream at the interceptors that she invoked the Queen's protection on these people—Nayr's clones must know she was down here—but she knew it would do no good.

She switched her distiller to the vacuum extraction setting and marched over to the woman with the lifeless child in her arms. "Keep moving," she ordered the others. "We'll catch up."

There was no way she'd compound this woman's grief by leaving her child's body by the side of the path. She placed her free hand on the young mother's shoulder and peered at her with steely intent. "I am so sorry."

The mother, clearly sensing what had to be done, began to wrap the body in a blanket. Her shoulders shook in silent grief. The drizzle hid her tears, but Zharla didn't need to see them to know they mixed with streaming rain. As people filed past, they brushed the young mother's back and muttered words of comfort.

What comfort could this mother feel now?

Zharla placed the nozzle of her distiller on an empty patch of mud and made sure the discharge vent pointed away from anyone. She squeezed the trigger and watched as the distiller squelched congealed earth and debris off to the side. The digging felt like it took forever, and Zharla worried that another sonic boom would sound at any moment, tolling another death for the ragged column.

After an eternity, but probably closer to thirty seconds, she'd made a hole big enough for the baby's tender body. Rain gushed down the young mother's cheeks as she laid him in the newly dug grave. Behind her, a man, a brother or cousin perhaps, crouched down and laid a hand on her back.

The mother raised puffy eyes and considered Zharla. "His name"—she choked back a sob—"was Zha." She looked down at the little body. "We named him after you."

The mother broke down, shoulders shaking once again, then she shrieked in anger and pain.

Zharla put a hand on her mouth and coughed. Tears welled. She knelt down and pressed two fingers onto the little body in the grave, then drew in a deep breath to keep her emotions at bay. "Rest in the Lady's embrace, Zha."

The man behind the mother sighed. "Go to the Lady of the Emerald Moon."

Gently, carefully, Zharla pushed the clumps of mud that the distiller had discharged back over the grave. The mother pounded the earthy muck next to the grave, her sobbing unabated.

Another sonic boom jerked Zharla back to their peril. She waited for the unmistakable cry of agony and sound of a body crumbling to the sodden earth. It didn't come. Instead, she looked up to see an interceptor hovering just over the jungle canopy, ahead, above the path, like the disembodied head of death. The bosonic hum of its microfusion engines sounded a dirge to the newly deceased and the soon-to-be dead.

On reflex, Zharla aimed and squeezed the trigger, but the distiller just sucked up air and discharged it out the vent, harmless. She slammed her hand against the side of the distiller in frustration and jammed the switch back to the kill position.

The rest of the column huddled in the underbrush, unsure how to handle this new enemy tactic. They pointed their distillers at the interceptor, its stubby nose cone arcing back and forth between the two sides of the path, but they didn't shoot their weapons.

"Mash it!" Zharla yelled, squeezing her own trigger with an angry *thu-thu-thunk*. "Bring it down!" *Thu-thu-thunk*.

A single distiller could do little against an interceptor. Its shields absorbed Zharla's charges with ease. By the time the others discharged their own weapons, the interceptor had already begun to evade.

The first person to shoot his weapon after Zharla, a middle-aged man with a paunch and a daughter by his side, caught the interceptor's single charge in the face. His head buckled and disappeared in a silvery red spray. His body wilted in a heap, like a flower withered under a penetrating desert sun.

His daughter, a girl of about fourteen, screamed her father's name and tried to take his arm out of the distiller. To arm herself. To take revenge.

In a whoosh of bosonic wash, the interceptor was gone. The girl almost had the distiller free of her father's corpse, and threatened real harm to those around her.

Zharla strode up, knelt, and put an arm around the girl's shoulders. "Calm, child. They'll be back." She hefted the distiller pack off of the corpse's back and unwound the cord from the arm. "Here, give me the weapon."

The girl's furious eyes softened when she saw who helped her. "Your Majesty, I . . ."

Zharla just squeezed her shoulder once more. "Let me take your revenge." She put the dead man's distiller pack onto her own back, right over Ahrik's distiller pack. She grunted back the extra weight, then shoved her off-hand into the dead man's distiller. It felt unnatural, but she knew she'd need two distillers to do what she planned.

She looked at those staring at her, their eyes husks of uncertainty, despair. "Let me take revenge," she said, "for all of you."

Confused silence reigned, until the daughter made a desperate motion with her hand. "How, Your Majesty?"

Zharla looked down the path. "You all wait here, and pretend like you're burying this man." She raised both distillers, the metal dull and mud-stained in the bleak late afternoon light. "I'll go up ahead. Don't shoot at the next interceptor, whatever you do, not until I give the signal."

She suspected the interceptor pilots wouldn't reinforce their rear shields, just the front. She also suspected they felt hubris at picking off helpless civilians and exhausted soldiers. Two distillers might be just enough.

She ran down the path another forty meters, and her heart leaped for joy, for around the next bend, where the others couldn't see, the rendezvous point peeked through the opening into the clearing, with the crumbling observation towers of the old transit station.

She prayed that Renla would be there.

Zharla laid face down on the path, so the next interceptor pilot would see a dead body, not the Queen. She chanced a look back at the others, their numbers diminished from some two hundred to about fifty. She forced down a simmering rage and cleared her mind. Timing was essential. And she only had one chance at this.

A sonic boom pierced the sky once again. She waited, hoping for the bass, bosonic hum of the interceptor engine instead of a cry of pain from another of their number. She pled with the Lady to make the pilot arrogant enough to hover close.

After a painful beat of waiting, she heard the welcome sound of the boson drive overhead, buzzing like a mechanized Angel of Death. She counted to five, to make sure the pilot would be fully taken in by the game. Let him think he's tormenting them.

In a single motion, Zharla rolled over onto her back and rested her distillers on her bent knees. She'd guessed the angle right, and she squeezed the triggers with all her might. *Thu-thu-thunk, thu-thu-thunk, thu-thu-thunk, thu-thu-thunk.*

The pilot tried to maneuver the craft to face her, but his move only served to gouge the craft more. Zharla's barrage ate a gaping hole in the interceptor's rear, and as the pilot turned his craft, the hole extended forward, nearly shearing off the interceptor's port lobe.

The interceptor dropped with a thud, spraying mud and debris in every direction. Zharla rose and ran toward the wreckage, screaming at the others to destroy the pilot's internal compiler.

By the time she gotten there, they'd dragged him out of the ruined cockpit and begun pumping his body full of distiller charges, screaming inchoate curses at all he represented.

But they didn't destroy the internal compiler.

"His compiler!" she screamed, then leveled a distiller at his neck and squeezed the trigger. She heaved a breath and looked around. "They transmit their location with compilers implanted in their necks."

The girl, the dead man's daughter, came forward and placed a hand on Zharla's shoulder. Her eyes burned with an eternal thirst for revenge. "May my father's wrath never wane from the nether reaches of death."

"He did not die in vain," answered Zharla. "I swear it. I will live a thousand years and not exact enough justice for what the Tyrant has done this day."

All around her, they cheered, slapped backs, and hugged at their little victory. Zharla knew it could swiftly turn into utter defeat, but she needed them to hope now, above all. "Hurry," she yelled over the crowd, pointing forward. "The rendezvous point is just around the bend."

The smoldering fire of revenge glowed in Zharla's heart as she watched the refugees straggle by. So many innocent people, dead at her own son's hand. No longer was her life one of regret. Hers was now a life of revenge.

Somehow, she'd always known this day would come, the day she forsook her own son.

2 removed his pieces from the *chartak* board and huffed in defeat. Nayr draped his arm around 2's shoulders and said, "You win some, you lose some."

Right now, Nayr was winning. Not only in the game of *chartak* laid out on the table before them, but in life. With Mother's absence, Nayr realized that his power was ascendant, and with the Usurper out of the picture no one could challenge him. His sons, the mighty 100,000 of Nayr, ruled the planet. The Usurper and Shahl and Renla still nagged at him, but Nayr's sons were about to take care of the Usurper problem once and for all.

2 sighed and reached for the candy bowl.

"Ho, 2," said 3, from his place across the table. "Will it be sugar or spice?"

2 picked up a little ball from the bowl and popped it in his mouth. He chewed, then smiled. "Spice."

Nayr had given his command company the afternoon off, to reward his sons for their hard-earned victories. Victory at Peshron and Meran were imminent. And soon Hof Chelek too would be cleansed of disloyalty and faithlessness.

Sometimes, security meant starting with a clean slate.

2 leaned back on the couch and gave a contented sigh, eyelids fluttering, body succumbing to the flood of ecstasy. 6, sitting next to 3, across the table, took his turn. 5, the last of their *chartak* quintet, leaned forward and reached into the bowl. He grunted in disappointment as he munched. "Sugar."

Nayr sucked in a draught of air, the smell of camaraderie and new furniture in his nostrils. His new headquarters, just outside Mekele Eshel, was a gem at the center of the Eshel, far away from Ahrik's old center of power, in tired, dusty Meran. This brand new officers club was the exclusive reserve of Nayr and his most loyal sons.

All around them, tables were packed with the sons of Nayr. Sweet susurrations of victorious conversation lilted about the room as the Ketel of Nayr revelled in its newfound glory.

Win.

Soon his sons would be the only officers in the Army, and soon Nayr would be in complete control of the planet, especially since he was rid of Meran forever, with all of its problems, like in-mountain malcontents and refugee filth. They wanted to go off-planet anyway, which was as good as being dead, as far as Nayr could tell. He saved them some trouble.

And he was done with Shahl and his pesky daughter, the little girl that Mother demanded he not harm. Pitiful sentiment. How did Mother think he kept the peace?

Keeping the peace means making hard choices.

6 rolled a piece of candy around his mouth, then took his turn. "Sugar." He glanced over at 2, then at Nayr. "Your turn, Father."

2 snored. Nayr smiled, then rubbed his neck and stared at the *chartak* board. He was surprised by 3's last move, and he didn't see how he could keep 3 from winning, much less win himself. How tables turn in a game of *chartak*.

5 chuckled and gestured toward 2. "What's in that new spice, Father?"

Nayr moved his pieces on the board, an effort to forestall 3's inevitable triumph. "Only the best for my sons," said Nayr, without looking back at 2. He gave a wicked, conspiratorial smile. "New formula, they said."

"They," in this case, was the servants at the officers club. Nayr brought the most loyal servants from the palace in Meran, before the city was pacified.

While 3 pondered his next move, Nayr checked his wrist compiler to make sure the comms were still linked with his internal compiler. He wanted to know as soon as the Ketel of Ahrik operation was set to go.

3 caught him checking, then pinged Nayr over the tendril link. *Father, last report was that the seekerbots were dispersed across all population centers in the Eshel and the Kereu. Your sons are checking the nanobio payloads, and they'll let us know as soon as they're ready for you to give the order.*

Check, Nayr replied. *Keep me posted.*

3 nodded and took his turn. He popped a ball from the bowl into his mouth, frowning. "Sugar."

Nayr's wrist compiler dinged. He whipped his wrist around. Just a message from Mother. He wished he could block her, but one doesn't block the Queen.

Her message scrolled up the tiny display: *I left gifts for your men at the officers club.*

He furrowed his brow and replied, *Where are you, Mother?*

Stay away from the officers club today.

Nayr cocked his head, perplexed. Mother signed off without explaining the odd warning. Her profile went off the grid, too, as if she were sending him a message then disappearing once again.

He shrugged. She would come back eventually.

He looked around the officers club and wondered what gifts she referred to.

5 mulled his next move. A serving boy rushed in their direction, a fine specimen of freneticism, his forehead gleaming as he wove around tables packed with Nayr's choicest sons. Nayr waved him down and patted the boy's thigh. "Five *hender* teas."

The boy nodded. "Yes, sir."

"Father," said 3. He smiled and nodded at 2. "You might want to make it four."

Nayr glanced in 2's direction, about to correct the order, but froze instead. His world swam for a beat. 2 lay still, eyes closed, but foam speckled the corners of his mouth.

Then he heard 5 say, "Hmm, spice."

When had he reached for another?

"Sweet Lady," said 3, voice laced with sinking realization.

3, cast Nayr. *Save 5.*

Nayr shot his fingers to 2's neck, but he knew it was too late. He knew what gift Mother, or the Usurper acting through Mother, had intended for him. Renla might be wrapped up in the conspiracy, too. Nayr looked over at 5. His body had already begun to seize up.

Nayr smashed his hand into the bowl. Balls of sugar and spice, indistinguishable from one another, flew in every direction. The bowl shattered into a hundred pieces.

Heads turned from all over the club, and an uncomfortable hush descended. Around the room, a half-dozen small commotions flared up. Nayr looked around to see his sons clustered around prone comrades. Whispered questions of "Poison?" and "Is Father safe?" rippled throughout the great room.

Father, cast 3 over the tendril link, sighing audibly. *Seekerbots are in place. Ready for your order.*

Nayr answered 3's thought with a look. His vision blurred with rage. He accessed his internal compiler and opened the file called Revenge: "Kill Ahrik. Kill Shahl. Punish Renla. Beware of Mother."

3, he cast. *Launch the nanobios over the whole planet. Everywhere. Kill the Ketel of Ahrik. Destroy anything that tries to get through the portal, even if it means pursuit to the other side.*

Hunched over 5's now lifeless body, 3 nodded, his expression vacant. Nayr slumped into the couch, pondering two more dear friends, victims of faithlessness and treachery.

Had Mother turned against him? Could it be?

Nayr bored his gaze into his director of operations. *3,* he cast, *find the Queen.*

Ahrik woke to the bright light of day streaming into his room. Wait. Shouldn't he be on the moon? Blueish light bounced off of colorless walls, making the room feel bigger than it really was. The moon didn't have daylight. Not like this.

His eyes darted, trying to make sense of his surroundings. His body felt heavy. Limbs like lead.

A chair groaned against someone shifting their weight, close by. "We thought the natural light would make you more comfortable, sir."

The voice came from his right, and he tried to move his head in that direction, but settled for straining his eyeballs until he caught a glimpse of a uniform and the insignia of the Fighting 11th. He was definitely on the moon. The suss and whir of healing equipment padded the air with its melancholy refrain.

Ahrik grimaced. At least he had control over his facial muscles. "I can tell the light's fake," he said, scanning the room for any other inhabitants, squeezing pain into his eyes in the process. "Why can't I move?"

The man chuckled and stood. An orderly. "Commander Renla has already been called, sir. She asked to be notified as soon as you came to."

Ahrik sent his mind into his extremities. They didn't feel damaged, and he didn't remember being in a crash, or passing out. He narrowed his eyes. With all the insanity he'd seen in the last few weeks, it was just possible that he was a prisoner. "Why won't my limbs move?"

"Sir, we had to . . . ah . . . maybe I should let Commander Re—"

"I want you to tell me, orderly."

The orderly cleared his throat and shuffled in the direction of the door. It hissed open. "Sir, I—"

Footsteps from down the corridor saved him. The orderly breathed a sigh of relief. Ahrik glowered.

Renla strode in and stopped at the side of his bed. Others came with her, but Ahrik couldn't tell who or how many. Was Zharla with them? He paused on this thought. Did he really care?

Renla patted his hand. "I'm sorry for the sedation, sir. We had to be sure you weren't a threat to yourself, or others." She paused. "And we found something while you were under."

Renla exchanged a look with some of the others in the room. Ahrik had never known her to be this unsettled or unsure of herself. It was . . . endearing.

"Well?" asked Ahrik, with a bit more impatience than he intended.

"I . . . can't tell you . . . I just have to show you." She nodded, and someone pressed a button, followed by a surge of pain through his spine. He arched his back in reflex, vaguely happy that he could do so now, despite the pain, and then the pain faded and feeling rushed into his limbs.

Blood pumped through his veins and he gulped in air to compensate. Renla waited for his breathing to recover a bit, then nodded to someone else. One of her soldiers moved forward with a facial display cradled in his hands. His insignia marked him as research or intelligence, and he moved the contraption toward Ahrik's head with extreme care. "May I, sir?" He licked his lips, like a scientist on the verge of some world-changing discovery. "It's the prototype, so it might not fit perfectly."

Someone helped Ahrik sit up. He grunted his thanks, then eyed the scientist with uncertainty. "So, I'm a lab rat?"

Renla sighed. "We wanted to wait until you were completely better, sir, but the situation has escalated and we're getting disturbing signals from gravside and . . . well . . . let's try this."

"How bad is it, Renla?" he asked. The cockle of whispers in the room made Ahrik think that the situation was very bad indeed.

She bit her lip, a worrying sign. "It could be terrible, sir, but it could also be nothing. We're trying to understand what happened to your men on Peshron and in Meran, how the Tyrant located them so easily."

Ahrik nodded at the contraption the scientist held, which resembled a thin crown of metal wires with a compiler coupling dangling off the back. "And this," Ahrik asked, "what is it?"

"A tendril hack."

Ahrik shrank back. He looked at Renla in disbelief. "Tendril comms are unhackable."

Renla shrugged. "We think Nayr figured out how to do it, and if—"

"If he can hack the tendril link, then he can track me and my sons." Worry washed over Ahrik's face. He dipped his head toward the scientist. "Put it on." With his head bowed, he looked up his forehead at Renla. "How far can you repeat the signal?"

Renla smiled, but concern lined her eyes. "All of Dom, sir. And Moon."

The base of Ahrik's skull tingled where the contraption's coupler rested against the skin over his internal compiler.

"Sorry to do this to you, sir, but you're the first commander with clones to make it up here. We don't think it'll work at lower echelons of a ketel."

Ahrik pressed his eyes shut and focused his breathing. *Ketel of Ahrik*, he cast over the tendril link.

Renla whispered, "There might be a delay."

Ahrik gasped, and his mind burst into awareness, a vividness he hadn't tasted since he'd been with all his ketel together, years ago. Everywhere on the moon and Dom, he sensed his sons. "Oh."

"Sir?"

"You're sure this has coverage over the whole of Dom?"

"Yes, and Moon."

Ahrik's face turned grim. "There are only four members of my ketel here on the moo—"

Father. Help.

Someone over the tendril link. Fear. Pain. Running from some unseen terror. On the far side of Dom.

Before Ahrik could do nothing, not even respond, and the tendril presence winked out. Dead.

Ahrik took a deep breath and tried to calm his nerves, refusing to believe what was happening. He focused his mind and reached with his thoughts, deep into his ketel's lowest echelons. Sweat beaded on his forehead. "So few," he said. His world began to swim. He searched the worried faces of those surrounding him in the healing room. "So few still alive."

A nervous discussion broke out, whispered and tense. Renla reached for him, as if to stop the experiment, but her hand froze in midair when he shook his head.

"I have to know what Nayr has done." Blood coursed through his chest and neck. His head grew heavy. He forced himself to search through his tendril network, but he knew what he would find. Two weeks ago, over fifteen hundred of his sons still lived, but now he found only emptiness.

Father, someone cast to him. Uncertainty, exertion, and anger in his thoughts, as if fleeing some unexpected danger. This was one of his retired sons, discharged years ago for medical reasons, and Ahrik sensed he was hobbled by some injury sustained in defense of the Eshel, and of women's rule.

Ahrik's eyes burned. His chest churned with anguish at the tragedy and injustice that pulsed through his mind. With the time delay, he knew that everything coming over the tendril link had already happened. There was nothing he could do, no comfort he could give in his sons' dying moments.

This one, too, blinked out, but just before that terrible moment of suspended nothingness, Ahrik glimpsed what this injured, retired soldier saw: two hands, his hands, shriveled and black, death reaching and clawing up his arm. Then unspeakable agony as the Black, whatever it was, spread to his internal organs, leaving the brain for last, along with a vivid and gut-wrenching record of his final seconds of agony.

What focus and courage it took for this retired soldier to center his breathing and cast his dying throes onto the tendril link.

Ahrik balled up the bedsheet in his fist and ground his teeth. He would never see such courage again. He forced himself to stay on the tendril link, to search for his sons. To be sure. The healing room faded into inconsequence around him as he cast, cast, cast to his sons and begged the tendril link to hold so he could suffer with his men.

The outcome, he knew, was inevitable. One by one, his sons remaining gravside went dark, leaving a gaping stillness in his mind.

Hawk. He felt nothing from Hawk.

Ahrik's consciousness began to fade, and he felt himself being sucked down into this nether trench, as if the Black could spread its tentacles over the tendril link as well. Was that possible? Ahrik hadn't thought a tendril hack was possible, but here he was, able to communicate with his sons across inconceivable distances.

Ahrik's breathing became shallow. He drifted toward awareness of the healing room, but still lingered in the no man's land between the tendril link, the planet, and the moon, half aware of nothingness on one side and spurts of activity on the other. Voices, orders, purposeful movement.

Then silence, silence and dim lights. When his awareness wandered back to the healing room, back to the present, the Black still loomed in his mind, ready to engulf him.

Renla stood by his bed, but all the others were gone. The contraption was gone, as were the buzz and hum of the healing equipment. Renla's eyes were red and puffy. Tears stained her face. Worry creased her brow.

Ahrik felt the sheen of sweat and tears on his own face. He touched a finger to his own cheek, then reached a hand out to stroke the side of Renla's face.

She let him, and familiarity leapt between them, like electricity yearning between two nodes. She knew his pain, the helplessness of losing lives with so many more years yet to live. She knew the gaping hole yawning in his heart, a space more vacant and alone than any that time or comfort or victory could heal.

Death would be better, if not for the knowledge that someone else lived who understood him, who said with her eyes that she would stay by his side, and mourn, however long it took.

He dropped his hand after brushing her cheek. Would she reciprocate?

"Sir . . . Ahrik," she whispered. "I'm so sorry."

He furrowed his brow. "You saw?"

In answer, she merely nodded toward the compiler display near the bed. So, not only could they hack tendril comms, but they could interpret and record them, too.

Ahrik choked on a sob. "They died well."

Her face glazed with hatred and she gave a furious shake of her head. "They died too soon."

He stared into the middle distance, as if it might hold answers. His mind drifted through desolation and mourning for a beat, then resolved into the only thing he knew. "We can fight him, Renla, but should we?"

"Do we have a choice, sir?"

"I realized something there, Renla, staring into the Black, or whatever you call it." He turned a mournful eye on her. "He doesn't want to kill me. Nayr wants to destroy me, to make me live with the sorrow of losing everything I hold dear."

She squeezed his hand, and new tears formed at the corners of her eyes. She leaned in and kissed his cheek, with more tenderness than Ahrik thought possible, certainly with more compassion than Zharla had ever graced him with. "Don't let him win," she said. "Stay strong."

His heart pounded with the anticipation of what could have been. "I'd rather stand and fight," he said. "And die."

She caressed his cheek where she'd kissed it and shook her head again, as firm as the kiss was tender. "No, Ahrik. I will fight. You must go."

"I do not run from battle."

"You still have clones to lead, four here on Moon, and many soldiers who will follow you, to fight on the White Planet. They need a leader who stands for freedom. For *cheret*."

He scoffed and began to push himself off the bed. "My ketel is dead. Nayr has sown the seeds of revenge in my heart. My hatred for him digs deep, deep and unyielding." He sucked in a vengeful breath. "I don't stand for freedom, Renla. I stand for death. For revenge."

She put a hand on his chest. "I can't let you stand here with me, and die."

He brushed his fingers over the outside of her hand. "I'd rather die with you than wonder what could have been."

Renla half-turned and covered her mouth. Her shoulders shook. Ahrik cringed to see her turmoil. He reached out to caress her back. "Renla, we can win, I—"

"No!" She spun around, slapping his hand away. "I saw what he did, what he's capable of. He'll send that Black here, too, and you'll end up just like the others, a blackened, twisted shell of yourself." She stepped back and glared at him, her face red and streaked. "You're dead already if you stay. Now is not the time to stand and fight."

"I don't know how to run."

Renla threw her hands up in exasperation. "She needs you, okay! I love you and everything about you, but this, between us? Impossible. Especially now. Zharla deserves every shred of loyalty you can muster, and she can't beat Nayr alone."

"How are we supposed to fight him on a strange, new planet, with no resources?"

"I'm giving you a chance, Ahrik. All our research has been uploaded to a shuttle compiler in Hangar Bay Four. Your sons are waiting for you."

"Let me stay."

"Your brother needs you, too. He can't find his wife alone. Sera needs her parents. Make a difference for Sera, Ahrik."

"Come with me, Renla."

"We both know the meaning of duty."

Ahrik clenched his jaw, defeated.

Her electromag crackled. "One, this is command. That hostile fleet is charging up boson drives on the elevator stations, over."

She breathed out in frustration and switched open the channel. "Check, command. Be there in three, out."

She leveled a fierce gaze at Ahrik and wiped her eyes. "Nayr is coming for me. Go, while you still can."

Ahrik nodded and complied, but every step felt like a slog through the cold sludge of regret and self-loathing.

14 Battle

RENLA DREW OUT HER BREATH as long as she could, to delay the inexorable finality of what she was about to do. Toes tapped and fingers fidgeted with nervous energy throughout the command bunker under Station Prime, on Moon.

Lyn brushed her shoulder against Renla's and gave her a look that said, "There's no going back from this."

Renla gave her a quick nod and opened the electromag channel. "Rail Gun Control, on my mark."

Rail Gun Control crackled back: "Target coordinates loaded, ma'am. Rail gun primed. On your mark."

The lights in the bunker dimmed as the rail gun sucked up energy from all over Moon. Two hundred of the Tyrant's military and security installations were about to be on the wrong end of energy that Renla had been storing for weeks. Even with the massive storage capacity they'd built, energy use across Moon was reduced to barely survivable levels to make the barrage possible.

Someone in ops whispered, all too audibly, "Hope we did the math right."

As nervous laughter reverberated through the bunker, Lyn leaned in and whispered so only Renla could hear, "Ma'am, you sure you don't want to send an ultimatum first?"

Renla gave her aide an icy stare. "The Tyrant declared total war, not us. Meran will need a radiation containment field for generations, Peshron is rubble, and the Tyrant used genetic targeting to fry Ahrik's clones from the inside. There's only one way to stop that kind of evil."

Every city gravside that had shown even an inclination to rebel against the Tyrant's rule lived in utter fear. All over Dom, from the Eshel to the Kereu, hundreds of thousands of people, maybe even millions, had fallen victim to his tectonics or atomics or atmospherics. Tens of thousands, far fewer than should have, streamed to the Emerald Moon, and fewer still made it through the Tyrant's harassing patrols, through the portal, to the White Planet beyond. The Tyrant's genocide had turned half the planet and the space around the portal into a graveyard.

It was time to do some real damage, but Renla had still spent a sleepless night, while Ahrik recuperated from his ordeal in Peshron, wondering whether using the rail gun was right or wrong. Renla finally decided that she had to give those paltry thousands who had escaped Nayr's murderous drones a chance to get off Dom and make it to Moon, then to the White Planet.

But Nayr had dozens of bases in populated areas on Dom. If the rail gun calculations were off by even a fraction of a degree, the high energy slugs would miss their targets and turn even more innocent lives into craters of smoking ash.

She had to do something to cripple the Tyrant's infrastructure of death and destruction. No one else could. She'd rather have the lives of innocents on her conscience after doing something worthwhile than after doing nothing at all.

Renla tightened her grip on the electromag control. Her heart thumped in her chest. "Rail Gun Control, this is one. Go."

An eternal moment passed, where a hundred eyes looked at the lighting to see if a power drain would signal the rail gun charge passing. They weren't even sure it would work. They couldn't exactly test it without the Tyrant finding out.

Renla pulled at a curl behind her ear and bit her lip. Nayr's retribution would be sure and swift.

The lighting dimmed almost to black, and static electricity strummed through the command bunker, the wake of a giant electric current passing overhead. High above them, on the surface, a slug fed spurred by atomic energy sped along a hyperconductive rail three meters in diameter, on its way to blast the first target: the Black Eye north of what was once Meran.

Renla looked at her staff. "Intel, your sensors better be online. If we're off by even a second of lat or long, I want to know."

The rail ran from Moon's equator on the far side, over the pole, to a point twenty degrees down the near side. The targeting system shuttled magnetic blocks up and down the rail so the energy slugs left at the correct trajectory, to hit Dom at the right time and place. Every time the rail faced the correct longitude as Dom spun on its axis, the targeting system launched another bolt.

Every ten or fifteen seconds, the rail gun shuddered to life, sometimes two or three times in quick succession. After a few minutes of flickering lights and buzzing air, Renla turned to her aide. "Lyn, see that the defenses are prepared."

"Yes, ma'am." Lyn saluted and left.

"Intel," said Renla, "any report on those elevator stations?" After the Black Eye, the twenty-four elevator stations were highest on the targeting list. They were the source of the Tyrant's sorties against the fleeing refugee ships, and the location of the massing attack fleet.

The intel chief pursed her lips in response to Renla's question. "Not ye . . . hold a minute . . . three stations have come in range . . ." She trailed off and furrowed her brow into her compiler display. The tension in the command bunker ratcheted up as the silence grew, all eyes fixed on the intel chief, then evaporated with an audible sigh as she brightened into a smile. "Two direct hits and one glancing blow. One station severed from its cable and is adrift, with seventy percent damage. The other two have sustained forty and twenty percent damage."

The intel chief looked up at her commander, and the bunker erupted with cheers and back slapping. Renla looked on with satisfaction as her staff reveled in their success, even though she knew it would be fleeting.

"Intel," said Renla, "roll results on the bunker compiler display." A grid appeared, a column of target names, with information on location, and either estimated damage or time to impact in rows after each target.

The elevator station targets had the most information, since they were closest. Five stations were listed as having been struck, with only one more direct hit beyond what the intel chief had announced earlier.

Renla scanned the results. Some of the larger bases gravside were devastated, based on their size and concentration of assets, but smaller command and control nodes and intelligence collection points had mostly been spared.

Renla surveyed her staff's jubilation. Who could tell what fate would unleash when the passions of war jangled loose? Had they merely stung the Tyrant, or had they crippled him enough to give the refugees a chance? How elusive was that sprite called victory.

After about half the target list cycled down the display—one hundred launches, with about seventy-five hits—a member of the intel staff looked at his compiler display and nudged his chief. The intel chief looked her concern at Renla, beckoning Renla with her eyes.

Renla stood her ground. "Give me the bad with the good, intel."

The intel chief frowned. "Multiple launches from elevator stations 3 through 9," she said.

The tentative optimism petered out of the command bunker. Those were the stations that hadn't come in range of the rail gun yet.

"I confirm over four hundred interceptor launches," said ops. "ETA from 3 to 4 hours, depending on how they form up for their attack."

Renla furrowed her brow. "Any carrier launches? Is this the main fleet?"

"No carrier launches yet, ma'am," said Intel, "so this is probably just reprisal."

Renla rushed to open the electromag channel. "Rail Gun Control, this is one. Continue your attack *at all costs*. Press refugees into service if you have to. Make sure those interceptors have nowhere to return."

"Check, ma'am," answered Rail Gun Control. A descant of determination carried over the static in the response, and Renla's heart sang with the pride of a commander whose trust in her soldiers was well-placed. For now, she had the enemy right where she wanted, and all she had to do was let her diggers finish the job.

But the future beyond today scudded with dark clouds of uncertainty. Nayr would come, with his thousands and tens of thousands, to sow revenge and destruction in the cold, green lignite of the Emerald Moon. Then he might move on to the White Planet. He was not one to weather defeat well.

Renla couldn't show that uncertainty to her dear diggers now, though, so she turned to her staff and pumped a fist. This battle wasn't over by any means, but they'd surprised the enemy and given the refugees from Dom a chance at survival. Seeing her exuberance, smiles spread throughout the staff in the command bunker, the news about the four hundred enemy interceptors forgotten, for the moment. They believed in the cause of freedom, really believed. *Cheret.*

This was Renla's most important fight, in the hearts of the women and men under her command. Her duty, more sacred even than devotion to her friend, the Queen, was to give the Fighting 11th the power to accomplish the impossible, to defend the helpless and enshrine liberty in every human heart, whether that heart beat on Dom or Moon. She saw that now, where she hadn't before.

She opened the electromag. "Two, this is one. It's going to get hot where you are."

"Check, ma'am," sizzled Lyn's voice over the channel, "we're ready."

Thus primed, Renla and her motley diggers of the Fighting 11th waited for the full fury of the Tyrant's drones to dash against their defenses like storm surge against a jagged sea wall. Their defenses would hold. They'd prepared them from the second Renla stepped onto Station Prime and saw the effects of the bioweapon. This fight was weeks in the making.

The rail gun, the new interceptor launch tubes, the targeting system using the new electromag detection system to defeat the enemy's cloaking technology, the enhanced distiller pods with larger, hardened reactor cores, the electromag communications system, all were innovations of the Fighting 11th that they knew the Tyrant's drones had no answer for.

So, though doubt needled her breast, Renla stood with the confidence of thousands and opened the general comms channel. "Diggers, this is our chance at history. Let it be written that the Fighting 11th did not stand idly by while tyranny sank its claws into the human race. Let it be known that we fought for freedom. We fight for humanity."

Renla closed the channel, hand trembling, and turned to keep her staff from seeing the worry that crossed her face. They were about to write a history that no one would record. No one would read the story of their last stand. The refugees who fled Dom for Moon would have to flee again, to the White Planet, and someone would have to hold the line, to screen the refugees' flight. Who would remember her chosen few, her sisterhood of valor, her motley band of rebels? The Fighting 11th was winning, for now, but how long could it withstand the stormy ire of the Ketel of Nayr?

So Renla waited, with her brave diggers, for the demons of war to unleash their hell fury. She waited, knowing that hope was her only choice, since the alternative was despair and defeat. History left no room for those who lost.

And Renla was determined to win.

Three hours later, Rail Gun Control crackled over the electromag. "One, we've lost targeting and main power supply."

Nayr poised the pill over his tongue, but then the alert leaped into his thoughts. *Father,* cast 3 over the tendril link, *we are under attack.*

Nayr grumbled and stashed the pill in his breast pocket. He was already beginning to feel the shake in his legs. He mumbled something like thanks to the buzztender and pushed himself off the stool. His security detail rose with him. Nayr didn't relish the long walk to the station where his shuttle awaited, but Mekele's mountain depths were the only place he wasn't hassled nowadays.

And now add on another headache. An attack. Probably just a local fire that 3 could put out. "Let's go," Nayr sighed to his detail. *On my way*, he cast back to 3.

Father, 3 cast, a sense of urgency in the thought. *I recommend you get airborne quickly.*

Nayr strode out into the murky stone corridor. He didn't care to filter the annoyance out of his reply. *Got it. I'm sure it's nothing we can't handle. Win.*

Frustration. *Win*, 3 cast back.

The Ketel of Nayr was the most powerful force on the planet. Why should 3 doubt? Nayr needed to nip 3's doubt in the bud.

Nayr's boots clattered against the stone pavers. At this late hour, well after curfew, Mekele's deep in-mountain inhabitants were supposed to be ensconced in their hovels.

Two members of his security detail ran ahead to secure the route. The other four stayed behind with him. Nayr fingered the tiny lump in his breast pocket. He probably had enough time to pop it in his mouth without anyone seeing. The corridor was deserted, and his detail was fiercely loyal, or sufficiently afraid, Nayr made sure of that.

His fingers worked open the flap of the pocket. His mouth salivated. Then a gaggle of teens ran around the corner. Nayr's detail leapt ahead for protection. The teens froze at the sight of the remaining detail of well-armed soldiers, quieted down, and hugged the walls to let them pass.

3, Nayr cast in annoyance, *is it morning, or are people breaking curfew?*

It is morning, Father. Are you—

Calm down. I'm almost to my shuttle.

Nayr patted down the flap of his pocket, just to be sure the pill was safe. His hand shook, and he swore under his breath. If people were out already, he'd have to leave the pill until he got back to the shuttle.

Up ahead, the light from Mekele's central cavern glowed from around the final bend in the corridor. He patted his pocket once again. Just a few more minutes.

They got to the two members of the security detail who'd rushed ahead, but Nayr started when he saw the worried expressions they wore.

"What is it?" he asked as he passed by them. Let the others keep up. He slowed, though, when he sensed the silent tension in the cavern itself. If it was morning already, even with all the refugees that had fled, he expected more activity here, in in-mountain Mekele. Nothing moved, though, except the buzz of the automated caller machine, announcing the news on a loop, news he approved daily.

Nayr stopped. "What's going o—"

The mountain rumbled and shook. A shockwave passed under, over, and through them. He looked at the security detail lead. "Earthquake?"

The security detail lead shook his head as he checked his internal compiler. Had it been an earthquake, the mountain's countering mechanisms would have stabilized it much better. They shouldn't have felt that much of a shockwave.

After the initial disorientation, a visceral urge took over Nayr's mind: run. He sprinted toward the shuttle, ahead of his men. They'd keep up.

Furious, he focused his mind and cast to 3, *How close was that?*

Are you airborne, Father? Unexpressed pleading swam through 3's thought.

Nayr needed to have a talk with him about decorum over the tendril link.

Nayr got to the shuttle and slammed his palm down on the reader. The happy hum of the boson drive told him that the pilot had kept the rig warm. At least someone in his ketel could be trusted to do his job.

The hatch hissed open, and Nayr sprang from the rear cabin into the cockpit, then locked himself into the restraints of the command seat. "Go," he ordered.

The pilot swiveled his head with consternation. "Father? What about the security detail?"

Nayr, nonplussed, noted sounds of a fight raging outside the shuttle. He transluced the hull and saw his security detail pinned down behind a row of stalls. That's why it was so quiet in the cavern. The rebels prepared an ambush, and they warned off the citizenry. Traitors, all of them.

The rebels' projectiles zipped and slapped against the shuttle's energy shield. How dare they attack his shuttle?

Father, cast 3, *we believe you are in imminent danger.*

Nayr sighed and shrugged at the pilot. "The security detail will cover my retreat. Lift off."

The pilot nodded and turned to his work, but Nayr saw how he gulped, then squeezed his eyes shut, as if uncomfortable with the task at hand. No matter. Sometimes you had to do distasteful things. Nayr didn't like the thought of leaving his sons to die, but what could he do? He also didn't like pacifying cities with tectonics and atmospherics, but the security of the planet sometimes demanded it.

The shuttle heaved toward the escape shaft from Mekele mountain, built especially for Nayr's shuttle. How else could he frequent in-mountain buzz bars without being seen?

I'm airborne, 3, he cast.

No response. Would being in the shaft prevent tendril comms? He furrowed his brow. His tendril link should be omnipresent over the whole planet.

The shuttle burst from the mountain's bulk and into the morning light. Nayr stroked his chin. How had so much time passed?

The main spire of his gleaming new headquarters rushed toward them from the eastern horizon. 3 would be there, ready to tell him how he'd taken care of this latest headache.

Then the spire disintegrated in an explosion of raw energy. Nayr's eyes grew wide and his breath turned to vacuum in his chest. The explosion swarmed over the other structures visible from this distance. The lifting early morning sky twisted in an angry mix of blues and reds.

Nayr wrestled with his senses. *3,* he cast, *status.*

The shuttle slowed. It wobbled in the shockwave.

3, harried: *Attack planet-wide. From the moon. Ketel in the air. Rendezvous at Station 1. Planning counterattack. Over.*

The moon. Renla. Just as he'd suspected. She was a traitor after all. Nayr would deal with her soon enough. Nayr, jaw clenched: *3, are the atmospherics and tectonics set on all rebel cities?*

3, confused: *Yes, Father . . . but this attack came from the Emerald Moon.*

Nayr, impatient: *My shuttle was just attacked. Launch tectonics and atmospherics against all cities.*

3, shocked: *All cities, Father? We've selected targets to balance refugee exodus with the ability to sustain the planet's econo—*

Nayr, angry: *That. Is. An. Order.*

3, pliant: *Yes, Father. Sorry, Father. At once, Father.*

Nayr could tell that 3 was holding something back, like he had something else to say. Probably more unacceptable doubts about their cause. Nayr was glad 3 left that thought uncast.

"Father?" asked the pilot. "Back to Mekele?"

3, wary: *Father, if the cities empty out, it will be harder to recruit more soldiers for the assault force.*

Nayr, hiding his confusion: *Explain.*

3, anxious: *The ketel has lost too many men, Father. We can't pacify the moon, much less go through the portal, without a more substantial force.*

Nayr felt the pilot's eyes on him. Did he judge his commander with thoughts of doubt and negativity, like 3 and Nayr's other senior aides? Everywhere, enemies, everywhere.

Nayr allayed his fears into submission with the thought of all the good he had done for the planet. He had built a just and lasting peace. And now? Treachery was the recompense.

He set his chin with a grave look at the pilot. "Station 1."

Nayr glanced down to find something in his hand. When had he taken the pill out of his pocket? No matter. He popped it in his mouth as the shuttle altered course and accelerated toward the stratosphere and Station 1.

Nayr found 3 on the tendril link. *Launch the counterattack, then conscript them all.*

All, Father?

Nayr considered this with a stroke of his chin, as the pleasing buzz seeped into his veins and leached out all worry and care. *I take it back, 3. Don't conscript anyone with rebel connections. Just kill* them. *Any other refugees, they're yours.*

A pause followed, longer than Nayr liked. What was wrong with 3?

Yes, Father. Without delay.

Nayr opened the file called Revenge and edited it: "Kill Ahrik. Kill Shahl. Kill Renla. Rescue Mother. Watch 3."

Renla's command bunker deep beneath Station Prime shuddered from an explosion on the surface. The moon plunged into darkness. She immediately opened the general channel on her electromag. "We knew they'd hit the main generator first. Go to minimum auxiliary power to reduce energy signatures. They won't stay on your scopes for long, so pick them off when you can."

The dim green lights of the auxiliary power system flickered to life. Renla looked around the bunker at her command group, thirty of her most experienced staff. They represented all the functions necessary in a fight: operations, personnel, intelligence, futures, logistics.

Everyone in the bunker, and on Moon for that matter, knew that Nayr's inevitable response to the rail gun attack meant a fight for their lives. Every able-bodied woman and man on Moon, born on Moon or Dom, was either engaged in the fight or helping with the evacuation of children, the sick, and the elderly.

Renla switched to her private channel with Lyn, who was on the far side of Moon, at the evacuation center. "Two, this is one, over."

"Copy, one."

"The bombardment has begun. Are those refugee ships in their tubes, ready to launch?"

"We need more time, ma'am."

Renla pursed her lips. "We'll hold them off as long as we can."

Renla turned to the ops section, seated nearest to her in the bunker. "We *only* scramble our interceptors if the enemy stops their short-loiter bombing runs and concentrates for an attack. We can't expose our force unnecessarily."

"Check, ma'am," said ops.

"Ma'am," said intel, "we count seventy-five unique interceptors with Ketel of Nayr transponders on short-loiter bombing runs all over Moon. One carrier is waiting just out of range, in the Nejru Gulch between the Moon and Dom gravity wells."

"Good," answered Renla. "That means they don't know where we are for sure." But she bit her lip. In reality, she didn't know if her motley force would survive the night. She opened the general electromag channel one last time, before the fight really began. "Dig on, Fighting 11th. *Cheret.*" Freedom. "Command out."

They had to go electromag silent so the Tyrant's drones couldn't get a bead on their positions. She still had the private, hardened grid link to Lyn, and they'd been able to set up a few hardened grid links to other units, but there was no guarantee these would hold up under what she knew was coming.

Hundreds of Moonborn civilians had joined her force after the Fighting 11th's operation at the elevator stations, when she and Lyn narrowly escaped disaster. Most of the hand commanders she had reached out to sent troops to reinforce her, but only in small numbers. Then Nayr shut down the transport link to Moon and purged the officer corps. By seeding her green units with the hundred and fifty soldiers that the others sent, she was able to cobble together a reinforced combat hand, almost 3,000 in all.

Problem was, most of her new recruits were Moonborn farmers and miners, drawn by the promise of freedom and steady meals, if not tasty ones. Most of them could barely use their weapons, much less maintain discipline or fight as teams.

But they had heart. They sang their battle songs with a conviction she'd never seen in a fighting force. She knew how fragile this passion could be, which was why Nayr's interceptors zipping in to bombard the moon worried her so much. The Fighting 11th needed a win. Not an ambiguous victory, as at the elevator stations, when she'd lost some of her best diggers, but an outright victory.

She hoped the rail gun attack would provoke Nayr into doing something rash, and she hoped that technology and innovation would then give her an edge. Her research team figured out how to capture electromag waves as visual information, and this research was now integrated into their automated targeting system. The night optics that her pilots, commanders, and subcommanders were now equipped with used the same technology. Nayr might have the advantage of speed and numbers and clear logistical lines, as well as cloaking tech and shields for the larger ships like carriers, but the Fighting 11th could see the interceptors when they slowed down to bombard, even if they were cloaked.

The battle reports trickled in, an eerie counterpoise to the dimness. Every once in a while, an atomic would get through the defensive distiller barrage and ravage the surface, but her diggers gave as good as they got. Their hardened bunkers and radiation containment fields limited most of the surface damage to the infrastructure that Nayr's drones already knew about, like the primary power generation system and the mining tunnels. These were built before comms with gravside went dark, before Nayr overthrew the legitimate government.

A half hour into the bombardment, intel spoke up. "Ma'am, twenty-nine enemy interceptors confirmed killed."

Ops scoffed. "There are more where those came from."

Futures nodded. "And they'll keep sending them."

Renla gritted her teeth, then held up her hand to stop the squabble. "Remember who the enemy is. We win by not losing, so let me know if they change tactics. They launched three more craft than are running the bombing sorties, in addition to that carrier."

There were at least a hundred more interceptors on that carrier.

Renla switched on the link to Lyn. "Two?"

Lyn's voice crackled back. "Almost read—"

Static.

"Ma'am," said ops, "we just lost the grid network."

Renla fought the worry out of her eyes. "Get it back. I have to know the status of those civilians."

The intel lead looked up from her compiler display. "Ma'am," she said. "The enemy carrier has shifted to an elliptical orbit. We give a sixty percent chance they'll attempt a surface assault."

Renla nodded, her face grim. One carrier could carry five or six thousand assault troops, depending on how extensive the interceptor arsenal was. Her little force probably wouldn't last long against a determined assault, especially if they found their new network of tunnels and launch tubes. She motioned toward ops and futures. "Give me an assessment of what kind of assault force we'll be up against."

"Yes, ma'am," they said.

The enemy interceptors kept coming, in wave after wave. Even when Renla's markswomen missed the interceptors themselves, her automated distiller targeting systems got most of the atomics they sent down.

Another atomic rocked Renla's sector of the surface. Her bunker shook, and dust showered from the ceiling, floating down in a fine mist.

"Ma'am," said personnel, "that last atomic knocked primary life support offline. Secondary power generation and life support systems now in operation."

This was a setback, but the Fighting 11th were combat engineers. They had secondary and tertiary backups for all essential systems, and the network of defensive strong points and bunkers they built was like nothing Nayr's drones ever faced on Dom. All civilians were concentrated in hardened but simple living quarters buried deep inside Moon, massive metal boxes that could double as refugee ships, two thousand refugees to a ship. In extremis, Renla could order the ships to launch, and they would streak from their launch tubes on preprogrammed trajectories to the dimensional portal, then on to the White Planet, where they would throw themselves at the mercy of an alien civilization.

With the punishment her diggers were meting out, she hoped they didn't have to go that far.

"Personnel," said Renla, "update status of the civilians with two. Are they ready to launch?" She turned to ops. "Unit status and casualty summaries, please."

The reports appeared on her compiler display and a pit opened up in Renla's stomach. "How are all units showing green when I've got three companies with thirty percent casualties?"

"Ma'am," said Ops, "They've maintained their distiller discharge rates, and they have better kill-to-sortie ratios than all but the two most experienced companies."

Renla shook her head. Those three companies with heavy casualties were three of her greenest, with Moonborn recruits making up around half their ranks. Such courage.

Renla looked around the command bunker. "If the Fighting 11th survives the night, it'll be because of those green diggers."

Suddenly, a sense of confusion radiated from the intel section. "Ma'am," said the chief, her voice shaky, "the carrier has changed its orbit again. Looks like it's going to slingshot back to Dom."

Ops: "Copy that, ma'am. The last two waves of enemy interceptors did not drop atomics."

Renla scowled. "If they didn't drop atomics, then what in contumacy *did* they drop?" She rose from her chair and looked around the room. "And can anyone get me two?"

Ops and intel exchanged a helpless glance. Personnel said, "No units have reported explosions, ma'am."

Futures motioned for Renla's attention. "I've got an idea, but you won't like it, ma'am."

Renla narrowed her eyes at the futures chief. "Give me something."

"Nanobios, ma'am."

Renla scrunched up her face in question. Doubt and uncertainty snaked their way into her confidence. "But we neutralized the bioweapon after the attack on Moon, back when people were trying to get off this rock, instead of onto it. The spectral filtration system did that."

The futures chief tapped a few commands into her compiler, then stood. Her three-dimensional schematic showed two balls, one the diameter of an armspan, the other the size of a pinhead, barely noticeable in the dim, green light. She coughed and pointed to the larger sphere. "Imagine the bios we track with spectral filtration are this big." She then pointed to the tiny sphere. "Nanobios would be this small in comparison. Spectral filtration has no hope of catching them."

The intel chief shook her head. "They were supposed to be years away from weaponizing them. If they already figured it out . . ."

A heavy silence settled over the command bunker. The staff looked at each other, then at Renla. She couldn't leave them like this, but she had no idea what to do. She put on a brave face. "We don't know that they're nanobios." She looked at intel. "Is that carrier leaving Moon's orbit?"

The intel chief checked her compiler display, then nodded. Her face told Renla she also wasn't convinced by her commander's confidence.

Renla clasped her hands behind her back and forced herself to take a happy tone. "If they've given up, then we've won."

The moment she said it, she knew it wasn't true. The words rang hollow against the soulless stone walls of the bunker. As if in response, the electromag pinged once.

"Ma'am," said Ops, "link to two is back up."

"One, this is two." Lyn's voice trembled with panic. "We have a problem."

What little confidence remained in Renla's breast evaporated, like water dancing on a hot stove. She sucked in her breath. She knew the problem before Lyn even spoke. Nanobios were invading Moon. "Launch, Lyn. Launch all of them. Get those civilians out of here." She whirled toward ops. "Sound air alarm on all channels. Don exosuits. Vent air from all pressurized spaces. One minute."

Renla reached for her helmet and slumped into her chair. She squeezed an armrest. This might look like a win on the outside, but it sure felt like a loss. Half of those green diggers wouldn't even get their exosuits on in time.

Renla promised herself that she would make Nayr pay for every life he ended tonight, whether Doman or Moonborn. Freedom always comes with a price, and Nayr was going to pay it.

15 Superiority of Numbers

AHRIK GRASPED A HANDHOLD and leaned into the rear cabin of the shuttle. He donned the bitter mask of command, for perhaps the last time. "Get your exosuits on," he said to his four clones as they strapped into their jump seats. "After launch, two of you man the crew-served distiller aft, and the other two man the port and starboard distillers."

The men saluted from their jump seats, but not as quickly or as sharply as he hoped they would. Ahrik knew the beginnings of insurrection when he saw it. They may not have recognized it yet, but Ahrik had been there before, a soldier on the cusp of rebellion. He saw the slight hesitation in their faces, the stolen glances to see what others would do, the moment of wavering volition before years of military habit kicked in.

Were these the only remaining clones of the 10,000 he had started with all those years ago? He'd grown up with his 10,000, fought with them, and now almost all lay in their eternal repose, a bitter sacrifice to the insatiable appetite of war. If these last four blamed Ahrik for the death of their comrades, he wouldn't hold it against them.

They eyed him with a faint sense of annoyance. At being commanded by a man who arrogated power to himself. Who was he anymore, anyway? How much longer could he lead, truly?

"Sir," echoed the pilot's voice from the cockpit, with a calmness that defied their desperate situation. His shoulder patches marked him as a pilot from Renla's Fighting 11th. "The nanobios have reached our sector."

Ahrik tightened his grip on the handhold and faced his last four clones. "Once we're near the portal, mash anything that's not a refugee ship, check?"

They nodded. "Check."

"First," said Ahrik.

"To the fight," they answered, without the vigor of battle cries long past.

He resolved the hatch to the rear cabin as he turned back into the cockpit. He gripped a bulkhead, gloved fingers curling over grease and grime. That might have been the last time he heard his ketel's battle slogan, or anything at all, for that matter.

First to the fight. Last to die.

He plopped into the co-pilot's seat and strapped in. The electromag crackled to life with Renla's voice, the tones strained, almost panicked. "Command here. I'm transmitting rendezvous coordinates on the White Planet, just in case Zharla comes through here. We have reason to believe that Shahl is headed there, too."

Ahrik scrounge a wrist compiler from a compartment at the back of the cabin and downloaded the coordinates into it. He didn't know if he'd have the presence of mind, or the time, to do it later. He slapped the compiler in his wrist, next to the steel band reminding him of his sons who had died.

Renla crackled over the electromag once again, a descant of panic in her voice. "Get out of here. I don't know what the nanobios will do to your launch tube. Command out."

The pilot grunted and punched the controls. The shuttle shuddered, but did not move. The pilot swore, then unbuckled himself and crawled under the control console. He poked his head out and nodded to the base of Ahrik's seat. "Hand me that hammer there?"

He didn't say "sir." Ahrik didn't care.

The pilot hammered at the underside of the control console. "Welcome to Renla's Fighting 11th"—*bam*—"where we jury-rig"—*bam, bam*—"everything."

Ahrik jiggled the controls to transluce the hull on his side of the cockpit. His jaw dropped at what he saw. "Pilot, the wall of our launch bay is melting."

Bam, bam!

Chunks of cobalt blue rock fell away as the wall rippled and began to fold like poorly-cooked pastry dough. Ahrik reached for his helmet and slapped it on.

"Sir?" buzzed a voice in his helmet. The clones from the rear.

Bam!

"I see it. Helmets on."

The pilot's legs squirmed for a better angle under the console. His voice, unconcerned, was faint from outside Ahrik's helmet. "Figure we have about thirty seconds."

The pilot's lack of urgency filled Ahrik with alarm. *Bam, bam!* Ahrik examined the flight controls. "Shall I . . . hit something?"

The pilot's hands and head appeared as he scooted out from under the console and slapped the hammer back onto the magnetic strip at the foot of Ahrik's seat with a dull clang of finality, like the toll of a funeral bell. He slammed his own helmet on his head and swiped at a switch on the control panel. The boson drive bloomed to life. The hum reached a fever pitch in a matter of seconds, which was less time than Ahrik thought they had.

Ahead of them, the launch tube shimmered blue-black. The pilot sucked in a breath, as if preparing to experience sharp pain. He leaned forward. His voice crackled over the shuttle's internal comm. "This is gonna sting."

An ominous sucking sound balanced the airlock to vacuum in the bay outside. They paused, another eternity, then lurched forward, the blackness of space racing toward them at an improbable speed. Renla had made her launch tubes so efficient that Ahrik even felt the acceleration in his chest, despite the inertial stabilizers that he assumed were functional.

Until they cleared it, Ahrik didn't think the tube would hold. Blue rock sloughed off the walls in limp strips, and vertigo wrapped around his mind in the two seconds it took to clear into space.

The sensation of being suspended in space swam over Ahrik as they left the reference point of the tube. With nothing but space around them, it felt like they'd stopped moving, even though he still felt the acceleration and knew, in his heart if not his mind, that they had passed into the vast danger of space, where a dozen of Nayr's interceptors wanted to slime them into space junk.

He checked their speed on his display. They were moving faster than he'd ever known a shuttle to move. "What's our target speed, pilot?"

The pilot shrugged as he plotted a course in a wide arc toward the portal to the White Planet. "Hmm . . . faster than the Tyrant's missiles, hopefully. Hadn't put much thought into it."

Ahrik familiarized himself with the forward weapon controls. Renla's mechanics had fitted the shuttle with two clusters of makeshift missiles, tipped with boson bombs that could bring down a shield momentarily, in addition to the standard large-gauge distillers. One shuttle armed like this couldn't do much damage against a carrier, but it could rip an interceptor in half, if it could catch one with its shields down.

The pilot hummed a dark warning, uncharacteristic for him. "Decelerate, sir, or proceed?"

Piqued at the pilot's tone, Ahrik looked up. His heart fell to his feet. At least two dozen distress signals chimed onto his display. The portal was close now, but all around them dead and dying refugee ships drifted through space, the macabre jetsam of a massacre. Most of the ships had been torn apart by the force of the *nayra's* kinetic weapons. Others were cored and shredded by distiller charges. The tiny specks of headlamps from drifting exosuits rushed by, as if floating on some alternate timeline.

"Sweet Lady," muttered Ahrik. If he hailed these distress signals, the *nayra* would know exactly where they were, and probably guess it was Ahrik. His heart grew heavy, and Ahrik realized that the refugee ships made it out of failing launch tubes on the moon only to meet bloodthirsty *nayra* at the portal. He wondered if Hawk had made it to the White Planet, or Shahl. Did Nayr really want Shahl dead? Maybe Zharla was right, and there was still hope for him.

"Sir?" asked the pilot again.

Ahrik clenched his teeth. Just how important was he, really? He considered Zharla and Shahl, his family of sorts. How many other families like his would Nayr destroy before he was stopped? The unsuspecting inhabitants of the White Planet needed someone to help them organize a defense. Someone to warn them, at least. Dom was finished. At least the White Planet held out hope. Was Ahrik truly the one to be that leader for the White Planet, after how he'd failed Dom?

His face darkened. "Get through the portal."

The pilot nodded with characteristic nonchalance and tapped the console's display, then furrowed his brow. "They've tagged us."

Ahrik checked his own display and commed to the back. "We have five bogies on approach. Looks like they're tired of easy prey."

The lead clone's voice crackled back: "Check, sir."

The pilot smiled an apology. "Hope you guys didn't eat a big breakfast. We're gonna take evasive action, and the inertial stabilizers don't work so great on this rig."

Ahrik primed the forward distillers and tagged the bogies with his missile targeting system. "You get us through that portal at max speed. We'll take care of the rest."

The pilot took a deep breath and engaged the remote piloting control, eyelids fluttering. Ahrik's eyes widened in surprise. "You have an internal compiler for remote piloting? Are you keteli?"

"Not a clone." He pointed to the base of his helmet. "Just another one of Commander Renla's innovations. She figured we might need it to even the odds. Remote cognitive control is the only thing that works right on this rig." He smiled. "Dig on."

"First to the . . . Dig on."

Their shuttle lurched and accelerated in a new direction, a vector to squeeze through the *nayra's* closing cordon.

Ahrik grunted. He launched missiles at the first two bogies. He only had six, so he had to make them count. If the enemy still had missiles left, they hadn't launched them.

Ahrik wondered if the Tyrant's interceptors had explosive- or boson-tipped missiles. He turned to the pilot. "How are the shields on this rig?"

The pilot shrugged. "Like I said, the remote cognitive control is the only thing that always works right."

Ahrik commed to the back. "We have very little margin for error. Put the distillers on target as soon as our missiles hit. We can't let their shields regenerate."

"Check, sir."

"Here we go," said the pilot.

Ahrik examined his display. The five interceptors launched missiles, about two dozen of them. They knew who was in this shuttle, then. Nayr wanted to kill him after all.

"Forget about those interceptors," said the pilot over the shuttle's general channel. "We need our distillers to knock out missiles."

Their shuttle echoed with the hollow chirp of the side and aft distillers. *Thu-thu-thunk, thu-thu-thunk.*

The pilot jerked the shuttle to starboard, then dipped and banked hard to port, underneath the lifeless hulk of a refugee transporter. Ahrik's stomach tightened, and he grunted to keep blood in his head. Through the translucent hull, Ahrik saw a half dozen missiles tear into the refugee transporter and shred it apart in a ball of flame. Debris pinged against their shield as the pilot weaved and dodged the gruesome shrapnel of violence.

Ahrik narrowed his wavering focus on finding more of those missiles. He had to be ready to mash targets if missiles or interceptors crossed the forward distillers' arc. Targets shifted this way and that as the shuttle careened and yawed and slid and dipped. Ahrik's head lolled, but he focused on breathing, on staying alert.

The shuttle darted behind another derelict refugee ship, dodging flotsam and debris, using the derelict ship as a screen against another volley of missiles. Ahrik checked his console display. Their boson missiles had hit two of the interceptors, but there was so much jetsam around them that he didn't see how they could range the interceptors with their distillers, at least not in time.

"Bingo," said the pilot. "Hold on."

The shuttle shot forward, through a narrow hole in the derelict ship, zipping past steel girders, mangled piping, and bodies with faces frozen in laments of horror. Two more enemy missiles detonated against the derelict ship behind them, and the shuttle pilot rolled and swerved to avoid the hull rocking into them.

Ahrik heard gagging over the comm channel to the rear.

They shot out the other side as another missile slammed into the hull of the derelict ship. The shuttle buckled with the shockwave. Four more missiles bore down on them from behind, but Ahrik heard a *thu-thu-thunk*, then cheering from the rear.

The pilot jerked the shuttle to port and punched the boson drive, hurling them toward the portal, a floating sentinel, its marker buoys blinking happily, unaware of the carnage that wandered before them. Ahrik checked his display. Four interceptors raced through the debris to engage them. Where was the fifth interceptor?

Ahrik tagged the interceptors he hadn't hit already and launched two more boson missiles. One failed to launch. Ahrik slammed a fist onto his armrest. "What'll it be next? The boson drive?"

"Hey, don't jinx it." The pilot leaned his head to the right, and the shuttle rolled to starboard and through the gap closing between two massive shards of space debris.

The shuttle buckled and jerked into a slow yaw as it plunged through. The pilot let out an angry moan.

"Sir," a clone commed from the rear. "Lost starboard distiller."

Suddenly, an interceptor slid in front of them, shield weak from one of Ahrik's missiles, broadside showing, probably surprised by the unnatural vector they had taken after skating through the debris.

Ahrik didn't hesitate. He squeezed off a three-second burst. Its regenerating shield absorbed the first two seconds, but the last second cut through the hull like a scythe. The interceptor erupted in a cloud of elemental mist and debris. The rounded nose spun off and slammed into a slab of metal that had once belonged to the hull of a military transporter, maybe even one of Ahrik's, from the contingent he'd sent under Hawk's command.

Ahrik hadn't sensed Hawk over the tendril hack back on the moon. Did that mean he'd made a run for the White Planet and made it, or had he failed too?

Distillers chattered from the rear of the shuttle and the lead clone's voice crackled over the comm. "We got one, too."

The pilot fought with the yaw. "Three more."

The two that Ahrik could still see on his display launched more missiles—how many did they have?—and spun in pursuit of the shuttle as it shot past. The pilot oriented on the portal once again and rammed the boson drive into full acceleration.

The shuttle sprang forward. The portal careened toward them. The rear distillers chattered. Ahrik checked his display. Three of four missiles neutralized.

Then the boson drive went silent and fear descended on the cockpit.

"Pilot . . ."

He kicked at the console. Nothing. The fourth missile exploded somewhere in the baffle made by their boson drive, and the shuttle lurched. The pilot unstrapped and pushed off from his seat.

Ahrik clicked open the comm to his clones with his tongue. "Damage?"

Silence.

Ahrik unstrapped and leaped toward the rear, slapping his hand against the control to dissolve the hatch. Air rushed by him as the hatch dissolved.

Three heads turned as he entered, eyes wide. A mess of metal and wiring remained where the rear distiller had been, and the fourth head turned, more slowly, belonging to a clone that had been blown against the opposite bulkhead. He raised a fist in defiance, but Ahrik could tell he was not okay. The lead clone, manning the port distiller, left his post to help his comrade.

The hull transluce flickered in and out, showing one interceptor approaching from port and one from the rear. The two interceptors' frontal shields shimmered, fully regenerated. Ahrik's missile must have missed. Their distiller tubes nodded with menace as the interceptors shuddered to a stop, not fifty meters away. Their missile tubes were empty.

"Why ain't they mushin' us?" asked the clone seated on the deck, against the opposite bulkhead.

Two short raps with the hammer—*bam, bam*—echoed from the cockpit.

Ahrik narrowed his eyes. "They might want us alive."

Bam!

The clone leader chuckled. "Sir, they might wunt *yuh* ulive."

A pause, then they lost artigrav. On instinct, Ahrik responded to the float by kicking off a strut, so as not to be stuck in the middle of the cabin. He floated to the ceiling. The hull transluced and he saw two missile trails arcing underneath their shuttle and toward the interceptors. The interceptors would be unlikely to see the missiles coming, with the distance so short.

Ahrik glanced toward the cockpit, through the open hatch, and the pilot looked back and smiled. Then their own hull shimmered. The pilot had diverted power from the artigrav to bring their shields up.

Ahrik kicked off the ceiling and shoved his hands into the portside distiller controls. He squeezed the triggers just as one of their two remaining boson missiles hit the interceptor to their port. The interceptor wagged back with the impact, and its shields faded. Ahrik's distiller charges slammed into its nose. He saw the pilot's alarm as his ship caved in around him, then burst apart.

The pitter-patter of the other interceptor's distiller charges hitting their shields rippled through the rear cabin. Their boson drive came to life—finally—and the shuttle pitched to avoid the deadly stream of matter scramblers. Their shield blinkered, and a line of holes melted through their hull.

The shuttle rolled as it pitched, easing the interceptor toward the port distiller's arc. Ahrik jammed the distiller as far as it would go in that direction, but the line of holes melting into their hull paced toward him, a morbid cadence of approaching doom.

A charge punched through the hull and slammed one of the clones back against the opposite hull. He gave a withering gasp over the comm as he flew, trailing crystal droplets of blood. The last clone flew to his aid.

Ahrik would only get one shot at this. He flexed his hands over the triggers inside the twin distiller casings.

His heart pounded in his helmet, and his breath sounded a focused drumbeat in his mind. Be the last one to die. Them or the interceptor pilot. A patient death game, an eternity passing in an instant, an inexorable contest of wills.

Out of the corner of his eye, Ahrik saw a hole open up by his left hand. He forced down his alarm and focused on the interceptor. Almost there. He ducked as another hole opened up, this time near his head.

Suddenly, the shuttle dropped. Ahrik rammed up the distiller, cursing his lack of focus. The line of holes jerked up with the shuttle's movement, but just then the interceptor slipped into range of the distiller's arc.

Ahrik squeezed. A stream of tracers flew through the blackness and hit the interceptor's undercarriage. Its shield absorbed them. No. Had their missile missed? Another dud?

Ahrik couldn't give up. They had no other hope, and a man does desperate things when he's out of hope. He screamed into his helmet.

Calm and cool, the interceptor stopped shooting and rotated in space. The interceptor pilot knew they were as good as dead. He just wanted to draw out the moment of agony and terror as long as possible.

Ahrik screamed into his helmet and kept the trigger depressed. Never give up. Show them no fear.

The interceptor drew a bead on them, head on now. Ahrik saw the bastard smile. He almost felt the interceptor's distillers prime, their imaginary hum rippling through his spine.

Then Ahrik felt a click underneath the shuttle, and another missile arced toward the interceptor. He paused in his screaming and shouting and shooting and let out a slow breath of air. The missile that hadn't launched earlier. Their pilot had figured out how to launch it.

Steady. This was it.

The interceptor pilot's face registered alarm when the missile struck the nose. He had waited too long. The folly of hubris. Die, demon of Nayr.

Ahrik squeezed. The interceptor bloomed apart. Then, sweet silence.

Comms came back online, as did artigrav and life support. "Sir . . . come," said the pilot.

Ahrik heard pain in his voice.

When he got back to the cockpit, Ahrik saw that the pilot's right shoulder was missing. Smooth, melted flesh formed the cavity where his shoulder used to be. When the pilot had dipped the shuttle to give them more time against that last interceptor, he'd sacrificed himself. His right arm hung limp, dangling from an improbable swatch of flesh.

Ahrik noticed that a section of the pilot's chair was also missing, a portion of his torso along with it. Ahrik assessed the injuries. He felt helpless. Spleen. A kidney. Most of the large intestine. Gone. Even though distillers cauterized flesh, they still mangled the insides. Internal bleeding would kill him before his external injuries did.

The pilot winced. "Pilot . . . rig." He pointed with this good hand. "Not much . . . juice left"—he coughed—"can make it . . . through portal . . . rendezvous . . . White Planet"—he coughed, and his eyes widened with alarm and pain—"programmed . . . into nav."

Ahrik, tentative, inserted his hands into the controls and toggled the display to summarize system status. He saw lots of red, but the portal drew closer, a graveyard of ships and lives floating by in a slow parade. Ahrik doubted he could get the shuttle to move faster.

One of the indicators on his display showed the growing list of distress signals they'd received. He scrolled through refugee ship after refugee ship. Helplessness overcame him by degrees as he scrolled through. Then his gaze fell on a name he recognized: his own personal shuttle, the one that Hawk took when last they parted in Meran.

Hawk had made a run for the White Planet after all. Elation surged in Ahrik's breast for a moment, before he remembered that his shuttle couldn't hold more than twenty people, packed tightly. And that was before the main hatch in the rear was mangled by a *nayri* missile. Their shuttle had no way to mate with another ship.

Had any of his sons made it through the portal to the White Planet?

Ahrik brought up the distress signal and peered at the schematic on the holo display. The ship was definitely Ahrik's. Maybe Hawk had launched from Dom before Ahrik, so that Renla's tendril hack scan didn't pick him up. Ahrik tried to remember if Renla had pointed the tendril repeaters in the direction of the portal. A painful fog clouded his memory.

Ahrik peered through the flickering hull and into space. Hawk's ship, if it was indeed his ship, drifted nearby, somewhere in this wreck of debris and shattered hopes.

Ahrik glanced at the pilot. His helmet lolled to the side. His body slumped against his restraints. Gone.

"Go to the Lady," said Ahrik, placing a hand on his left shoulder.

The portal drew nearer.

He peered into the lumpy mess of space around the shuttle, his eyes sifting through ragged debris, drifting derelicts, and careening shards of metal to find a speck of a shuttle, like finding a tick in a bowl of black pepper.

Father.

Hawk. Over the tendril link. Ahrik's blood went cold. Was Hawk still alive? Ahrik's shuttle was almost on top of the portal now, limping along. If they stopped to save Hawk, could they reprogram the nav to get them to the rendezvous point on the White Planet? If he left Hawk, how could he live with himself?

Then he saw Hawk's shuttle. Two drifting refugee ships rammed into one another, and Hawk's shuttle emerged from behind them, rising out of the blossoming debris. A shard of a hull bashed into Hawk's shuttle and jerked it in Ahrik's general direction. Its markings were clear.

Father.

Ahrik squeezed his eyes shut.

"Sir," commed the clone leader from the back. "Shuttle t'sturboard bears murkings frum th'Ketel uv Ahrik. One uv ours?"

They were nearly to the portal. They were so close that the blinking buoys crowded Ahrik's vision, but they could still turn back.

Then Ahrik remembered the tendril hack. If Nayr could hack the tendril link to track Ahrik's sons, then he could also spoof a distress signal from one of his sons. Was Hawk's distress signal genuine? Could Ahrik afford to find out?

An alarm tore Ahrik's attention back to the central console display. The fifth interceptor bore down on them from the rear. Was this a trap? If they turned aside now to answer Hawk's distress signal, or what might be his distress signal, the interceptor would finish them off, but if they proceeded through the portal they had a good chance of making it to the rendezvous point, assuming the interceptor didn't follow.

"Sir?" asked the clone leader again, over the internal comm.

A bead of sweat ran down Ahrik's forehead and into his eye. He steeled himself for the guilt he would have at not knowing whether he could have saved a few more of his sons.

From the other end of the comm line, the silence screamed at Ahrik with rage at leaving one of their own to die out here. But they would all die if they turned back now.

Ahrik gave the boson drive everything he could. They slipped through the portal and into another dimension of time and space. Silent agony beat at Ahrik's mind. Hawk. He was more than a loyal pilot and two. He was a friend.

Ahrik clicked on the comm. "If that interceptor follows us through, slime him."

The clone leader did not acknowledge the order. In a voice of barely concealed rage, he muttered, "We lost Touch. He wuz my best healer."

Which one was Touch? Ahrik had only three clones left, three sons. He would have to learn their names if he wanted to lead them. If he even dared to risk having more lives on his conscience.

The interceptor did not follow them through.

The White Planet loomed before them, and doubt gnawed at Ahrik's chest. His heartbeat sped up. Could he lead his last three sons now?

Would they follow?

The clone leader emerged from the rear, his teeth clenched, and switched to a private command channel. "Did yuh see thut shuttle buck there? Wuz it Hawk's?"

"The shuttle was dead. It was a trap."

The clone leader narrowed his eyes with distrust and returned to the rear.

Esh'a stared death in the face. A young woman, her body frail and overworked, stared up from the packed dirt and coughed into the thin mountain air. Red spittle lurched from her mouth. A hush fell over the miners around them.

"Give her some space," said Esh'a, kneeling down beside the young woman. Esh'a hadn't even bothered to learn her name. No one learned real names here, at the mine. People died too quickly. Esh'a was glad for years of hard work and strenuous physical training back on Moon. It made her strong.

Here, on this new planet, with its thin air, mine work made for a harsh taskmaster. Thoughts of her daughter Sera drove Esh'a on and gave her strength while others succumbed to a nameless disease in this strange place.

But this young woman was different. She reminded Esh'a of Sera. Long, auburn hair, with a feisty determination to defy the odds. A fighter in spirit, even if her body was weak. Esh'a couldn't watch her die, not like this. "You, Spike, help me move her." When they had to call to one another, they used only nicknames. "We can't let the *nayra* find her."

Spike glanced at Esh'a, but went on stabbing at the stony, volcanic ground with the pointed end of his long, metal staff. If the soldiers guarding them had access to modern mining technology, they didn't waste it on refugees and slaves.

Spike grunted. "She'll die. They'll bury her. Or burn her. We'll keep working."

"Spike." Esh'a sighed and rose up, padded over to the large man, one of those not afflicted by the shallow cough, blurred vision, and trembling hands that many others had. Like Sera had.

Was Sera still alive?

Esh'a rested her hand on Spike's forearm, the tension and anger burned in the muscles under his skin as he raised and lowered, raised and lowered his metal staff. Volcanic rock, dirt, and twigs exploded out each time he slammed his spike into the ground.

Esh'a applied gentle pressure. She would need Spike's strength and the respect he commanded with the others if she was to carry her plan through, a plan she had begun contemplating the moment the young woman collapsed in a coughing heap on the ground. "Let's help this one live."

Spike stopped and narrowed his eyes at her. "Then what? You know what the soldiers will do to us if they find out."

"We hide her, nurse her back to health."

Spike grunted and relaunched his attack on the rocky ground. "Sounds like a death wish to me."

Esh'a peered at the miners gathering around them. The young woman coughed once more and groaned, then her breathing grew even more shallow. She didn't have much time.

Esh'a glared. "Then what, Spike? If we give up on life, we give up on what it means to be human."

One of the miners in the small crowd, with vacant eyes and a rinsing pan in his hand, cleared his throat. "We stopped being human long ago, when the *nayra* brought us here as slaves."

"No." Esh'a dropped to one knee and unhitched her canteen from her belt. She shook it. Not much left. She ran her tongue over her parched lips, then closed her eyes and prepared herself to sleep thirsty that night.

Esh'a worked her grimy thumbs under the lip of the stopper and popped it off, then eased the spigot onto the young woman's lips. The young woman seemed to draw strength from the few drops of water that flowed into her parched mouth. Her eyes fluttered open, and a weak smile stretched over her face.

After Esh'a emptied the last few drops of her water into the young woman's mouth, she glared at the other miners, first at Spike and Pan, then at the rest. They understood perfectly well what Esh'a had done, even if the young woman was not lucid enough to understand. These mountains were cool, but they were dry. Very dry. The breeze carried the scent of pine on the air, but the needles would snap at the lightest pressure. Esh'a cast her gaze at those gathered round. "We are human."

Most of the miners stared at her, dumbfounded. Water rations were still a day away. Spike stepped forward. "I'll share my water with you till the rations come."

Pan called out, "I will, too."

"Me too," said another, then another, and another, until all twenty or so miners in their work group had stopped their pounding, hammering, sifting, panning, separating, and sorting, and called out that they too would help Esh'a fend off her thirst.

Esh'a beamed. She hadn't felt a part of something like this since, well, since Sera had gotten sick, back when their family hadn't a care in the world and their life had passed from one happy moment to another. This was what it meant to be human.

"Ho, slaves!"

Fear rippled through the small crowd, and miners crouched, like frightened prey ready to run.

A hundred meters away, one of the Tyrant's soldiers bounded toward them. The soldiers were nearly superhuman back home, but here, in the lower grav, they could leap five meters at a time with ease.

The miners scattered back to their work, all except Esh'a and Spike, who stood looking at each other for a beat. Then, without a word, Spike leaned down and gathered the young woman in his arms. Spike scrambled over the rocky terrain with his precious burden, toward a stand of pine about twenty meters farther up a small rise.

"Ho, there!" the soldier called again as he skidded to a stop near Esh'a. He grimaced in Spike's direction. "Where yuh goin' with that gurl, slave?"

Spike ignored him. Alarm sprang into Esh'a's chest. These soldiers harbored little regard for life, human or not. The soldier raised his distiller, and the chilling hum of the weapon charging sounded its doom on the crisp mountain air.

Esh'a jumped forward, but not fast enough to keep the soldier from unleashing his malice. A single matter scrambler charge sprang from the weapon—*thunk*—and Esh'a heard Spike give a doleful grunt. Esh'a leaped and slammed her head down onto the soldier's chest, like a steel point striking volcanic rock. The soldier was surprised, or out of practice, or dull from months of guarding half-starved slaves, because he staggered back in shock. Acting on instinct remembered from years of military training, so long ago, Esh'a shook the grogginess from her head, collected her legs underneath her, and lashed out with a kick aimed at the soldier's neck, which was surprisingly easy to do in the lower gravity. Her foot connected with a satisfying crunch, and the soldier brought his off-hand to his neck as he choked on his voice box.

Esh'a moved in close to beat his distiller. She slapped the weapon away and jabbed his kidney with a fist to double him over, and then used her elbows to batter his temples.

She beat him longer than she needed to, but weeks of oppression and penury released themselves in the violence. This soldier represented all the death and injustice that Esh'a had seen, the pain of not knowing whether her family was alive or dead.

The soldier's eyes rolled back into his head, and Esh'a ignored the pain in her elbows as blood spurted from his ears. The soldier crumpled to the ground, and she ripped his distiller off and pounded the side of his head until it grew pliable. Even then, she pressed her furious attack. Esh'a knew what Spike's grunt meant, that he would not rise again. For all the miners who'd suffered, and for the dehumanizing oppression this soldier had inflicted, Esh'a had to finish what she started. Power coursed through her body as she gave the soldier his due.

A hand gripped Esh'a by the shoulder. She sprang up and whipped herself around, the hate high on her blood. Pan stared her in the face, and his eyes flickered toward Spike, confirming what she suspected.

She took a step toward the bodies of Spike and the young woman, but Pan held a hand out and shook his head, eyes flashing a warning. He raised an eyebrow in the direction of the body at her feet. "How long before his friends show up?"

She frowned at him, unwilling to tell him the true odds of success for the hasty plan she had just set in motion. She reached down and tore off the soldier's kall pack so she could use the distiller herself, then she looked at the miners gathered around. "My name is Esh'a."

The miners gasped at hearing her true name.

She gripped the weapon. "I am from Moon, but I'm not Moonborn. My Moonborn daughter fell sick, and our algae crop failed, so I went gravside to provide for my family. But then the *nayra* kidnapped me and brought me here. I don't know if my husband and daughter are alive or dead, or if they have any clue where to look for me."

She spat at the dead soldier on the ground. "We all have a story. We all have something or someone to fight for. Or against." She raised the distiller in the air. "Fight now. Fight to write your story. Fight so someone will remember your name."

Murmurs of assent rippled through the assembled miners, and Esh'a gained heart. "There are only twenty of them," she said, "but two hundred of us." She tested the distiller's prime, and it gave off an ominous hum. "They'll be back. We'll be ready."

Clusters of three and four miners, driven by the prospect of freedom, or at least release, ran off to warn the other nine groups of miners. A cluster of others carried the bodies of Spike and the young woman and nestled them in the stand of pines, out of sight. The rest of the miners ignored the soldier's body and returned to their work, as if nothing were wrong, as if the corpse laying on the ground were the most natural thing on the White Planet.

Esh'a picked her way toward the stand of pine, to set her position. When she passed Spike and the young woman's bodies, she had to look away. Spike had tried to shield the young woman, but the soldier had set the distiller to its maximum charge. The matter scramblers had gone through both of them. They didn't have a chance.

Esh'a caught a glimpse of the young woman's face before she looked away. Peaceful, happy. No pain. A face that knew freedom, at long last. Esh'a wondered how many more would free themselves in this way before the day was out.

Esh'a dug her position with the vacuum setting on the distiller, expelling the refuse on the ground behind a clump of rocks, where the next group of soldiers wouldn't see as they approached. Esh'a examined the kall readout on the distiller, and it was much lower than she expected it would be.

The *nayra* probably wasted their kall.

Before long, five soldiers came bounding over the ridge and clustered in a huddle around their fallen comrade. Esh'a had the high ground and a clear field of vision. She aimed her weapon, slowed her breathing, and waited for just the right moment.

Pan walked by the group of soldiers with a small pile of dirt in his pan.

"You," said one of the soldiers. "Come here."

Pan hesitated, and the soldier leveled his distiller at Pan's chest, but Esh'a squeezed the trigger—*thunk*—and the soldier's head evaporated in a red-gray mist. The other soldiers crouched and looked around, trying to find the source. Esh'a dropped two more before they could react. *Thunk. Thunk.* They were caught in the open.

A blood-curdling shout went through the other miners, and they swarmed toward the remaining two soldiers, brandishing their tools as weapons. The soldiers, before they succumbed to the angry mass of miners, sprayed distiller charges in a wild spasm of violence. The skirmish took less than ten seconds, leaving in its wake a flower of bludgeoned and steaming bodies, some writhing in pain, some still, and some casting eyes about warily, as if not believing that it could really be over, or that it had happened at all, or that they were lucky enough to be alive.

As she began to count the cost, Esh'a vomited what little remained in her stomach toward the pile of rocks behind her position. She paused to catch her breath and process the surge of adrenaline in her blood.

In the distance she heard the angry *thu-thu-thunk* of distillers and the agonized cries of wounded and dying miners, but she also heard the cheers of miners as they overcame their oppressors.

She was about to scramble out of her hole when a sound behind her froze her in place, the sound of combat boots crunching over rocks. Miners' feet didn't make that sound, not here, because they were only given soft-soled shoes, to make it harder to flee. Then, a dark and forbidding voice said, "Huld it right there."

A distiller primed. She waited for the dreaded *thunk*, and the end of her mortal pain.

Renla surveyed the bleak scene. Such a strain against reason. What evil brought humanity to such depths? Outside her office window, on the Station Prime platform, hundreds of refugees from Dom waited in switchbacks, faces hollow. Hungry children wailed their agony to anyone who might care, while her diggers, some of them conscripted Moonborn, distributed their personal rations to the most vulnerable. A few diggers had to draw weapons on refugees who tried to take food from the children. Such desperation.

This was the last refugee ship to make it off Dom.

Renla crossed her arms over her chest and sighed. "Lyn, when I first stepped onto this platform, it was full of Moonborn, but also of hope. Hope for an escape, for a solution to a confounding situation. Now, it is packed with people from Dom, but also with despair."

Lyn shook her head. "We turned back the Tyrant's first wave, ma'am. Those people back then had just as few options as these." She moved to open the door. "We have to give them hope. Even if they die, we can free them from despair before they do."

Renla shook her head. "Despair and hope bringing Moon and Dom together." She eyed her two. "War makes strange bedfellows."

Lyn smiled with mock surprise. "Ma'am, if I didn't know better, I'd say you've found a soft spot for people from Moon."

Renla grunted. "I just want to destroy Nayr and his system of evil."

Lyn considered the throng of refugees. "He'll be back, and with even greater force than before."

"You're right," said Renla, rising and moving toward the door, "but I think these people will revolt if we tell them we're conscripting them to fight in the 11th."

Renla thought how much the last few months defied hope. They'd won victories of sorts at the elevator stations and with the rail gun, but tens of thousands of refugees still launched on ships bound for the White Planet, with Moon as a waystation. Renla still didn't know if the nanobios were under control, but she had lost half of her new recruits when she vented atmosphere to keep the nanobios from spreading. Renla had rescued Ahrik from Peshron, but Zharla had stayed on Dom, then Renla had launched the rail gun attack and turned back the counterattack. That was almost three weeks ago, so Renla didn't know if her old friend was alive or dead.

With a heavy heart, Renla palmed open the door and let the anguish and fear wash over her. There was no use trying to staunch it now. If Zharla wasn't on this ship, then she was almost certainly dead.

This war had made victims of them all.

A few of the lucky ones had made it through the portal, but most didn't, after Nayr started sending his patrols. She prayed, not for the first time, that those who fled would find more charity on the White Planet than in the charnel hell Nayr had made out of Dom and Moon and everywhere in between.

Renla slowed her step when she exited her office. Tension rested like a pall over the Station Prime platform. She expected stress and impatience about families being separated, but this? Didn't these refugees know that she was trying to save them? These refugees from Dom were less grateful than the Moonborn that had squatted on her platform all those weeks before. Renla shook her head.

She and her diggers had done so much for the refugees. Renla had assigned an entire squadron, the 11–2 Hellbats, to keep the portal clear for the refugee ships, and still Ahrik had only barely made it through. She couldn't spare any more forces. The nanobios could still take over Moon. Its environment became less livable every day, and she needed her diggers to prepare for Nayr's inevitable second assault.

Her womanpower needs were critical.

At the far end of the platform, one of her subcommanders called out instructions to the refugees exiting the switchbacks. "Children to the right. One adult may accompany them." He motioned this way and that with his arms. "Everyone else to the left."

Grumbles of agitation rippled through the crowd. "Split up?" ". . . going to go?" Murmurs echoed. ". . . to the mines?" ". . . stay together." Refugee heads turned in every direction, as if they would be able to find a way off this rock, forsaken by all, deity and mortal alike. ". . . won't leave my grandkids . . ." ". . . not going to the mines."

Someone raised their arms in exasperation and gave the subcommander a cold glare. "What's going on?"

Renla quickened her pace toward the end of the platform, her eyes focused on the subcommander.

The subcommander's face flushed with impatience. He glared at his challenger and took on an insolent air. "Look, I don't make the rules."

Renla frowned. The subcommander was just about at the end of his tether. She didn't blame him. Nine hours on a task a digger wasn't trained for was bound to put him on edge.

Lyn gave her a look. Renla's two felt the tension, as well.

They were almost to the end of the platform when a man began to push and shove, shouldering his way toward the temporary barrier that kept the refugees in line. Just as Lyn was passing the barrier, the man emerged from the crowd.

Lyn stopped to confront him, her hands up in appeasement. "Okay, okay. Calm do—"

The man swung his fist. He caught Lyn unawares, right on the chin. Her head whipped back, and she staggered toward the wall. Her eyes were wide with shock.

People near them gasped. The man, muttering something about freedom, threw his leg over the barrier, but Renla closed on him in one step. She said nothing, just planted her feet, cocked her arm, and jammed her elbow into the side of his head.

Her arm guard caught him in the temple, and he slumped to the ground on the near side of the barrier.

Murmurs of uncertainty fluttered over the crowd. The subcommander stopped talking and stared. Two of his diggers rushed toward Renla. She picked the man up by the arm, surprised by how light he was. She felt a twinge of guilt at having to womanhandle him, since he didn't ask for the hardscrabble life on Dom that had left him malnourished for years, but there was nothing for it. She needed to make an example before things got out of hand.

She flung him against the wall, a meter or so away from where Lyn supported herself, rubbing her chin and working her jaw. Renla jabbed a finger into the man's face. "Stay. In. Line." Renla looked around at the crowd. "For the Lady's sake, we're trying to keep you alive."

A dozen whispered conversations burst out in the crowd, as if the blow to the man's head had reopened some ongoing debate in the crowd of refugees.

Renla couldn't process what they were saying. She had diggers to protect. She put a hand on Lyn's shoulder, to make sure she was okay. When her two nodded, Renla grabbed one of the subcommander's diggers by the arm and pulled her within whispering distance. "Get the ready company here. Now."

Renla clenched her jaw. Her diggers were combat engineers, not riot forces, but she had no choice. She had to risk the violence that nobody wanted: her, her diggers, or the refugees.

The digger dashed off.

Renla refused to sacrifice the cause of freedom because a few short-sighted refugees couldn't see the bigger picture, even if they were poor and desperate. If she didn't stop the Tyrant, if the Fighting 11th didn't stand up, no one would. He would win, and his swarming masses would smear evil all over the world, and the merciless grip of hate would expand, even to the White Planet. And she had no idea if the White Planet could stand up to the Tyrant and his force of supersoldiers.

The conversations in the crowd fanned out and erupted into exclamation and anger. A refugee whispered, close enough for Renla to hear, "She must be a moonie lover." Similar comments echoed through the crowd. Renla felt an icy frustration descend on her heart. She would brook no specious whining, not while more important things were at stake.

She sprang to the raised platform where the frazzled subcommander stood. He shuffled off, his face telling a tale of gratitude. It was a black metal box, really, not a platform, but it put her in a position to see the crowd.

A sense of futility assaulted her when she jumped onto the box. A few heads turned in her direction, but not enough. Most of the refugees continued their feisty conferences in groups of three or four, full of disdain for the moonies who received them. When faces turned in her direction, she saw not a hint of kindness or gratitude, only resentment.

Their pettiness disgusted her. How dare they call themselves Domans.

The line of refugees extended back to the other end of the platform. There, the line turned and disappeared into the corridor leading to the next bay, where Station Prime Control sent all the refugee ships. Renla sighed with newfound empathy for the subcommander's predicament.

How would this end?

Palms moist, Renla held up her hands for silence, as she had a hundred times in front of large groups of people.

They ignored her.

"Okay, okay," she called out, in her best command voice.

More people started pushing and shoving. Shouts of "food" and "get a move on" and "go home" broke out in the crowd. The ready company filed into the bay, some hundred strong, then spread down the platform in an ominous line, hands already inside their distillers. The refugees paused their scuffles and debates to cast nervous glances in the direction of the ready company.

The situation was slipping away from Renla, in slow motion, like fine sand falling through the cracks in a fist closed too tight. Where had she gone wrong?

"Hey," someone near the front called, "are you going to kill us, too, just like Nayr's thugs killed our families and friends?"

"Are you going to feed us to the moonies? They eat their own here, don't they?" asked someone else.

A few diggers from the ready company slid into the space between Renla and the temporary barrier. The crowd of refugees was now cornered between the ready company and the bay wall, adding a dose of nervousness to the rising tension.

Renla's face grew grim in response to the shouted question, desperate. She shrugged off her distiller pack and let it fall to the ground with a metallic clang. A few heads turned at the new sound, but only a few. At the far end, refugees were shouting at her diggers in the ready company, oblivious to her presence some hundred meters away.

A deep anger lurked inside this group. She hadn't counted on that when she began to welcome Doman refugees to Station Prime. Most refugees were grateful for a warm meal and a safe place to sleep, but this group harbored a deeper fear and desperation. What had they seen? What had they lived?

To their credit, her diggers remained impassive, looking to her for some sign, some order to act. To do what exactly, Renla still had no clue. Shoot defenseless refugees? Renla shuddered with revulsion and frustration at the impossible choice before her.

Renla suppressed her frustration and raised her hands. A few more glanced her way. "We're the good guys." She stomped her foot. Her heel made a thud on the box. "We're the good guys!"

She'd gotten the attention of about a third of the crowd now. A few heads turned near the middle of the hangar bay, but at the far end refugees still shouted insults at her diggers, some of them Moonborn, for whom the insults were especially harsh. Desperate, she grasped at the first idea that came to mind.

She had no time for anything else. The Tyrant would be here any day, maybe any hour.

"We need your help," she shouted to the crowd.

A few people in the front guffawed. Should she tell them what she really needed from them? Could she ask people who had nothing at all to give their lives, in hopes of squeezing out a few more days or hours of life for those who survived? What chance did they have, really, against the Tyrant's horde?

At the far end, someone tried to climb over the barrier, and two of her diggers moved in to cart him off. A second refugee took a swing at one of them. The situation was shifting underfoot. Renla's chest seized with indecision.

As if sensing her uncertainty, a woman at the front challenged her, "If you're the good guys, why won't you tell us what's really going on?" The woman pointed to the two lines that the subcommander had been directing people toward. "Where do these lines go?"

Renla's shoulders slumped, but she held her head high. An act. The mask of command. "We need you to fight." She scanned the crowd for a friendly face, but found none. "The Tyrant is coming. If he takes Moon, then no one else escapes to the White Planet."

The crowd erupted in a cauldron of curses and shouts. "I don't want to die here!" someone shouted. "Back to the ship!" screamed another. "Let's leave for the White Planet now!" called another.

Renla had lost them, if she ever had them to begin with. She leaped down from the box and worked on her distiller pack once again. She shoved her arm into her distiller. She needed every one of her diggers to fight the Tyrant. Better to sacrifice a few people who didn't get it so that those who saw reason could live.

Down at the far end of the platform, members of the ready company leveled their distillers at the crowd. They'd seen Renla arm herself. They knew what it meant. They had passed the point of reconciliation, of explaining with level heads the merits of a unified front, of giving Renla the womanpower she needed. Renla set her jaw and accepted a grisly future, one decided by violence.

How had they gotten here, to this place Renla would always regret? They were the good guys.

She raised her distiller, and as one the reserve company did the same. Renla called out, "Keep them in line, diggers of the Fighting 11th."

"Hold!" A clear voice of command pierced the chaos and fear and adrenaline. A voice accustomed to being obeyed, with a descant of power, a conviction of utmost certainty.

Renla started. She recognized the voice.

A hush settled over the crowd. Not just over those near the front, where Renla was, but throughout the crowd. Movement near the middle of the platform, just across from Renla's office, gave away the location of the voice.

A woman raised her hands in a gesture of command when she got to the barrier.

"Stay this madness," the woman called. She sat on the barrier, ready to throw her leg over, and two of Renla's diggers approached, weapons at the ready.

"Let her through," Renla called, working through the mix of shock, at seeing her here, and elation, at seeing her alive. The Queen probably could have disarmed the diggers herself, but at last Renla saw a clear path out of the vale of violence in which she tarried.

Zharla jumped the barrier with a litheness and grace that only she could, then strode down the platform. The outer layer of her clothing was dirty, ragged, but Renla saw an advanced black bioflauge combat suit peek through. Her face was dirty and tear-stained, and a little worn, but proud and undaunted.

Murmurs of "The Queen" and "I knew it was her" ruffled through the crowd now.

Zharla strode to Renla and embraced her, held her tight for a moment. "How I've missed you, dear Re'le."

Flustered, all Renla could think to say was, "Yes, Your Majesty."

Zharla smiled at Renla and took hold of her distiller. "I'll take that."

Zharla shook off her outer rags and hoisted the distiller pack onto her own shoulders, then plunged her hand into the weapon's arm holster. She pounced onto the box, like a panther armed with righteous fury. She turned to the crowd. "The true enemy is coming."

All faces turned in her direction, attention rapt.

Zharla poked her own chest. "Of anyone here, I know the enemy best. He's my son. He will not give up until he wins, until he controls all he sees." She leaned toward the crowd, sinking her rhetorical claws into them with practiced skill. She lowered her voice, and they leaned in with her. "But if we fight together, we can beat him."

Whispers rustled through the crowd, but Zharla raised her voice again. "We only lose if we give up, if we fight each other instead of the enemy. Moonies. Domans. These labels don't matter now, in the face of death." She raised the distiller high above her head. "I fight for you. We fight for each other. If I die in defense of freedom, then you will remember me, just like I will remember you."

She slapped the side of the distiller. The sound made Renla jump, enraptured as she was by Zharla's words, by her presence.

"We can win this fight," the Queen continued. "*Cheret!*" She clenched her fist and shook it at the crowd, arm muscles quivering with tension. "We fight for freedom."

The refugees erupted with cheers and chanting, "*Che-ret. Che-ret. Che-ret.*" Ululations of joy peeled out from the women, tolling their approval. Refugees surged toward the line to the left, meant for those who would be conscripted into Renla's motley force, shuffling their children into the care of the aged, to the right.

Zharla stepped down from the box and handed Renla her distiller. "I'm sorry I didn't do that earlier," she whispered to Renla. Zharla flicked away a tear. "After what I saw gravside . . . what Nayr did to Dom . . . I . . . had nothing left."

Refugees inclined their heads in Zharla's direction as they passed, smiling, acknowledging her with, "Your Majesty."

Renla drew close to her friend and turned her back to the refugees, her aspect as hard as stone. "I don't know how long we can keep the portal open, Your Majesty. We need to get you to the White Planet. I've established a rendezvous point for you and Ahrik. We think Shahl might be headed to a point near there."

Zharla smiled and looked over Renla's shoulder at the refugees. Her eyes saddened when she turned to Renla once again. "Give these refugees their moment of hope, Renla. Many of them will die." Zharla squeezed Renla's hand in hers, like she'd done hundreds of times in their shared youth. "I'm not as important as you think in all this, you know. I may die, you may die, but if we lose hope, then we have no chance of turning back Nayr at the White Planet." She looked across the platform. "Many more are counting on us that what you see here."

Renla nodded. "Probably millions."

"The White Planet doesn't know what's coming." Zharla smiled, with effort, and set off toward the middle of the platform at a dignified pace.

Renla's pace was pensive beside her. She'd been so focused on beating the Tyrant that she'd lost sight of the deeper fight. "Hope," she said.

"That's why we fight," said Zharla.

Renla sighed. "You still need to leave, Your Majesty."

Lyn strode up to Renla, inclining her head in Zharla's direction and casting a worried look at Renla. "Ma'am," she whispered, "he's accelerated launch preparations."

Renla narrowed her eyes in concern. "How bad is it?"

"A massive force, ma'am." Her eyes flickered in an unspoken struggle with despair. "Seven carriers. Probably a thousand interceptors and fifty thousand assault troops. We estimate he'll launch within a day."

Renla bit her lip. Fifty thousand was probably a low estimate, with seven carriers. Was he bound for Moon, or for the portal to the White Planet? Millions depended on her guessing right.

"Lyn," said Renla, "take Her Majesty to my shuttle. Order my pilot to get her to Ahrik at the rally point on the White Planet, then train these new recruits to defend this rock."

Zharla reached to her wrist and unwound a pendant, the necklace that Shahl had given Zharla, before she chose, in her rashness, to wed Ahrik instead. She pressed the necklace into Renla's hand. "It gave me strength when I needed it most." She sighed. "I don't know where he and his daughter are now, but I know they'll never give up. Their courage gives us strength."

Renla nodded and smiled at the Queen, but feared that saying anything at all would let her emotions gush out.

Lyn looked from the Queen to her commander. "Are we defending Moon, ma'am, or the portal?"

Renla sucked in a long breath. "Prepare Harkov Station for launch, and ready interceptors in the remaining launch tubes. We will stop the Tyrant from reaching the White Planet." She didn't add the grim coda that sprang to her mind, the one she saw behind Lyn's eyes. If the Tyrant assaulted Moon instead of the portal, these refugees and tens of thousands of others would be slaughtered.

Renla gripped her aide's shoulder and drew close to whisper, "Is the backup plan ready?"

Anger flashed in Lyn's narrowing eyes, but she pulled a transmitter from her pocket and stuffed it into Renla's hand with a curt nod. "Ma'am, you know we shouldn't use this."

She stormed off without a word, followed by a concerned Zharla.

Renla reassumed the mask of command and scanned the crowd of refugees after her two friends left. These refugees might be dead in a few hours. Then she thought of the millions on the White Planet who would never know the price that Renla and the Fighting 11th were about to pay.

The price of hope.

16 Effects of Victory

THE DISPLAY WENT BLANK and the automatic pilot cut off mid-sentence. Anda gripped the bulkhead. He planted his feet against the ferocious shaking. Everything rattled, from deck plates and hull connectors to compiler tube casings and what few jump seats the makers of this death rig had deigned to install.

All around them, faces cast about in the flickering light, searching for an answer to their fear. Her knuckles white, Sera held fast to Anda's waist. She coughed, and Anda steeled his soul for the pain and grief that awaited him. And her. And Esh'a.

Death, come quick.

Death, stay thy hand.

The automatic pilot's metallic voice tore into his fear once again. *Brace. Inertial stabilizers are—*

It cut off again. Anda frowned. *That can't be normal.*

Anda gazed around the cabin. He would find no answers in the faces he saw here. These people were miners, farmers, and small traders, not space travelers. What was wrong with the inertials? Were they about to be burned by entry into the White Planet's atmosphere? Or crushed by impact on the surface? Did they have enough left in the boson drive for one last deceleration?

Anda struggled to a standing position and coaxed Sera up with him. They had to be ready to flee or move or something.

"Abbi," said Sera. "I'm frightened."

Anda stroked her long hair, scanning the hull for potential separation points. As if that would help. "Shhhh."

The mother standing next to Anda and Sera gripped one child by the hand while the other clung to a leg. She shrugged her shoulders and implored a helpless look at Anda. "Isn't this better than dying from starvation and disease on Moon?"

The ship buckled, and everyone froze, eyes pegged on the nearest section of hull. The ship held, but the baseline rattling resumed, fierce and insistent.

Anda sighed in response to the woman, and cast a tender gaze on his daughter. "Someday," he said, "life will not be so cheap."

The woman scoffed and shook her head, then looked to her own children. "Tell that to my dead husband."

Anda looked away. He had no words for the death that stalked their reality, that haunted their fears. For all Anda knew, Esh'a might be just as dead as this woman's husband.

He scanned his surroundings for a way out. The rattling couldn't last forever. His short time in space, a decade and a half ago, had taught him that much, at least. Eventually, the ship would slow enough that the atmosphere wouldn't batter it like this anymore. If the ship didn't break up on entry into the atmosphere, they'd land, or crash, and then their problems would really start.

But the mystery of Nayr's threat haunted Anda's mind more than imminent death. How could Nayr link Sera's life with Anda's? The thought churned his stomach. Would Nayr hunt them down, or was his plan already in motion? How could the nanos inside Sera possibly communicate with those inside Anda? He had to know. He had to know if they would be running in vain or if Nayr could not seal their fate.

Anda stood on his tiptoes and looked toward the rear. Even if he could find what he needed forward, they would never make it past the main hatch. If they didn't crash, the hatch would be jammed with people, and some would probably die in the press to debark. Anda didn't want Sera to be one of them. Life had become so cheap.

They needed to find a safer place to survive the crash landing. Anda knew it was coming.

The main cabin carried so many people, and had so few jump seats, that the impact would kill them if the inertial stabilizers failed, or even faltered momentarily. Anda expected that, in the best case, many of the refugees in the cabin would be maimed.

Anda craned his neck around the bulkhead. Better to move while everyone else was frozen by fear of the ship falling apart, instead of driven by panic to the closest exit after they'd crashed.

Ah, there. He saw something in the rear passageway. Desperation transformed into the beginnings of a plan.

"Come, Serit," he whispered. He gave the mother beside them a smile. "Excuse us."

Shock painted the woman's face. "Making for the rear?" She made way, but pointed toward the exit hatch that was forward of them. "That's the fastest way out of here."

He gave a sheepish smile and gestured at Sera. "Small bladder."

He and Sera shuffled and stumbled and excused themselves toward the rear. A clutch of refugees hugged the wall in the rear passageway, and they threw strange glances in Anda's direction as he and Sera approached, but they made way for them all the same.

Then the rattling stopped, without warning, and a sensation of gentle weightlessness, little more than a slight upward pressure on the limbs, settled over the ship.

"Did the inertial stabilizers just kick in?" someone asked. Someone else gave a weak cheer, a feeble hope, and others followed suit. Down the passageway and through the cabin beyond, more refugees cheered their salvation.

Anda furrowed his brow. He knew a death rig when he saw one. He would celebrate when Sera and he were on the ground, alive, but even then he knew that they had an entire planet to contend with, and they had to find his wife, all while eluding or frustrating Nayr's murderous intent.

He didn't like his own chances, but maybe he could do something for his daughter.

They waded through what remained of the cheering refugees. He and Sera trundled to a stop outside a hatch with "Healing Supply" emblazoned on a sign above it.

Anda allowed himself a brief smile.

Sera frowned and studied the letters. "H-e-a-l... Abbi, what's in here?"

"You're doing well with your reading." He squeezed her hand and lowered his voice, so the refugees down the passageway wouldn't hear. "Safety lies behind this hatch." *And answers.*

Anda tried the palm reader. It glowed red. The hatch didn't open. He stroked his chin. *Why would a refugee ship with no crew need a locked hatch?*

Realization flashed like a strobe over the havoc of his mind. The door would only open if the automatic pilot program allowed it.

And he knew what he had to do to fool the program.

Despair pushed the air out of his lungs. He didn't know if they had minutes or seconds before they crashed, and he had to act. Fast.

Anda clenched his fists in frustration, then looked forward, down the passageway, at the huddled refugees, whose former fear at the rattling and shaking of the ship had fled in favor of hopeful expectation. A few had begun to smile, gather pitiful belongings, and shuffle in the direction of the main hatch, at the forward end of the cabin.

They thought they were going to land, not crash. Could he disabuse them of this, their premature hope? Did he dare?

He had to get to another exit hatch. Now.

Too many people huddled in the main cabin on this deck. He glanced toward the ladders across the passageway from the healing supply closet. The main cabins on the other two decks would tell the same story: more people than he could fight through to get to one of the main hatches. He looked even farther toward the rear, where they had boarded the ship, before Nayr turned Meran into an irradiated wasteland. There'd be fewer people that direction, since the rear hatch opened off a narrow passageway, instead of a relatively spacious cabin.

Anda grabbed Sera's hand and pulled her toward the passageway to the rear hatch. They came to a dogleg around the corner from the healing supply closet, where two right-angled bends in the passageway prevented someone from seeing straight from the rear hatch to the main hatch. Anda paused and looked both ways to make sure they were alone, then crouched down and fixed his eyes on his precious daughter. "Serit," he said, "you need to keep up. We don't have much time."

Sera coughed, then nodded. "Okay."

She reached to hold his hand again, but he caught her hand and pressed it to his chest instead. "No, I may need to push people out of the way, maybe even keep some people from hurting us, so I need both hands free."

Warning, rang the automatic pilot's voice over the ship's comm system. *Impact imminent.*

The voices from the main cabin hushed to an uncertain murmur at the automatic pilot's announcement.

Sera searched the air for an explanation for the voice, but Anda found her gaze and focused her. She nodded her understanding, but her eyes trembled with apprehension.

Anda hugged her. "We only do this because we have to." He tried to pass her his courage with the embrace, then held her by the shoulders. "For Imma."

She beamed through a fog of fear. "For Imma."

From the dogleg, they raced toward the rear of the ship, through twisting passageways, joints and panels cobbled together from a half-dozen cannibalized ships. Tiny refugee cabins opened off these narrow warrens, and Anda smelled the leavings of close-quartered humans, ripped clothes and discarded food, and objects that had probably seemed lighter and more important when they were originally retrieved, in haste, back on Moon or Dom.

Nayr had killed tens of thousands, maybe more, but he'd ruined many more lives than that. To the survivors, life meant something much deeper now, an inexorable force of love that no violence could extinguish.

Love of family, or unquenchable revenge.

Nothing like a war to give some perspective.

It didn't have to be this way. He chided himself for agreeing to let Esh'a leave them all those months ago. Better to have suffered through all this together, to have given each other strength, than to risk straining the bonds of love even more.

They came upon the rear hatch on this, the ship's middle deck. Anda's legs grew weak. A woman and man, muscle-bound and nasty-looking, waited by the exit hatch. They hadn't seen Anda, so he grunted blood into his legs and attacked. He leapt between them and threw his shoulder into the door with a thud, then worked the mechanical locking lever up and down, hoping to loosen it before they had time to react.

"Hey," said the woman.

Warning. Impact imminent.

A man's fingers alighted on his shoulder. Anda ignored him, drew back his weight, and slammed his shoulder into the hatch again.

"Ho, friend." The woman gripped his other shoulder, her grip a bit more insistent than the man's. "It'll be okay."

The locking mechanism jiggled loose. Just one more good shove should do it. He didn't need to open the hatch, just crack it.

Just enough to fool the automatic pilot program into thinking they had experienced a hull breach emergency.

Two hands pressed down, hard, when he drew his weight to jam his shoulder into the hatch a third time. But he followed the pressure downward, then wriggled free and thrust his legs toward the hatch. The woman gasped in surprise at his agility and quickness, and the hatch gave a deep pucker as the seal broke and air rushed out.

Now the healing supply closet would unlock.

Through the crack, the ground rushed by, dry and emotionless desert, a lot closer than Anda had hoped it would be. Time was short.

A red light flickered on over the hatch, then blinked out. Defective. *Warning,* came a metallic voice, different from the automatic pilot, a local warning for those near the hatch. *Hull breach. Warning. Hull bre—*

The voice cut off. Also defective.

Death rig.

Anda expected two sets of hands to pull him back, but only the woman's fingers dug into his shoulders. The pain lanced through his neck, but a deeper sense of panic gripped his mind. Where was the man?

Sera.

"Abb—"

Anda tried to whirl his body around, but only succeeded in craning his neck, for the grip the woman had on him.

The man held Sera, arms pinned to her side, his hand over her mouth. He sneered at Anda. "I always wanted a daughter, ya know?"

The ship buckled again, and an alarm ripped through the ship, unlike anything Anda had yet heard. *Brrrah . . . warning . . . brrrah . . . impact imminent . . . brrrah . . . brrrah . . . brrrah.*

For a split second, just enough, the woman and man diverted their attention. Anda saw the terror in Sera's eyes. He snapped. Every inhibition melted away, and every ounce of energy focused on saving his daughter.

He sank his nails into the woman's wrists, then plunged down and twisted, yanking his arms forward to pull her down and toward the hatch. With a gasp of surprise, the woman's body hurtled forward, but Anda misjudged the force of the air passing over the hull, outside the hatch. Her arm jammed into the crack and she cried out in pain.

Anda paused at her cry. He sucked in his breath. He hadn't wanted to hurt the woman, just escape. His instinct had gotten the better of him.

"No!" shouted the man, who released Sera and lunged for the woman.

"I . . ." Anda began, but turned to find Sera, to rush back to the healing supply closet before it was too late.

The man, tugging on the woman's waist, craned his head around to Anda, eyes wild and pleading at the force of the air rushing by outside. "Help me."

The hatch lurched open a few centimeters more, and with a cry of alarm the woman's body slipped farther out. The ground racing by below told Anda he had very little time to get back to the healing supply closet.

Brrrah. Warning. Brrrah. Impact imminent. Brrrah.

She would die, both the woman and man would, if that hatch gave. But they had threatened his precious little girl, his Serit. What could forgive that?

He turned to go, his hand opening to grab hold of his daughter, but a blur of white cotton skipped through his peripheral vision instead. Sera planted her feet alongside the man, grabbed the woman's leg, and pulled. She turned her head. "Abbi!"

The hatch lurched open a bit more, and half of the woman's torso went through. Anda sprang forward and planted a foot on the hatch jamb. He grabbed Sera with one hand and the woman's flailing arm with the other. Anda nudged the man. "1 . . . 2 . . . 3 . . . pull!"

They all three pulled, and the woman sprang free from certain death. The four of them fell in a heap on the floor. The woman sucked in her breath and held her arm close to her body.

The man rose on one knee to tend to her. He turned to Anda. "What I said earlier . . ."

Anda just looked out the hatch. He made out individual shrubs and squat desert trees now, and the ship was not slowing down like it should. Anda met the man's eyes. No time for apologies. "Follow me."

Brrrah. Warning. Brrrah. Impact imminent. Brrrah.

Anda took Sera by the hand and ran back through the warren of narrow passageways toward the healing supply closet. He didn't bother to check whether the man and woman followed, or kept up.

Anda was glad they weren't on the lowest deck. He didn't give the refugees down there much chance at survival. He grunted. He didn't give themselves much chance at survival.

The ship began to rattle again, with only slightly less violence than before. Was this air turbulence, or were they close enough to skim the tops of the trees? Everything was happening so fast that their speed and trajectory were impossible to judge.

Warning. Impact imminent.

"That warning came quicker than the others," said the man. They were still behind Anda and Sera, after all.

"Almost there," replied Anda.

They arrived back at the dogleg by the healing supply closet. Anda guided Sera to the forward corner of the dogleg, just around the corner from the supply closet. "Brace here."

The man eased the woman down next to Sera. She winced when she bumped her arm against the wall.

Warning. Impact imminent.

Anda crouched down next to Sera. "I'll be right back. I need to get something from the healing supply closet."

"Healing supply?" asked the man, glancing at his wife. "I'll come with you."

Anda rushed around the corner. He caught sight of the main cabin. Refugees had squished their way toward the exit. The woman they'd passed earlier, the one with the two children, glanced in his direction as he pressed his palm to the reader outside the closet. Her face told a tale of worry, her hopeful determination gone.

Warning. Impact imminent.

The hatch in front of Anda made a click and he slid it open in the old-fashioned way, into the wall. The lights flickered on. Anda whipped the bag off his shoulder, wrapping the strap around his wrist, and scoured the shelves with his eyes. Bags of fluids, syringes, bottle after bottle of medicines, but not what he sought.

Packages of bandages lined one wall, and the man made for them. "To make a sling," he said.

Anda scanned, frantic now. There, next to the bandages that the man was raiding. A blood analysis kit. Anda reached. His fingers closed over the reinforced paper package.

He almost had a good grip on the blood analysis kit, but then the floor fell out from under him. Or, rather, he took flight, and his body smashed into the forward wall. The loudest sound he'd ever heard consumed them. Anda and the man tumbled together in a crash of limbs and bodies, and then the force of impact squeezed them to the base of the forward wall, near the floor.

The lights went dark. Anda's head hit something hard and his world closed into a swirling vortex of pain.

Screams.

Black.

Quiet.

Time.

Stillness.

Light flashed into Anda's consciousness from some far-off place. Strange voices, warbling but guttural, hummed from the passageway. Dust choked the air. The strap of his bag was still wrapped around his wrist, but the blood analysis kit was gone.

Anda tried to raise himself up on an elbow, but the weight of the man and a stab of pain in his head forced him back down.

The voices came closer. *Is Sera okay?*

Anda felt around for the analysis kit, then shoved at the man with his elbow, in an effort to wake him. He whispered, "Can you move?"

Streams of light flashed through the passageway, spearing the dusty haze. He couldn't tell if they came from forward or aft. The voices mumbled to one another again, uncertainty roiling their hum, as if assessing a new situation. Refugees from the other decks, perhaps, looking for survivors, or aliens inspecting a crash site?

Someone coughed, timid and afraid, out in the passageway. Sera. She was alive. The voices stopped.

Alarm flooded into Anda's core. He grunted through the pain and pushed on the man. The man's weight shifted, then his body slid off. Anda's hand found purchase on the man's neck, icy cold with stillness and death. How long had Anda been out?

He forced aching joints and stiff muscles into motion. He felt around once more in the flickering light, then felt the packaging of the analysis kit. Satchel in one hand and kit in the other, he broke into a frantic crawl toward the door.

He peeked around the jamb of the hatch. The light that searched the murk came from forward, not the rear. They hadn't gotten this far back yet.

"*Hoobala baar,*" said one to another.

They were aliens, then. A shiver crawled down Anda's back. If he was going to reach Sera, he had to chance that they were friendly. Would they shoot first and ask questions later, like the *nayra*? Could the aliens tell the difference between a refugee ship and an invasion carrier?

He took a deep breath, then sprang through the hatch and toward the rear. His foot caught on something and he hurtled forward, out of control. He turned his body in the air to cradle the kit, and landed with a thud on the deck. Pain lanced through his shoulder.

"*Ajay!*" yelled a voice behind him.

He ignored the pain searing through his body and scrambled to the dogleg, away from the alien voices, where Sera and the woman had taken shelter. He rounded the corner on all fours and, in the twisting light, just made out the woman's form.

Where was Sera?

"Abbi," she whispered, then coughed again.

"Serit," he whispered back, scanning the darkness. "I'm here."

"*Hoobala,*" said the voice behind him, with an air of command. This alien was a soldier. Anda didn't stop and turn to see if a weapon had raised in his direction. He didn't have to. He knew the assumption of authority when he heard it. He knew when a voice had cold steel to back it up.

Anda scooted farther into the dogleg, expecting to be shot, ignoring the danger. He had to find his daughter. *Please, Lady, let him miss in the darkness.*

"*Hoobala.*" An additional tone of warning as more footfalls slowed behind him.

Anda felt for the woman's form. The lights came closer, slow and tentative. They must be as scared of him as he was of them. The fickle light improved, and he made out the woman's face. He recoiled at her mouth, yawning in a rictus of horror, and her eyes, wide with pain and death.

Then he saw the rod sticking out from her chest, and he saw her shattered arm, and understood how she must have ignored her fear and her pain to shield his daughter from the rod hurtling toward them in that terrifying moment of impact. Guilt and gratitude washed over him at once, at this act of heroism that he would never be able to repay, a redemption for supposed sins committed.

He should have forgiven her, in his heart, when she was yet alive. Who was he to judge another soul?

A small hand reached out from underneath the woman's body. Fingers wriggled with frantic apprehension. "Abbi, help me."

Footsteps behind him. A shaft of light focused on his back, its warmth oddly chilling.

Anda gripped Sera's hand. "Are you hurt?"

"*Hoobala*," the voice commanded. "*Jaloov*."

"No, Abbi, just scared."

Anda turned, and saw nothing but lights piercing the darkness, in every direction it seemed, sweeping back and forth, blinding him. The clink of weapons and gear and the tromp of boots filled the space with menace.

Anda slumped down with resignation and squeezed his daughter's hand in return. He gulped back the dryness in his mouth. "Me too, Serit. Me too."

Nayr could tell when his people lied to him. He didn't even need to access the tendril link to check on their thoughts. Their eyes shifted everywhere but toward him, and sweat limned more than a few foreheads. The circulated air of the space elevator they rose on emitted a slightly more stale smell than when the trip had begun, two hours earlier.

"Well?" Nayr heaved a deep breath and took in the receding planet. The golden hues of its land masses gave way to the pale blue-gray of its shallow oceans as the elevator sped up through the atmosphere. Nayr tapped his foot.

"Father, your Grand Army would be ready, but—"

"But? Come now, 3, you know I don't like excuses."

"Yes, Father. Sorry, Father."

"Or apologies."

"Yes, Father." 3 stood at attention, frozen in a visual embrace with Nayr, as if unsure of what to say next.

Nayr gazed at the thirty-odd people who filled the elevator cabin. The only pair of eyes that met his belonged to 3. Nayr raised an inquisitive eyebrow at his ops chief. "Why. Is. My. Grand. Army. Not. Ready?

3 gulped. "Father, all seven carriers are ready, and the Ketel of Nayr can leave at a moment's notice, but—"

"Excuses?"

3 motioned to someone behind him. "Not an excuse, Father, a reason: recruitment is difficult."

A disturbing hush gripped the cabin. Nayr could tell there was more to the story. He narrowed his eyes and fingered his distiller almost as an afterthought. Almost. "Go on."

"Father, many cities have revolted."

Nayr grunted. "And been pacified. I know."

"And many of their inhabitants have fled the planet for the moon ... and beyond." 3 cast a nervous glance at those nearest him.

Wild embers of hate flashed in Nayr's chest. The thought of Mother and what her captors could do to her, far away, made his eyes burn. Renla was complicit, up on the moon, so the nanobios were only a down payment, a prelude to the cost she would pay. "They have captured the Queen, 3, and all you can tell me is that there are not enough people to fill my Grand Army?" Nayr scoffed, with a sneer for his ops chief. "Why do I keep you around?"

The flash of disappointment on 3's face quickly gave way to a veneer of confidence, like a lap cat fawning to impress its betters. "I thought you'd never ask, Father."

3 motioned behind him once again, with a bit more urgency this time, and two individuals came forward who, Nayr gathered, were supposed to be soldiers. Their combat blouses, nearly devoid of decoration or grime, or any evidence at all that their wearers had earned them, hung loose on their frames. One, a man, wore an expression like a village tough, but Nayr could see his knees quiver inside his older-model bioflauge trousers. His qasfin wasn't even fastened on correctly. It was so loose it would slap against his thigh if he tried to run. Assuming he wasn't shot for incompetence first.

The other, a woman, reminded him too much of that upstart, Renla. She had short curls, just the wrong shade, and a strained expression. Like dough that rises too long and then is stretched overmuch to compensate.

Nayr gulped back the taste of bile in his mouth, then turned to 3. "How am I supposed to invade the White Planet and find the Queen with soldiers like these?"

3 cleared his throat. The young woman's eyes darted to the man. Her lover, maybe? She took an involuntary step back. Nayr slipped his hand into his distiller and smiled at how much he was going to enjoy teaching his people the meaning of loyalty.

He nodded to the man and flicked his distiller to life, then rested the business end under the man's chin. The man's eyes widened as the distiller's hum grew, like the hungry growl of a predator before feasting on a vanquished foe. A drop of sweat meandered down the man's temple. Nayr almost felt the man's breath catch in his throat.

Nayr smiled. "Are you a soldier in my Grand Army?"

The man nodded almost imperceptibly. Beside him, out of the corner of his vision, Nayr saw hate simmer in the woman's eyes. Yes, they were connected, Nayr was sure of it now.

The hush of the others in the elevator cabin left a deafening silence. Nayr smiled inwardly. They watched intently for his latest wisdom.

Nayr nodded at the man. "Are you ready for your first order?"

Another barely perceptible nod, little more than a head titter.

"Don't move," said Nayr. With that, in a fluid motion, he whipped the distiller over and pointed it into the woman's face.

The woman gasped.

Nayr flicked off the distiller's microcore and squeezed the trigger, so it clicked without releasing its charge.

The woman pressed her eyes shut.

"No!" the man said, raising his hand to stop Nayr, then freezing his hand mid-grip on Nayr's arm when he realized what was happening and seeing that the woman's head had not evaporated into elemental mist after all.

Nayr clucked and used his free hand to unsheathe his qasfin and flick the man's hand away with it. Nayr sighed. "You didn't follow my order."

"Father . . ." whispered 3 beside him.

Nayr stowed his distiller on his pack and tapped the man's chest with his qasfin, the killing point of the curved blade poking into the man's blouse for emphasis. "All I ask of my people is loyalty." Nayr glared at the others in the space elevator cabin. "Is that too much to ask?"

Murmurs of "no" rippled throughout the cabin.

Nayr shook his head. "How are we supposed to save the Queen with such sorry soldiers?" He twisted the killing point on the man's chest, so that it sliced a hole. Red began to seep out as Nayr continue to twist, but the man stood ramrod straight.

"Father . . ." said 3.

Nayr drew back his qasfin, and the man collapsed, unconscious. Nayr was sure he was still alive, but faking. The woman and one of his other people dragged the man toward the other side of the cabin. Nayr watched him go, his face dead and expressionless.

Invading the White Planet was going to be harder than he had thought.

"3."

"Father?"

"How many carriers have we slated for my Grand Army?"

"Seven, Father."

"Make it ten."

"Yes, Father."

Anxious murmurs rippled through the cabin once again.

"Silence!"

Respect returned.

"3."

"Father?"

"Have you increased the capacity of the carriers?"

"Yes, Father, in four of the carriers. We can get fifty thousand in those four, but it'll be tight."

Nayr motioned toward the man they dragged away. "I want two hundred thousand of those soldiers in the first six carriers of the convoy. They're much less valuable than my ketelis."

A moment of briefest hesitation. "Yes, Father." 3 narrowed his eyes. "It will take time to recruit more."

"I don't care. Drain the countryside. Empty the cities. Prove to me that my people are loyal."

"Yes, Father."

"And I want to be able to spoof command communications in the convoy so it looks like my orders are coming from the fifth carrier in the convoy, instead of the last."

"Yes, Father. Anything else?"

"Win."

"Win, Father."

"Win," said the others in the cabin, but without the fervor that Nayr liked to hear.

He accessed his internal compiler and called up the Revenge file. He overwrote one word and read the rest of the names there: "Kill Ahrik. Kill Shahl. Kill Renla. Rescue Mother. Humble 3." Then he added: "Prepare for the reckoning."

Ahrik's eyes winked open and sunlight panned across his face. He shook off the daze, unsure when he'd fallen asleep. An alarm sounded, a far off pinging, outside his helmet. His eyes wandered around the cockpit. The dead pilot sat, statuesque and macabre, strapped into his seat, body mangled, helmet lolling to starboard. Ahrik reached up to adjust his own helmet, but touched his face instead. Where was his helmet?

The alarm grew louder, and a faint panic rose in the back of his head. He needed to do something. Now.

But what? His head nodded, and his gaze fell to the control panel. Lights flashed an angry red. Oxygen. Hull integrity. Artigrav. Those systems should be working. Was this rig really that bad off after their narrow escape from those interceptors?

He reached to unstrap himself, then felt himself float and drift back into his chair as the shuttle turned. His helmet. It hung on the armrest. Groggy, he lifted it to his head and felt it lock home with a fulfilling slurp.

Air rushed into his helmet from his exosuit reserves, and along with it his senses. Awareness hit him with an undercurrent of anxiety. They were about to enter the White Planet's atmosphere, and the shuttle's autopilot was turning the shuttle to thrust the boson drive against gravity. Their hull leaked oxygen from the blasted rear cabin, a rear that wouldn't withstand atmospheric entry, not with their shield in its sorry state.

Ahrik assessed the situation. He scanned the console and reviewed their planned trajectory over the White Planet. He saw the location of the rally point, then saw another point that they would also fly over, a suspected mining camp. A chance at redemption, to right what went wrong on Dom. Shahl's wife Esh'a might be there, and if she was then he could begin to heal the mistrust and hate that had haunted him on Dom. It had all gone wrong when he fell out with his brother, before Zharla had even chosen a husband.

It wasn't much, but it was a start. A new start, on a new planet.

He pushed off from his chair, toward the hatch to the rear. He misjudged the increasing gravity, though, and made it only halfway before crunching back into the chair. He gripped a bulkhead and furrowed his brow, then pulled himself toward the rear. The hatch was open when they passed through the portal. The others should have come forward, too. Anyone left in the rear was looking death square in the face. He had to get those men into the cockpit, to safety.

He froze, on the verge of punching open the hatch. Next to the hatch controls, the oxygen control casing hung open, like someone had accessed it in a rush, then not closed it properly. A warning flashed in his mind. He opened the oxygen control casing all the way, then stared in shock at the reserve tank controls. Someone had set the cockpit reserve tanks on a slow draw while his helmet was off, then closed the cockpit hatch, gradually decreasing his oxygen until he passed out.

One of his men, or all of them—he couldn't be sure—wanted him dead.

He had to get off this shuttle.

Ahrik clenched his jaw. He still had to save them, if he could. They were so low on the ketel hierarchy that they'd only experienced atmospheric entry in the space elevators and the massive carriers. They probably didn't know that the rear cabin was about to burn up, with them inside.

Ahrik punched open the hatch and peered into the rear cabin. Rushing air beat against his chest as the pressure between the cabins equalized. Three helmeted heads turned toward him, the clone leader, the injured keteli, and the last one, who was smaller than the others, but considerably stronger. With their helmets on, Ahrik couldn't tell which face held surprise and regret that he'd survived the assassination attempt.

Had they drawn the cockpit oxygen into the reserve tanks any faster, he would be dead.

Touch, the clone that had died in the fight, lay beside his comrades, arms folded over his chest in the death salute.

Seeing that the rest had their helmets fixed, Ahrik turned back to the oxygen control casing and set all the air in the shuttle to draw into the reserve tanks. Then he motioned to them to top up their exosuit reserves by tubing into the tanks.

He twisted back toward the control console, careful not to let the deceleration slam him into his chair again, and checked the shuttle's trajectory. He did some calculations using his internal compiler. This entry was going to be dicey. Very dicey.

Ahrik undid the pilot's restraints and angled the pilot's stiffening body toward the rear. He frowned. No time for a proper burial. This man was a hero for sacrificing himself to save those he didn't know. Ahrik lunged off of the pilot's chair and slipped through the hatch to the rear with the body, steadying himself on the hatch jamb as he passed.

Ahrik let the pilot's body slide to a stop next to Touch's body, a prayer to the Lady of the Emerald Moon on his lips, to carry them both to the afterlife and the eternal embrace of their heroic peers. He forced the pilot's arms as best he could into the death salute. Ahrik rued the undignified burial, but thought of it as one final sacrifice for the dead men's comrades.

Ahrik was too far away from the clones in the tendril network to be able to think directly into their minds. He tried his suit comms. "Into the cockpit."

They didn't move, whether out of disobedience or a comms breakdown, Ahrik couldn't tell. He motioned them into the cockpit, examining each face in turn. Which was the assassin, and which the conspirators?

The clone leader locked eyes with him as he passed, but only for a beat. Too little information to make a conclusion.

The wounded man, the one who'd been blown back by the missile explosion that mangled the hull, hobbled past with eyes averted. He gripped his ribs with one hand. The chest of his exosuit was blackened from the blast. Ahrik read fierce anger in his body language, but it would have been very difficult for a wounded man to rig the cockpit's oxygen in zero gravity.

The stocky clone smiled curtly and nodded with good, military deference.

Ahrik breathed out in frustration. At least one of them was acting, but he couldn't tell which.

He suppressed his anger and lurking fear of death. He'd probably be dead soon enough anyway, with the way his odds had turned.

He hooked his toes under a strut and examined the shuttle's emergency pods. Of the six pods on the shuttle, four had been shredded by missile shrapnel and the interceptor's projectiles before they passed through the portal.

A furious, keening whine screamed out, vivid enough even to be heard through the vacuum gap of his exosuit. Ahrik didn't recognize this alarm. He whipped his head toward the cockpit and saw the clone leader drift toward him, his eyes wide with panic, glued to something behind Ahrik. Ahrik gulped, then shifted his body around and followed the clone leader's alarmed gaze. The rear of the hull was no longer a dull metal gray, but a pulsing, living orange.

The same exosuit technology that kept out the cold of space also kept out the heat of atmospheric entry, but he knew the suits couldn't withstand that much heat for long.

He had seconds before a fiery death engulfed him. He pursed his lips and chose one of the two emergency pods that didn't look damaged, unlatched it, and pushed off toward the cockpit. A sharp pain seared through his feet and legs as he pushed off. The clone leader, one hand on the jamb of the hatch, heaved the pod into the cockpit. Ahrik followed the pod through, the clone leader's hand on his sleeve, yanking him in with the other two clones.

Ahrik's faceplate slammed against the pod as the clone leader jostled to close the hatch behind Ahrik. One leg was pinned against the pilot's chair, one hand caught between the pod and the clone leader's chest.

A faint whoosh told Ahrik that the clone leader got the hatch closed. Ahrik felt a hand on his helmet, and the clone leader's voice came over the command channel, respect tinged with regret. "Thank you, sir."

Ahrik frowned. Was it a group assassination plot, then, and the clone leader wanted to apologize on behalf of the group with his thanks? Ahrik pushed the emergency pod against the growing force of gravity, maneuvering it in the cramped cockpit. It didn't move very far.

Ahrik clicked on the command channel to the clone leader and furrowed his brow. His distrust grew. "Pressurize the cockpit. The oxygen control casing is there, behind your left shoulder."

"Yes, sir." The clone leader nodded, but Ahrik saw the hesitation as he complied. The other helmets in the cockpit turned to eye the clone leader with suspicion.

Air rushed into the cockpit from the holding tanks.

Ahrik removed his helmet and nodded at the wounded keteli and the stocky one. "Sit down in those two chairs. We need the space." He felt a pang of regret at the harshness in his voice. "Sorry." He sighed, a gesture that Ahrik hoped the clones interpreted as kind. "What are your names?" Then, to the wounded keteli: "Are . . . are you hurt badly?"

The stocky clone nodded. "I'm Tank." He looked a question at the others. "Sir."

The wounded keteli grunted as he worked his helmet off. "I'm Hilt." Still clutching his side, Hilt said, "I'll live."

Tension flowed into the cockpit when he didn't say "sir." The other ketelis traded nervous looks. The clone leader removed his helmet and growled at his men, then acknowledged Ahrik with a salute. "Sir, m'name is Flank."

The wounded keteli, Hilt, said nothing more, just leveled an ice-cold stare at the middle distance to his front.

The bang and rattle of the shuttle falling apart on the other side of the hatch averted Ahrik's attention. He glanced at the control panel. The shield had just enough juice to keep the cockpit intact, and they'd sucked most of the oxygen out of the tanks in the rear before the atmosphere began to thicken. The shuttle began processing air from outside.

The clone leader, Flank, shifted beside Ahrik, then looked around nervously. "Sir, th'men ur probubly wunderin' why we have thus emurgency pud in the cockpit."

"I'm getting off before we reach the rally point."

Hilt glared. "So yuh cun abandun us, too?" Tank placed a hand on Hilt's shoulder, in a gesture that could have meant either "bide your time, our chance will come" or "calm down, keteli."

"Hilt," said Flank, a warning tone in his voice. Ahrik narrowed his eyes. Was Flank being nice to hide the fact that he's just tried to frag Ahrik, or was he genuinely surprised by the other two clones' insubordinate behavior?

Hilt squeezed the armrests of the pilot's chair. "Flank, we have tuh tull 'im sometime!" Hilt cast his icy glare at the other clones. "Thur's unly three uf us left."

The cockpit jerked and a loud sound, like metal ripping, shuddered through the shuttle. The rear cabin was gone.

"Sir," said Flank, with a careful glance at the others. "We dun't understand whut's goin' un."

Ahrik pursed his lips. "Nayr has turned Dom into a wasteland. Hate consumes him, and I could not stop him."

Hilt, apparently healthy enough to register discontent, clenched and unclenched his good hand with simmering anger. "Why duh we care?"

Flank fidgeted, unsure of himself, clearly uncomfortable with palace politics, not to mention with the tension between his commander and the men he led.

Tank stared absently out the hull, that same fake smile on his face, then turned to Ahrik as if a thought had just occurred to him. "Whut do yuh suggest?"

Ahrik squeezed his way to the control panel and brought up the schematic of their approach. He pointed to the rally point, nestled in a mountain range in a sparsely populated area, where he and Shahl and Zharla could evade Nayr's forces long enough to warn the planet's inhabitants of the danger they faced and, hopefully, mount a credible defense. "This shuttle," said Ahrik, "will set you down near the rally point. Secure the area as best you can. Avoid any locals till I arrive."

"Where yuh goin', sir?" asked Flank.

"I have some things to set right." He pointed to a location short of the rally point, but along their flight path. "You'll drop me here instead."

Flank tapped the emergency pod. "Yuh trust the 'nertial stabulizers on this thing t'break yur fall?"

Ahrik gestured to the cockpit around them. "We trust what we have."

Flank nodded, but Ahrik noted a glint in his eye that said he was glad to see Ahrik go. The feeling was mutual.

Ahrik nodded toward the distiller racked on the hull. "Keep an eye on that thing. We'll need it where we're going."

"Check."

Flank also didn't say "sir".

Ahrik's drop area moved underneath them on the schematic, and he opened the emergency pod. Renla had made the pods to withstand a space battle, so he was pretty sure it would survive full-grav impact. But he wasn't certain.

He wriggled out of his exosuit and made sure that the wrist compiler with the coordinates Renla had given him was snugly in place. He couldn't afford to miss the rally point.

He sat down in the man-sized pod, then tucked his legs inside, angling his feet so they fit into the pod's thin, rounded tail. He wriggled his shoulders into place next and drew in as deep a breath as he could. He wouldn't be able to breath naturally inside the pod.

Tank was about to set the lid in place, an earthbound casket, when Flank rubbed his chin and said, "Uh-oh."

"Tell me," said Ahrik, his eyes narrow.

"Thur's a thumb-size chink in the tail'f thus thing."

Ahrik gulped, but put on a brave face. "Close it up. I only have one chance to make this drop." He adjusted Biriq on his thigh, then said, "First."

Tank closed the lid. Ahrik didn't hear the response, and he knew, in his heart, that they hadn't said it. He'd lost them. They were no longer his men. They no longer believed in the Ketel of Ahrik.

"To the fight," he said to himself. His voice sounded tinny and afraid, hollow inside the confines of the pod. Then he felt the pod being manhandled toward the hatch. Then a mighty rush of air, and the sensation of falling, faster and faster, toward impending doom.

He wondered when the inertial stabilizers would kick in. The wind rushed faster and faster outside, whistling through the chink in the tail. Ahrik thought just how little he'd prepared for these to be his final moments.

If the inertial stabilizers didn't kick in, he wouldn't know it until it was too late.

The pod met the ground with a sickening crunch, and he cried out in alarm. Pain shot through his ankle. The pod tumbled a few times and came to a rest. He chanced a shallow breath. He was dizzy and rattled, but alive.

The stabilizers had worked. Not perfectly, but well enough. Thank you, Renla.

The pod ran through a series of external environment checks, marked by a sequence of calming beeps, at odds with the violence of the landing. The lid swished open, and he squinted into a bright blue sky and tall, lush trees that smelled distinctly of pine.

A back-lit figure appeared in his vision, blocking out the pleasing view. He pointed a weapon at Ahrik's head, his voice a study in menace. "Get out. Nice and slow."

Renla rose from her command seat and approached the hull of Harkov Station. Hands clasped behind her back, she ordered, "Transluce the hull."

She stared through the hull of the command module, one of three spherical modules in Harkov, and considered the fragility of human life. An uncomfortable hush settled over the staff behind her. The whispered discussions over tactical objectives, the last-minute orders to outlying interceptor units, the fervent rush of personnel entering and exiting the command module, all died down into rapt attention at the spectral scene that unfolded in the space outside Harkov.

A graveyard of refugee ships, debris, and bodies drifted along a thousand vectors in the space around the portal to the White Planet. The portal, shimmering in the fabric of space, floated like a stealthy, grim sentry some ten thousand meters away. It had trailed Moon's gravity well, presumably, since time immemorial, but the human race had known of it only since the War for the Emerald Moon, a decade-and-a-half ago. Two rows of blinking buoys marked the gateway to another dimension of space. Renla's space engineers had cleared a path through the wreckage, their ships' positions represented by tiny points of light projected onto the hull by Harkov Station's compiler.

The dark husk of a boxy refugee ship drifted toward the portal at the wrong angle, striking the portal amidships. The ship twisted into the tension of the portal's gravity well, then snapped in two, flinging a slurry of detritus out from the wreckage, further littering the scene with lives once lived. Had they found any survivors out there? Renla grimaced. Would it matter?

In the foreground, the remains of an interceptor drifted across the view, blazoned with unit markings from the 11–2 Hellbats, the squadron

Renla had charged with defending the approaches to the portal. The interceptor's nose had been torn open with terrible explosive force. Angry spines of metal splayed out at unnatural angles. Where the pilot had been, only vacuum remained. A pilot's helmet drifted in the interceptor's wake, along with a trail of vacuum tubes, compiler casings, and boson drive components from the interceptor's interior, a funerary procession marching across Renla's clouded vision.

Renla stiffened, breathed in, and blinked back tears. She turned to her staff, meeting the gaze of the fifty-odd people fixed on her. A seat creaked, and someone sniffed. The hum of the air circulation system sounded its dirge. The stale air stung her eyes like the dying embers of a pyre. She cleared her throat. "That is why we're here, diggers of the Fighting 11th. We fight so people out there get a chance at a better life, so they might enjoy a shred of humanity in a new home." Then she whispered, "*Cheret.*"

"*Cheret,*" they all repeated in unison. Their faces were somber, their eyes focused on the middle distance.

Renla nodded at Lyn, her aide, who stood at her post behind the command seat.

Lyn snapped to attention and nodded back, but her face twisted with anguish for the atrocities displayed before them. She bore none of the youthful exuberance she had when Renla first met her, on the shuttle bound for her command on the Emerald Moon. Lyn was a war leader now.

Lyn swiveled on her heel and strode up the stairs leading from the command seat to the entrance to the central module. "Diggers," she barked, "the Tyrant's task force will be in range in less than ten minutes. Engineers, shroud those portal buoys and get the decoy buoys working. Ops, get those explosive mines in place on the other side of the fake portal. Nothing like giving the Tyrant a nasty surprise to start our little ambush." Lyn stopped at the top of the stairs, without a hint of irony at having used the word "little", and spun on her heel. "Comms, be ready to spoof their sensors the second we spring the ambush. Make them believe we're everywhere."

A flurry of "Yes, ma'ams" blossomed around the room, and Lyn smiled at Renla.

Renla bit her lip, sat, and faced her chair away from her staff. Life was so fragile.

"Go opaque," she ordered. The harrowing scene outside the hull vanished, replaced by dull metal. She needed to reduce Harkov's electromag signature as much as possible before the Tyrant appeared.

She looked down at the inside of her armrest, where her backup plan nestled in a small alcove. She had only to twist and press the button to incinerate everything within five thousand meters of the portal, using the atomics Lyn had arranged, against her will. Renla didn't want to use it, but even if she did, would it be enough?

Renla glanced up at Lyn at the top of the stairs. Lyn furrowed her brow, then followed Renla's gaze. Panic washed over Lyn's face for a moment, and she shook her head in brief fury. Only Lyn knew about Renla's backup plan, and she'd spent the hour before they launched trying to talk Renla out of it. "We can keep fighting on Moon, ma'am," she'd said. "Why guarantee Moon's defeat when so many lives remain to be saved?" In response to Lyn's panic at the top of the stairs in Harkov, Renla closed her eyes in a gesture of reassurance.

Only if there was no other way.

"Ma'am." A voice from off to the left snapped Renla back to the present. Intel. "Three bogeys on approach at hypersonic. Seekerbots, ma'am."

"All units go dark and silent," said Renla. In space, seekerbots keyed in on electromag signatures. If Renla's standard looked like all the other debris in the vicinity, the path to the false portal would light up like a bonfire. Their plan would work, as long as the Tyrant came in fast. If he came in slow and steady, he'd overwhelm Renla's tiny force. She prayed that the Lady of the Emerald Moon would give them the strength to turn back this tide of evil.

"Ops," said Renla, "final order to all units: fix your kill zone, wait for the signal, trust your comrades. *Cheret u-met*." Freedom or death. "Dig on. Command out."

The hush of battle descended on the room, the helpless feeling that victory now lay in the hands of others. The orders were given. Renla couldn't risk issuing orders until the Tyrant's main force hit the ambush site, and after the battle was joined the friction of war would surely make something go wrong.

She fingered the pendant that Zharla had given Renla before she left, the flame of peace that Shahl gave to Zharla so many years ago, before their world was destroyed by war and carnage. Renla closed her eyes in prayer once again, that someone might live to know the peace that had abandoned her.

She swivelled her creaky seat to face intel. "Update on those seekerbots."

"Ma'am, they've branched off their original trajectory to three random vectors through the debris field. If they know the portal markers have changed, they don't show it."

Renla growled with satisfaction. "May the Tyrant's genocide of the people on Dom and Moon come back to bite him." The debris from the drones' attacks on the refugees concealed the Fighting 11th's ambush.

Renla bit her lip and assessed her soldiers' mood with narrowed eye. She couldn't remember anymore who was Moonborn and who wasn't. They'd given her so much. She needed just a little more.

Lyn sauntered her way back down the stairs. She cast her watchful gaze this way and that.

Intel: "Ma'am, enemy convoy is within scope range. We count . . . ten carriers, ma'am."

The room gasped. Renla leaped from her chair. "Silence." She glared. "We knew the odds." Renla set her chin, but her heart sank to her gut. The Tyrant had at least seventy thousand supersoldiers with him, enough to lay waste to the White Planet, just like he'd done to their home, using tectonics and atmospherics and atomics.

What other ground assault forces did he have inside those extra carriers? Renla clenched her teeth. He'd have enough interceptors to defend his carriers through the portal, too. She strode toward the hull, to hide her shaking knees and to give herself a few beats to think. How would they survive this?

She turned on her heel and avoided eye contact with Lyn. Renla knew what her aide's gaze held, a realization of their worst fears. But Renla couldn't succumb to fear now. She summoned every bit of false courage she found in the wasteland of her heart. "Intel, give me an assessment of ancillary ship strength. Comms, see if you can figure out which carrier the Tyrant is in. Ops, we still have the most important advantage: surprise."

She walked toward the nearest staff desk and planted her knuckles on the cold metal surface. The chill flowed up her arms and straight to her core as she scanned the fearful faces of her brave diggers. "We can win this. We are the Fighting 11th. Every carrier that doesn't make it through the portal is seven thousand fewer murderers that the people of the White Planet have to deal with."

The intel chief cleared her throat. "Ma'am, there are four sweepers per carrier, but the number of interceptors is unknown, and the carriers themselves have enhanced missile pods." Sweepers had enough power to blast or push anything out of their way, and interceptors were so small that they'd be impossible to find in the detritus around the portal.

Renla turned toward the hull once again and pursed her lips. "Energy shields?"

"Full front, ma'am, and they are approaching at about 4,500 meters per second. Two minutes till they reach the portal."

The task force was moving so fast there was no way the Tyrant could pick his way through the debris. A shred of luck. But Renla's staff had planned for seven carriers. Her tiny force could take out two or three carriers outright, and maybe cripple one or two more, but ten?

She turned to face her staff and rose to her full height. She saw the brave front in their eyes, the acceptance of their fate. *Cheret u-met*. "Ignore the ancillary ships. The carriers are the main objective. The engineers have done their jobs. Their explosives will clog up the area around the portal and induce panic. After we hit the first carrier and the rest realize they're at the wrong place, we just have to maintain the chaos long enough for our interceptors to do their work."

"Ma'am." Ops. "One seekerbot discovered and engaged one of our interceptors. The seekerbot was destroyed, but the other two seekerbots immediately dispersed microbots. They've already homed in on twelve of our interceptors. Permission to deploy electromag defenses."

"Only when absolutely necessary. Give away as few of our interceptors as possible." Renla only had fifty interceptors in her force. "Get the interceptors moving if you have to." The only defense against microbots was to fry them just before they latched onto the hull. If her interceptors stayed put, the Tyrant would know Renla's entire disposition before he even got to the kill zone.

Intel: "Ma'am, sixty seconds till the convoy reaches the false portal."

Comms: "Signal density is greatest from carriers two, three, and five, but it's not clear that all those are genuine, ma'am."

Renla sat in her chair and called up the armrest display. A schematic showed those three carriers near the center of the convoy. This new information wasn't enough to deviate from the plan. "Monitor those ships when we spring the ambush. If the Tyrant himself is with them, and he probably is, then we want to make sure we attack his ship."

Ops: "Ma'am, seekerbots two and three homed in on the first seekerbot's last location. Interceptors in the area engaged and destroyed them. Fifteen of our interceptors are compromised with microbots, but they're moving around the battlefield to mimic tugbot behavior."

Renla sighed, a baleful sound, one that comes with ordering others to die for a greater cause. "Ensure that the compromised interceptors lead the attack. We need to preserve the element of surprise as long as possible."

Intel: "Thirty seconds, ma'am."

"Transluce the hull," said Renla, "and project friendly ship locations."

Outside Harkov, the Tyrant's convoy lunged past, single file, decelerating as they approached the portal, or what they thought was the portal. Sweepers blasted a path before the carriers, and the carriers' powerful frontal shields flicked aside any debris that the sweepers missed.

Lyn approached and placed a hand on Renla's shoulder. "They desecrate our dead, like a cold wind blowing through the first leaves of autumn."

Renla squeezed her two's hand and stood, a soft gaze in her eyes. "Today we avenge our dead." She looked around the command module. "Today we begin the rebirth of the human race in a new home."

Zharla's last words sprang to her mind. *Strength when I needed it most.* Renla tried to force the emotion down her throat. Then she screamed in fury, a guttural, inhuman cry. As her scream died on Harkov's hull, she turned to the crew and pointed toward the portal. "Ops, detonate the explosives on the first carrier amidships. Full frontal shield on Harkov. It's time to send this spawn of hell back where it belongs."

Her staff cheered. "*Cheret,*" some cried out.

At the false portal, a massive ring of explosives erupted around the first carrier, shearing it clean asunder. Harkov's shields went up, and Renla's interceptors down by the portal pounced on the second carrier. Throughout the convoy, the Tyrant's interceptors shot from their launch tubes.

Renla's eyes widened in disbelief. Even from this far away, she saw them swarm out like the breath of death itself.

Intel: "Ma'am, carrier two is adrift, and carriers three and four have rammed it aside."

Carriers five and six passed in front of Harkov. Renla smiled. "Our ruse is working. Comms, do they know we're here?"

Comms: "Ma'am, signals density spiked from carrier five when we hit carrier one. No indication they're aware of us. Too busy worrying about the spoof. The Tyrant is likely in carrier five."

Renla gritted her teeth. "Then let's give them something else to worry about. Open up Harkov on carrier five."

Two dozen large caliber distiller weapons opened up from Harkov. Their charges slammed into the starboard hull of the carrier. It buckled, slid from its spot in the convoy, then began to turn toward Harkov.

Was she wounded and angry, or drifting? Renla gripped her armrests. "Launch reserve interceptors."

"Ma'am," said Lyn, "our flanks will be exposed."

Renla glanced at Lyn, then set her jaw. "Yes, but only for a moment."

A swarm of interceptors from carrier five bore down on Harkov.

Ops: "Ma'am, shall we order reserve interceptors to defend Harkov?"

"No. Carrier five is the main objective."

Intel: "Carrier three has veered off. She's wounded, ma'am."

Comms: "Ma'am, they've found the real portal. The convoy has adjusted course."

Ops: "Ma'am, we're down to twenty-seven interceptors, eight in the reserve and nineteen in the ambush force. The ambush force has moved on to carrier four."

Renla growled in frustration. With only nineteen interceptors left in the ambush force, and that swarm of drone interceptors coming at them, they probably wouldn't be able to touch carrier four. Her pilots out by the portal were as good as dead.

Intel: "Enemy interceptors from carrier five will be in range of Harkov in ten seconds."

Renla looked over to Harkov's pilot. "Engage the boson drive."

"Ma'am?"

Renla knew they couldn't win and live. *Cheret u-met.* "We'll send as many of them to hell as we can."

"Yes, ma'am," said the pilot. "Brace for impact."

Harkov lurched forward, then shuddered as Nayr's drones attacked her unprotected flanks. Carrier five lumbered to turn toward the true portal.

Intel: "Ma'am, carrier five has primed it's missile pods."

"She knows we're going to ram her," said Lyn over Renla's shoulder, a smile in her voice. "She's trying to run away."

One by one, the carrier's missile pods lit up. Tiny points of light on Harkov's hull showed Renla and the crew where the missiles were and how long they had until fate consumed them. One by one, Harkov's distillers sputtered and winked out as the Tyrant's interceptors engaged the station's flanks.

"Ma'am," said Intel, her voice almost at a whisper, "forty seconds to missile impact."

"Intel, how fast can they arm?" Renla asked. "The Tyrant thinks he's won, but he does not know our courage." Face dark, she turned to the pilot. "Speed up. Beat those missiles."

"Yes, ma'am."

"Diggers," said Renla, "prepare to abandon Harkov. You can still make it back to Moon."

She hoped.

Her command staff, except for the pilot and the ops and intel chiefs, moved toward escape pods in Harkov's rear. There was nothing more they could do in this battle.

Ops: "Shields holding, ma'am, but we're losing Harkov's flank modules."

"Get out of here, ops."

An ethereal creaking whined through the station, but then a brief rush of air cut it off, and the station sprang forward. The tang of ozone hung on the air as the life support systems failed.

Pilot: "Ma'am, we lost the starboard module."

Renla coughed. "Intel, will we beat the missiles?"

"Not clear, ma'am." She gulped down a breath of the acrid air. "The missiles are already hypersonic. Might be upgraded from the last model." Cough. "Half are armed already." Cough. "Depends on our shields."

"Intel and pilot, go." Renla reached into her armrest and extracted the atomic detonator. "Lyn."

"Ma'am," said Lyn, "don't ask me to leave you now."

The *tha-tha-tha-woo* of escape pods launching from Harkov thrummed throughout the command module. Renla peered into her two's face and handed her the detonator. "*Cheret u-met*. Kill as many as possible."

Lyn gave the death salute, arms crossed in an X on her chest. Her eyes were moist. "*Cheret u-met*." She paused. "Did you know, ma'am, that I am Moonborn?"

Renla smiled. "Deep down, I always knew." She steeled her face. "Go."

Renla tightened her restraining harness and gazed into Lyn's eyes, to give her two the courage she would need. "For our new home."

When Lyn didn't move, Renla gritted her teeth and turned away. "Go, Lyn. That detonator needs to be close enough to the portal to set off the atomic."

Lyn's footfalls sprinted up the stairs, and Renla fixed her helmet in place, then set steely eyes on carrier five, and fate. Many of the carrier's missiles careened off Harkov's powerful frontal shield, not yet armed, but a few exploded, weakening the shield and slowing Harkov's momentum.

Light from the missile blasts stung Renla's eyes, but she forced herself to look death in the face. Her eyes burned wet from the bursts of light. The shuddering whine of ripping metal told Renla that Harkov's port module had nearly succumbed to Nayr's interceptors. In spite of the missiles and interceptors, Harkov approached the carrier at fearsome speed.

Lyn couldn't have much time left. Renla set her helmet to inform her when Lyn launched.

Something snapped in Harkov's innards, and the artigrav gave out. Renla gripped her armrests, but strapped in as she was she realized the futility of doing so and let go.

A deep and satisfying *ping* sounded in Renla's helmet in the seconds before impact. *Farewell, Lyn.*

Renla coughed. The air in her suit was souring. Did she have a leak? Renla bit her lip. Didn't matter.

Harkov's forward shield struck the carrier amidships. In the utter silence of space, the carrier's hull crumpled like paper. A gap tore open. Sudden vacuum sucked men and equipment into space before Renla's eyes. One of the Tyrant's drones locked eyes with her as the force of the expulsion slammed him against the shield, his face masked with horror. A shard of bulkhead struck his back and smeared him into space.

Harkov's shield disintegrated, and the thunderous roar of colliding air pockets filled Renla's command module, audible even through the vacuum insulation of her exosuit. The impact forced her body against the harness and knocked the breath out of her. In a squeal of twisting metal, Harkov groaned, then the port module snapped away. Through the translucent hull, Renla saw the starboard module, separated earlier, careen on a separate trajectory into one of the carrier's hangar bays. It burst into flame. The force of the explosion altered the command module's vector and drove it farther into the belly of the carrier.

A fissure snaked open in the command module's hull, and a rush of air told Renla that the end neared. A rupture grumbled behind Harkov, or what remained of it, growing as it rippled toward the command module. Renla craned her head back, lungs burning from lack of oxygen, and saw the rear of the command module crumple inward.

Debris from the rear rushed toward Renla and the fissure in the forward hull, following the last of Harkov's atmosphere into space. Two shards of metal sliced at Renla's suit, one on her upper arm and one on the inside of her thigh, where she'd concealed the targeting list all those weeks before. Pain speared her leg and arm. Renla glanced down to see blood squirt out in tiny, frozen droplets from her thigh. Air rushed out of her suit, and the numbness of frigid space spidered out from the two suit punctures. Didn't matter.

Like a piece of gravel dislodged from a shoe, Harkov sprang into space on the other side of the carrier, forced out by the carrier's escaping atmosphere. Harkov, or what was left of it, drifted into the space battle, and Renla squinted through blurry eyes at the death splayed out before her. The sun had rounded Moon, casting a pale orange pall over the scene.

Darkness crept into the rim of her vision. She unstrapped and drifted with Harkov's escaping atmosphere toward the fissure in the hull. Numbness crept up her extremities, searching for her core. A cough racked her chest. Ice filled her lungs.

The rising sun glinted over interceptors skittering through space, a morbid ice dance in three dimensions. Smaller glints marked Harkov's escape pods, her crew making a desperate gamble for life. But interceptors followed them, and the interceptors' distillers found them. One, two, three pods evaporated in clouds of elemental crystal. A fourth and fifth burst apart.

Then hope glimmered in Renla's pounding heart. The pods turned toward the carrier instead of making for the moon. *To the end, they fight. Cheret.*

She grunted back unconsciousness. *U-met.* Her muscles and lungs pled for oxygen. Panic rose through her neck. She struggled to form thoughts.

One glint sped toward the portal, weaving through debris and drifting ships, silent catacombs in the vastness of space. *Lyn.*

Then a familiar voice sounded in her helmet, over the all-frequency channel, a voice she felt she should know. "All ships, clear a path. Advance through the portal."

Lyn? No, not Lyn. Why was her head so fuzzy? Renla should know the voice. Who? She grunted to push one last burst of oxygen to her brain, then realization snapped her eyes wide with fear.

Nayr. Not dead. Failure.

But as darkness enveloped her vision and cold overcame her body, Lyn's streaking glint burst into a flash of energy, a ball of light and fire expanding from its epicenter, subatomic reactions consuming everything in their path.

Lyn. Success.

The last thing she saw was blinding light, and instead of cold, the deepest of warmth. Then sweet release. *Cheret.*

17 Cordon

ANDA SHIFTED SERA'S WEIGHT on his hip. She slept now, but in a slumber of fitfulness, not of rest. Over the last day since they had crashed on the White Planet, strength had drained from her.

He was down to four pills, and she wasn't getting any better.

Their turn in line was almost up, and he didn't know how he'd explain to these soldiers in static print camouflage that his daughter faced death if she didn't see a healer soon. He scanned the loose perimeter that the soldiers kept around the two hundred or so refugees, far fewer than Anda suspected started the trip. He only counted ten soldiers, but there could be more sitting in their squat, dun-colored vehicles that rumbled around on four wheels, touching the ground. Their engines gave off a metallic grumble and a faint smell of something foul burning.

Anda gazed toward the hills to the north, in the direction where Esh'a was, according to the beat-up compiler. The location was close, he knew, less than a hundred kilometers, and the topography didn't look too forbidding, at least on the sand model. He could carry Sera that far in two or three days.

If the pills lasted.

He opened his satchel and made sure the compiler and the blood analysis kit were there. When they were alone, and free from prying eyes, he could test their blood to see if the nanos that Nayr had put in their bodies really communicated with each other. That was the only way to know if the threat was real, or just bluster.

The only way to know who would live and who would die.

He squinted at the setting sun. If the soldiers became distracted, he could make a run for it, but their discipline and watchfulness was at least as impressive as any soldier in Ahrik's ketel. Anda thought of Ahrik and the others, and wondered if they'd made it off of Dom, or if they would be able to get here. Anda thought of Esh'a. She would have clear answers, like she always did.

He felt so alone.

He looked toward the mountains that stood off in the northern distance, beyond the hills. It couldn't be that hard of a walk. The evening air was dry and the terrain looked bleak, but he felt strong in this new planet's low gravity. He'd come this far. What could stop him from saving Sera now?

She stirred on his shoulder.

He shaded his eyes from the setting sun, then stroked her hair. Time for a new beginning. Was Esh'a looking for him and missing him, too?

"Abbi, can I get down?"

"No, Serit. It's almost our turn." He felt a twinge of guilt at the lie. If they had to make a run for it, in this lower gravity they'd be faster if he carried her.

The line opened up ahead of them, and a soldier seated on some sort of camp chair grunted at him in the aliens' guttural, loopy language. Anda could tell that the soldier was taller than him, even seated, but he couldn't tell just how large the soldier was with all the gear attached to his body. These soldiers went into battle weighed down like pack animals. The soldier had to reach around his weapon to grip the writing instrument that he used to scribble down names of refugees. His weapon, fitted into a sort of sleeve attached to his chest, was black and small enough to be held in one hand, but everything else on his body was big and bulky. How did he move, much less fight?

The soldier gargled something at Anda, which Anda took to be, "What are your names?" The soldier stared, expressionless, so Anda filled the silence by pointing at himself and saying, "Anda." Then, he pointed at his daughter and said, "Sera." He coughed and pointed at Sera again, to indicate that she was sick and needed attention.

The soldier cocked his head and furrowed his brow, an eerily familiar expression of confusion. The soldier's features were finer and longer than Anda was used to, but he was surprisingly humanoid. Arms. Legs. Hands with five fingers. Anda presumed he had feet inside his bulky boots, but Anda didn't know how he could lift them, they looked so heavy.

The soldier, a question on his face, pointed at Anda and said, "Ahnna," then coughed into his hand, like Anda had done.

Anda frowned and waved his hands to tell the soldier he had his name wrong, but another soldier watching over them nearby whipped his weapon up and pointed it at Anda's head, growling. His weapon was linger than the first soldier's and looked something like those that rebels back home had smuggled from this planet to fight with, back in the war, but this weapon was bulkier, well-greased, and had scopes and tubes added on, none of which looked friendly.

Anda backed off, palms up, then pointed to himself again. Very slowly, he said, "An-da." Then at his daughter. "Ce-ra."

The first soldier scratched something onto the paper in front of him. The writing struck Anda as blocky and slow. Lots of straight lines and lifting of the writing utensil off the paper. The soldier made the same scratches on two strips of a flexible material. It didn't look like paper, but the scratches remained all the same. He smiled and handed the first strip to Anda, then motioned to Sera and gestured with a hand around his wrist. "Say-ra," he said.

Anda peered down at the strip, then gathered that it was a bracelet, with an ingenious little peg that a tab sticking out from the strip would fold onto.

"Hold out your hand, Serit." Anda affixed Sera's strip, and turned back to the soldier for his own, but the soldier had dropped Anda's strip and removed his weapon from its sleeve. His communications device, a slimmer, sleeker version of the electromags Anda saw in the war, chattered with static and alarmed voices. The soldier stood, eyes scanning the sky. He shouted an order to the others, and they began to fan out in a widening perimeter, weapons pointed upwards. The soldier who'd menaced Anda with his weapon produced a ballish lump of metal from behind his back, probably a bomb, and stuffed it into one of the tubes attached to his weapon.

The soldiers motioned for the refugees to stay down, and worried murmurs rippled through the crowd. Anda wanted to tell them to remain calm, to trust these soldiers and their bulky equipment, but a creeping sense of danger forewarned him.

Sera squeezed her arms around his neck. She wouldn't want to get down now.

An ear-splitting whine ripped open the impending dusk, a roar from the direction of the setting sun. Two alien aircraft, traveling at a ferocious speed, screamed across the sky, darts trailing flame. Were they damaged? Their lateral movement hampered?

The two aircraft swerved and streaked up into the sky, as if avoiding some other objects up there. They began to circle high above, like hawks, or vultures. Anda couldn't tell which.

Sera shrieked in fright. As Anda crouched, he tried to comfort her with a hand on her back.

Then Anda heard the terrifying, basso hum of a boson drive descending toward them. An interceptor. The crowd of refugees cowered. Some cried out in fear at recognizing the sound. The alien soldiers scanned the crowd, nervous, their slim electromags crackling with garbled voices.

Anda narrowed his eyes against the sun and peered into the blue expanse, tracking the source of the hum. After what seemed like an eternity, he caught the faint shimmer of the interceptor's cloak as it weaved and bobbed among the alien craft, toying with them.

The interceptor descended until it hovered over the crowd, on the opposite side from Anda and Sera, over by the wreckage of the refugee ship. The alien dart aircraft up in the sky made no move to challenge the interceptor. Were their scanners that rudimentary? Did they not know what it would do, what it and others like it had already done?

Sera's breath came warm and fast in his ear.

The soldiers still swept their weapons across the sky. Their electromags still chattered with static and alarm. Anda was shocked. They really couldn't see what was happening, couldn't detect the descending interceptor.

A feeling of dread mounted in Anda's chest. He knew what that interceptor intended, as did everyone else in the crowd of refugees. As more and more of the refugees perceived the interceptor, a hush descended. They gathered loved ones and meager possessions close, poised for flight, like wary prey.

The interceptor decloaked, and the alien soldiers shouted at one another and trained their weapons on it. The soldier closest to Anda, the one who'd scratched their names down, shouted an order and spoke into his electromag. This was their leader, to be sure.

A *nayri* clone leaped out of the interceptor's rear hatch and brandished his distiller, its forbidding hum ramping up on the evening breeze. Anda shivered, whether at the dropping temperature or the horror unfolding before him, he couldn't be sure.

"Shahl Jeber-li," one of the clones shouted.

Relief fluttered over Anda's sense of building doom. The refugees' heads turned this way and that in confusion. They would only recognize him as Anda, not Shahl.

But how long did he have, really? He crouched down to make himself and Sera as small as possible. He shifted her to his back. "Hang on, Serit," he said.

Not many refugees had a daughter of Sera's age with them, and eventually the *nayri* would give a description. Anda's sense of creeping doom rose to panic when the *nayri* began relaying that very description.

Anda refused to wait for death to find them. He filled his lungs with air, then screamed, "Run!"

He sprang up to dart between two of the alien soldiers, but he became aware, in the moment he did so, with terrifying clarity, that none of the other refugees had moved a muscle. He had miscalculated, and his mortality crystallized in delicate, fragile relief.

In slow motion, the *nayri's* distiller revved up, then the sound he dreaded sliced through the silence. *Thu-wunk.* But his foot caught on something. He fell. Sera landed on top of him, startled into silence. The distiller charge hit home with smack.

But Anda wasn't hit. Sera squirmed. He felt no pain. He looked up, and the alien soldiers' leader dropped his weapon. A hole gaped in his chest, and he stared down at it in silent alarm.

The soldiers screamed, then opened up with their weapons on the interceptor and the *nayri*. *Pa-pa-pa-pa-pa-pa-pa.*

The violence of the sound spurred the refugees into action. They scattered. The *nayri* responded. *Thu-thu-thunk.* Two more alien soldiers fell. Refugees screamed and wailed from that direction, then the *nayri's* distiller went silent. The alien soldiers' weapons, as Anda had expected, had no effect on the interceptor. Its boson engine thrummed.

The interceptor was not preparing for a battle, but for a massacre.

Another raucous sound shredded the morning. *Whup-whup-whup.* As if out of nowhere, another aircraft emerged, this time flying close to the ground, like a black metal hornet closing in for a kill. Its forward weapon opened up with a tinny but ferocious *brrrrrrrap*. Four missiles shot from tube pods on its underbelly. *Wha-whoosh.*

The interceptor rose and slid to meet this new threat. The refugees' shrieks died down as they dispersed to the four winds, driven by the clamor and panic of battle. Anda and Sera fled toward the mountains to the north.

The black hornet craft hovered to a stop, midair. *Whup-whup. Brrrrrrrap.* Dust swirled. Anda covered his mouth and narrowed his eyes to slits as he crouch-ran for the hills. Sera clung to his back for dear life and coughed. Anda smelled violence and destruction on the air. When they reached a shadowy depression in the sandy ground, he swiveled her around to his front and cradled her close, then went to one knee to survey their options.

The interceptor swiveled onto the hovering hornet, like a wounded tiger limping toward unsuspecting prey. The hornet aircraft's weapons had some effect on the interceptor, after all. Just not enough.

Thu-wunk.

Brrrrra—

The hovering metal hornet disintegrated from the nose and flew apart in a storm of rancor and steel. Anda threw himself on the ground, using his body to protect his daughter. She screamed again, at the din, at the dust, at the palpable hate. Wreckage flew in a thousand directions, then the remains of the metal hornet fell, slack, to the ground. The earth shook beneath them.

The lower gravity assisted the refugees' flight. Some soldiers tried to corral them, while others closed in on the *nayri* clone, now lying on the ground.

As pieces of the metal hornet splashed all around, the two flying darts swooped down on the wounded interceptor, which was now rotating to face them. Flames burst from the darts' wings. *Ka-ka-ka-ka-ka-ka-ka*. The ground underneath the interceptor erupted with furious geysers of earth. The force of the darts' projectiles drove the interceptor into the flayed ground, and it struggled to make the turn.

What power! What new weapons were these, that could destabilize an interceptor's boson drive?

Anda cradled Sera and stumbled away from this new violence, his mind now one with the mad scramble of refugees fleeing the scene of carnage and destruction. He tripped and fell, then clawed at the earth underneath him, but froze when his hand felt cold steel. He looked down. A soldier's handheld weapon. He considered it, then stuffed it into a thigh pocket and stumbled on, the weapon slapping against his leg.

He pushed himself into a crouch and shifted Sera to his back once again, ready to run. A loud *whoosh-bang* broke over the din of battle. He turned to see two missiles streak into the interceptor from the alien dart aircraft, up above. Instead of absorbing the blasts like it had the hornet craft's missiles, the interceptor exploded in a ball of flame. Anda ducked, but the force of the explosion knocked him to his knees. An alien soldier near him, who had been trying to keep refugees from fleeing, dove to the ground, hands on his head. Was he hit?

Anda was up and running before he saw what the soldier would do. Time played against Anda. He focused his eyes on the undulating hills and the mountains beyond, with their cover of trees and foliage. If the soldiers caught him again, so be it, but they had hundreds of other refugees to worry about, and Anda had no way to communicate to them how important it was that he get away.

He had no other way to save Sera, or to find Esh'a once again.

The *nayra* were coming for him, perhaps to finish what the nanos started, or maybe as an insurance policy against Nayr's vacant threats.

Anda held a steady pace, to account for Sera's weight, even as slight as it was.

He ran about five kilometers, then stopped just over a rise, lungs heaving. The gravity hadn't helped him as much as he thought it would, or maybe the drain of adrenaline worked against him as danger receded. "I'm sorry, Serit. You need to walk. Serit?"

Frantic, he pulled Sera around, then breathed easy. Sleeping. Then he realized that her sleep might be a bad sign.

"Abbi?"

Her voice was weak. He needed to analyze her blood, to see if his worst fears would be realized.

He sat down with her on the ground, then pulled the weapon from his thigh pocket to examine it. He saw the trigger immediately, as well as the short barrel from which, he assumed, the metal projectiles flew. It had a number of knobs and other moving parts, but he wasn't about to test it out. No sense announcing his position by having this thing go off.

"Can I see, Abbi?" asked Sera.

He frowned. "No. This is dangerous."

With the weapon in his hand, he flipped onto his belly and peered through a stand of scrub brush in the fading light of sunset. Pyres of smoke ascended from the downed interceptor and hornet, and the refugee ship smoldered beyond them. Soldiers scrambled like ants around the battlefield—more must have come since he fled—and a billow of dust off to the right told him that more were on route. More of the hovering hornets circled above, although these were more stubby than the one that had crashed, their *whap whap* not as deep-throated and forbidding as the first hornet's had been. Some had turned on beams of light to scan the ground around the battlefield in ever expanding circles.

Anda cast his eyes over the hills. Clusters of refugees bobbed and weaved and ran, while others huddled in the lightbeams of the soldiers' vehicles, captive once again. The sight pricked his heart, for fear what would happen to them. Would these aliens protect the refugees' human dignity, or were they as uncaring as the *nayra*?

He drew a deep breath against the terror of knowing, to steel himself for what would come next, and reached for the blood analysis kit. In the fading light, he read the instructions and realized that this was a single-use kit. Of course. He should have grabbed two kits to analyze both of their blood.

He huffed in frustration.

A small hand rested on his arm, delicate with worry. "Are you okay, Abbi?"

He met her eyes and tried to smile. He knew what he had to do. He squeezed her hand and tried to hide the lie on his face. "Yes, Serit."

He brought out the handheld compiler from his satchel and synced it to the blood analysis kit, then adjusted the settings. He had one shot at this, so he had to make it count. He held Sera's gaze for a beat. "This will prick a bit."

She pursed her lips and pressed her hand to the wooden container hanging from his neck. "For Imma."

He smelled vanilla, even though the container was tightly closed.

"For Imma," he said. His ears burned with the thought that Sera could die, or worse, lose hope, and he resolved to do all in his power to prevent both.

Sera winced at the initial prick, then Anda studied the readout with a fervent awareness of their mortality. Her vitals were normal, but there was definitely something foreign in her blood. As the kit did its work, the terrifying picture became clear: Sera's illness had nothing to do with a virus or bacteria, but with the millions of nanos floating around in her body.

He reached for the metal canister of pills. He didn't want to use one if she wasn't coughing, but he had to know. He had to know the extent of Nayr's evil.

Sera shifted in discomfort. "Am I okay, Abbi?"

Anda twisted the lid off the canister and gave her a thin smile. "I think . . . I hope so."

Sera gulped.

Anda studied the readout on his hand-held compiler, to see how the nanos swirled and moved and acted in her bloodstream. He pinched a pill out of the canister and held it out to his daughter. If the pill did what he thought they would to the nanos, then he would know the very thing he absolutely did not want to know.

"Take this."

"To eat?"

Anda nodded.

She frowned. "How many are left?"

Anda's eyes trembled with fear and self-loathing at what he had become, a man who lies to his daughter, supposedly for her own good. He promised himself this would be the last lie he told her. "For Imma."

"For Imma." She gave him a knowing look, a look that pierced his heart and made his blood run cold, as if she understood what was really going on.

No, Sera, do not lose your sweet innocence. Not like this.

He had to press on. He blinked back the tears that threatened the corners of his eyes, then he nodded.

She gulped down the pill.

Three left.

Immediately the nanos in her blood went dormant, as if suppressed by whatever was in the pill.

Anda's head swam. All this time, from the moment she began to cough on Moon, through all their travails, from the escape from Moon to the flight from Nayr's murderous thugs, she had never really been sick at all. Nayr, or someone close to him, had put these nanos on Moon, and from there into her body, before she ever set foot on Home.

Then it hit him. The same thing that had infected his algae tanks on Moon must have infected Sera as well. And everyone else born on Moon. With this realization grew a fire, an incandescent fury at the evil that Nayr represented, and at his own inability to do anything about it.

"Abbi," Sera whispered, croaked really.

But he could not respond or answer or divert his attention. He could not think past this rage that consumed his mind as he watched the readout on his old, beaten compiler, showing the muted nano activity slowly reactivating, the wavelengths gradually transforming back to a baseline frequency of activity and emissions. He squeezed his eyes shut.

"Abbi."

He breathed out in frustration. "Not now."

His hands trembled as he turned the metal canister over and considered the forbidding message carved underneath: *A life for a life.*

The message intimated one piece of information, one nettlesome unknown, that, if true, would complete Nayr's circle of evil. Did the nanos in Sera's body really communicate with those inside his own body? The pain of knowing was almost too great, for he bore no desire to face the doom that knowing portended, but the grief he knew it would cause Esh'a to lose Sera swirled with his fury and shock, imploring him to know.

Knowledge meant death. And life. Better to know than to wander through a valley of indecision.

"Abbi, there's—"

"Serit. Not. Now." He sucked in a deep breath, then handed her the compiler. "Hold this up so I can see the display."

Her tender little body shook, and she hesitated before cradling the compiler in her lithe fingers. "Like this?"

He breathed in again. "Yes. And whatever you do, keep it where I can see it."

She nodded with fearful solemnity.

"And don't stop me." He glared at her to emphasize the seriousness of that last statement. "Whatever you do, don't try to stop me."

Concern creased her face, and she began to lower the compiler, but Anda grunted at her and she brought it back up. The display wobbled with the shaking of her little body.

He breathed in once more, slower this time, then let it out. He wrapped his hands around his own neck and pressed on his windpipe.

"Abbi!"

The menace in Anda's grunt froze her. Tears streamed down her face, but she did not waver in her duty, nor did she cry out again. He thought how proud he was at her trust and obedience, then thought how odd it was to have such a thought at such a time, as he died before her eyes.

His lungs screamed for oxygen and his hands fought to weaken their grip, but he could not give in. He had to know.

Eyes wide, he focused as best he could on the display that Sera held up. The breath would have left his body, if he'd had any left. Not only did the wavelengths on the display flatten out, suggesting reduced nano activity in Sera's blood, but the overall estimate of the number of nanos in Sera's blood decreased, slowly at first, but as he tightened the vice around his own neck and fought against the natural urge to gasp for air, the number of nanos dropped off precipitously.

Were the nanos dying?

If their nanos were connected, then the longer he choked himself, the more the nanos would die in Sera's body and the healthier she would be.

He clenched his teeth, to make his distress last as long as possible, to kill as many of the nanos as he could before his will gave out, or he fainted.

The number of nanos kept going down on the display, and the pressure built in his neck and eyes, as if life itself could burst through. He tightened his will with each involuntary spasm in his gut and each burning beat in his chest. He could not give in. For Sera.

His legs and arms trembled, so he bit into his tongue to distract himself from the nearly overwhelming urge to expel the carbon dioxide from his lungs and live.

But the nanos kept going down, and he'd rather fade away like this than face the alternative, to see his own daughter waste away by degrees, another nameless victim of Nayr's terror.

"Abbi?" Sera's eyes widened in fear, but she held the compiler steady.

The rim of his vision began to blur, and he struggled to focus on the pulsing wavelength and the numbers ticking down next to it on the display. He was so close. So. Close. To. Zer—

Black. Silence.

A beat of weightlessness. Painless, at last.

A sound, far away.

Heartbeats. His own, pulsing through his temples. Breath, life, and a measure of relief.

Sera tugged on his sleeve and whispered, "Abbi?"

Her voice trembled, and her tears caressed his cheek.

He looked up at her from the ground. Sand and pebbles clung to his face. His vision cleared, and he saw that she stared toward the hills. The alarm in her voice sent a shiver of fear into his stomach. He followed her gaze, then tried to process the odd rumble and clank that came toward them.

One of the alien vehicles.

His alarm grew as he hobbled to his knees, then to his feet, like a marionette with one too many broken strings. He must keep Sera safe. Now, more than ever before, he needed to get her to Esh'a. Her life depended on it.

Sera gripped him by the arm, to steady him, for what good that did. "I . . . I tried to tell you, Abbi. I saw the lights coming over the moun—"

"Stay behind me, Serit," Anda mumbled. His words felt barely coherent. "Maybe he hasn't seen us yet."

From the direction of the mountains, a vehicle bumped over the rough ground. This vehicle was more boxy than the soldiers' vehicles, and noisier, its clink and clank carrying over the hundred meters or so that separated them. From its forward face, two lightbeams jerked and leaped this way and that. Anda imagined that in daylight the vehicle would be bright red.

They were exposed. If they ran, they were more likely to be seen. Better to hold still, and hope the vehicle passed.

Then with dawning horror, Anda remembered the blood kit and the compiler. He whipped around to face Sera. "The kit. Is it still in?"

She handed him the compiler. "I didn't know what to do."

Anda sighed with relief. The compiler was still reading her blood. He was about to swipe the kit off and pull it from her arm when he noticed the number of nanos.

He froze mid-sigh. The numbers crept up. The nanos were reproducing. Slowly, but reproducing all the same.

He wanted to collapse back to the ground, but Sera needed him to be strong. The vehicle's lights danced all around them. He reached into his thigh pocket and fingered the weapon he'd found on the ground. Should he draw? Was this alien hostile?

Maybe he should wait.

"Abbi? Are you okay?"

He sucked in the cool night air, the smell suddenly crisp and refreshing after the heat of the day and the trauma of his ordeal. "Here, Serit, let's take that kit out."

The kit slid out easily and dissolved into the air, then he pressed a patch of NewSkin onto her arm. The two of them, father and daughter, smiled at each other, one last moment of sweetness before the new bitterness that the approaching vehicle augured.

Anda turned to face the growling, jouncing vehicle. Such an uncouth way to move. With such crude technology, it made sense that Domans had gotten to this planet first, instead of Dom being the target of discovery.

Anda drew the weapon and pointed it toward the vehicle. He held it with two hands. He hadn't gotten a good look at how the soldier held the weapon in the chaos of battle, so he wasn't sure he was doing it right.

The muzzle quivered and shook, the weapon unnatural and heavy in his hands.

The red vehicle skidded to a stop about twenty meters away, then stood still, lightbeams blinding them. The vehicle's engine rattled. A cloud of dust washed over them, the taste chalky in Anda's mouth. The smell of the vehicle's chemical reaction engine wafted toward them.

Anda wrinkled his nose. Uncivilized.

Sera coughed and clutched his trouser leg.

The lightbeams dimmed, and Anda could once again make out the outline of the vehicle. A door on the side creaked open, and two palms appeared, pale in the paltry light of the whitish moon and distant stars. A head appeared behind the hands as the figure emerged, wearing some sort of wide-brimmed hat, which seemed an odd device to wear at night.

The man—it seemed to be a man—gargled something in his language. Anda noted a tinge of fear. The man said something else, short and choppy, and reached, ever so slowly, into the door, where Anda couldn't see.

Anda reached for Sera's hand and crouched. "Get ready to run, Serit."

The man with the odd hat made reassuring sounds and held up a clear bottle of liquid. Water. Anda realized all of a sudden how parched he was. He'd run off of the ship with the kit and compiler, but no water.

Sera squeezed his hand. "I'm thirsty."

The man tossed the bottle in their direction, and it flopped to a rest by Anda's foot. When he reached down to grab it, he realized that he still held the weapon in his hand. Too late, he realized what had happened, and when he looked up he saw the man moving toward them at a crouch, a long weapon of his own pointed at Anda's head.

He said something else, but Anda heard no fear this time, only a voice of command.

Nayr glared at 3, expectant.

3 shifted his weight. To his credit, he didn't break eye contact. "No, Father. We have not found her body."

"She's out there," said Nayr. "I heard her voice on the electromag transmission we intercepted."

"Father, the probability she's alive . . . after the rebel atomic . . . is next to zero."

Nayr pushed back on his hoverchair and stood. He paced around his desk and cocked his head at 3. "Are you challenging me?"

3 gulped. "No, Father."

Nayr held up air quotes. "'Next to zero' isn't good enough. If Renla is really dead, I have to know for sure." Nayr rubbed his chin and considered his options. He needed someone he could trust to run the next phase of the operation. He reached out over the tendril link to 6, who was running the search for Renla's body. 6, cast Nayr, *have you found her?*

3 shuffled his feet and peered out the transluced hull of Nayr's office, above the bridge on the last carrier that came through the portal. "Father, seven carriers made it through the portal. None of your sons from the Ketel of Nayr were lost, only recent conscripts. We can see the White Planet." 3 pointed to the shimmering blue-white globe, and made as if to curl his fingers around it. "Let's take it."

Nayr sighed. "You're one of my best sons, 3, maybe the best that's still alive." He gave his head a slow shake, his eyes moist. "But you're not 2 . . ."

3 shifted his weight, clearly uncomfortable.

Father, cast 6, *the first wave of seekerbots has returned. They found nothing, but we have two more waves of seekerbots still to return.*

3 cleared his throat. "Thank you for the compliment, Father."

Nayr sighed. "You ask too many questions."

"Only in private, Father, and only because I have your best interests at heart."

Acknowledged, 6. How many seekerbots do we have left?

Nayr didn't know what to make of this new turn in 3. Nayr narrowed his eyes. "When I decide something, I need you to execute."

3 clenched his jaw and studied his commander, as if on the cusp of some fateful decision. "I'm worried that we'll lose the men, Father. The radiation back there on the other side of the portal will degrade the seekerbots we sent to find Renla's body." He drew a deep breath. "We need the seekerbots to scout out the White Planet."

6: *Father, we have ninety left.*

Nayr: *Send them back through the portal. Find Renla.*

Nayr shrugged at 3. "Send interceptors to scout the White Planet."

"That'll take a long time, Father. Finding three people on an alien planet is like finding a grain of sand on a beach. We need to be more efficient."

"We'll embargo the planet. We'll find them eventually."

Father, cast 6, *the second batch of seekerbots has returned through the portal. Before it melted, one seekerbot uploaded a recording of a commander's exosuit drifting in space.*

Anticipation flared in Nayr's chest, but he kept it out of his response to 3. No need to entrust the untrustworthy with this kind of information. Nayr furrowed his brow. "Do you trust me, 3?"

"Without question, Father." 3 stood up a bit straighter, as if putting a stamp of emphasis on his fidelity.

Nayr swept forward and grasped 3 by the shoulders in a gesture of fatherly concern. "I receive reports from across the ketel. I know how to guide us to victory."

"Of course, Father."

Nayr: *6, ramp up production of seekerbots. Provide an estimate of when we'll have enough to find the traitors on the White Planet and rescue the Queen.*

6: *Yes, Father.*

Nayr squeezed 3's shoulders and leaned in to kiss his forehead, then pulled back to examine his face. "Do I need to teach you the value of trust?"

"No, Father. My trust in you is complete."

Father, cast 6, *we have confirmed that Commander Renla is dead. Tugbots have been sent to retrieve her body.*

Very good, Nayr cast back. *Win.*

Win.

With a satisfying inward smile, Nayr accessed Revenge, erased the words "Kill Renla," and altered his entry for 3: "Kill Ahrik. Kill Shahl. Rescue Mother. Take care of 3."

3 shifted his weight, as if anxious to leave, but Nayr froze him with a look. "We've got her body now," said Nayr. "Renla is dead."

3 smiled. "Congratula—"

"Silence!" Nayr's eyes flashed at 3's smugness. "This will be the last time you challenge me, understood?"

All emotion drained from 3's face, and he took on an air of placid quiescence. "Understood, Father."

Nayr put his face a few finger widths from 3's, so he could see how angry Nayr was. "Dismissed." Nayr scoffed. His upper lip curled. "Win."

"Win, Father."

18 Stratagem

ESH'A POKED AT THE FIRE and studied the sparks as they floated up into the night, toward a cold, unheralded death. Her life, and the lives of all those around the campfire, could extinguish like those sparks, in the blink of an eye.

Esh'a knew she was lucky to be alive. One of the soldiers had crept up behind her ambush site during the revolt, but a well-thrown stone from Pan had given Esh'a just enough time to shoot first.

The revolt itself had only been the start of their problems. Every night, a few more dropped off, succumbing to the cold or to sickness or to hunger. Some had slunk off to fend for themselves and hadn't returned. Of the two hundred or so miners who had revolted with Esh'a a week earlier, only about sixty remained.

In the days since the revolt, the mining groups that rose up together with so much promise had devolved into four factions, trusting only those with whom they had slaved for months. The factions mostly kept to themselves, except for moments like this, when they would all be affected by the decision of one.

They still didn't bother to learn each other's names.

Esh'a hadn't counted on that, or on the soldiers' hasty retreat, leaving most of their supplies, weapons, and the mangled bodies of their comrades for weather and wild dogs to ravage. That was no kind of military ethic that Esh'a knew, but maybe that was how things worked in the mighty Ketel of Nayr. Everyone saved their own skin.

And now she sat at the campfire with the leaders of the other three factions to decide next steps, munching on the day's ration, a sliver of roast squirrel. She sucked a bone dry, then tossed it into the fire, eyeing the other three faction leaders. "We're better off staying together," she said.

The faction leader across the fire scoffed. "Are you kidding? Sixty aliens walk into a town, if we even find one in this mountain wilderness, and they'll shoot us on the spot."

To her right, another faction leader agreed. "We should split up, each group to a different cardinal point."

Esh'a shook her head. "We don't know how big or small this wilderness is. There could be a city of a million people just over that mountain over there. We know this planet is more densely populated than Dom. If one group finds a city, how will they tell the others? We rebelled together. We should live together."

The leader to the left guffawed, her skin pale from a lifetime of mining on the Emerald Moon, then here, on the White Planet. "Ya," she said, sarcastic, her scraggly hair swishing this way and that, "and we'll die together. There's only so much squirrel to eat, and large groups of people frighten the skinny deer we see." She patted her qasfin, which the faction leaders carried, liberated after the soldiers' retreat. "It's hard to hunt spooked deer with stones and qasfina."

The leader across the fire stood and threw another scrap of wood on the flames, their only means of fending off the cold that settled at night. The days were dry and hot, the sun piercing at such a high elevation, but at night the temperature sank to just above freezing. As Esh'a watched the sparks flee up from the new wood, she pulled her outer shirt close around her neck. She shivered in anticipation of how cold she'd feel that night.

The leader who'd just thrown the wood onto the fire put his hands on his hips and looked at Esh'a. "You're outvoted. We split up."

Esh'a threw up her hands. "So that's it, then? Everyone just save their own ski—"

A commotion sounded off to their left. She and the other leaders readied themselves at a crouch and slipped qasfina out of sheaths. Boots crunched on the rocky ground, just outside the firelight. Why hadn't the pickets sounded the alarm?

Esh'a sensed something was wrong. She felt it in the air. She half-hoped it was some local authority there to arrest them. At least that way she'd have something in her belly besides the failing promise of freedom.

A burly miner broke the firelight, one arm in a distiller, left over from the soldiers' retreat but dead now because they had no kall packs to power it. The burly miner pulled a man behind, bioflauge suit ragged, face sunken by too few meals. He was a soldier. Esh'a could tell by his bearing, the rigid shoulders and alert eyes, darting, taking everything in.

He also feigned defeat, probably for his captor's benefit. But she couldn't tell much more than that, since the burly miner kept blocking her view.

"Ma'am," grumbled Burly to his faction leader, the woman with the pale skin and scraggly hair, "he's only said one word since I uncorked his capsule: 'Esh'a'."

All faces turned to look at Esh'a, and she narrowed her eyes into the dimness at the edge of the firelight, studying his features. A crawling sensation under her skin told her she should know him.

Pale Face sneered at Esh'a, then cocked her head at Burly. In the same sarcastic tone she'd used before, she asked, "Did you encourage him to say more?"

Burly nodded, grabbed a fistful of the captive's short hair, and yanked his head into the firelight. The captive's silence had won him a monstrous bruise on his temple, which Esh'a hadn't seen in the dimness at the edge of the light. A trickle of blood ran from his upper lip to his chin.

His unit markings were torn off, but she didn't need those to recognize him. She fought back the urge to gasp, and then to tell Burly just how lucky he was that his captive didn't take umbrage with the rough treatment. Even unarmed, hungry, and beaten up, she would choose Ahrik Jeber-li over anyone, any day.

He was beaten up, but he was not beaten. He was also the second-most hated man on Dom or Moon.

When she looked around the fire at her fellow rebels, she suppressed a scoff of surprise. She saw it in their faces: not a one of them, lifelong inhabitants of Moon, recognized the greatest enemy to their freedom, the man who had defeated them in the so-called War for the Emerald Moon, who hunted the rebels on Moon for years since. Maybe they couldn't imagine that the king consort could descend as low as this.

And if they found out that Ahrik was her brother-in-law, they'd kill her on the spot. Esh'a knew the risk she had taken when she married Ahrik's brother, all those years ago, but they'd lived in exile for so long, with her husband under an assumed name, that she never thought it would matter.

Until now. For the second time in a week, death stared her in the face. True, Ahrik had put his life in danger coming after her, but she didn't know whether it would be better to kill him or free him. If she freed him, they had a small chance at escape together, as loathsome as it would be to flee with a man she despised. If she killed him, her secret would be safe, unless the other miners figured out who he was before she succeeded.

A thought struck her: what if he knew where Anda and Sera were?

She had to find out why he'd come, why he spouted her name. She stood and sheathed her qasfin, her face as blank as slate. She nodded toward him. "If he asked for me, I might as well figure out what he wants."

Pale Face sprang up and moved between Esh'a and Ahrik. "Not so fast. He came down in my sector, and one of my men took him captive." She snarled in Ahrik's direction, hair flopping over her eyes. "I want to know how he got here and why he came."

The tension around the fire grew thick and hot. The pop and crackle of burning pine accentuated a hundred petty conflicts and differences of opinion that were coming to a head all at once. Across the fire, the two male faction leaders fingered the hilts of their qasfina. Miners from each of the factions, women and men both, shuffled toward the firelight, drawn to the tense air like moths to a flame.

Esh'a sized up her challenger. Esh'a had more military training than Pale Face, but Pale Face was a good ten years younger, and she was feisty. The odds of keeping the other leaders and their factions out of a fight also looked grim. If it came to blows, she and her miners would be outnumbered three-to-one.

Unless . . .

"Fine," said Esh'a, running her tongue over her top teeth, as if taking stock of the situation. "You can interrogate him, but I want to be present."

Pale Face folded her arms over her chest and gazed at the others around the fire, then cast a pointed look at Esh'a. "Are you really making demands?"

Esh'a raised her eyebrows in mock surprise, palms up in conciliation. "Oh no, I'm not making demands." She smiled in false appeasement and looked at the others just like Pale Face had, then shrugged. "We all want to know his mysteries. If he's valuable, then we want him in one piece."

She gave Ahrik a hard stare. The magnitude of her bluff weighed on her mind like an anchor. Esh'a was trusting a murderer, responsible for the deaths of thousands, to stay quiet until she could get to him. He had only to speak a few words, and she would be mob fodder.

Across the fire, one of the other leaders stroked his chin, then glanced at Pale Face. "She's right, you know. No use fighting over this."

To Esh'a's right, the last leader nodded. "Agree."

Pale Face frowned. Her shoulders slumped and the tension drifted away, to die in the night. She looked a pout at the others, a sure sign of tactical defeat. "Fine, we interrogate at first light," she said to Esh'a, then pointed to herself. "But we do this in *my* sector, not yours."

Esh'a looked away and shrugged, as if she didn't care. Then, as the crowd melted away to the different faction areas, Esh'a moved to linger in a dark stand of pine, just out of earshot, while Pale Face gave her miners instructions on what to do with the captive. The clear pungence of pine sap filled her nostrils as she breathed the cold night air.

She waited. The crystal night sky revealed a bright pantheon of stars and a brilliant crescent moon. Esh'a frowned. All that light would make her design difficult to accomplish.

But the light did make it easy to see where Pale Face stashed Ahrik. Esh'a flanked Pale Face and Burly at a safe distance as they meandered toward their faction area, pulling Ahrik along behind. Ahrik limped, and every once in a while Ahrik would stumble, but Esh'a was sure it was intentional, a soft test of his captors' resolve, probing for escape options.

They made their way to a cluster of pine trees near Pale Face's lean-to, in the center of their faction area. Burly tied Ahrik to a tree and slapped him across the face, for good measure. Ahrik's head lolled forward, as if he'd felt it. Esh'a began to wonder if he really was weakened.

Esh'a crouched in the darkness outside the Pale Face faction camp. Ahrik's head hung forward, as if defeated, while Pale Face's faction wound down the day, retreating to lean-tos and mumbling good nights. Three pickets wandered about the perimeter, to give the impression of safety, but Esh'a could tell they didn't really mean it. People were exhausted from the lack of food and from the faction leaders' bickering, so there was little inclination to exert more effort than necessary.

Esh'a found a bed of pine needles to cushion her lean posterior, then drew the whetstone from her qasfin sheath. She sharpened her blade in time with the soft rustle of the wind and the whisper of chirping insects. She kept an eye on Ahrik, who pretended to sleep.

The night grew colder as the moon crawled to the horizon. Esh'a's hands quivered with the cold, but she kept running the whetstone over the blade, to keep her mind off it. The chirping of insects faded with the settling chill. Esh'a tested the sharpness of her blade. It would do.

The Pale Face faction's fires died down. Esh'a counted the pickets, all three accounted for, then glanced up to check on Ahrik. His head turned, slowly, this way and that, testing his environment once again. She had not heard human movement since the moon hit fifteen degrees from the horizon, so she wondered what he could be searching for.

Esh'a narrowed her eyes. Was he alone, or was someone else out here, in the dark? Did the internal compiler planted at the base of his skull give him extra powers of perception? Esh'a surveyed the area once more. If someone else was out here, some confederate still at liberty, she couldn't see him. But she still had no way to determine whether Ahrik was friend or foe.

She had to know. As soon as Burly had dragged him into the firelight, she knew her time with these miners was at an end. Regardless of circumstances or personal loyalty, these miners remained united by an infinite hatred for Ahrik, the Butcher of Kafron.

But Esh'a and Ahrik were blood, a fact she could no longer avoid. Whatever new realities this war had created, even if Ahrik fought now against the Tyrant, and even if Esh'a had risked her own hide in the fight against Ahrik fourteen years ago, her marriage to Ahrik's brother trumped all. She was tainted in the miners' eyes, and as good as dead if she stayed.

Esh'a crept forward a few meters at a time, stopping to listen and watch at each interval. The pickets were easy enough to avoid, but her focus remained on Ahrik and whether he gave any indication of noticing her presence.

She kept herself downwind and approached from behind the tree he was tied to. This made it hard to discern his head movements, but was prudent given how dangerous this man was. A cold-blooded killer.

A few paces distant, Esh'a's foot hit a twig wrong. She tried to shift her weight. Too late. It made a merciless crack, and Ahrik's head whipped up. He yanked at his bindings on Esh'a's side of the tree, but made no more sound.

Esh'a paused to see if the moment would pass, or if the sound would attract any attention from the Pale Face faction. The only sounds she heard were Ahrik's angry breathing and the passing night breeze.

Esh'a shivered. She smelled the dying embers of Pale Face's fires.

She inched forward, reached her qasfin around the tree, and pressed the killing point to Ahrik's neck, where a simple pull, twist, and yank would puncture his windpipe and slice his jugular in two.

He let out a slow breath, but still said nothing. Esh'a flexed her fingers around the hilt of the qasfin. "How do I know which side you're on?"

He grunted. "Everyone's on their own side now."

Esh'a applied the slightest of pressure. She knew he felt it when he sucked in his breath. Esh'a clenched her teeth. "How. Do. I. Know?"

Ahrik sighed. "That ball of fat with the dead distiller is still alive, isn't he?"

"Not good enough, Ahrik."

By the way her blade moved, she could tell he shrugged. "Shahl will be happy that I found you."

Esh'a crept around the tree, making sure to keep the curve of her blade at Ahrik's throat. She pressed one knee onto his thighs so he couldn't strike her with a knee or foot. With her blade forcing his head back against the tree, she put her face close to his and glared. "Your brother and I have spent fourteen years hiding from you. I need more than that to trust you."

Ahrik pursed his lips, but looked back at her without malice. His eyes told her that he understood her caution. "The ball of fat emptied my pockets, but I stashed my wrist compiler where he wouldn't think to look. Our rally point is about fifteen kilometers from here, and that compiler tells us where it is."

She scrunched up her face in disgust, then looked down at his crotch, then back at Ahrik's face. He nodded, and with her off-hand she unsealed the access flap of his combat suit and shuddered as she felt for the wrist compiler, trying not to touch anything else. She extracted the compiler and examined the small display. It was completely blank.

"Put it in on my wrist to activate it," he said, wincing at the bite of the blade on his neck.

She narrowed her eyes to slits and her voice to a hiss, and didn't move her qasfin. "I don't think so, Butcher." She stuffed the compiler in her pocket. "You could have some sort of weapon in this thing."

Ahrik closed his eyes and took short, shallow breaths as the blade began to draw blood. "Shahl . . . meet . . . us. Have to . . . work . . . together."

"Okay," she said, relaxing her blade enough to let Ahrik breathe normally. She kept the pressure on his legs. "Let's say I believe that there's a rally point. How do I know you won't kill me in my sleep?" She looked up into the trees, as if searching for some other way to verify Ahrik's loyalty.

"Sera," he said, interrupting her, a glint of hope in his voice. "Your daughter is Sera."

Esh'a scowled, then lowered her voice in warning. "If she's been harmed . . ."

Ahrik cast his eyes down. "The Tyrant, Nayr, was poisoning Sera, Shahl rescued her, and Renla said he knew how to get to the rally point."

Esh'a drew her qasfin away from his neck, but kept one hand on his chest and enough weight on his legs to keep him from lashing out at her.

Ahrik shook his head. "Nayr has killed millions. Enough of killing. Enough of death." Ahrik's eyes glassed over with emotion, a humanity she didn't know he was capable of. He blinked back tears. "I have a special debt to repay to the Tyrant."

That sense of shared oppression and hatred of Nayr was enough for Esh'a. She lifted herself from his legs and reached around the tree to slice the rough rope that Burly had used to bind Ahrik's hands. She helped Ahrik up, and he nodded his thanks.

She sheathed her qasfin. "Let's go. quick."

Feet swished on pine needles behind her. Esh'a whirled. Through the night, Burly bore down on her. "Where do you think you're going with our prisoner?"

Her hand went back to her qasfin, but she was too slow. Burly's hulking mass filled her vision, and the carbon composite housing of his distiller, now used as a club, rushed toward her face with sickening speed.

Motion flashed in her peripheral vision. Ahrik darted around her, parried and redirected the other man's blow, then jammed his fingers into the man's voice box. Burly coughed, but rushed at Ahrik all the same. Ahrik danced out of his path, but rewarded Burly's charge with an elbow to the chin.

As Burly rushed by, Esh'a dodged, then stuck out her leg to trip him. He crashed to the ground with a dull thud and a deflating breath of air. Esh'a pounced on his back and placed the point of her blade on his neck. "Scream and you die."

As Burly coughed and sputtered on the rough ground, Ahrik untied the rope around his hands and used it to bind the man's hands and feet behind his back. Burly wriggled on the ground to get a better look at Ahrik, but did not make a sound.

Ahrik stood and winced as he worked his foot around in circles, then he stopped and gave Burly a curious expression. Esh'a followed Ahrik's gaze to find Burly, suddenly still, with his eyes locked on Ahrik, a vicious gleam of recognition on his face.

Esh'a grunted and pressed the point of her blade ever so slightly into his neck, just enough to draw a wince of pain from Burly. "He recognizes you. If I kill him, we don't have to worry about him making a fuss."

Ahrik just shook his head and tore a piece of Burly's overshirt. He wrapped the strip of cloth, tight, over the man's tongue and around his head, then stepped back to survey his handiwork.

"There," he said, looking at Esh'a. "Shall we?"

Esh'a cocked her hand back to smack Burly in the back of the head, but Ahrik lunged to stop her. "No," he whispered. "Violence creates more problems than it solves."

Burly gave a muffle of agreement, but Esh'a jabbed him in the ribs with her toe to shut him up. "Sometimes violence keeps us alive," she responded. She shook her head and pulled the wrist compiler out of her pocket. She handed it to Ahrik. "Unlock this for me, then."

"Fine," said Ahrik, tapping on the display, "but I'll have to unlock it again after twenty minutes."

"It's like you don't trust me."

"Trust moves two ways. I can't outrun you with my twisted ankle, and you're armed." His eyes were steady.

Esh'a accepted the wrist compiler back from him and grunted, then relieved Burly of his distiller and pack, working the pack onto her shoulders. "Fine," she said, "lead the way. If you trip into a hole or fall off a cliff or something, at least I'll have some warning."

Without a word, or even turning to see if she would follow, Ahrik took off at a trot, his gait hobbled by a limp, but faster than Esh'a thought possible on a twisted ankle. Esh'a dashed after him, wary.

With any luck, the miners would just let them go. Esh'a doubted that. The most they could hope for was for death to give them a head start.

Zharla, weary eyes suddenly alert, frowned at Renla's pilot. "What's wrong?"

The pilot leaned forward and tapped his control console. His eyes wide, he gulped and slumped down into his seat. "This can't be right."

Zharla got up from the command seat in the shuttle cockpit and sat in the empty copilot seat, to get a better view of the control console.

The shuttle orbited the White Planet while they waited for the rally point to slip over the horizon. The horror of passing through the portal, with its graveyard of refugee ships, had cast a pall over their two-person voyage. Zharla wondered how many refugee ships had actually made it through the portal.

Was Shahl still alive? Had he found his wife? Zharla shook these thoughts from her mind, to focus on the less painful question of whether they would survive the next few hours.

They wanted to make an easy, controlled descent to the White Planet. They saw no reason to alarm local authorities with a high velocity approach. They didn't want to get blasted out of the sky because some local mistook them for an alien projectile, or an oddly shaped meteor.

The pilot pursed his lips and stole a nervous glance at Zharla, then tapped at the control panel again. "Your Majesty," he said. "I . . . um . . . don't know how to say this."

"Out with it."

A wave of sadness and far-off longing washed over his face. He looked down. "The Tyrant's ships made it through the portal."

Zharla sank in the copilot seat as the implications sank in. She didn't need confirmation of what she knew in her heart to be true: Renla was dead. She had failed. "How many ships?" Zharla asked.

The pilot quirked his mouth. "Hard to say, Your Majesty, with the portal on the other side of the planet . . . at least three or four carriers, though."

Zharla's shoulders slumped with the mental calculation. "That's over twenty thousand clones." She shook her head and took in the beautiful watery haze panning underneath them. She nodded toward the planet and its unsuspecting inhabitants. "They aren't ready for the Tyrant down there."

The pilot shrugged. "Why do you care about them, Your Majesty, when so many of our own drift lifeless in space?"

"We're about to throw ourselves at the mercy of these aliens." Zharla swiveled her chair toward the pilot. "We have nowhere else to flee. Our fates are linked."

The pilot scoffed. "Your Majesty, how many planets will your son destroy before he realizes that?"

Zharla winced at the mention of her son. The pain that the pilot's remark evinced must have shown on her face, because remorse immediately overcame his gaze.

"I'm sorry, Your Majesty, that was insensitive. Your son . . ." He trailed off and studied the controls for a beat.

Zharla shook her head to show that she'd let the comment stand. "Your comment is justified. We've all lost people dear to us." Zharla choked back a sob as she thought of Renla, and so many others, and the son she should have raised better. Such a heavy weight on her conscience.

The pilot focused on the controls with brooding silence. Dozens of his closest friends were probably dead now because of her son.

"You know," said Zharla, "Nayr didn't start out evil."

The pilot cocked his head, considering this. "Who does?" He glared forward. "Your Majesty."

Zharla let a tear of regret slip down her cheek, then watched the deep blue ocean ease by below, no large land mass in sight, even from this height. "Such a wealth of water," she said.

The control console chimed, and the pilot leaned forward. "Ah," he said, forcing a smile. "Time to . . . uh oh."

Zharla examined the schematic on the control console. Two dots of light raced toward their position from the opposite side of the planet. Zharla furrowed her brow. "Interceptors, or White Planet vessels?"

The pilot squeezed forward the boson drive control, and the shuttle sprang forward and down. "The Tyran—Nayr's drones, probably."

"Do they know I'm in this shuttle?"

Through the forward hull, the shield began to glow red as they accelerated into the descent. The hull shuddered. The pilot fought to keep the shuttle controls steady. "I don't intend to find out, Your Majesty."

Zharla scanned the schematic once more. Still the two dots gained. "How are they still gaining?" she asked.

"We're fighting atmosphere. They're not." The pilot grunted in frustration, then nodded toward the schematic. "But that's not our only problem, see?"

Two more dots appeared on the compiler display, approaching from the opposite horizon, from the land mass the shuttle aimed for. Beyond the two dots, the rally point pulsed in the middle of a small mountain range, a few hundred kilometers inland.

Zharla shook her head as a flame of deep longing settled on her heart. "This land reminds me of the Eshel."

"Your Majesty," said the pilot, his voice a bit testy, "it might remind you of nothing but death unless you get to one of those distillers in the rear."

Zharla leaped up and slid to the rear cabin. "I'm on the starboard side."

"Check, Your Majesty," said the pilot. "They're coming fast. We can't let the drones know where we land. We need to shoot first."

Zharla paused while slipping her hands into the grips of the starboard radial distiller. She called to the cockpit. "What if they're not Nayr's?"

"We still have to . . . oh."

"I'm not starting an interplanetary war with the aliens that we're asking for refuge."

The pilot cursed. The hull transluced. He was one of Renla's best pilots, but he didn't have answers for this new set of questions.

"Just evade if you can," she said. "If they're alien, we'll see what their vessels can do."

He muttered something unintelligible. "Check, Your Majesty," he said, louder. "We engage the locals only as a last resort."

Outside the hull, the glow of the shield dulled from angry red to an almost festive orange as they decelerated. Zharla checked the schematic next to the starboard distiller controls, attached to the bulkhead at eye level. Nayr's interceptors still gained, though not as fast, while in front of them the two alien vessels split apart. One sped up, as if to engage the interceptors. One slowed and veered toward them.

Static burst over the electromag in the shuttle, followed by a piercing whine. Zharla's breath caught in her throat. Her chest tightened. Was this some sort of alien weapon?

After the whine subsided, she gulped down a breath and called to the front, "Pilot, what was that?"

A pause. "I think the pilot of one of the alien vessels just tried to hail us over an electromag frequency, but our compiler could only interpret it as noise." Another pause. "Your Majesty, should we allow the alien vessel to engage us, or . . . ?"

Zharla pursed her lips. "We will not shoot first." She flexed her hands over the distiller grips and breathed out at the dangerous game they played. She realized how hungry she was. She licked her parched lips. "We have to make it to that rally point."

"Check, Your Majesty. Make it to the rally point. Setting automatic pilot to guide us in."

Both cabins of the shuttle erupted with the static and noisy whine again. This time, the cacophony felt more insistent, less forgiving, but Zharla couldn't tell if that was her fear talking or if the alien vessel was about to blast them from the sky.

The aliens were close now. Zharla looked forward to follow them through the translucent hull. She squinted, and the faster one streaked by, a silver grey dart cutting through the morning sky. The vessel wasn't rounded like theirs, and it had large foils extending from its flanks and fire spurting from its rear. It screamed of power. Zharla's knees trembled at the sight.

The static and whine cut through the shuttle once more after the first alien vessel shot past, toward Nayr's interceptors. Zharla checked the schematic. The second, slower alien vessel began a wide arc across their starboard flank, right through the kill zone of Zharla's radial distiller. She could end this quickly, before this vessel got around and sent a missile into their baffles.

"Your Majesty," came the pilot's warning voice from the cockpit.

Her trigger fingers shuffled down, for a better grip. She tracked the alien vessel as it crossed her kill zone. All she had to do was squeeze. The targeting system would do most of the work.

Another burst of static and whine echoed through the shuttle. The alien was definitely trying to communicate. She only had about thirty degrees of arc left before the vessel would be at their rear.

"Pilot, accelerate and ease to starboard. Let's see what he does."

The alien vessel adjusted its bearing and speed to compensate for their shift. Zharla checked the schematic, and her blood ran cold. The two interceptors behind them veered apart, forcing the fast alien to choose which to follow. They were going to engage. "Pilot . . . "

"I see it. Preparing to reorient on rally point." A pause. "Maintaining speed and bearing."

Zharla focused on the schematic. The faster alien vessel sped up even more, then followed one of the interceptors. To her horror, and as she fully expected, the second interceptor pursued the fast alien vessel instead of continuing to pursue their shuttle.

They eased back toward the rally point, attitude as unthreatening as possible. Zharla craned her head around to see the fight unfolding to their rear. The alien vessel following them slid in behind them, but kept its distance. Beyond, the other alien vessel and the two interceptors burst into a random fluidity of motion, all at once.

With lightning speed, faster than Zharla thought possible, the three craft dove and weaved and dodged. The alien pilot was good, but outnumbered, and outmaneuvered by Nayr's more agile interceptors.

The alien vessel following them realized what was happening. It accelerated, flame at its rear, but before it veered off to engage the interceptors flame shot from its flank foils. The shuttle's rear shield shuddered, and then hot metal ripped through the rear cabin and into the cockpit.

Zharla squeezed into the marginal safety of the starboard distiller alcove. "Go, pilot!"

The shuttle leaped forward. Zharla's feet swept out from underneath her and she struggled to maintain her grip on the distiller. The burst of metal projectiles must have knocked out the inertial stabilizers.

Zharla worked her feet onto a bulkhead and pushed herself fully into the alcove. She heaved herself to the schematic, pain radiating through her fingers and wrists, the tension in her muscles almost unbearable. She scanned the display, and her heart sank to her feet. They had accelerated out of range of the alien vessel following them, but Nayr's interceptors, after dispensing with the first alien vessel, converged on the second.

This time, the alien vessel was ready. It didn't discharge its metal projectile weapons, but launched a volley of missiles. One interceptor exploded in a ball of flame, and the other buckled in an awkward direction.

The alien moved in to finish off his opponent, but the interceptor pilot wouldn't be surprised twice. The interceptor slid, yawed, and twisted in a way that defied the physics of the alien vessel.

The interceptor discharged its forward distillers, and the alien vessel broke apart. The interceptor turned to pursue the shuttle, but paused. A trail of smoke flowed from its port lobe.

"Pilot, the second interceptor is not pursuing." No response. "Pilot?"

"Your . . . Majes . . . ty."

The shuttle's speed became constant, and the overtaxed inertials caught up. Zharla, alarm building from her gut to her temples, worked her feet to the deck and trudged to the cockpit, gripping bulkheads along the way.

"Pilo—"

She scanned the cockpit for the healing kit. "Stay with me, pilot." She spotted the kit and moved toward it, but too fast. Her feet slipped on an expanding puddle of blood. She banged her knees on the deck. She reached up and ripped the healing kit from the wall, then tore it open and found the NewSkin bandages as she moved to the pilot's side. "What's your name?"

"Unnnh . . ."

She unstrapped his restraints and laid him on the deck. As she did so, she saw a perfectly round hole in the back of the pilot's chair. She gritted her teeth. Either the lung or the artery in his arm.

"You'll be okay. Tell me your name." Why hadn't she learned more about him earlier?

"Ah . . . ren." He winced with pain.

Zharla searched for the exit wound as she ripped open his tunic. There. The alien projectile had taken out a bit of rib and grazed the his arm, but missed the artery. She sighed with relief. "Ahren. A good Merani name. You're not a clone, so tell me about your family. Is there a girl?"

Ahren's head swayed in random directions, an inscrutable gesture. Zharla tore open two NewSkin packages and slapped one onto the inside of Ahren's arm and the other to his side. He arched his back in pain and gave Zharla a wild glare, then he went unconscious.

Zharla checked his vitals. Pulse weak. She rooted in the healing kit for fluids, saw none. Forehead damp with sudden perspiration, she looked to the wall rack where the healing kit had hung. There. An intravenous.

She sprang to her feet and grabbed the intravenous packet and slid back to the deck next to Ahren. She squished the packet in her hand and scratched at the side to activate the pokebot. She tore up the sleeve on Ahren's good arm and nestled the packet in the crook of his elbow. The pokebot did the rest, found the vein and started to pump life-giving fluid into Ahren's body.

But the puddle of blood still grew. His clothes were so soaked in it she couldn't tell where it came from. Ahren's breathing grew shallow.

"Ahren!" Zharla screamed. She grunted through her teeth. "Ahren, tell me where else you're hit!"

The control console beeped. Then kept beeping.

Zharla ignored it. She ran her eyes over his chair, to see if any other projectiles had pierced it. She sucked in her breath. Of course. One of the projectiles had grazed the chair's undercarriage. His leg.

The beeping from the console grew louder, more insistent. "*Proximity warning*," said a metallic voice.

She paused while unsealing Ahren's boot, to decide whether she should try to guide the shuttle in, but then thought it was better to save him if she could. If the automatic pilot and the inertials weren't working, they'd be jumbled and knocked around the cabin on impact, and would probably die anyway.

She yanked off his boot. Blood gushed out. She ripped open another NewSkin packet and wiped at the blood on his ankle, to find the wound.

She slapped on the NewSkin, then stole a frantic glance at the control console. But the only thing she saw was an alien planet rushing toward them through the translucent hull of the shuttle, the mountain crags unforgiving and the verdant trees spread like a carpet of needles below them. Dark storm clouds, like the ones she'd fled from at Peshron, brewed on the horizon.

Warning. Impact imminent.

She threw herself over Ahren's body without thinking, a protective but meaningless instinct if the inertial stabilizers and automatic pilot didn't do their job.

Then she remembered nothing.

"3, I am master of all I see." Nayr let a new pill dissolve on his tongue and surveyed the planet before him. His ops chief stood rigid beside him. "I can almost taste the sweetness of revenge. Soon Ahrik and Shahl will be dead, and Mother rescued."

And 3 humbled.

Nayr's hand began to shake. He gripped the handrail overlooking his carrier's command bay and breathed in with satisfaction. The command bay hummed with hundreds of his sons, busy preparing search-and-destroy orders for teams to insert onto the alien world, each with a handful of seekerbots and a swath of landmass to cover. Nayr would teach the inhabitants of the White Planet to harbor criminals and vagabonds.

Did they not ask why hundreds, maybe even thousands, of people dropped from space onto their planet? Or whether it was right to take them in? Did they not know that peace was gained by hard labor and toil, and not by sloth?

Nayr spoke to his operations chief, without turning. "How did that rogue shuttle get away?"

"Two alien vessels helped it escape, Father."

"*Pfft*. Why should that matter? Was Mother on the shuttle?"

"It was Renla's shuttle, so it was probably someone important, Father."

Nayr knew at that moment that 3 had failed him for the last time. Sadness twinged within his breast, for the magnificent son that 3 could have been. "3," said Nayr, "are the search-and-detroy teams ready to deploy? Are the atmospherics and tectonics in place?"

"Father," said 3. "Perhaps we should give them more time to answer the ultimatum."

Nayr whipped his head around. "We already discussed this." He glared at the other staff principals standing with him on the observation deck. "Who has doubts?"

They looked at each other. They avoided his gaze. None raised his hand, but 3 stepped closer to Nayr. "Father," 3 whispered. "I do not doubt you, but we don't yet know what their military is capable of."

Nayr stepped away and cast a sidelong glance at 3, until recently his closest, most trusted subordinate. "You doubt the power of the Ketel of Nayr," he whispered. Nayr shook his head with a rhythm of disappointment. "After 2, 4, and 5 died, I trusted you to be my greatest support. Then, after the search for the body of Renla, I still trusted you, even after you questioned me."

Uncomfortable murmurs rustled behind them. Nayr took in the White Planet. "We got to their planet first, not the other way around. I like our chances."

"Father, I am your greatest suppor—"

Nayr put his right arm around 3's shoulder and drew him close. He smiled at his erstwhile friend, then slipped his left hand into his distiller and eased it off its latch, silent, like he'd practiced a thousand times, then leveled it behind his back at 3. Nayr smiled. "It'll be all right."

He squeezed the trigger, once, and, after a *thunk* from the distiller, 3 slumped away from Nayr and over the railing. 3 clawed for the railing on his way over, but missed, his eyes wide with astonishment. Nayr heard a dull smack, and from the deck below, 3 raised up on two hands and took one last breath, then collapsed to the floor and lay still.

Nayr cocked his head at 3, considering his disloyalty, then narrowed his eyes at the rest of his staff principals. "Anyone else have a moral compass that needs adjusting?"

Murmurs of "No, Father" and the shaking of heads reverberated around the observation platform. Nayr wagged his finger at them. "Hear this. We did not strike first, but we will strike last. Win."

"Win!" they shouted in unison, the gusto behind the battle slogan music to Nayr's ears.

Nayr examined the number tapes on the breasts of his commanders and subcommanders in the first row. "You. 8. You're the new ops chief. Give your subcommander command of your arm of the ketel."

8 saluted, a dignified and appreciative action. "Yes, Father."

"Now," said Nayr, looking around at the group once again. "If we haven't gotten a response to our ultimatum after sending it in every language known to us, including mathematical symbology, over every known electromag frequency, then why have we not launched our search-and-destroy teams?"

"Yes, Father," said 8. "Right away, Father."

Nayr gripped the railing again and inspected the planet below. Brilliant white clouds swirled and eddied over vast oceans of deep blue, nothing like the shallow, algae-infested oceans back home. Verdant continents hemmed in the oceans. Such a wealth of resources, wasted in a foolhardy errand, giving succor to usurpers and leeches.

Alongside his carrier in orbit, six other carriers cordoned off the planet, constant patrols running between the carriers, in a variety of orbits. The carriers and patrols were cloaked, but Nayr didn't care if the locals knew they were there, or even if they resisted. He could just launch his atomics at them, from seven directions.

After all, winning means making hard choices. That's what Mother and Ahrik and Shahl and Renla and 3 taught him. Victory always comes at a cost.

Renla and 3 were dead. He accessed the revenge file with his internal compiler and revised it: "Kill Ahrik. Kill Shahl. Rescue Mother."

Dear, sweet Mother.

Nayr turned to 8. "Release a few atmospherics and tectonics. Let's test the aliens' will, shall we?"

19 | Invasion

ANDA'S EYES WIDENED with concern. Sera's body convulsed as another coughing fit attacked her body, the first one since the night before, when the animal farmer with the hat had detained them.

He thought the nanos would take longer to reproduce. He only had two pills left, and they had to last until he found Esh'a, or until . . .

He refused to finish the thought. He would only consider that as a last resort.

He furrowed his brow. Sera's coughing showed no signs of letting up. Should he let it run its course, and keep the two pills in reserve, or suppress the nanos with one of them? Knowing what he knew now, about how Nayr had planted the nanos in their bodies, he didn't want to give in to his nephew's evil. Each pill Sera swallowed just brought her death one step closer.

To distract himself, he peered out the transparent side partition of the vehicle they rode in, sizing up the storm clouds that gathered like sentinels of doom over the valley below them.

Both they and the storm clouds were converging on the coordinates where Esh'a should be. They were in a race for Sera's life.

So he rubbed Sera's back and tried to comfort her against the jostling of the vehicle, then fixed his gaze once more on the darkening storm. *Please let her live*, he prayed to the Lady of the Emerald Moon, in an effort to convince himself that prayer would do some good.

Distant thunder rolled through the storm clouds menacing the valley below. Last night, after the farmer had apprehended them, a storm and temblor had swept the land with such power that they had to hole up in the farmer's home, part captives and part guests, before setting out in the morning for the coordinates in the old compiler's sand model. This planet boasted so much water, so much life, and now this bounty threatened to keep them from getting to the place they absolutely had to reach.

Sera's life depended on it.

Beside them in the vehicle, the animal farmer mumbled something in his language, evidently a question, laced with mild alarm, which Anda interpreted as, "Is she okay?"

Anda made a calming motion with his hand, and the farmer squirmed in his seat and squinted into the setting light and the black, wind-swept path the vehicle was on. Sera's body shook and rattled with each cough.

Her cough was getting worse.

The animal farmer mumbled. Anda stared out the window and gulped, rubbing her back.

Then Sera coughed blood all over the forward panel of the farmer's vehicle. The farmer shouted. Anda dug into his satchel for the metal canister. Sera began to hyperventilate between coughs, her sleeve now over her mouth, her eyes as wide as the moon.

The farmer slowed his vehicle, almost to a stop, and pursed his lips, as if considering a weighty decision. Anda got the pill under Sera's tongue, and her coughing evaporated, like the dew before the sun. The farmer grunted with surprise and accelerated once again, but not before he pointed to a compartment that contained some sort of fibered cleaning cloths, among other papers.

Anda wiped down the panel, then rummaged around in his satchel for the compiler. Would the compiler's inertial navigator really work? Could it tell him how far they were from the coordinates?

He craned his neck down to check on Sera. Smiling. Crisis averted, for now. One pill left.

He sighed with relief when the terrain map came up on the compiler, showing both the rally point and a small, blue blip where they were at that moment. The display flickered, and he peered at the valley spreading out under the darkening clouds, in an effort to orient and get the bearing they needed. Landmarks were becoming difficult to discern as the sun crept behind the mountains above them, on their left, but he thought he made out a bare, rocky ridge directly between them and where the coordinates should be.

He was about to look back down at his compiler when a streak of red hot silver glinted across the sky and landed with a puff near the bare ridge. For a split second, he thought he saw two lobes on the craft, like the shuttles from Home. Zharla? Ahrik?

He couldn't process this, though, because at that moment his compiler chirped, the display flickered once more, and then the thing died. His breath grew frantic. The farmer gave him a look. Sera stirred. The vehicle began to slow once more.

Anda jiggled the compiler, but it refused to respond. A space opened up in his gut, and he felt the blood drain from his face. They were lost without the map.

Unless . . .

The vehicle slowed even more, but Anda ignored it.

He swiveled his head in the direction of the barren ridge. To his horror, he saw flames. Zharla. Ahrik.

Was there some way to tell the farmer to go toward that ridge? He looked back to the farmer, his eyes prepared with the entreaty, but then he noticed that the vehicle had slowed even more, and he saw the look of concern on the farmer's face.

He followed the farmer's gaze, fixed to the front. They approached the lip of a rise, and blue and red flashing lights glanced off of the black vehicle path, red earth, and rich pine trees.

They kept slowing down.

Anda stared from the farmer to the lights and back, eyes set with consternation. Didn't the farmer realize that Sera's life was at stake, and maybe Ahrik's or Zharla's too? Anda's palms grew sweaty. They had to get to those coordinates.

The farmer jerked his vehicle to avoid a large crack in the black road. Without inertial stabilizers, such manic piloting jostled Anda and Sera around the cabin. Anda checked to be sure her restraining harness was secure, but also to be sure he could release their harnesses at a moment's notice, if they needed to escape. Could this farmer be in league with Nayr?

Anda didn't like the look of those lights, or the worried look on the farmer's face. Actually, it was the same look of distrust he'd seen on the farmer's face when he apprehended them the previous night, but before he had brought them home and his kind wife talked to him in soothing tones, then fed them and gave them a place to sleep, and let them stay there during the temblor and storm, until the farmer ordered them into his vehicle and drove them into the mountains.

Now, with the lights flashing ahead, the look of distrust was back, this time with a tinge of malice. Anda held his breath. The vehicle slowed to a crawl, and Anda made out another vehicle ahead, the source of the flashing lights.

Suddenly, the farmer seemed determined to strike up a conversation. Somehow, he didn't understand that they were aliens, not from a different place on the White Planet, where they spoke a slightly different language, but from a different planet entirely.

"Hoobala joobala icko?" The farmer swerved to avoid a fallen tree on the black vehicle path, then muttered something under his breath, which Anda took to be a curse. He then repeated his question: *"Hoobala joobala icko?"*

Anda perceived it as a question because of the pregnant pause that followed. He smiled at the farmer, squeezed Sera close, then shrugged with a look of apology. He cast a nervous look in the direction of the crash site on the barren ridge. A thin spire of smoke had begun to drift into the sky.

He knew the farmer was getting them to their location faster than they could have gotten there on foot, but he sensed that the farmer was miffed at Anda's silence. Anda had no choice but to be mute. He couldn't trust the farmer, not with that look on his face, and the fiction that he was from this planet and just didn't understand the farmer's language was better than to speak up and confirm that he was from another planet.

Anda had almost spoken once, back at the farmer's house, when the farmer couple saw his compiler. They had looked with wonder at the novelty of new technology, but the man recognized the terrain around the coordinates immediately. He and his wife had held a hurried, whispered conference, then he looked at Anda with purpose, removed his headgear for the first time, and said something that Anda took as, "Be ready to leave soon."

Then the temblor came, barely even a shake back home, after which the farmer couple huddled in their sitting room and spoke in nervous tones all night and into the early morning, watching moving pictures of devastation from some other place or places on their boxy communications device. With this odd behavior, they made no move to take Anda and Sera anywhere.

The farmer kept his weapon close the whole night, so Anda dared not make a run for it. He merely observed his surroundings while Sera, thankfully, succumbed to her exhaustion and slept, without coughing. After so much frantic flight, Anda was grateful for the rest himself, even if he'd rather have been moving closer to the coordinates.

They left late the this morning, after a quick but filling meal of something like gruel, crisped bread, and a round, tart fruit. They jumbled into the farmer's rickety vehicle, with his long weapon hanging in the rear window of the main cabin and some sort of seat in the open cargo area in the rear, like something one would use to sit on a large beast. In the wan morning light, as they boarded the vehicle, Anda had heard some sort of animal call, halfway between a high-pitched laugh and a throaty grumble, and Anda had concluded that the farming couple farmed animals instead of plants.

Now, in the waning afternoon light, on the black vehicle path, they approached the flashing lights at a crawl. Wind whipped around the vehicle. They veered around another crack in the black road. The farmer flexed his fingers on the piloting controls and let out a tense breath. Anda saw in the farmer's face that these conditions were not normal.

Then the farmer stole a nervous glance in Anda's direction and said something in a comforting tone. Anda's stomach churned. He sensed the lie in his voice. Sera looked up at Anda in alarm. Even she felt it.

"Abbi, wh—"

"Shhhh, quiet now, Serit," he whispered, hoping that the farmer wouldn't discern the strange sounds of their language.

Up ahead, a large vehicle lay overturned on the side of the road. The large silver casing attached to its rear was blackened and smoking, and suited figures scrambled around as if they had just smothered some angry inferno. Two men stood next to the wreckage, one apparently civilian, dressed much like the farmer, and the other in uniform, although in a different uniform from the ones the alien soldiers had worn back at the refugee ship crash site. This uniform consisted of solid, dark colors, not patterns with a wide range of green hues.

The flashing lights came from a smaller vehicle, stopped on the opposite side of the road from the first, overturned one. The smaller vehicle had an official look, colored black, with white letters and other markings on its body.

The man in uniform noticed the farmer's vehicle and made a motion with his hands, patting the air with his palms down.

Anda had no idea how to interpret this motion, but a feeling of panic surged through him as the farmer stopped. *Why is he stopping?* With all his might, Anda wished he could explain to the farmer his need to deliver Sera to Esh'a before her time ran out.

Before his time ran out.

Anda choked back a sob. After all this, he wouldn't get to see his dear Esh'a again. Anda saw no point in trusting hope now. His only hope was to get Sera to safety in time.

That hope leaked out of him as the farmer pressed a button and the transparent partition between the interior and exterior descended. Outside, the wind howled nature's fury.

Anda felt the blood drain from his face. He and Sera would be taken into custody by this uniformed official, who carried himself like a peace forces officer. Surely Anda and Sera hadn't hidden their true provenance well enough. They looked a bit like locals, but their speech, their mannerisms, their mute acceptance of everything thrown at them gave them away as children of space, born a dimension away.

Sera would die, and Anda would have to watch.

The farmer looked at Anda askance and said something curt, tinged with threat. He hoped it was "let me do the talking," or some such, but a sense of foreboding settled over his mind like the dark green clouds that had begun settling into the valley from the forbidding horizon. The farmer considered Anda for a beat.

He was about to turn them in.

They were done.

Anda looked around the cabin for a way out, wishing he'd paid better attention to how to exit the vehicle. He slowly released his and Sera's restraining harnesses. Thunder clapped down in the valley. Anda jumped and looked for the spire of smoke. Flames at its base now glowed an angry red. His arms tensed around Sera. She groaned in fear.

The farmer patted Anda's arm and said something that was supposed to be reassuring. Was this an implicit threat or did it represent a genuine desire to get them beyond this checkpoint?

Anda gulped. If the farmer tried to deliver them to the Tyrant's thugs, or if the man in uniform tried to take them into custody, he and Sera would have to make a run for it, into that storm. Anda tried to remain calm, to time their escape for just the right moment.

The uniformed man tipped his headgear to the farmer and leaned into the wind. The farmer and uniformed man greeted each other, exchanged a few words, then looked at Anda and Sera. The uniformed man waggled his fingers in Sera's direction and smiled, unaware what little meaning the motion held for her. When Sera didn't respond, the uniformed man grunted and cocked his head, but then the farmer grinned and looked at Sera as if he knew her, reached down, and tousled her hair.

Sera froze. The action was foreign and strange, but she giggled with delight. "It tickles, Abbi!"

Anda seized up in fear for a moment, then joined his laughter with hers, in hopes that the uniformed man wouldn't notice her strange speech.

It was enough. The uniformed man bent back and laughed into the coming storm. "*Ooie hoobaloo boogaloo kay.*"

The uniformed man slapped the side of the vehicle with a metallic thud and motioned them to continue moving. The farmer closed his transparent partition and piloted off, accelerating over the rise. As soon as he was out of sight of the checkpoint, though, he slowed once again and stopped at the side of the road.

Anda readied himself to exit the vehicle once again, but the farmer didn't try to stop him, or even look at him. Instead, he drilled his stare into the piloting wheel, his breath heaving in deep gulps. His eyes told Anda that he was in the midst of a deep personal struggle, a decision between vicious opposites.

The farmer held his hand to his chest and took a deep, long breath. He looked at Anda with a mix of sadness and fear, then out at the looming clouds, tonguing the inside of his cheek as if considering the implications of what he was about to do. He gripped his piloting wheel and avoided Anda's gaze. He pursed his lips, then said one word: "*Goah*."

Anda perceived the word's meaning, even having never heard it before. He looked out into the growling fury of the storm and the angry fire on the ridge below, now not more than five hundred meters away, a livid beacon.

But this took him away from the coordinates. Despair crawled over Anda's consciousness.

How was he supposed to get to the coordinates from here? Anda tried to remember the contour guides on his dead compiler's terrain map. The coordinates must still be over thirty kilometers away, but he guessed that if he got to the crash site where the fire was and kept going, they would still make it.

But now, on the side of the black vehicle path, a deep ravine also lay between them and the crash site. Off of the black path, the terrain looked rough, the vegetation dense and tall. The wind whipped outside, and rain began to pitter, then pour, then whip, the slant nearly parallel to the path's black surface.

With it, a weight of realization sank into Anda's consciousness. The farmer had no connection to the Tyrant, but this storm was definitely the work of Nayr. So was the temblor. These events were not normal, and the farmer had no desire to get caught up in whatever this was. Anda saw it all over the man's face and in his body language.

Anda and Sera's time with the farmer was done.

Another realization wormed its way into his mind, leaving a deeper disquiet. The Tyrant had followed him and Sera here, to sow their lives with his chaos, so Anda had to deliver Sera to Esh'a before it was too late, before the nanos produced another coughing attack and he ran out of pills, her condition beyond repair. Esh'a was the only one who could keep Sera safe from the Tyrant.

He knew, in that moment of terrible finality, when he finally accepted what he had to do, that out of love for his daughter he would embrace his greatest fear. He wouldn't see Esh'a again. He felt it in his heart. Anda wouldn't see his daughter grow into a strong young woman, to greet the destiny he saw for her, a woman so strong she could save a nation.

He pulled Sera into in his arms.

The farmer reached over and unlatched the door. It swung open. "*Goah,*" he said.

The storm pounded outside. Sera looked at Anda with understanding, then pulled her collar up over her ears and climbed onto his back. Anda took one last, pitiful look at the farmer, then passed with Sera into the storm.

Zharla woke to heat. She coughed. Wisps of smoke searched the ceiling of the shuttle's cockpit for a way out. The hull flickered in and out of transluscence, and she saw flames licking the outer hull of the shuttle.

Zharla's whole body ached. Sharp pain jabbed at her back. Awareness crept back to her senses. She must have landed on the control panel.

Then she snapped to full appreciation of the danger. Get out. She had to get out. She planted a hand to push off the hull, but recoiled at the heat and pain that resulted. Zharla clenched her fist and slammed it against the control panel, with just enough force to roll herself off.

She fell into a soft, squishy mess. Her hand seared with pain where she'd punched the control panel. From the deck, the iron tang of coagulated blood assaulted her nostrils. She had to get away from the shuttle. Find the rally point. Find Ahrik. Find a way to fight Nayr.

She pushed herself off the floor with a grunt. Something popped near the nose of the shuttle, then something massive slammed against the hull. Fear at this unfamiliar sound froze Zharla for a beat, then the temperature inside the shuttle ratcheted up. The urge to escape enveloped her consciousness until it became the only thought she could consider.

She saw the pilot, his body prone against the rear bulkhead of the cockpit, just inside the hatch to the rear compartment. The impact must have thrown him back.

"Ahren," she whispered, because her parched throat couldn't produce a louder sound.

The pilot didn't move. She dragged herself, sliding through gore—why wouldn't her legs work?—until she could rest against the bulkhead next to Ahren. She cleared her throat and moistened her mouth with what little spit remained in her.

"Ahren," she gasped. She felt for a pulse, found only a flutter.

He emitted a faint groan, a desperate grasping at life.

Zharla jiggled her legs. Good. They just lacked blood flow. No structural damage. She pushed against the bulkhead with her hands and gathered her still-tingling legs underneath herself, then stood, wobbling, and gripped two handfuls of the pilot's uniform, at the shoulders.

She sucked in a breath, to gather the strength to heave Ahren into the rear compartment, away from the heat, but the sound of groaning metal tore her attention back to the nose of the shuttle. A burning tree tore a ragged gash in the hull. Fire leaped onto the control panel, and a wall of heat washed over Zharla.

She gave a guttural cry of anger and pushed off the deck, throwing her head back with the effort. Ahren slid along the deck with surprising ease, but he gave another groan, this one of pain. Zharla paused with Ahren halfway through the hatch, unsure if she was doing more harm than good, but then the hull shuddered once more and the ceiling of the cockpit caved down in flame.

She hoisted Ahren into the rear just in time to avoid the cockpit's collapse. Heat assaulted them, and Zharla had to look away as she dragged Ahren toward the rear hatch. She felt the redness on her face and smelled the tartness of singed hair and eyebrows. She stole a glance behind her and was grateful that the shuttle's crash system had dissolved the rear hatch on impact.

The hull shuddered. A fissure snaked across the ceiling of the rear cabin, and the deck shifted under her feet, forcing her to check her balance. She planted her foot as she stepped away from the heat, pulling Ahren, and felt rocky ground. Fresh, cool air crawled up her back. After three more stumbling steps, Ahren was clear of the shuttle, too. Zharla looked to the sky. Night was coming.

She sniffed the air. A storm was coming, too, a furious and angry storm.

Ahren groaned once again, a sound like the failing breeze of summer.

"No!" She pulled him farther from the burning shuttle.

Then the cockpit exploded, hurtling Zharla back and wrenching her hands away from Ahren's uniform.

"No!" she screamed, after she came to rest at the foot of a tree, her back blossoming with new pain, from jagged volcanic rock and tough bark. She scrambled up to a crouch. "Ahren!"

Thunder tore through the evening, so deep and close that it resonated in Zharla's chest. She cowered, out of reflex, but then a fire awoke within her breast. She could deal no more in fear and self-doubt. No force of nature or will of woman could keep her from saving this young pilot from the death that gaped open to devour him. One more death would be one death too many. One more moment of pain would be one pain too many.

She scraped a knee as she crawled back to Ahren's side, but she would not be deterred now. Such needless pain and suffering she could no longer countenance. She cursed the day she bore her son, and brought his evil into her world, and this one.

She cursed herself, as well. Most women would have aborted a pregnancy after being raped, but not her. Her sense of nobility won through then, but at what cost? She thought then that the unborn child should have a chance at life, that he bore no guilt for the violence that made him, but how could she not have seen what would come of it? And when Nayr was older, how could she not have seen what a toxic mix his inner rage would make with power?

Now her seed was the harbinger of death. She should have seen his terror coming, but the unsuspecting people of the White Planet now had no chance. Oh terrible day, when she infested her world and this with Nayr's insatiable thirst for power! Oh terrible day, when she prevailed upon Ahrik to let the boy take power without a fight! Oh terrible day, when she could have killed her son outright, but did not.

She cradled Ahren's head with trembling fingers. His face blanched. The heat of the blaze on her face told her she had no choice but to move him. As she grabbed his uniform to drag him away from the blaze, millions of other ruined lives clawed at her conscience and dragged her slowly toward despair, a pit tentacled with guilt and lost dreams.

She had to save this one poor soul.

Ahren's fingers grazed her wrist. "Death comes," he said.

She tugged on his uniform and dragged him toward safety. "Hang on, Ahren."

He gave a negating grunt, and she stopped. His eyes bore a knowing look, and he pointed one finger in her direction. "You are . . . hope."

The flames from the shuttle crash licked the treetops, threatening to encircle them, but Zharla did not care. She knelt next to him. "I am a tired and broken woman."

"You . . . must . . . live."

"Where are you injured, Ahren?" She peered into the night and the brewing storm clouds above with wilding eyes, darting and hopeless. "I can get help."

He gave a reproving shake of his head, barely more than a shiver, and pressed two shaky fingers to her wrist. "Save . . . our people." He winced in agony. "Make . . . peace . . . deserved . . . Dom."

Her shoulders sank as she rested his head on the ground. "Live, Ahren."

His eyes examined her, pierced her soul with the inevitability of it all. He knew as well as she how this night would end.

His eyes lost focus for a beat.

She wept, and let the sobs wrack her body. So much death, and for what? Why hadn't she stopped this ruinous war when she had the chance? Blinded by false promises of peace, she would now have yet another death to lay on her conscience. "Stay with me, Ahren. Help me build the peace we deserve. Please."

He smiled with his eyes. "You . . . live."

Ahren breathed his last, and a torrent poured from the ominous green clouds. The burning carcass of the shuttle hissed and steamed in complaint at the deluge, which soon enough came down in sheets of warm water, borne by some fast-moving wind from a warmer clime.

The blaze retreated, but persisted in fits and starts, and Zharla turned her rage on the sky and the storm and whatever fate oversaw this new world. "Why? Why wait till now?" Her body convulsed with a sob. Was fate in this world as callous as the Lady of the Emerald Moon, to let war ruin yet another planet? She shouted at the heavens, for she had not faith to implore the Lady of the Emerald Moon, "Ten minutes earlier, and the rain would have saved him!"

She cried out her agony and pain and despair and heartache. The storm seeped into the seams of her bioflauge suit, but she did not care. She had nothing left to give. How could she right the wrongs she had permitted, other than to give life to the belief that her son must die?

Death was the only way to stop Nayr. Her deepest dream, of a peace forged in her name, would die with him.

After an eternity, the rain subsided, having washed the world, but not her heart. The thunder and lightning receded, to dance and sing on the horizon. Zharla collapsed back against a mountain pine and looked out over the moonlit mountain valleys layered before her. The moon peeked through thinning clouds, spreading its soft white light over the forest, a wealth of wood and water on this verdant planet.

In this new world, she was nothing, powerless even to deter her son from genocide. Better just to wait here, and die.

Footsteps crunched on the rocky ground behind her, but she did not bother to turn around. Death would bring its sweet release soon enough.

A hand pressed to her shoulder, soft and comforting, familiar. "Zharla?"

She started, as if out of a long slumber, and turned her head. "Shahl?"

He held Sera close, hunched over to protect her from the storm. "I saw the fire." His smile caught moonbeams. "I'm so glad we found you."

She gave him a blank stare, then looked from Sera to him and back. The hope in Shahl's eyes and the quiet dignity in Sera's cold, shivering body mocked Zharla's pain, her spent aspirations. "Glad?" How could he be glad, with peace nothing but a cruel memory, with her hopes smashed? She nodded toward Ahren's body. "I need to bury him."

Without comment, Shahl set Sera down, and the two of them, along with Zharla, lifted Ahren from the now soft earth and nestled his body among the trees. The white moon plied its way up the sky, and they piled stone after stone on the body. They covered the head last, and before they did Sera pressed Ahren's eyes closed with two small pebbles.

Zharla shook her head. What happened to the girl's innocence? She sent a reproving look in Shahl's direction. "How did death become so familiar?"

Shahl just rubbed Zharla's arm and sighed. "I think Esh'a is close by."

Zharla pulled away. "There's nothing for me there."

"We'll be there."

Zharla looked away, up the mountain, anywhere but at Shahl's penetrating eyes. "I burn with jealousy," she said, "for the life you lead. That should have been my life."

Sera walked up and curled her hand inside Shahl's. He shrugged. "I have nothing to give you. I'm trying to put my own family back together, and my own hopes hang by mere threads."

"You have love."

Shahl glanced at her with a look like the thin hope of spring blossoms after a frost. "We all have love. You'll see."

Shahl squeezed Sera's hand and set off into the failing night, picking his way carefully through the trees with his daughter. "Are you coming?"

Zharla slumped down against the rough bark of the pine and let the breath drain out of her. Death would be nothing more than losing the will to live. It would be so easy.

But seeing Shahl and Sera together touched a long-buried ray of something, maybe hope, a feeling she had felt the day Nayr was born, the promise of a life not yet lived. Even if Nayr was far beyond her power to mold and cherish now, perhaps others would not be. Ahrik and Shahl and his wife and their daughter could never be the family she'd always wanted, but they still might give her the chance to love again.

Just before Shahl and Sera melted into the night, Zharla unfolded herself from the ground and stumbled after them. She called, "Shahl, Ahrik should be just over that next rise."

Dying embers smoked and fumed, and the light of predawn slid over the eastern horizon.

Esh'a shielded her eyes from the rising sun. She looked behind them. Movement crawled in the valley behind them. The Pale Face faction and the rest were out for blood, by the looks of it. Ahead of them, a spire of smoke clawed its way into the crisp morning, probably a crash site, against the backdrop of a sturdy, pine-laden ridge.

She frowned at Ahrik's ankle. "I don't think we can make it to the rally point before they catch us." she said. She took off the wrist compiler and handed it to him. "Unlocking this every twenty minutes is slowing us down, and I'm certain you can't outrun me now."

Ahrik grunted in pain and reached for the wrist compiler, then struggled to rise from the ground. Esh'a didn't move a muscle to help him. Every time she looked at him, she saw only the man who had hunted her people for years. If the other miners caught up to them, she could just leave him. What was one more death, in a whole sea of despair?

Ahrik leaned against a pine, its bark rough and sappy. He didn't meet her gaze, but pressed a finger to the wrist compiler to unlock it for another twenty minutes. "I'm okay," he said. "Just needed a quick rest." A cloud of breath puffed out of his lungs and into the brisk morning air, an indication that he was not okay.

He pushed off from the tree and wobbled a bit before limping in the direction of the crash site. "We have to make it. If that ship is one of ours, it might have *kall* packs for that distiller you've been lugging around."

He wiped his nose against the chill. "We'll need that distiller for what's coming."

Esh'a looked back toward the valley once again. "There could be over fifty of them, if Pale Face rallied my old faction." She gave Ahrik a pointed look. "And rallying them wouldn't be hard, since I stole a prisoner, and the prisoner happens to be 'The Butcher'."

"One distiller and a little creativity can even the odds," said Ahrik over his shoulder as he stumbled through the trees. "Besides, they're weak and hungry."

"They also don't walk with a limp." She shook her head as she trudged after him. She wanted to club him and turn him over to the miners, but his wrist compiler held the map to the rally point, where Anda and Sera waited, and only he could unlock the compiler. She hated it, but their fates were linked.

They trudged on in silence. Esh'a could tell that Ahrik was trying his best not to grimace and grunt with pain, and she derived perverse pleasure from witnessing his discomfort.

The wispy spire of smoke grew closer. Soon enough the smell of smoldering wood and scorched metal tinged the air. Far-off voices rustled on the wind behind them, voices hungry for revenge.

Esh'a narrowed her eyes and exchanged a glance with Ahrik. He gritted his teeth and looked toward the crash site with renewed determination, then broke into a lopsided run. Esh'a shot off after him. Like him, she kept her center of gravity low and searched for the bulkiest beds of pine needles to place her feet.

Through the trees, Esh'a caught sight of crushed metal and ruined, blackened trees. The hull, smeared with ash and grime, glared at them through wisps of smoke. They burst into the ragged clearing created by the impact of the ship.

It was one of theirs.

Ahrik stopped short and sucked in his breath. He looked at Esh'a with panic, but there was no time to consider why. The voices behind them grew closer. Shouting echoed through the trees.

Ahrik grunted with pain as he scrambled toward the front of the ship, where the hull was a jagged ruin, a thick tree trunk having crushed it to half its normal size. He peered through shards of metal and into the cockpit. Esh'a leaned in behind him, her hand on the hull. The metal was still warm.

He stole a glance in the direction of the voices and pierced her with a purposeful look. "Check the perimeter. I'll go inside."

He circled the hull on the ridge side of the crash and entered the ruined shuttle through the open rear hatch.

Esh'a circled the shuttle in the opposite direction, but paused when she rounded the starboard lobe. Someone had dragged something, or a somebody, over the dirt. The fresh tracks led up the hill, in the direction Esh'a guessed that the rally point lay. She cast about with her eyes and saw a pile of rocks through the trees. Someone was dead, and someone was left alive.

Something heavy made a dull thud inside the shuttle, to her right. Esh'a spun in surprise and leveled her distiller at the wreck, then realized that the weapon was useless. "Ahrik?" she hissed.

The shouting from the way they'd come grew nearer still. Footsteps beat and crashed through the trees, crunching over rough, rocky soil.

The color drained from her face. She looked for something besides the dead distiller to use as a weapon, then thought that it might be better to run, and leave Ahrik to his just deserts.

She readied herself to flee, but Ahrik appeared in the rear hatch, bearing a load.

From the direction they'd come, the indistinct voices morphed into actual words. She recognized Pale Face's voice and at least one other faction leader.

"A freshly broken twig," said Pale Face. "I told you they would make for this wreck."

If she ran now, she might not be able to find the rally point in this vast forest, not without Ahrik, and even if she did find it she'd have to explain how she got there and Ahrik didn't. If she left Ahrik now, Pale Face and her faction would kill him for sure.

Ahrik stumbled against the hatch and dropped something with a bang. The voices of the pursuers on the other side of the shuttle hushed. Even the birds stopped their chirping, as if they too anticipated battle. "Careful now," hissed Pale Face. "Spread out."

Esh'a could almost feel them circling a perimeter around the shuttle.

Ahrik stepped gingerly out of the warbled hatch, cradling two *kall* packs in one hand and a cluster of boson bombs in the other.

"What was that?" asked someone on the other side of the shuttle. The other faction leader.

Ahrik shot Esh'a a glance, then worked the inside of his cheek as if he was about to do something very rash.

Alarm sprang onto Esh'a's face.

After a pause, the footfalls resumed. It wouldn't be long before they rounded the shuttle.

Ahrik gave her a look of the most startlingly false confidence, then filled his lungs with air. In a voice as crisp as the mountain morning that surrounded them, he called, "Don't move any closer. The shuttle isn't stable."

The footsteps paused once again. From a crouch, Ahrik eased a *kall* pack toward Esh'a. She eased it into the pack on her back, then primed the weapon with her thumb inside the weapon. It emitted a baritone hum.

Someone gasped off to their left, just around the corner of the shuttle. "What's that? Hold on over there," Pale Face said. A pause. "Just give us the prisoner, Esh'a. We know who he is. You can go free."

Esh'a looked in Pale Face's direction. The head of her shadow showed ragged dreadlocks, swaying this way and that on the ground. She was confused, unsure.

Esh'a mulled her proposal. It would be no less than Ahrik deserved, after everything he'd done. She glanced down toward Ahrik to see his reaction, to gauge whether she could look at him square in the face, see death there, and live with herself.

She had a live distiller now. She could guarantee her own safety. She would live, at least today.

But when she looked down at Ahrik, his face did not bear defiance or self-pity, but resolution and acceptance. To her shock, he extended his wrist compiler to her.

"It's unlocked permanently," he whispered.

She held out her arm and he slapped it on her wrist. She narrowed her eyes at him. A wave of uncertainty and confused trust invaded her mind. She could run right now, and solve a lot of problems all at once.

"Esh'a?" asked Pale Face.

Esha looked at Ahrik, then at Pale Face's shadow, then back at Ahrik. He handed her another *kall* pack and gave her the same look of false confidence, but this time she read a new meaning in his face, that he would accept whatever she decided, that he would live or die with the consequences.

"Give me something, Esh'a," called Pale Face.

Esh'a gripped the second *kall* pack with her off hand, leaving Ahrik with the cluster of boson bombs. She gave a slow shake of her head, knowing somehow that she would regret what she was about to do. "Pale Face, stay back. The shuttle's about to blow."

Ahrik eased onto his haunches and mouthed the word "run," then he twisted a bomb off his cluster, activated the timer, and tossed it into the shuttle.

Esh'a bolted, following the path made by someone being dragged through the dirt. Ahrik's footfalls followed, uneven. They sprinted up the rocky hill, toward the ridgeline, Ahrik gasping with pain.

"Sto—!" yelled Pale Face.

The sizzle of the boson bombs cut her off. The air sang with the buzz of matter scramblers zipping in every direction inside the shuttle. Magnified like a bell in the confines of the hull, the zing and pop made for a sickening din. Shouts of "Bombs!" and "Run!" rang out over the melee of sound.

Esh'a ran on, half-hoping that Ahrik, behind her, would catch a scrambler in the back.

The cacophony of destruction petered out, and Pale Face shouted behind them, "Esh'a!"

Esh'a's breath caught in her throat. Was she still following them?

Ahrik crashed to the path. Esh'a spun, her distiller at the ready. Ahrik pushed himself up, one elbow bloodied by the fall, the cluster of bombs still cradled in the other. Fifteen meters farther down the path, Pale Face scrambled toward them. Her footing slipped. She looked up, clutching one arm, her face a mask of anger and pain. "Esh'a!"

Esh'a squeezed off a charge from her distiller, and elemental sludge splashed around Pale Face's ankles. The woman sneered and gave Esh'a an icy glare, but she advanced no more.

Ahrik scrambled to his feet at Esh'a's side. "Don't waste the *kall*."

"Waste it?" asked Esh'a. "Two packs is enough to hold off a small army for a week."

Ahrik shook his head. "Back home, yes, but not here."

"Esh'a!" yelled Pale Face. "Are you protecting the Butcher?"

Esh'a cocked her head at Ahrik. "We can't have her following us."

"Don't kill her."

"Esh'a!" Pale Face threw a stone at them with her good hand, brimming with rage.

Esh'a batted the stone away with her distiller, the carbon fiber casing emitting a tinny ping. She kept her eyes on Pale Face, but leaned toward Ahrik. "Do you have a better plan?"

Down in the clearing, the heads of miners began to pop out from cover. They would join Pale Face soon. Ahrik nodded toward the ruined shuttle. "I could have killed most of them with a few bombs, but I didn't."

"Esh'a," said Pale Face, "if you help him, then the lives of all those he's killed will be on your conscience!"

Esh'a scoffed and whispered, "These miners mean nothing to me, Ahrik. My way would be easier."

"Let her live."

"I will not endanger my family because I didn't kill her when I had the chance." Esh'a raised her distiller and aimed for Pale Face's head.

Ahrik touched her shoulder. He didn't leave it there, just grazed it with his own shoulder. Out of the corner of her eye, Esh'a saw Ahrik nod in the direction of the shuttle once more. "That's Renla's personal shuttle. I can tell by the markings."

"Your protégé Renla?"

Ahrik nodded. "She's probably dead. She wouldn't come here unless there was no battle left to fight."

"Shame on you, Esh'a!" screamed Pale Face.

Miners from different factions began to skirt the ruins of the shuttle, giving it a wide berth.

"There were at least two people on that shuttle, and one of them died," said Esh'a. She scanned the clearing. She saw about thirty miners, and clenched her jaw at Ahrik. "Let me do this."

"No. One of those two people on that shuttle was probably the Queen, my wife." He pursed his lips with regret. "I have a chance to make things right."

"Ha! How could you possibly atone—"

"Enough killing," he said. "Violence brought us here. Violence destroyed Dom. Violence made refugees of us all."

Esh'a lowered her weapon and considered him. Her face transformed with bitterness and pain. She counted on the fingers of her free hand. "Kal. Ren. Temra. Lela. Init. Par. Tewel. The entire town of Beta Station on Moon." She pointed her weapon at Ahrik. "*You* killed them. My friends. My people. And now your son has racked up the greatest butcher's bill of them all, the destruction of an entire planet. Tell me, Ahrik Jeber-li. Who will pay that bill now?" She poked the distiller into his chest. "Who. Pays?"

Another stone fell at their feet. "Esh'a! Do it! End this now!"

Her distiller's hum crescendoed, near to bursting with angry destruction.

He met her venomous glare with the calmness of a summer morn. "Blame me, if you want. Kill me, if you must. But know this: there will always be someone to blame. A life of war has taught me that much, at least." He nodded toward their surroundings. "Look around you, at this new world. Will we spoil this one, too? Tell me, sister, how does it end, the violence, the killing?"

"Esh'a! Think of what he's done." Pale Face's voice had come closer. "Justice, Esh'a. Give us justice!"

Esh'a whipped her distiller around and pointed it at Pale Face. "Get back."

Behind Pale Face, the miners had begun to cluster at the bottom of the path, on the near side of the shuttle.

"Esh'a," Ahrik whispered. "The path narrows up ahead. We can block it so they can't follow us." He shifted his weight and turned his back to the miners. "This may be our last chance to meet our families. They could leave if we don't make it to the rally point soon."

Esh'a looked from the miners to Ahrik and back. Her pain and bitterness wrestled with hope, tying her heart in impossible knots.

She stuck the distiller back in Ahrik's chest. She knew what she wanted to do, with a passion nearly beyond comprehension, as if a force beyond her frail ability to comprehend willed her to squeeze the trigger and bask in the glorious elixir of total victory. How easy it would be to grasp revenge for all of the Butcher's crimes.

"Pulling the trigger now would not feel like a waste, Butcher."

Ahrik merely drew a breath and gave her a look that said the choice was hers.

"Stand back," she said to the miners. Her shoulders slumped, but she kept the distiller trained on Ahrik.

She lowered the distiller altogether and looked at the ground by the miners' feet. "Let us go in peace."

"Traitor!" screamed Pale Face.

Her screaming followed them up to the ridgeline. Even after Ahrik blasted a minor landslide out of the cliff face, to block the path, still the fury of Pale Face's screams followed them. Not until they crested the ridge did the morning's birdsong and the penetrating mountain sun reclaim the land's natural state, a setting unconcerned with their petty human grievances.

A cool breeze wandered through the trees. Esh'a checked the wrist compiler, then looked ahead at the blanket of green forest spread out over the undulating terrain. Yet another ominous ridge lay in wait in the distance.

She reached out to support Ahrik, whose limp had worsened. "Only a few hundred more meters, brother. How's your ankle?"

20 What Is War?

AHRIK WOKE TO A FRIGID SHOCK of cold air and the chirping of a thousand birds. His face felt damp. The light of dawn broke over the ridgeline to the west, or was it east? He couldn't be sure, in this new place, since he didn't know which pole the aliens considered north, and which south. His breath came out in clouds of moisture, his life expelling itself into a foreign world.

He raised up on one elbow, and every part of his body complained. His back ached from a night spent tossing and turning on a bed of pine needles, and his arm tingled with sleepiness. He moved his leg and winced when pain shot from his twisted ankle.

"Yuh ukay, sir?" Flank sat cleaning a distiller, the one they'd taken from the shuttle. His qasfin, Biriq, lay on its sheath, next to him, already gleaming and razor sharp.

Ahrik knew those weapons would be of little use here. The kall packs for the distillers depleted at a furious rate on the White Planet, and the locals' reliance on remotely-delivered firepower made close-quarters combat almost irrelevant. He gave Flank a brave smile. "No need to 'sir' me anymore."

Ahrik held his breath as he worked himself into a seated position and rested his arms on his knees. The other two clones sat apart, eating, sharpening weapons, talking in the soft morning light. Ahrik sighed. "Do you know why war is a young man's game, Flank?"

Flank cocked his head to one side. "Young mun's game?"

"Sure. War. Interplanetary travel. Running from a tyrannical stepson." Ahrik shuddered that they couldn't fight Nayr on his terms anymore. "Why can't I do this?"

Flank scrubbed at a particularly nettlesome piece of grime, then sighed and gave Ahrik an inscrutable look. "Nuh idea, sir."

Ahrik paused in frustration at the "sir," but thought better of making any more of it than he already had. Old habits die hard. He took in a flock of birds, winging from a stand of pine on the breeze. So much wildlife here. "The reason, Flank, is that old men like us have too many dead friends. Young men don't know better. Their friends are still alive."

Flank worked his tongue around in his mouth. Ahrik had met him less than three days ago, but he could still tell something bothered his clone. "Sir," said Flank, with the slightest note of challenge, "yuh sayin' we should guv up?"

Ahrik shook his head. "No. Only that our little force will tire before the Tyrant does."

Flank rummaged through his pack and produced a ration bar. He broke off a piece and handed it to Ahrik, then cast a meaningful look at Zharla, Shahl, and Sera. Flank sneered in disdain. "If it wuz jus' us soldiers, we'd 'ave some udvantages."

Ahrik munched on his half of the ration bar and studied the ground at his feet. The thought had crossed his mind, too, but he couldn't leave Zharla and Shahl and his family to contend with fate. Sera's innocence would be a crime to destroy. How long would it take for Nayr to find them here, in the wilderness? How many would die before he won? Ahrik pondered what could be his last meaningful act as a leader of soldiers. He and his sons needed to stay together, and they had to melt into the local civilization. To disappear.

He swallowed and looked hard at Flank. "Do you remember what we used to be?"

Flank stopped eating and stared toward the ridgeline, a far off look in his eye. "We wuz legion, whun we called yuh 'Father'." He glanced at Ahrik. "But now we're jus' three, an' yuh say th'ketel is gone furever."

"I can't change what happened." Ahrik cast a mournful look at Flank, then pointed to where the civilians still slept. He furrowed his brow, because he couldn't see Esh'a anywhere. He pushed the thought from his mind and turned his attention back to Flank. "We never fought for ourselves, anyway. We fought for them."

Flank grimaced. Color rose in his face. "Things iz different now. Ain't nuthin' t'fight fur. Ain't no one needs prutectin'. We're all vuctums now."

Ahrik set his jaw and reached into his heart for his last wisps of inspiration. Would it be enough to convince this man to follow him? "Remember who we were, Flank, who we still are. Once a soldier, always a soldier."

"We jus' wunna survive."

"We need to live, not just survive."

Flank threw his partly-eaten ration bar back in his pack, then stood up. "Yuh'll die, sir, an' yur death wun't mean nuthin'." He looked down at his former commander, a vein popping out on his forehead. "I told th'uthers I'd try, but yuh give us no choice."

"So that's it, then?"

"Thut's it." Behind him, the other two clones saw Flank's signal and shouldered their own packs, casting wary glances in Ahrik's direction, interested in his reaction, but not prying.

Ahrik bit the inside of his cheek to suppress his annoyance at the insubordination that only a day earlier, when his ketel was still intact, would have been a tryable offense. He took a deep breath. "Where will you go?"

Flank shrugged, then reached down to pick up his pack. "We huv weapuns t'hunt wuth, an' th'weather don't seem too hursh. The fuster we get uway from th'crash site, the longer we live."

Ahrik stood, ignoring the fire that lanced through his ankle. He drew himself up and looked Flank in the eye. "Life is about more than survival."

Flank saluted, but his laugh made clear his true feelings. "An' war iz'bout more thun dyin'."

Ahrik returned the salute and watched his last three men trudge off up the slope, toward the lip of the ridge. A piece of Ahrik died in that moment. For the first time in his life, he was totally alone, like a man who jumps into space then loses his tether.

But something wouldn't let him give up. He wanted to leave behind the love triangle of Zharla, Shahl, and Esh'a to follow his men, but duty ran deeper than attachment, or passion, or even than love. His duty, as always, lay with his people, such as they were, that piece of him that he could never abandon.

He leaned on a tree, the bark rough under his hand, the needles pungent. The tree was at least twice as tall as any tree back home. Cautious at first, then with increasing vigor, he worked his ankle around, testing range of motion. The day of rest since he and Esh'a found the rally point and met the others had done his ankle good.

He pumped his foot on the ground, and when he was satisfied that he could use it without too much more damage, he sheathed Biriq and crept over to where Zharla lay huddled with Shahl and Sera. He winced all the way.

Seeing his brother and wife together made anger flare in his chest, but he breathed deeply to control it. Duty.

He knelt, careful to put as little weight as possible on his ankle, and brushed Zharla's shoulder with his hand.

Her eyes fluttered open. When she saw him, remorse flooded into her face. But almost as fast, her anger returned.

Ahrik had to look away. He never could endure her disapproval.

"What do you want?" she whispered.

He sighed with striations of regret. "I'm going to reconnoiter. Be back in an hour."

Zharla scoffed. "If Nayr comes, he comes. What's the use?"

Ahrik narrowed his eyes and nodded toward Sera. "You may have nothing to live for, Your Majesty, but that girl does. Give her the chance she deserves."

He eased himself up, ignoring the pain. He walked off after his men, choosing his steps carefully, the temptation to leave the civilians for good never greater than at that moment. He could go longer and farther with his men. They would find a way to blend in eventually. He'd seen the locals. They were taller, but humanoid.

He breathed easily. The lower gravity here meant he could cover more ground. The mountain air was crisp and clean, and the rising sun turned the sky a brilliant shade of blue. He slowed when he got to the last point he'd seen his men, looking for clues of their passage. He pressed on, and every minute or so, he stopped, knelt, and listened for the baseline sounds of the morning. Birds chirping. Pine needles swishing in the breeze.

He turned back to look over the ridge once, and he saw the whole valley below him carpeted in brilliant green pine trees. The light and bounty on this planet was so . . . powerful.

On he hobbled, tracking the very few clues his men left, a broken twig there, mashed needles there. The incline increased, but he still didn't have to work that hard. He could run forever in these conditions, if not for his ankle. He paused once more, then heard whispered voices.

He eased his head this way and that, locating the source of the sound. The voices were familiar, the language his own. His men. About fifty meters away, to the northwest, or what he assumed was northwest. He crept up on them, shifting his angle so he was downwind.

He knelt again when he was close enough to make out their words. Hilt, still clutching his ribs, stood in a clearing, in a campsite belonging to an alien, presumably. Flank sat on the ground, wincing in pain. Tank crouched, examining Flank's leg.

"...wus thut thing?" asked Tank.

"Dud yuh hear th'rattle befur it struck Flank?" asked Hilt, kneeling down.

Tank stroked his chin, furrowed his brow. "Yuh ukay t'walk, Flank?"

Flank shook his head. "Hurts bad." He said. He squeezed his eyes shut, the pain evident on his face. "Vusion blurry."

"I'll muk a smull uncision, see if I cun bleed't out." Tank reached into his pack and asked Hilt, "Cun yuh find somethin' useful 'round here?"

Hilt moved through the campsite, but it looked so well-kept that Ahrik doubted he'd find anything that wasn't secured. The vague remains of a fire lay inside a ring of stones, the coals clearly having been smothered with dirt. A dome of grey fabric, supported with curved struts, stood off to the left, and Hilt stood puzzling over how to open it up. Giving up on the dome, Hilt approached a blockish, blue vehicle, with an open holding area in the back. The vehicle sat on four black wheels that touched the ground. He placed his hand to the opening mechanism to gain access to the passenger compartment, to no avail.

Flank gave a sharp cry of pain, and his breathing became shallow. He clutched Tank's arm. Flank's eyes registered alarm. "Can't . . . feel . . . leg."

From the vehicle, panic flashed onto Hilt's face, and Tank rummaged around in his pack with evident frustration next to Flank. The two healthy clones exchanged worried looks.

Recognition clicked, and Ahrik hobbled into the clearing. He knew this wound. "Keep his leg below his heart," he said to his erstwhile sons.

Ahrik once saw a keteli poisoned like this, when they came to the other hemisphere of the White Planet, some fourteen years earlier. Calm and cool, Ahrik knelt down, grabbed Flank's lower leg, and sucked on the wound.

Blood and venom rushed into his mouth, and he spat them on the ground. He looked at Flank, whose face had blanched. Ahrik sucked and spat again, then twice more, just like he saw the man treated so long ago. "You'll be okay, Flank. Tank, dress his wound."

The two clones looked at him with a cold mix of guilt and respect, but neither moved to dress Flank's wound.

Ahrik stood and moved toward the vehicle. He'd seen a mechanism like this during the war, too. He gripped the metal handhold with his fingers and pressed on a button beside the handhold with his thumb. He pulled, and the door creaked open, using some sort of mechanical hinge attached to one side. He peered into the compartment and saw a series of controls, levers, knobs, and pedals, with a faded leather seat running the width of the compartment. A paper box sat on the seat. He opened it. Ammunition, like the rebels used in the War for the Emerald Moon, so long ago. But the ammunition was useless without the weapon to go with it, so he set the box down.

Then he saw a sheaf of paper, folded onto itself, with delicate markings in a variety of colors. A map. He snatched it up.

A voice startled him from behind. "Whut'd yuh find?"

He turned, the map behind his back, and found Tank standing too close, straining to look into the vehicle compartment. The distiller that Ahrik had entrusted to Flank now swayed from Tank's pack. His glare was not as deferential as it was earlier, in the shuttle, his cheery loyalty distant now, forgotten.

Ahrik pursed his lips and produced the map from behind his back. "We can put this to good use, once we figure out how to read it." He half-turned toward the vehicle seat and tilted his head at the ammunition box. "Whoever camped here is armed. We should leave."

Ahrik made a move to pass, but Tank placed a hand on Ahrik's chest. The physical contact was the surest evidence yet that the men he'd once commanded now regarded theirs as the position of giving commands.

Tank grunted and tossed his head in the direction of the others. "Yuh mean, *we* could muk good use uv this mup."

The words cut like a dagger. Ahrik was no longer one of them. His blood rushed to his feet. He gripped the frame of the vehicle door. If Tank tried to take the map by force at that moment, Ahrik could not stop him. Nor would Ahrik try.

Ahrik peered into Tank's face for some trace of rationality, some indication that he would countenance reason. "Let's talk about it with Hilt."

Tank dropped his hand and Ahrik pushed by him, careful not to show weakness by favoring his ankle. He squinted his eyes and clenched his teeth against the pain as he moved toward Hilt and Flank. Crouched at Flank's side, Hilt gave Ahrik's approach a suspicious look.

Ahrik's chest tightened with alarm. Flank lay flaccid now, face pale, breathing labored. What had Ahrik missed? The keteli he saw poisoned fourteen years earlier was fine after a few minutes, not worse.

Ahrik's shoulders slumped. "I . . . I don't know what happened."

Then Ahrik realized that even though that other keteli came from Ahrik's world, he'd been on this planet for months, if not years, while Flank had been here less than two days, with no chance to adapt to local pathogens or to develop antibodies against the local environment.

Flank's eyes shot open and he reached a feeble hand toward Ahrik. "I am dead, Father."

"No, we'll get you out of this," said Ahrik, crouching down, wincing at the pain in his ankle.

Flank gripped Ahrik's hand with surprising strength. "I . . . I drained the oxygen."

"We can move forward."

Tank snorted behind him. "Get uway frum Flank," he growled. "Yuh don't deserve t—"

Flank's breath became even shallower, and his neck swelled. "So . . . rry."

Flank's hand dropped from Ahrik's grip and his eyes glazed into the middle distance.

Hilt stood and folded his arms across his chest, an insolent look in his eyes. "Any mur tricks up yur sleeve?"

Ahrik sensed that false confidence was dangerous now, even more so to argue that Tank's incision on Flank's leg could just as well have worsened the situation. Ahrik tossed down the map and held his head high. "We need to buy Flank time. Maybe there's a med pack back at—"

Flank cried out once again and arched his back. His legs convulsed with disturbing violence.

Hilt motioned for Ahrik to move away. "Th'med pack burned up wuth uverythin' else in th'crush." He shook his head at Ahrik. "We dun't evun have nuthin' t'dull th'pain."

Ahrik refused to move. Maybe there was still a chance to regain his sons' trust. He searched Hilt and Tank's eyes for a sign of empathy. "We can't do noth—"

Flank stopped breathing. Ahrik leaned Flank's head back and opened his airway to begin artificial respiration, but at a grunt from Hilt, Tank grabbed Ahrik by the scruff and yanked him back. Ahrik flailed, then landed on his backside. He scrambled up to help Flank, but again Tank put a hand on Ahrik's chest, accompanied by a menacing shake of his head. The distiller clanked against Tank's leg, as if in punctuation.

Ahrik locked eyes with Tank. How did it come to this? "Tank, in the name of the Lady, do something for him. I order it."

"Dun't move," said Hilt, glaring at Tank. Hilt unhitched the distiller from Tank's pack and slipped his hand in. The weapon's hum lent a furious accent to the menace in his voice. "He lust th'right t'cummand us when he sucrificed his sons t'save his own hide."

Flank took a shallow breath and moaned. His eyes ripped open. He coughed, and then gasped for air, like a fish caught on land.

"His death will be on your hands," Ahrik said, clenching his fists, but utterly helpless.

Hilt chuckled. "No, no. Ut's ulready on yurs."

With that, he slammed the distiller into the side of Ahrik's head. Pain flashed, and his body slumped into darkness.

When Ahrik came to, the late morning sun beat down. The thin mountain air left little protection from the sun's penetrating rays. A dry, slicing heat had replaced the morning's frosty bite. His head throbbed. He ran his tongue over his parched mouth, and felt blood crusted on his swollen lip.

After his eyes adjusted to the light, as he expected, he saw that the map was gone and that Flank's body lay nearby, cold, pale, and peaceful, arms folded over his chest in the death salute. He couldn't leave him here. Flank deserved a proper burial, even if he'd turned against Ahrik once. Ahrik and his sons had lived through too much together.

Ahrik pushed himself up to a crouch and took a deep breath, grunting away the pain in his ankle, then lifted himself up the rest of the way. He stopped and took in the world around him. Birds, breezes, the smell of pine. Normal. He staggered over to the vehicle and peered into the holding area at the back. Even if he'd had one, he couldn't use a distiller to dig a grave like he could back home. The kall packs would be gone before he finished.

He needed to find a digging tool. The holding area contained an assortment of tools, and his eyes rested on one that would work, a flat, semicircular metal plate attached to a long wooden pole. He hefted it out, glad that it was light, like everything else on this planet.

He scurried back to Flank's body and listened once again. He sucked in his breath. A new sound carried on the wind, faint but coming his way. Whistling. Someone trying to mimic bird calls but doing a poor job of it.

He wasn't about to wait around for an alien to find him with a digging tool and a dead body. He leaned the digging tool against a nearby tree, took a deep breath, and worked Flank onto his shoulder. He steeled himself for the ache he would feel in his ankle later. Grateful for the lower gravity, he grabbed the tool and hobbled back into the forest.

Ahrik had put a good hundred meters between himself and the campsite when the whistling stopped abruptly. Ahrik froze. He crouched. Behind him, he heard the vehicle door squeak open and slam closed, then he heard the alien rummage through the tools in the vehicle's rear storage area. The alien shouted something, probably a curse, then went silent.

Ahrik eased his body around, still in a crouch, to see if the alien was following him. The alien looked this way and that, loading his, or possibly her, weapon. The alien trudged off in the opposite direction from Ahrik, moving further up the ridge.

Ahrik sighed with relief, but he knew he didn't have much time. If he and the others didn't move soon, that alien with the weapon would find them, and Ahrik didn't want to have to kill again.

He also had a grave to dig, preferably before the day's heat set in for real, so he moved with purpose back toward their clearing.

A burden that had been light enough when he set off from the alien campsite, after a while grew leaden. He had to stop and lean against a tree every few steps, but he dared not set down Flank's body, for fear he wouldn't be able to hoist him back up.

By the time he broke the treeline of the clearing, the sun sat high in the sky and his legs wobbled from the weight. His ankle throbbed. His growling stomach reminded him that he'd only eaten half a ration bar that day.

Sucking in great gulps of air, he laid Flank out on the stony ground. Ahrik hung his head for a moment, in a prayer for the dead man's soul, but looked up when he heard footfalls. Shahl.

Ahrik didn't even have the strength to greet him, but Shahl approached without breaking stride. His eyes were red-rimmed and swollen, but his pupils bore the focus and intensity of extreme anger. He snatched the digging tool from the ground. "I'll take care of this."

Without even a glance at Ahrik, Shahl began hammering away at the ground with the digging tool. Again and again he slashed at the earth, mounding rocks, sticks, and dirt all around him.

Then Ahrik heard muffled sobs, and saw Zharla staggering toward him, from the same direction Shahl had come. Her shoulders shook, and she crumpled to the ground beside Ahrik, her cheeks moist. She took a deep breath and cast a longing look at Shahl as he dug.

Ahrik scanned his surroundings. He fought the pity that rose inside him, pity laced with sadness, pity at the wreck his wife had become, sadness at his men abandoning him, at his inability to lead those who would not follow.

He was no longer the man he was once, when war was simple and violence led to decisive outcomes. In this new world of ambiguity, where others set the rules, he was nothing. Less than nothing.

He ran his parched tongue over his swollen lip and thought of the twisted past that led him here. Of what could have been. He cast about in his mind for some lodestar that might give him direction in an uncertain future. "Zharla," he asked, extending a gentle hand to her shoulder. "Where is Sera? Where is Esh'a?"

Zharla sniffed, eyes red, gaze distant. As expected, she recoiled from his touch. "Who?"

"I've always wondered what human regard lay in your heart." He looked up to the blue sky, so beguiling in its clarity. Death would come to them all, eventually. He turned back to Zharla and sighed. "Now I know."

Heart heavy, he rose on an unsteady ankle and took over from Shahl, knowing that this would not be the last grave he would dig. The hole widened, and Zharla broke into a keening wail of utmost, and self-absorbed, anguish.

Esh'a had woken early that morning, to ponder the turmoil within her breast. Her family was here at the rally point, and they were alive, but a menace lurked close, like death on the prowl. Maybe it was an old fighter's curse, her knack for sensing the calm before the storm.

Esh'a shivered, but not at the cool air. A teenage megalomaniac wanted to destroy them all, root and branch, and he would ravage this planet to do it, just like he had lain waste to Home and Moon. Their only hope was to stick together, but the Queen was trying to steal Esh'a's husband, Ahrik was moping over his lost command, and Anda was distracted, but by what, Esh'a couldn't fathom. She and Anda hadn't always had the best relationship, but he'd been tight-lipped about something since yesterday, when they had reunited.

Esh'a scratched at the ground with her toe, the sole of her shoe so thin she could feel every pebble, it seemed. How could she reconnect with her husband?

Footsteps crunched on cinders, and Esh'a turned. Sera smiled up at her.

The girl slipped her tender little hand inside her mother's. "Why are you all the way over here?" Sera asked. "Abbi is looking for you."

Esh'a doubted that. She hugged Sera close and drew strength from her daughter's inner resolve and kindness. Esh'a smiled, which didn't seem too hard, at least for a moment. "You're not coughing as much as you did before."

As if reminded of her condition, Sera coughed and gave Esh'a a sheepish grin, like she should apologize for something she could not control. "I like these mountains, Imma."

Esh'a peered through the trees at those mountains, her home for three long months of bone-chilling labor, digging kall out of the hardscrabble ground so that the Tyrant could feed his war machine. The day was beginning to warm as the sun crept toward late morning. The sky had shifted from the oranges and purples of sunrise to the clear blue warmth of day. They would sweat before long, under the beating sun.

The thin, dry air did wonders for Sera's breathing, or so Anda claimed, but Esh'a knew that sooner or later they'd need to heal her, to figure out what was really going on with this mystery illness.

Esh'a crouched down and slid an arm around Sera's shoulder. She squeezed her daughter close. "Serit," Esh'a asked, "do you feel like you're getting better?"

"Yes, Imma." Sera bounced on her heels. Her hand wriggled inside Esh'a's. But then she froze and her eyes grew wide.

Alarm built inside Esh'a's chest, and her whole body flashed with a chill. She couldn't move. Sera clutched her chest and winced, which was enough to slice back the tangle of indecision that clawed at Esh'a's breast.

Esh'a reached for her little girl and lifted her up just as the coughing fit tore through Sera's body, a reckless wave, worse than she'd ever seen. After a few steps in the direction of their makeshift camp, Esh'a didn't need to look down to see the smear of blood and tears on her shoulder.

Esh'a burst into the clearing. Anda looked up from where Ahrik hacked at the ground, digging a grave. Ahrik ignored her return, despite Sera's coughing. Instead, he focused on kicking and pulling at rocks in the ground. The Queen sat in the middle of the clearing, apparently more interested in bugs and cinders than in helping out. A body lay near the grave, one of Ahrik's clones. Esh'a shoved aside the question of how he died and where the other clones were, and made a beeline for Anda.

Anda looked at Sera, then with purpose at his pack. Esh'a broke off in that direction. The Queen rose, but Esh'a would never accept help from her.

She resolved in that moment that, as soon as this coughing fit was under control, she was getting her husband back. Royalty or not, no woman walked on Esh'a's turf. Anda might think it was nothing, but Esh'a saw how Her Majesty looked at Esh'a's man.

No more.

Esh'a skidded to a stop at Anda's pack, Sera convulsing on her shoulder. She crouched and reached to tear open the pack's main compartment with one hand.

"The metal canister in the side pocket. It . . ." Anda stumbled up behind her, obviously upset about something else, something he'd probably been talking about with That Other Woman and Ahrik.

Esh'a ripped open the side pocket. Something small rattled inside the canister as she yanked it out. She twisted it open to reveal a single white pill.

"It's the last one," said Anda, a disconcerting tremble in his voice.

Esh'a pinched the pill and popped it under Sera's tongue, between coughs.

Sera clamped her mouth shut and the coughing subsided, but Sera's eyes sent streams of tears down her reddened, swollen face. She gave a weak nod, indicating she was okay.

Esh'a breathed a sigh of relief and set her little girl down, then looked down at the canister in her hand. The lid bore an inscription, in ornate, engraved letters: *A life for a life.*

She furrowed her brow, but then heard That Other Woman approach from their rear, her footfalls like daggers raked across ice.

The anticipation of confronting the Queen flooded her spine, but she couldn't avoid the inevitable. She might as well get it over with now.

She stuffed the canister in her pocket, then whirled on her competitor. "You—"

Esh'a froze. The Queen's face was red and swollen, even more than Sera's. Her cheeks glistened with moisture. Esh'a gave Anda a confused look and lowered her voice. "Why's she crying?"

Anda broke eye contact with Esh'a. "I told her."

"That she'll have to deal with me if she doesn't back off?" The rush of the fight flared in Esh'a's nostrils. "I could take her."

Anda's eyes pleaded with his wife. His shoulders slumped. "I told her that I cannot love two women."

Esh'a narrowed her eyes. "You better say I'm the one . . ."

He cradled her shoulders with his hands. "Esh'a, I have been faithful to you for all these months." He gave her a tender smile, but she saw something else in his face, although she still couldn't figure out what. He drew in a reassuring breath. "I could never betray you."

Esh'a searched his eyes for any trace of doubt or infidelity, some hint that she shouldn't believe him. The moment passed as if through honey, slow and discolored. Did she trust him? His face still bore that unnamed something, but she could find no reason for distrust in the new creases of worry on his face. Besides, if she didn't trust him, could she live with the implications?

Before she could pull him into a forgiving embrace, a horrifying, high-pitched whine broke the morning. Esh'a's eyes darted to the sky, searching for the telltale speck against the blue, that angel of death.

"Seekerbot," whispered Anda, ripples of fear in his voice. He turned wide eyes on Esh'a. "Take Sera. Hide down the slope, where the trees are thicker."

"What will you do?"

Anda lowered his voice and leaned toward Esh'a, with an eyebrow raised in That Other Woman's direction. "Take the Queen up the slope, away from you two."

Esh'a pursed her lips and nodded. She gripped her little girl's hand. "Let's go."

As Anda crunched toward the Queen, Esh'a and Sera bounded down the slope. Esh'a peered up through the trees, to see if she could spy the seekerbot. The whine continued in a disconcerting ebb and piercing flow, punctuating Esh'a's rising anxiety.

But then a deeper buzz sounded on the air. Esh'a crouched with Sera beside a tree, frozen at the unfamiliar sound. She scanned the sky, then saw a strange, dark object silhouetted against the clouds, much larger than a seekerbot. A stocky central fuselage had flat appendages extending at odd angles. A bulbous dome sat below the forward section of the fuselage. The object's baritone buzz contrasted with the seekerbot's fell whine, as if competing with each other for Esh'a's fear.

Sera shivered. "I'm scared, Imma."

Crouching by a tree, Esh'a rubbed her between the shoulder blades. "Me too, Serit."

Esh'a glanced back toward the clearing. Anda and the Queen worked their way up the opposite slope, but it was plain that the Queen had no interest in leaving the clearing. She beat the midday air with her staccato protests, while Anda shushed her to keep her from giving away their position to the seekerbot.

Esh'a turned her attention back to the larger flying object. It gave a soft pop, then a projectile zipped down toward the clearing, trailing steam or smoke or something. Panic spiked in Esh'a's chest. Anda.

Sera. Esh'a dove against the tree and curled around Sera as the projectile screamed through the air. A ferocious explosion ripped open the morning. It concussed the day with a wave of power and heat. The force of the blast pressed into Esh'a's back and whipped at her already thin clothes. In an instant, nothing mattered but the violence of fire and fury that shredded their peace into chaos.

Silence descended as suddenly as the explosion that rent the clear blue sky. Esh'a's senses swirled. Nothing made sense. As if from far away, the deeper buzz continued, an ethereal, monotonous sound.

Esh'a couldn't quite place what the sound meant, but then a few beats passed and coherence returned in an ever-expanding circle of comprehension. Esh'a slowly grasped the environment around the tree where they cowered. She looked up to see the strange object veer through the sky in a wide arc, then realized that the seekerbot's whine had ceased. The alien aircraft had destroyed the seekerbot.

Esh'a breathed a sigh of relief. "Are you okay, Serit?"

Her little girl nodded, and Esh'a extracted the canister from her pocket. "Who gave this to Abbi?"

Sera wrinkled her nose in disgust and said, "My bad cousin."

Esh'a raised a panicked gaze back to the clearing. Horror flooded her soul at what she saw. Ahrik rose from protecting the dead body of his soldier, to continue digging the grave, and the Queen wailed into the sky. They had snapped.

But seeing her husband, her dear Anda, compounded her terror. He hurled himself at Ahrik's pack and pulled out a qasfin. The other two were unaware, fixated on their madness.

Esh'a ran, stumbling, through the trees. "Anda?" she called, still not quite certain how loudly she should speak.

If he heard her, he ignored her. Ahrik's blade gleamed in his hand as he drew it from its sheath, the noonday sun glinting off its wicked curve. The buzz of the alien aircraft faded away, and a terrible silence filled the void in Esh'a's heart.

Her mouth went as dry as the mountain air.

No.

Anda gave a furtive glance at his brother and the Queen, then set the killing point of the curved blade to his own neck. He cast a mournful eye on Esh'a, as if to apologize and plead all at once. Death once again stared Esh'a in the face, but this face was as calm, determined, and accepting as the sunrise she'd seen that morning.

No.

Horrible realization dawned on Esh'a. *A life for a life.* The Tyrant must have given Anda enough pills to keep Sera alive until they got here, but now Anda had to choose between his own life and his daughter's.

No, not like this. It couldn't be. Anda had chosen to sacrifice himself for Sera, and Esh'a was utterly powerless. She was too far away, and the cast of his face told her she couldn't have prevented this, even were she closer. Anda had waited for his chance, when no one could stop him.

"Ahrik!" she screamed. If she could jostle him from his melancholy trance, he could overpower Anda. *Please, brother.*

The strength drained from Esh'a's legs. She steadied herself on a tree. Further thought and word failed her, beyond the terror of losing her dearest friend.

"Imma?"

Her senses spun once again, worse than they had with the explosion. Sera. She still had to protect Sera.

Esh'a fought against the vertigo threatening to envelope her. She sucked in a lungful of air, to scream at Anda to stop, at Ahrik to stop him, and at the Queen to stop her delirious wail. To do something.

She squeezed Sera's hand and opened her mouth to scream, but movement in the trees beyond the clearing cut her off. A humanoid form crept toward the treeline on the opposite end of the clearing, sweeping a weapon back and forth.

An alien woman, and a soldier, by the way she moved. The explosion must have drawn her here.

The woman raised her weapon. At Esh'a and Sera? In a split second decision, Esh'a grabbed her little girl's hand and started to run down the slope. Into the wilderness. Away from danger.

She knew Anda. Nothing could stop him once he decided to sacrifice himself for his daughter.

Esha ran, Sera beside her, into the safety of the wilderness. Now Esh'a was the only one who could keep Sera safe.

The morning had dawned pure, and the noon sun burned bright, giving off the perfect light with which to die. The vision of his own hand gripping his father's old qasfin panned across Anda's mind as if in a dream, as if some other him had begun living the last moments of his own life.

The worn grains of the leather grip pressed against his palm, the murderous gleam of the noonday sun glinting off the razor edge, the unearthly keen of a spurned Queen slicing through the dread silence after the seekerbot's destruction, the crushing realization that he knew his dear Esh'a must feel now, all wove infinite threads of pain and love and grit, the stirring vibrance of death.

For from death must come life, or so he repeated to himself over and over again. Sera must live. *A life for a life.* If Esh'a could get away from here, away from Ahrik and Zharla, away from danger, then their sweet girl would live. Days of dawning fate and mental anguish, steeling himself for his moment of sacrifice, had led him and his life's twisted journey to this, their merciful repose, in redemption's sweet embrace.

Esh'a and Sera deserved none of the suffering they endured, and now his inevitable sacrifice would set them free, free of Sera's illness and free of this accursed war, at least the part of it that fate had blamed on him.

He raised the upper point of the blade to the left side of his windpipe. All he had to do was press and yank to sever the windpipe and the jugular. Just as real as his impending mortality, he felt the scream of shock and surprise welling up from Esh'a's core, ready to burst and bring his plan to a shuddering stop, for he could not go through with it knowing that his wife looked on with eyes of tenderness and a broken heart.

"Ahrik!" Esh'a screamed.

Flee, Esh'a, flee. Fate has cast my die.

But he heard no scream from down the mountain, only Zharla's keening wail and the sing-song clatter of Ahrik digging a grave.

But wait. Only the keening wail pierced his ear. Too late, he heard Ahrik stumble over the rocky ground toward him. Anda tried to plunge the point of the blade into his windpipe—please make it quick—but Ahrik stayed his hand. Anda saw the veins in his brother's wrist, smelled his sweat, and pushed with all his might against his brother's will.

Anda heard the beginnings of a word rattle in Ahrik's throat, but a gasp cut it off. Ahrik's body tightened with ripcord tension, suspended between fight and flight.

Zharla stopped screaming. Her hush ushered in a new danger.

Anda scanned with his eyes to find the source of their fear. His eyes grew wide with alarm, for out of the trees slunk a woman, tall, well-built, with a no-nonsense glare. And armed. Her weapon swept from the direction of the slope below, from Sera and Esh'a, and stopped its arc at Ahrik.

"*Hoobala*," she ordered.

Ahrik's tension slipped, for half a beat, into the slightest indecision. His grip wavered. His weight shifted.

It was enough. Just enough.

Anda shoved his brother with his shoulder, weakening Ahrik's stance at the knee, to create the minutest of openings. He threw himself forward, then away to his left.

The ease of his death surprised him. He expected it to be a culmination of supreme will, but as he fell, the air and blood sliding from his neck, he realized just how easy it was to overcome all things.

As he fell, Anda saw a single *pter'a* bush at the edge of the clearing, not ten meters away, its small white flowers dancing in the gentle breeze, its stems rustling against hardy tufts of mountain grass. As he fell, and the last of his air escaped his body, his tongue caught the *pter'a* flowers' sweet redolence on that mountain breeze.

He smiled.

Sera would be happy. She would be healed, and grow strong.

Ahrik shouted. Zharla renewed her wail. The alien woman gasped. The rain-soaked earth met his shoulder without pain, but with feathery light and gladness, receiving him and wrapping him in its embrace, warmed by the brightest of suns. *A life for a life.*

Victory

Extras

Sierra Vista

Redemption of the White Planet
Book 3: Saga of the Emerald Moon
Chapter 3, "Sierra Vista"

I SLAM THE PHONE DOWN, then slam it down again for good measure. No way am I going to let my good-for-nothing ex take my baby girl from me for Christmas, not when the tart that destroyed our marriage is still in the picture.

I turn away from the phone, the residue of the violence I inflicted on it hanging in the air, and start at the wraith that creeps up from behind me.

I shiver.

She always creeps, silent, brooding. When I came across her and her companion, dehydrated and cold, on a hunting trip up the Mogollon Rim, I never thought they'd stay this long. That day was hard, that clear day in late August when the divorce was final. For whatever reason, call it a middle finger to my ex, or a way to have someone around, these two became my guests.

But the woman creeps me out. She doesn't respond to a thing I say, even when I try using my college Spanish. I hear her mutter to the man in their own language, I assume a native dialect of Mayan or Quechua or something, but she never says anything to me. She glides everywhere, never leaves the apartment, and pretends I'm not here.

Until now.

There she stands, the wisps of the aggrieved phone ringer twisting through the space between us. She stares right at me, not through me like she normally does, and she has something that looks like it wants to be empathy on her face. It might be pity. It's hard to tell with her picture-perfect, olive face and eyes that could turn water to ice.

Her look isn't much, but today I'll take it.

"My ex, ya know, acting up again. Wants to keep my baby from me this Christmas."

She cocks her head like she wants to understand, like a puppy might do if it felt it were the master and you the pet. Or a cat. Cats are like that, even when they're the pets.

Anyway, she gives me a look like pity, which seems hard to do with those perfectly icy eyes, and makes a comforting sound, then glides toward me. She doesn't step, she never steps, she glides forward and squeezes my hand in a tender and unexpected and powerful way, and if I walked on that side of the street I might actually swoon a bit, or at least my heart might palpitate, but then just when I think she might actually hug me or something she's gone, quicksilver out of the pan, and sliding back down the hall to the room that used to be a study but is now where my guests sleep.

Or at least where she sleeps. He sleeps on the couch in the front room.

I grunt. There's a lot I don't know about that lady. She hasn't said a word to me in the week I've known her, but she told me more in those three seconds than most people tell me in a year of yacking out their pie holes. Even when she crept in on me when I was in the shower, I could tell it wasn't voyeurism or anything. She just watched me to see how I did it, then left, like they don't have running water where they come from. The lady is deathly serious about everything, in her perfect, majestic way.

The dude, who's not quite as creepy-stunning as the lady, just sits on the couch and stares at me after I have it out with the phone receiver and the lady just glides off. He's in something like a lotus position on the couch, but in a flash he stands up with the air of a five-foot-seven underwear model who knows he has all the goods and sort of inclines his head in my direction. I have no idea what this means because, well, this is America and we don't do the whole social hierarchy thing so well. Besides, my ex's old clothes don't fit him well and do nothing to accentuate his confidence or the ripcord body that was able to get off the couch so quick.

He bows his head a titch lower, like he's waiting for me to acknowledge him. I do something similar with my head and the corners of his mouth turn up, not too much, and he works his mouth around something, like he's getting the taste of a fine wine, or what I think that would look like if I drank.

He raises an eyebrow. "Mai eks, ya'no, ackating up gehn. Wans t'keep ma'bebbie from me zis Krissmas."

I narrow my eyes, because that's creepy. I try to remember all the way back to high school Spanish class, because they must be from Nicaragua or Guatemala or something. "¿De donde eres?"

He works his mouth again. "De donde—"

"Nope," I say, "we ain't doin' this."

I guide him back to the couch. It's midmorning on a weekday, so I flip on the TV and click the dial till I get to PBS. Hallelujah. Grover is there with the word of the day. I give an important nod to the TV. "You need to learn the gift of gab, and I have better things to do than play Twenty Questions to figure out where you two are from."

I clomp back to my room. The anger at my dalliant ex has slowed to a simmer, and as I dress in my BDUs and get my gear ready for drill, I wonder how I'm supposed to figure out where they're from, or even if I want to know.

My ex is a border guard, so it gives me a great deal of pleasure to stick it to him and harbor a couple of wetbacks for a while.

I drive by Tina's place on the way to drill. I go in Bess, my baby blue '76 Chevy pickup. She has a jack job that I laid on when I rebuilt her in '92, the year I graduated from Mountain View and got a signing bonus for signing up.

Bess is my other baby, only slightly less important than my actual baby.

I put her in neutral and give her a little gas to let Tina know I'm out front. I fully expect the neighbor to pop out her door and yell at me to fix my muffler. Not that I care. I rent my place, but Tina owns hers and is going to outlive the crotchety hag next door by a long shot. I've got bigger fish to fry than worrying about curmudgeons.

I have to rev Bess a couple more times before Tina storms out, ruck over her shoulder, face sour. She tosses her ruck in the bed and yanks open the door. She slides onto the leather upholstery. Tina breaths out in frustration after slamming the door home. "Just freakin' go."

Except she doesn't say "freakin'." Tina has a mouth on her, but all this is going in my diary and my baby might read it someday. Besides which, I was raised Mormon, and old habits die hard, ya know?

I pull into the street and let Bess show what she can do. I nod over at Tina. "What's eatin' you? I always rev Bess like that."

"It ain't the truck." She rolls down the window and tosses out a wad of chaw. "My dang ex wants a piece of my reenlistment bonus."

"Mine wants my baby for the holidays." I grunt with empathy. "Put your belt on. We're gettin' on the highway."

"I ain't wearin' no goshdarn seatbelt till we get to the dang base." She works the window up, though. "Can your ex even do that?"

I pull onto highway 90 and head toward Fort Huachuca. "Only a judge can do that, and I am not going to let it come down to a judge decidin'. No sir."

Tina folds her arms in a pout. "I was planning to freaking renovate my kitchen."

There's nothing I can do to fix that, since I've got enough problems of my own, so I just let the comfortable silence set between us, like it always does. Then a question occurs to me, "Tina, did you pick up any Quechua or Mayan or something when you were posted to the Canal Zone?"

She clicks her teeth with a rude sound. "Or something?"

I shrug an apology. "I only speak Spanish and a smidgen of Arabic."

She grunts. "There are freaking hundreds of indigenous languages down there. Why do you ask?"

I take one look at the annoyance on her face and know that I shouldn't complicate things by bringing her into my very illegal harboring activities. I shrug and reach into my breast pocket for my ID as we pull toward the post main gate. "Just curious. Now get your belt on before the MPs cite me."

I'm grungy, hot, tired, and hungry when I drive up in Bess. I'm an intel officer, but the Army still finds a way to make us rough it when we go out on drill.

I bite back a curse because my ex's pansy sedan is parked in my spot when I roll up to the complex. For a second, I consider keying his car, then I realize that he's probably early dropping off my baby and has somewhere to be with his little tart.

I park in a visitor spot, muttering under my breath.

I huff my ruck up the stairs and notice that the little tart is actually sitting in the front seat of the pansy sedan. I can't help but scratch my face with my middle finger in her direction. Nothing major, nothing that would get me in trouble with a judge, just a little present to let her know I see her, without seeing her.

My legs burn by the time I get to the top of the stairs, and I ask myself why I agreed to take a top floor apartment without paying any less in rent.

Seeing my ex knocking on my door with one fist, though, holding my baby by the other hand, makes me forget all that. I charge.

The audacity on him, to rob my baby of a day with her father. What would he have done if I hadn't come home when I did, leave my baby on the stoop like some cast-off?

He bangs on the door, and I hear his voice echo down the concrete hallway and over the metal railing to the parking lot below, "I know you're in there! Open up!"

He might as well dial up the flame on my anger to boiling. My charge quickens. "Hey! Lay off my door!"

I catch the glint of metal on his chest as he turns. He joined the border patrol after we split, and now he walks around all high 'n' mighty. Turning over a new leaf, he said.

I stifle a gasp, because now I have two illegals on the other side of the door he's laying into. And I'm sticking my finger in his face and getting red in the neck and getting fed up with his shenanigans, which is probably all the excuse he needs to go ahead and kick that door down all himself.

No way can I back down now, though. My baby squeals and scurries to me, her eyes all lit up. Well, at least I won that battle right out the gate.

My ex sneers and jabs a finger toward my place. "If you're out here, who's in there?"

I gather up my baby in an embrace and plant my feet. I can't give an inch, not after what he's trying to pull this Christmas. "How dare you," I say, using my best fake outrage voice, which isn't hard in this case. "You have a lotta nerve rollin' in here unannounced with your little biddy in tow."

He crosses his arms with his typical, irksome defiance. "You're hidin' something. You're scared I might win the custody case, that I might get the holidays with my daughter, and then some."

"You're as crazy as always, you sick bastard. I've got nothin' to hide, no sir."

He gives a triumphant smile and moves his hands down to his hips with even more arrogance than usual. "Okay, then, open up the door. Somethin' smells good in there, but you just got back from drill. What gives?"

He wiggles his finger at me and gives his triumphant, know-it-all smile, the one that always drove me bat crazy when we were together and reminds me now why we're better off apart. I get a thrashing, choking feeling like jumping into a stormy sea with no life jacket because I have no idea how I'm supposed to answer.

I flex and unflex the fingers on the hand that's not gripping my baby, to calm down a bit before responding, and to breathe some blood back into my legs because I'm a bit woozy after sniffing the air and recognizing that my goose might be cooked and my sorry ex might have done the cooking. Goodbye to my career, goodbye to Bess, goodbye to my baby while I squander my best years in the slammer.

I gulp down a breath and focus on a point just over my ex's right shoulder to keep my balance and stay conscious. I nudge away his finger. "You need to mind your own business. I don't think you want me rootin' around in your past to figure out exactly when the tart came on the scene and exactly how our marriage ended. Do you?"

His eyes get red hot, which is gratifying beyond measure, then he brushes past me. His angry footfalls echo down the concrete floor and stucco walls, but he just can't help getting in one last dig, calling over his shoulder, "I'll find out what you're up to, and when I do that girl will be all mine!"

Idiot. My baby can understand everything you're sayin'. I really should shut up and open the door to my apartment and make sure the illegals haven't torn the place up or stolen every last thing of value, but since I also can't help getting in the last word, since that's just who I am, I yell back, "Keep that marriage-wrecker away from my baby, or you'll be sorry!"

I crouch down and smile at my baby with my eyes, then give her a proper hug. "How ya doin', baby?"

"I like comin' home, Mama, even tho' Daddy says it ain't home."

I squeeze her tight, like I won't ever let her leave me again. "Your father says crazy things sometimes." I lean back and stroke her long auburn hair, which in eight years of life I've trimmed but never really cut. "You're home now, baby."

I fumble the keys out of my pocket and manage to slip the door key into the lock, scared of what I'll find when I open it up. I pick up my ruck and motion for my baby to wait outside. The dead bolt clicks open with a sound like thunder, then the latch frees like a round being chambered. I push the door hard to counteract the hydraulic return mechanism, which the landlord keeps too tight, but I'm also careful not to let the door open too much, in case someone (like my ex) is trying to pry.

I gasp.

The TV is still on Sesame Street, and something amazing is sizzling on the stove. The pretty, mute woman stands behind the breakfast bar with a wooden spatula in her hand and a look on her face like a deer in headlights, but the man is crouched next to the coffee table with an easy, calculating stare that I can only describe as military and ice cold. His stance is balanced, arms out, ready for a fight. But what really gets my goat is that my hunting rifle is completely disassembled on the coffee table, my gun oil and cleaning rag to the side, and the weapon parts, organized with military precision, shine with a luster that I've never seen before, even on a new M-16.

Right then, I decide to stop thinking of them as illegals from over the border.

For the first time in years, I actually agree with my ex on something: something is very not right here, and I have to suss it out before he does. I creep over to the TV and turn off Elmo's annoying, high-pitched voice. I knead the air with my palms in a gesture of calm, or at least what I hope they'll interpret as calm, because at that moment, out of the corner of my eye, I see the mute woman ease the largest knife I have back into my knife block next to the stove. "It's okay," I say, attempting a smile. "Just me."

I wonder what possibly could have them so amped up that they'd be willing to kill whoever came through my door, because I see a lot more than cold, military calculation behind the man's eyes. I see genuine fear, like the trauma that he lived coming here was more than any one human should endure. Now, the lady I can tell is a complete basket case, because behind her cold and steely exterior I see not just fear, but guilt. A lot of it. And it makes me wonder if it has something to do with how I found them on the Mogollon Rim.

The man relaxes with what appears a Herculean effort, then he snaps to attention and salutes me with a fist on his chest and his head bowed. Every muscle moves with unerring efficiency, no energy or breath wasted, and I know for certain he's a military man, but for the life of me I can't guess which military that might be.

The woman moves the food off the stove and clicks off the burner, then glides around the breakfast bar to stand behind the couch. Our eyes are level, but I get the distinct impression that she's looking down on me in a regal, maternal sort of way.

Little feet shuffle through the door, still propped half-open with my ruck. "Mama?"

From behind the couch, the mute woman squeals—not a very regal sound—and fixes her gaze on the doorway behind me, her hands covering a gasp. My heart skips and my blood runs cold, though, because she rushes me—or my baby—and says the absolute last thing I would expect anyone to say who's never met my daughter: "Sarah."

I move to intercept, because no one that unstable is getting near my baby. Adrenaline pumps into my veins and the fight-or-flight reflex flips to fight because my first thought is protecting my baby. The man springs forward too, but I can't tell if it's to stop the woman or to help her knock me down to get to my daughter. Either way, I widen my stance and prepare for the worst, moving my baby to safety behind me with a sweep of my arm.

We three meet together all at once, but it's not a collision like I fear. One of my hands ends up clutching the woman's shirt, which I notice with chagrin is one of my faves. She flails her arms toward my baby, and even the slight push she gives me shows me that she's incredibly strong and would have no problem sweeping me out of the way if she chose. She jabbers to the man in their language, and it's the first time I've heard it spoken above a whisper. After getting over the fact that the woman, indeed, is not mute after all, part of my brain begins to process her speech as a confusing mix of something almost Semitic, with short vowels like Spanish and a lilting sing-song like Finnish, where the first syllable of every word gets the emphasis.

While I'm getting over hearing her speak for the first time, and understanding none of it except my daughter's name over and over, my left forearm presses against the man's chest. He feels even stronger than the woman, but thankfully he's not trying to get through me, either, but to keep us two ladies apart or, mostly, to keep the pretty, once-mute lady away from me, because strangely the man seems a little scared of her, too.

"Stop!" I demand.

The lady quiets down, muttering "Sarah," and the man relaxes and breathes out with relief. I heave a sigh and raise my palms slowly. I kick my ruck out from propping the door open, because folks outside have probably heard or seen more of our ruckus than I want them to. After the door closes, I bring my baby out from behind me and raise my arm in introduction, suddenly grateful that this hasn't played out like my worst fears told me it would.

"This is Sarah," I say.

Of course, all this raises a whole lot more questions that I'm even more determined to get to the bottom of.

The man surprises me by crouching, fists to the floor, and bowing his head. He rises with his easy grace and points to himself, smiling at my baby. "Ahrik."

Something funny happens on the woman's face. It transforms from wild-eyed recognition to narrow-eyed confusion to cock-eyed bewilderment. More jabbering, this time with my baby's name as a question in Ahrik's direction. He jabbers back, sharply, and she turns to my baby and smiles the most beautiful smile I've seen on two feet. She inclines her head but doesn't do the strange floor thing that Ahrik did. She closes her eyes for a moment, as if us knowing her name is a profound privilege. "Zharla."

My baby cuddles against my hip, suddenly embarrassed with the attention.

Me, I'm a little miffed at how these folks lived in my house and ate my food for a week but didn't find it in themselves even to tell me their names. I point to myself. "Yeah, and I'm Samantha, or Sam for short. Now, do you mind telling me what in tarnation is going on?"

Ahrik and Zharla give me blank stares, then she turns to him as if expecting him to be the one to answer. So, I give him an expectant raise of my eyebrow and nod to the disassembled hunting rifle on the coffee table. "Like, for starters, what the heck?"

(I actually say "heck," not like Tina, who would certainly drop an f-bomb here. Believe me, I'm sorely tempted to do that now.)

He babbles in his own language with a tone of apology, clearly frustrated at his inability to communicate, then he stops and holds up a hand, as if asking me for patience. He slips back to my study, converted into a bedroom for my guests, and returns with a dingy but unfired 5.56 round. Now, I know that's not mine because I don't keep military ammo in my house, only at my locker at the range. I breathe another sigh of relief that he hasn't found the .22-caliber ammo for my hunting rifle, which of course I store in a different place, and even more relieved that he didn't try to chamber the 5.56 round in my hunting rifle, since firing that round from my rifle would probably destroy the rifle and maim the person who fired it.

I hold out my hand and he gives me the round. The moisture in my mouth wicks away as I examine it. It's a full metal jacket, and the headstamp bears the cross-in-circle of a NATO-interchangeable round, but there's no lot or factory numbers and what I presume is the year of manufacture—1982—tells me the bullet is almost fifteen years old. The round also has sealant around the case mouth and primer, but it's mustard yellow instead of the reds, blues, or greens that I typically see. I reach down for the cleaning rag next to my rifle and rub down the round, confirming that there is no colored tip.

This round is as much a mystery as my two guests, and I'm beginning to feel very uncomfortable, and quite certain that I've gotten myself into something way more complicated than I ever wanted when I thumbed my nose at the system and my good-for-nothing ex and brought my enigmatic guests home from the Mogollon Rim.

I look down at my baby. "We need to teach these two English."

My baby sniffs the air and smiles. "I'm hungry, Mama."

"Well shoot," I say, stuffing the round in the thigh pocket of my BDUs and giving what I hope is an encouraging smile to my guests. "I hope you made enough for four."

The next weekend, over Columbus Day, my baby teaches our guests the alphabet and makes signs for everything in the house, while I try to teach them how to play Scrabble. The TV basically stays tuned to PBS all morning now, while my baby is at school and I'm at my intel job on base. On the weekends, though, we can actually make progress with English.

Zharla is crap at language-learning, but Ahrik is a real quick study. On Saturday morning he's losing Scrabble games to my baby with Sesame Street words like "cat" and "ball," but by Sunday morning she can't beat him anymore. That's when I show him the dictionary and how to use it, and by Monday morning I can't beat him anymore.

Zharla doesn't even bother to play. She just sits on the couch, listening and watching with mute attention, or goes into the study and does calisthenics or other exercises. I walk in on her once—when I go in to get the dictionary—and she's doing handstand pushups against the wall. I count ten just in the time I'm in there getting the dictionary, and she has a look of intensity on her face like I'm not even there, with a fire that would melt steel. I used to be more scared of Ahrik, but now I'm more scared of her. She's got major trauma issues, like the PTSD that I see in folks coming back from Panama and the Gulf War.

She and Ahrik are great cooks, though, and I'm happy to graduate from frozen pizza and TV dinners to whatever they throw together. I bring home Mexican from a stand just down the street once—they're all over the place in Sierra Vista—and they absolutely love the refried beans. Ahrik puts more hot sauce on his tacos than I would use in a year, but to each his own, you know?

I finally break down and call Tina about the 5.56 round. I have to fix up the phone with some duct tape.

"T," I say, "I need a favor."

"I mean, why else would you call?"

"You know I always give you a ride to base, right?"

She sighs. "Okay, what's up?"

"I need you to buy some ammo for me."

"Buy your own dang ammo, Sam."

"This one's special. 5.56 FMJ with yellow sealant. I'll swing by an' drop off a sample."

There's an uncomfortable hesitation on the other end of the line. "I ain't goin' to ask why I'm doin' this, but someday you'll tell me the whole freakin' story, right?"

"Yup, someday. And thanks." I close the connection, but this time I'm much more gentle about laying the receiver on the cradle.

I check the mail that day, and there's a court summons, addressed to me, Samantha R. Snow. Custody hearing. The week after Thanksgiving. I can't wait to tell the judge what a philandering putz my ex is, and how he deserves no more time with my baby than he's already got.

The Monday before Thanksgiving, when my baby is with my good-for-nothing ex, the neighbors complain about the bumping and scraping when Zharla exercises. So, I give Zharla a pair of running shoes and take her on a run. I start out slow, then realize she's not even breathing hard at all, so I turn toward Reservoir Hill. After two miles of staying with me on the flat, she sprints up the ascent, like the incline gives her more energy or something, and if I didn't know better I'd say she was descended from mountain lions, with how she bounds up from rock to rock. When I finally huff and puff to the top, she's sitting cross-legged on a boulder and doing some sort of meditation.

I admire the sunrise over the Arizona desert. "Good run." I smile at her and suck down a few swigs of water. "Thanks for comin' with."

She just looks at me and nods, but I can't tell if that means she understands and agrees or just acknowledges the fact that sounds came out of my yapper. She takes a deep breath and nods toward the Huachuca mountains in the distance. "Long?"

I rub my chin. "Do you mean 'how far' or 'how long' are the Huachucas?"

She hums in frustration. "How far."

"Couple miles or so. You want to run up there, too?" I wave my hand in front of my face and flutter my lips. "I'm beat now, but maybe another day, okay?"

"No," she says, then springs down from her meditative position on the boulder and points at me, then makes like she's shouldering a rifle and walking through the trees, then points at me again and back toward the Huachucas.

"Oh, you want to know about where I found you." I turn and point to the north. "That was up the Mogollon Rim, like three hundred miles from here."

She stares at me for a beat, and her intensity weakens my knees and sends shivers down my spine all at the same time. She steps toward me and caresses my shoulder, and I think she's trying to be friendly but not too friendly. She licks her lips, like she's forming words around an idea whose time has come. "We go."

It's a statement, not a question, and she launches off back down Reservoir Hill without waiting for a response. I can't tell if she means to go back home or to go back up the Rim.

Either way, something tells me I don't like where this is going.

I wake up the next morning, sore from my run, and Ahrik is gone. This is weird because the way he and Zharla bicker makes me think they're an item, but he's not on the couch or in the kitchen when I get up to do pushups, pullups, and situps. My APFT is coming up, and the quickest way to get kicked out of the Army is to fail that thing. Or get SIRVed, but I'm going to fight that one.

Maybe he's actually bunking with Zharla now. Huh.

I'm halfway through my sets, but I can't get Ahrik's absence out of my head. Some creeping doom lurks on the fringe of my consciousness. I know I have to do something, but I don't know what. I shake out my arms after three more pullups and creep back to the study. The creaking in the floor sounds like a bullhorn to my strained senses. I coax the doorknob to the right and ease the door open as slowly as I can, because I know just where the hinges groan. The thing sounds like a ghost croaking, I open the door so slow.

There's just enough light slicing through the blinds to make out only one lump on the bed. The lump moves, but before it turns over and sits up and turns into an awake human form I pull the door closed, ignoring the door groans that sound like an alarm clock now but that I know really aren't that loud. Anyway, if Zharla wakes up, she wakes up, but it won't look like I did it.

I pad back to the living room and scan for clues. Where would he go? Where *could* he go that he would be able to find his way back? I look in the panty and the fridge. No food appears to be missing. Besides, Zharla is still here, and he wouldn't leave her, would he? I go to the gun cabinet, but my hunting rifle is still there, now perfectly cleaned and assembled. At least he isn't stupid enough to take that.

What then?

That's when I see the key rack. My house keys are there, as well as the spare set, but where the Bess key should be there is a vacant hook, taunting me and screaming at me to move, move, move.

I move.

I slip my feet into the flip-flops by the door and grab the spare keys before pulling open the door and flapping down the cement hallway. Down the stairs. Flap, flap, flap. My sweats flutter around my legs and arms, too, just without the racket. I'm sure that half the building is awake by now, and I'm just as sure that something very bad is about to happen.

I round the corner of the brick stairwell and relief floods over me. Bess is still there, where she should be. Ahrik's sitting in the driver's seat, hands on the wheel, a look of steely concentration on his chiseled face. The light from the desert sunrise slants across the parking lot and into the cab, glinting off of Bess's blue body but doing nothing to lighten the dark circles around Ahrik's brooding eyes.

I place a hand on the hood as I race around to the passenger door. Still cold. He hasn't turned her on yet. Another wave of relief rushes over me. Maybe this won't be as bad as I fear.

I try the passenger door latch. Locked. I fight down a rising panic before realizing that I have the spare keys right there, in my hand. Ahrik looks over at me, forlorn and angry, but he doesn't reach over to keep me from opening the door, even though I know he has the strength to. My key hammers home with a thunk of satisfaction and I get the door open and slip onto the leather upholstery without incident. I venture to hope that we might get through this, whatever it is.

My hands are shaking, so I sit on them. No need to work Ahrik up any more than he already is. He's gone back to staring a hole in the steering wheel, so I clear my throat to get his attention. "Ahrik, what's up?"

He glances up, but then understanding creeps into his features and he heaves the deepest sigh I've ever seen a body heave. He looks an apology at me. "Need we help."

I open my palms. "With what?"

I might finally get some answers here, and I have to work to suppress the giddy fluttering in my belly, which is also doubling as nervousness.

He looks around outside, then nods off to the north. "Air cold more."

"It's fall, but it won't get much cooler than this."

He growls and hits the steering wheel.

I place a hand on his arm, ever so gentle, and squeeze.

He presses his lips together. "I sorry." He points off to the north again. "Cold more there."

"Where?"

"Sarah there."

I look to see where he's pointing, and it's definitely not toward my apartment, where Sarah is still sleeping in our bedroom. "No," I say, "my baby is here, with us." I reach for his hand and give it a good filial squeeze. "You're safe here. Everything is okay."

His head whips around, and the violence of it takes me aback. The foreboding comes back to the fringe of my consciousness, probing, pawing, stalking.

"No." He gives a long, slow shake of his head. "Me no safe. Zharla no safe. You no safe. You baby no safe. No person safe."

"That's ridiculous. I won't let anything happen to us, no s—"

"No." He shakes off my hand and points a finger toward the glove box. "No . . . paper."

I open the glove box, confused.

"No paper," he says. "No paper show way to . . . to . . ."

"A map? To where?"

"Yes, map. To . . . to . . ." He points to the north again. "To air cold."

It hits me. "To the Rim? To the Mogollon Rim, where I found you?"

He waggles his head back and forth in what I take as a nod.

I close the glove box, afraid to say what I'm about to say. "Why do you need to go back to the Rim?"

"Sarah there."

"But my baby—"

"No you baby. Sarah me." He points to himself.

"You have a daughter. You and Zharla have a daughter. Of course."

He shimmies his shoulders with a look of confusion on his face, and I can tell he doesn't understand, but he tries again. "Hair long. Same years. Same face." He sighs. "Same name."

"Is she lost?"

Another shoulder shimmy of confusion.

Then Zharla rounds the corner of the stairwell, all dressed and ready to go, with a bag full of something. Food and water, I assume. I put two and two together. Zharla doesn't meet my gaze, and neither will Ahrik. She walks up and stands outside the driver side window, staring at Ahrik with pity, like he's done something wrong or failed at some important task.

He just stares back into the steering wheel. "Need we help."

I look back and forth between them, then make a decision I know I'll regret. But I can't help it. I know what it's like to be missing my baby. I know that ache and that helplessness. I know what it'll cost me, because I'll probably miss my court date. My ex will get fifty-fifty custody, and he'll have my baby for the holidays, and that little tart will probably still be in the picture, or some other tart will, because that's what a philandering, good-for-nothing putz my ex is, but my baby will be safe. She'll be fed. She'll go to school. I'll know where she is, and I know I'll get to see her again.

If there's another little girl out there, and she needs to be found, then we'll find her.

I pat his hand and give Zharla a reassuring smile through the glass. "We'll find her. I'll help you." I hesitate. "But I need to call a friend for help."

"Go now?"

"Today, we'll go."

I call the attorney as soon as her office opens, to tell her I can't make the court date, and that I know what this means. Christmas will be different this year, but the other Sarah will be found and Ahrik and Zharla will know where she is. They won't have the ache of missing their girl.

I call Tina, too. "Why'd you freakin' wake me up, S?"

"Want to go camping?"

"You askin' or tellin'? By the way, I dug around a bit on that 5.56 round, and you got yourself a little problem."

I shrug, even though I know she can't see. What's one more problem when I already have so many? "Tell me about it on the way. I'll pick you up in six zero mikes."

As I throw gear in the back of Bess, I know I'm doing the right thing, even though I know I'm in way deeper than I should be.

Acknowledgments

I WROTE THIS BOOK on the bus, commuting to and from work in Abu Dhabi. I am very grateful for all those who have encouraged and supported me in the creative process. Readers have given me positive feedback, especially the family members and friends who read early drafts of this book, including Hannah Toronto, Rebecca Toronto, and Sharon Benjamin. Writing group members Jason Palmatier, Shayne Easson, Kevin Kauffmann, Rob Riddell, and Jason Krenkel gave very helpful support and feedback, with sharp eyes that liberated the manuscript from a number of contradictions. Sharman Toronto also provided a timely and punctilious review that caught errors that I missed on the first, well, twelve proofreads.

I also couldn't have done this without the support of friends, family, and anonymous backers on Kickstarter. Their support paid for the cover design, printing, and marketing to help make the launch a success. Whether I sell a hundred books or ten thousand, their faith in my unproven writing career has earned my everlasting loyalty.

My greatest debt of gratitude is to my wife, who sees talent and potential in me that I sometimes do not even see in myself. She truly is never more than a heartbeat away. Thank you.

About the Author

After teaching military operations and strategy to military officers for ten years, Nathan W. Toronto became a management consultant in Washington, DC, where he devotes as much time as he can to writing fiction. He has lived in ten countries and visited some two dozen others, developing a firm belief that Mexican food is the best, at least for lunch and dinner. His breakfast belief is just as unequivocal: no Sunday is complete without waffles in the morning. In a previous move, Nathan had two fish and a turtle, but he's now petless. Four children are enough.

www.nathantoronto.com

www.ingramcontent.com/pod-product-compliance
Lightning Source LLC
Chambersburg PA
CBHW020307030826
48979CB00029B/2279/J

* 9 7 8 0 9 9 7 6 5 5 0 7 0 *